AnneM

Copyright 2017 To Gain
AnneMarie Brear

To Gain What's Lost

Published novels:

2

AnneMarie Brear

To Gain What's Lost

Happy the man, and happy he alone,
He who can call to-day his own:
He who, secure within, can say:
'To-morrow do thy worst, for I've liv'd to-day.'
- John Dryden, *Imitation of Horace, Book III, Ode 29*

Chapter 1

Yorkshire, England.
March 1864

The setting sun tinged the distant ranges a hue of bronze. Through the shallow valley, a delicate breeze gently caressed the leaves on the trees as the new spring flowers nodded their heads in accompaniment. A rare Goshawk soared, gliding on the air currents, its cry shattering the silence, and a daring hare paused in its feast of fresh grass. Ewes plodded by, laden down from the weight of their unborn offspring.

To the lone rider on top of the hill, the scene below filled her with pleasure. This was her home. The sprawling estate and surrounding acres of land were nestled peacefully amongst the rolling, undulating hills east of the Vale of York. It had been in her family for generations, and God willing, it would continue that way for years to come. The three-storied house, whose grey slates and numerous chimneys were just visible over the trees, was built from blocks of pale cream sandstone, quarried locally. The outer buildings had been constructed with the same stone to blend in with the house, making the whole estate look grand but not austere, welcoming rather than imposing.

Anna Claire Thornton sighed reluctantly and rose from the craggy outcrop, on which she rested whenever she rode this way. She called her horse twice before he abandoned the tuft of sweet grass and came to her. Once mounted, Anna sat quietly for a few moments still looking down at the Thornton Estate. Deliberately, she was going home late, not wanting to exchange the peaceful countryside for the mayhem inside the house. If her mother and sister realized she was still out riding with only an hour left before they went to a ball, they'd be appalled. Even with the help of their personal maids, it took them all afternoon to dress for such an occasion.

It was with some unwillingness, a short time later, that Anna rode into the cobbled stable yard behind the house. Two lads raced each other to hold her horse.

Bert, the head groomsman, came out of the large tack room to Anna's left. 'Oye, you pair! Get back to polishin' the carriage. T'master expects it to look its best tonight.' As the boys scurried off, grinning and pushing each other, Bert took hold of the horse's bridle. 'Did you have a good ride, Miss?'

'Yes, thank you.' She dismounted and gave Jasper the small apple she kept in her coat pocket for him.

'Me instructions from the master are to tell you to go straight inside once you returned, Miss.'

Anna sighed. 'Yes, I know I'm late. Though I may even plead a headache yet.'

'Aye…well...The message was over an hour ago, Miss.' He gave her a look that said she'd best get on before all hell broke loose.

'I'll see if I can get inside undetected then.' She sighed and headed for the house.

A large garden separated the house from the
stables. Anna gazed at the flourishing flowerbeds but
knew she didn't have time to stop and pick a bloom
or two. Gathering up the skirts of her blue riding
habit, she quickened her step. Meandering white
gravelled paths went off either towards the tiered
formal gardens and small lake that was on the right
side of the house or toward the service areas on the
left. Beyond the laundry, the lane went for about a
mile to the estate's home farm, which supplied the
house with fresh meat and dairy and made the estate
nearly self-sufficient.

Several doors led into the house and Anna usually
made for the kitchen to have a chat with Mrs. Wilson,
their cook, and the maids, and maybe to sample some
of Mrs. Wilson's delicious pastries, but she couldn't
afford the time today. Her mother and sister naturally
frowned upon this informality. Both considered it
beneath them to converse with the staff in any social
way, but Anna found a kind of comfort from these
down-to-earth people. In a way, they were family to
her just as much as her own flesh and blood. They,
the odd assortment of servants, filled a gap in a side
of her nature that her family couldn't.

She claimed no close friends within her own
circle. Females her own age bored her with their lack
of sensibilities. The staff treated her with respect and
kindness, but what was more, they were frank with
her about all aspects of their lives. They let her share
their joys and sorrows and showed her another world
outside the one she was born into. For that, she would
be eternally grateful.

Slipping through the gardens, she ran around to the conservatory at the side of the house. The ornate glass structure was built off a small sitting room between the formal dining room and the drawing room. Entering the hallway, Anna turned away from the large entrance hall and main stairway. She headed for the servants' staircase at the end of the hall, hoping not to meet her sister's or mother's maids on the way to her room, for they would quickly tattle on her.

'I think it would be advisable for you to be quick, my dear,' her father said, surprising her as he stepped out of the library opposite the stairs.

'Oh, Papa! You gave me a fright.'

'So, intent on sneaking in, were you?' Thomas Thornton teased.

'It'll not take me very long to get ready.' Anna flashed him a cheeky grin. 'Maisie will have everything all ready.'

'You've less than an hour. I believe your mother and sister have had the servants running like mad all day. Your maid must have said something to keep them satisfied and away from your room while you were out riding.' Thomas shook his head. 'You know your mother has to be punctual.' He frowned, the laughter leaving his grey eyes. 'It would be advantageous for us to keep your mother happy. Lately...well, never mind that, just be quick, pet.'

Anna nibbled her bottom lip as concern etched his face. Recently, her mother's mood swings had been very erratic. A strange, uneasy feeling Anna didn't understand tingled her spine.

Shrugging as though he shifted some hidden burden, he patted her gently on the back. 'Be down shortly, dearest.'

She made it to her room unseen. Her personal maid, Maisie, waited with a face red from exertion, her dark hair awry.

'Oh, Miss, thank goodness you back.' She rushed to help Anna undress. 'I've got a bath ready. My, it's been a job tryin' to keep it hot. Up and down those stairs I've been, Miss. Me legs are nearly worn away.'

Relaxing in the hot bath, Anna let Maisie air her grievances. She sat watching with a little smile as Maisie ran back and forth from the dressing room to the bedroom, spreading out all the paraphernalia needed to prepare Anna for the night's entertainment. An assortment of corsets and undergarments littered the bed.

'Miss, we must get your hair washed and then I can start dryin' it, for the mistress will be ready to go and you'll only be half dressed.'

Within ten minutes, Anna was washed, dried and scented. Maisie assisted her in putting on the many layers of underclothing required. At last, the gown was fitted over bloomers, chemise, petticoats, and crinoline cage. Anna crossed to the mirror to study her image, hoping her mother wouldn't find fault. The azure blue of the gown brought out the colour of her blue-green eyes and suited her thick honey blonde hair. She ran her hands over the dress. It was a plain uncomplicated cut, but it shaped beautifully over her bust and waist with yards of material flaring out in shimmering splendour.

She disliked frivolous dresses and her wardrobe was considered simple by the standards of her class. However, every item of clothing she wore was made of the finest fabric and material available in England, cut and tailored by the best seamstress in York.

In contrast to her sister, Arabella, the swaying tide of current fashion was of no interest to her. Momentarily, Anna wondered about her sister's attire for tonight, but the thought soon faded from lack of interest. At just eighteen, Arabella was four years Anna's junior. Both sisters were tall, slender and of the same fair colouring, but there the similarities ended. They had little in common, except their mutual dislike for each other, which had begun when they were children.

A knock sounded on the door as Anna selected jewellery, and a smiling face appeared from around the door. 'May I come in?'

'Yes, dearest, of course. Really, Maggie, when do you ever need permission to come into my room?' Anna smiled, and then noticed her youngest sister's nightdress. 'You're ready for bed early.'

'Mother said I'm not to go downstairs after you've left. I must stay up in my room and work on my embroidering.' Maggie screwed up her nose. 'It is not up to standard.'

Joining Anna at the dressing table, Maggie studied their reflections in the mirror. 'You look beautiful. How I wish I could go.' She sighed, fiddling with her long dark tresses that were so like their mother's.

'Your time will come soon enough. After a while it all becomes a bit tedious.' Anna smiled. 'I wish I didn't have to go.'

'Yes, well, it's all right to say that once you have attended a ball, but I have not. Mama said I will have to be at least seventeen before I am able to go. Which is rather unfair. Arabella was out at sixteen.'

Anna couldn't help laughing. Maggie looked so forlorn. At thirteen, the four years to wait seemed to her a lifetime. 'Fasten this for me, will you? You silly thing.' She smiled and held out the selected sapphire and diamond necklace.

Maggie grinned, her sunny nature coming to the fore as she pretended to waltz around the room clasping the necklace to her chest.

'Be careful. Papa would be upset if you broke his gift.' She had hardly worn the expensive necklace and matching earrings she'd received as a twenty-first birthday present a few months earlier.

After fastening the necklace around Anna's neck, Maggie flopped onto the huge four-poster bed in a fit of giggles just as Louise Thornton sailed into the room.

Their mother looked magnificent. Her hair, even at forty-five, was as black as a raven's wing, and tonight it was immaculately arranged high on her head. The diamond and pearl choker at her throat suited the burgundy velvet and lace gown perfectly. She looked regal, untouchable.

Maggie quickly sat up and straightened her nightgown, while Maisie hurriedly put the finishing touches to Anna's hair.

'Should you not be with Miss Foster, Magdalene?' Their mother spoke of her daughter's governess in a tone that brooked no argument.

Maggie stared at the floor. 'Miss Foster is having her meal, Mother, so I took the opportunity to watch Anna prepare for tonight.'

Louise's eyes narrowed. 'Anna does not have the time to talk to you. Please return to your room. I am sure Miss Foster has left something for you to do.'

'Yes, Mother. Good night, Anna.' Maggie, her shoulders slumped, left the room.

Anna rose from her dressing stool and put on her elbow length evening gloves. She smothered a flare of anger at her mother's harshness. 'Could you speak a little more kindly to Maggie, Mother? She is extremely sensitive.' Aware of her mother's dislike of Maggie and herself, Anna always tried to shield her sister from Louise's harsh words. The whole estate knew of Louise's preferences in regards to her children. Tom and Arabella enjoyed the pleasure of being their mother's favourites.

Anna often listened to her father's excuses for her mother's behaviour, but the older she became the less she respected her mother. On marrying Thomas, it was said Louise had wanted to fill the house with children to make him happy in return for all he'd done for her, even though she wasn't particularly maternal. However, the uncomfortable pregnancy and Anna's long, torturous birth remained forever in her mind. It took her a long time to get over it, and consequently she didn't care for, or indeed have anything to do with, the baby. Not only that, but the thought of having more children became abhorrent to her.

Fate though, decreed otherwise, for Tom and Arabella were born in quick succession. Louise then believed that because she had given the estate an heir, she was free from childbirth for good. However, with great horror and embarrassment, she became pregnant again five years after Arabella's birth. Innocent Maggie bore the brunt of being that mistake.

'Never instruct me on how to speak to my own daughter, Anna.' Louise's stare was glacial. 'Now, if you are finally ready, we shall leave.'

Maisie gave Anna her silk wrap and guided her feet into silver satin slippers.

Her mother paused at the door. 'I do not approve of your hair, Anna. It makes you look wanton.'

Anna peered into the mirror. The thick tresses were scooped up onto the top of her head and secured with tortoise shell combs, leaving wispy tendrils to hang daintily around her face. Personally, she liked the effect. It softened the style of the dress and gave her a fresh, carefree appearance. She smiled to herself. Obviously, her mother preferred the perfect, polished finish that was the standard practice of her station for their social class, but Anna enjoyed being unique. Hadn't she got a reputation for it? 'You know nothing can be done with my hair when it's newly washed, Mother.' She shrugged, dismissing the stinging words.

Her mother tutted and left the room.

Anna crossed the room and then lingered by the door. 'Once you've everything in order, Maisie, you might like to go and spend the evening with your mother. I don't mind. Tell her I will try to call in tomorrow for a quick cup of tea with her.'

'Thank you, Miss. Mam will be so pleased. You know how much she thinks of you.'

'Make sure you're back before we are.' Anna chuckled. 'I will never get out of this dress on my own.'

Grinning, Maisie nodded. 'Aye, I will, Miss. I promise.'

At the bottom of the staircase, Anna saw her mother's scowling face and turned her attention to her father.

'What a lucky man I am, to be escorting three of the most beautiful women in the country.' Thomas signalled Evans, the butler, to open the doors. The family walked out into the cool evening and the footman assisted them into the waiting carriage.

Arabella, dressed in a pink gown decorated in numerous frills and bows, chatted endlessly about what the women would be wearing and who would be present, as the carriage wheels sped over the bumpy road to York.

Anna ignored her sister's inane babble and stared out at the growing darkness. Arabella's prattle grew dim as Anna's thoughts crowded in. Of late, she felt bored, restless, and uncertain about her future. The activities women of her class enjoyed as a way of filling in their day were unattractive to her. She spent the odd day at different charities, yet she needed more to fill this void in her.

How she was going to find something to sustain this growing need, this wanting in her, she didn't know. The long rides she took up into the hills and valleys around her home were becoming increasingly frequent. Her mother had even stopped insisting she take a groom with her, for it did no good. Anna dismissed him once they got beyond view of the house. High on the rises surrounding the estate, she could be free, free to be herself. She could forget that down below her life felt meaningless.

Her mother and Arabella no longer asked if she wanted to go with them to visit the numerous family friends scattered across the region. They knew she disliked the repetitious discussions of fashions and gossip, which were the main topics of conversation. They felt embarrassed by her speeches about the poor and other uncomfortable issues. Could she help it if her forthright manner offended some? She knew she irritated them with her views that all people were equal and only wealth the divider. Her belief in educating the working class and bettering the lives of the poor meant acquaintances thought her odd. Men became uncomfortable when she told them the business world interested her. Most didn't understand when she discussed the ways she invested her own inheritance from her grandfather. It appalled them. Such things they considered strictly a man's domain, but Anna enjoyed being a part of that restricted world. She dealt with her own solicitor, instead of leaving it in her father's hands.

At one time she thought she simply needed a husband, but on reflection, she knew this wouldn't be enough to satisfy her unless the man was someone exceptional, someone who would allow her the freedom to express her own opinions and sadly, that type of man was rare.

Anna hated the position some women of her class endured. The pitiable creatures; meant only to be pretty adornments for their husbands, the breeder of male heirs and yet expected to be happy with their lot

14

in life. She was annoyed women had little or no control over their lives. No sympathetic ear would listen to their cries, for unhappiness must not be discussed under any circumstances. Women must accept their 'fate,' whether it be an abusive husband or being trapped in a loveless marriage. Whatever the reason, they must keep up the façade of being happy in this, their privileged existence.

Watching the black night glide past the small window of the carriage, she sighed and glanced across to catch her father's look. He gave her a small smile.

'I heard a rumour from Esther Redding that Sir Hugh's nephew will be there tonight,' Arabella said, breathless with anticipation. 'Do you think it is true, Mama? Has Lady Harriet mentioned anything to you?'

'I am not sure he is expected tonight, but his arrival is imminent.' Louise sniffed her disapproval. 'Though, *if* he is in attendance this evening, he is not the sort of man you should be interested in, my dear.'

Arabella leaned a little closer to her mother. 'Why not, Mama? I was told he is quite dashing and handsome—mysterious as well, for he's so rarely in England. He is always on his travels around the world.' Arabella's eyes were wide with excitement.

Thomas raised an eyebrow. 'You seem to know a lot about him, Arabella.'

Arabella blinked, obviously trying hard to look innocent. 'It's only what I have been told, Papa.'

'Well, I met him today at my club.'

Arabella stared. 'You met him? Then he must be coming tonight. Why did you not tell us?'

Anna rolled her eyes at her sister. Since Lady Harriet's first mention of her nephew, Arabella had been desperate to meet him and have him become part of her social crowd.

'I did not realize it was any concern of yours, Arabella, whom I speak with at the club.' Thomas gazed at his wife and Anna. 'Matt Cowan is a likable chap, and we talked for hours. Hugh Conway joined us, and we went for a meal together. In fact—' Thomas peered at Arabella. 'I may be doing business with him. He is coming to the house next week to discuss it. I don't want him being put off from visiting for fear he will be fawned over by you, Arabella. You will not embarrass us by judging him to see if he fits the bill as a future husband. Do I make myself clear?'

'Well, really, Papa. As if I would?' Arabella scoffed, indignant. 'Besides, he doesn't have claim to any title.'

Thomas laughed. 'You will be waiting a long time if it's a title you are wanting, my girl.'

'In truth, Papa, I have a wide circle of friends and acquaintances. I am invited to all the functions held in the area. So, you never know. Would it not surprise you if I married an Earl or a Viscount?'

Hearing the smugness in her sister's tone, Anna smiled blankly at her, letting her know she didn't care in the slightest whether she, herself, dined with royalty or with pigs. The last thing on her mind was trying to capture a husband and be at his beck and call. If she should ever marry, it would be to a man who respected her independence and intelligence and not to someone who thought her main use was keeping his house comfortable.

Perhaps she should once again make plans to travel. Last year she'd been all set to go abroad to Italy and Spain, but her mother had complained loudly that Anna was not to travel without her parents and since neither wanted to go with her, the whole thing had been abandoned. She mustn't be put off again, even if that meant finding a suitable companion to go with her.

The carriage slowed its pace as they passed under Monk Bar and entered the streets of York. Along Deansgate the numerous transports became clogged together in the narrow street. Looking out the window again, Anna saw, above the rooftops, the twin towers of York Minster, the splendid cathedral. She gazed at the beggars lining the road. They looked up, hopeful for some coins to be thrown out the window of the carriage. Anna would have done so gladly but knew through experience the consequences, for within seconds the carriage would be surrounded by street urchins, vagabonds, and shady characters from the dark alleys, all impeding the vehicle's progress, waiting for more money to be thrown out.

'Draw the curtains please, Anna,' Louise ordered.

She knew her mother didn't want to be reminded of the poor while she anticipated spending an evening at an opulent ball. Louise didn't want to see the unfortunates sneer at them in resentment. Her mother never hid her dislike of the impoverished populace.

Though Anna closed the curtains, the harsh sounds and pungent smells of the city drifted into the carriage's interior. She moved the curtain aside barely an inch, so her mother wouldn't notice, but so Anna could see out. She watched people hurry through the streets, finishing their last-minute shopping or heading for home after a long, tiring day's work.

The carriage slowed again as they entered Stonegate, busy with traffic. A couple stood at the edge of the road, dressed in thin ragged clothes with wooden clogs on their feet. The woman's hands covered her face. Her shoulders were hunched in great distress. A child pulled at her skirt. Anna craned her neck to catch a last glimpse of the woman as the man put his arm around her shoulders to comfort her. As it always did, Anna's heart went out to them. The scene, all too common in the crowded city, didn't help to lift Anna out of the despondency that for some reason was on her tonight. Letting the curtain drop back into place, she sighed.

Watkins, their carriage driver, brought the horses to a complete stop as they encountered a crush of vehicles in St Leonard's Place, not far from the Conways' home.

Her father opened the window and called out to Watkins', asking why they had stopped then listened to the reply. 'How many are there in front of us, then?' he asked.

'At least ten or twelve, sir.'

'Blast. We shall be here all night at this rate.'

'Language, Thomas,' Louise muttered. 'Why Harriet had to invite half the city is beyond me. A small dinner party would have sufficed.'

'Oh no, Mama, not for George and Violet's important birthdays,' cried Arabella. Their birthdays are close together and they will be twenty-one and eighteen. A ball is much more suitable than a dinner party.'

Anna checked her amusement at her sister's dismay. Arabella wanted a glittering masquerade ball for her next birthday. She'd read how they were popular on the continent, and only the best would do for Arabella. However, Anna knew she would have a fight on her hands with their mother. Louise maintained strict standards on the Thorntons' social activities.

'We will walk,' declared Thomas.

'What? Walk? I think not,' Louise scoffed.

'Well, it's either that or wait here for half the night. I know which *I* prefer.'

Anna pulled her silk wrap more firmly around her shoulders, ready to alight from the carriage. 'I think it is a good idea, Mother. At least this way we can be where it is comfortable and have some refreshments, while the others are out in the night air awaiting their turn to enter the house.'

Thomas opened the door, telling Watkins their intention of walking. 'It's only a hundred yards or so, come along. I'd like a drink.'

'Really Mama,' complained Arabella, as her father helped her on to the pavement. 'It is most embarrassing.'

* * *

Matthew Cowan stared at the whisky he swirled gently at the bottom of his glass. The man to his left had been talking non-stop for ten minutes, and Matt still didn't know what the fool was gibbering on about.

In one swift movement, Matt swallowed the rest of the whiskey and leaned back against the pillar behind him. Letting the man continue his jabbering, Matt surveyed the room.

His uncle and aunt, along with his cousins, greeted their guests near the front doors. People milled around the large elaborate room, watching and discussing each new arrival. Matt also noticed many of the glances that came in his direction and the way women whispered behind their fans as they walked past. He didn't mind that they talked about him. Sir Hugh's adventurous and mysterious nephew, an enigma, was how they thought of him. Why, people asked themselves, would a man who is wealthy in his own right, as well as having a noble family and good connections, go off into the wilds of South American jungles looking for gemstones? Actually mining alongside the natives he employs? A strange man indeed.

Smiling now at a young woman who was staring at him, Matt winked at her. She immediately blushed and turned away, covering her face with her fan. The girl's mother moved them further away from him, obviously afraid her young daughter might be eaten alive by the man from the jungle. Matt grinned. As a healthy, hot-blooded male, he enjoyed women appraising him, just as much as he got pleasure from judging them in return. He was honest enough to admit his looks drew a lot of women. If a certain woman appealed to him, he took full advantage of it, though he'd never been in a meaningful relationship in his life and had no intentions of changing now.

The sound of laughter brought him out of his reverie. Matt glanced up at the doorway and caught sight of one of the most arresting women he'd encountered in a long time. The woman laughed heartily at some comment made by his uncle. From his position in the corner, Matt was able to study her without her knowledge. He liked what he saw. He admired her golden tresses, arranged to make her look like a Roman goddess. At this distance it was hard to determine the colour of her eyes, but he could see her even white teeth. His gaze followed the slender curve of her neck and shoulders down past the swell of her bust to her small waist. She was a vision of perfection in her shimmering blue gown. He wished he were a painter, to capture her in oils.

'Your glass is empty,' Matt suddenly told the perspiring man beside him, stopping the flow of words about wool prices in mid-sentence. 'I'll get us another,' he said and left before the gaping man could reply.

The crowded reception hall made it difficult to reach his uncle. Once there, he found the beauty gone. 'Who was the woman in blue?'

'My boy, many women are in blue tonight,' Sir Hugh said with a wink.

'Not like this one'

Violet Conway turned to her father. 'I think Matt is asking after Anna Thornton, Papa.'

'Yes, of course. Anna.' Sir Hugh briefly stepped away from his wife and daughter. 'Understand Matt, the Thornton family are good friends of ours, and I'm particularly fond of Anna. She is a wonderful girl and defiantly not one to enter into a dalliance with. Pick someone else to flirt with tonight.'

'Don't be so coarse, Uncle. I merely asked you who she is, that is all.'

'Aye, lad.' His uncle eyed him. 'And I'm merely telling you straight that Anna is not an empty-headed dimwit who'll giggle at your flattery. She is intelligent and will not be patronized by anyone.'

Matt pursed his lips. 'She sounds interesting. A woman who knows her own mind is a rare thing indeed.'

'It's a bit sad really, because many men dislike clever ladies. Some men prefer their women to be docile, which makes the men appear smarter than they really are. I'm concerned Anna will remain a spinster. It'll take the right sort of man to understand her ways and not want to change her.' Sir Hugh gave a disgruntled sniff and moved back to his wife.

Matt turned and headed for the ballroom. He had the sudden urge to dance with a woman in blue.

Chapter 2

A kaleidoscope of colours swirled in the grand ballroom. Hanging from the high ceiling, crystal chandeliers reflected the brilliance of the gold silk wallpaper making the room seem as though Midas had touched it. Potted ferns and palms screened corners so ladies could cool down after an energetic reel and regain their composure.

Anna watched the couples twirling around the dance floor. Her foot tapped in time with the music played by the small orchestra on a raised dais. Arabella danced with a severe-looking, high-bred young chap wearing an intense expression, as though this waltz was the most important event in his life, and he must not make a fool of himself. Anna chuckled, sympathizing with the poor fellow, for Arabella never tolerated anyone who made her look ridiculous.

Her father now came into view as he swung Mrs. Priscilla Weldon close. He gave Anna a wink before swirling away again. Anna grinned and twisted to her mother to comment, but Louise was in deep discussion with the lady on her right.

'Anna,' spoke a quiet voice behind her.

Turning, she let out a delighted cry. 'Edwin!' She happily embraced her and Tom's childhood friend. 'I didn't know you were back in England.'

He smiled warmly, not letting go of her hands. 'I arrived home yesterday evening. Mother and Father have stayed on.'

'Welcome home, Edwin,' Louise said, excusing herself from her conversation. 'Are your parents well?'

'Yes, thank you, Mrs. Thornton.' He bowed slightly.

'Good.' Louise gave a small, thin smile and then turned her back on them.

'How is Tom?' Edwin grinned. 'I received a letter from him a few months ago, and it was the last I heard.'

'You know Tom. He is not the best correspondent. He rarely writes home.' Anna waved her hand in dismissal. 'Anyway, Tom is very well and shall be home soon for Easter.' Sitting, she waited for Edwin to join her. 'Tell me all about your trip and the places you visited. You have been gone over a year. I thought you might never come home.'

Misery swiftly etched Edwin's face before he could control it. 'I wish I had never gone…Oh, I guess it was all right. We saw some beautiful countries and cities and met some interesting people.'

Anna studied him, seeing the sadness on his thin face. Edwin had lost weight, which he didn't have much of in the first place. He looked older and sadder since he went away. Edwin was the epitome of a gentleman, a very gentle man. Only once during their ten-year friendship had she witnessed his anger, when

Tom broke his model sailboat that had taken many months to build. As children, Edwin was often the peacemaker between Anna and Tom, never taking sides. He was always able to calm her impetuous and fiery nature and reaffirm Tom's budding manliness. She and Tom were the decision makers, the risk takers, he the faithful follower.

'Your father made your life difficult, didn't he?' She took his hand in sympathy. 'I guess he didn't take the news of you having weak lungs very well?'

'I tried to stay out of his way as much as possible.' Edwin wrinkled his nose as if he smelt something unpleasant. 'He couldn't help being disappointed. Father so desperately wanted me to follow him into the military. He'd even arranged for me to join his former regiment.'

'Don't defend him, Edwin. I know what he is capable of. I've seen how he bullies you and your mother. I've even been the recipient of his behaviour myself.'

Edwin looked around, frightened that Anna may have drawn attention to them. 'I think I may go and avail myself of some refreshment. Would you care for some?'

She held back a groan at his self-consciousness. He was such a mouse at times. Thankfully, only one man, an attractive man standing not far away, watched them. 'Do stay, Edwin. Don't be upset with me. You know my temper.'

'Yes, I know it.' He sighed, as if the weight of the world rested on his shoulders. 'Still, I think I will find a drink.' Edwin gave her a small bow and left.

During a pause between dances, Arabella glided through the crowd to sit close to Anna and Louise. She arranged herself in the middle of them like a queen, and her faithful followers, in their gowns of every colour, gathered around her like lost sheep.

'Will you dance with Simon Palmer-Horne again, Arabella?' asked one excited young lady, waving her fan at great speed.

'I think he is divine,' gushed another, her eyes overly bright.

Arabella tilted her head. 'No, I don't think I will. After all, he is not titled, is he?' The girls gasped.

'He may not have a title, Arabella, but he is immensely wealthy. As his wife you'd be treated like a princess,' Bernice Pringle touted. 'My Mama says he's a fine catch.'

Arabella glanced at Bernice. 'I have wealth, Bernice. What I want is a title and to live in London. I'm tired of the country. Everyone who is anyone lives in London.'

Chuckling, Anna shook her head. 'Good lord, sister, just listen to yourself. You are so ignorant.'

'Why am I?'

'*Why* is a title so important?'

The young ladies tittered behind their fans. Arabella gave Anna a hateful stare. 'I suppose you're content to marry some poor pig farmer, are you?'

'If I loved him, it would not matter what he was.'

'Yes, well, being a farmer's wife would suit you admirably.'

'It's the person you marry that is significant, not the name.' Anna sighed. A quick stab of pain hit her heart at the contempt in Arabella's eyes. It hurt to fight with her so much, yet, in the past, each time she reached out to breach the gap, Arabella refused the offer.

Anna rose from her seat, not wanting to be near her sister a minute longer. Gathering her skirts, she negotiated her way through the chairs.

'I hope you aren't leaving on my account, Miss Thornton?'

A hurried look at the speaker caused Anna to trip on a chair leg and stumbled against a marble column. She bumped her wrist as she tried to stop herself from falling.

'Miss Thornton!' He clasped her arm to steady her.

Arabella's high-pitched laugh rang out behind them. 'Anna's so desperate for a man, she has to throw herself at one.'

His cold stare silenced Arabella's amusement. 'It's a pity when vulgarity strips away one's beauty.'

She blushed, and again the young women chuckled behind their fans this time at her expense.

Anna slowly gazed up at him. A sudden tingling in her stomach alarmed her as she stared into dark grey eyes, edged in long black lashes. His tanned face had laugh lines, showing an active sense of humour. Warmth rose like a tide into her face. He was the man who had been watching her earlier.

'Are you badly hurt?' A concerned frown wrinkled his brow.

'No. Thank you.' Anna rubbed her wrist. It pained a little, but she was more embarrassed than anything else. She wanted out of this room. The noise vibrated in her ears and heat sucked at her skin.

'Would you care for some wine?'

'No. Thank you.'

'Some air perhaps?' His deep voice washed over her in a soothing caress.

She nodded, acutely aware of him while everything around them seemed to blur.

His smile was for her alone, intimate and compelling. Taking her elbow, he guided her through the throng of people.

Anna's heart pounded in her chest. She glanced up at the handsome man beside her as they reached the balcony. Who was he? She certainly would've remembered him if they'd met before. Such height and dark Adonis looks made him stand out from the average man.

He hesitated. 'Would you like to sit down or walk?'

Secluded lamps lit the gravel paths for guests to stroll and smell the garden's night fragrance. It was the ideal setting for a man who might ask a certain question of his beloved.

She swallowed, unused to this breathlessness that plagued her. 'To walk, I think.'

They stepped down from the wide terrace. After a slight pause, they turned to the left and wandered along the garden paths in silence for a few minutes, until Anna stopped by a large pond. An owl hooted.

'We have not been properly introduced, Mr...?'

'Matthew Cowan at your service, Miss Thornton.'

Her eyes widened. 'So, you know me. That is an unfair advantage, Mr. Cowan.'

'I hope you'll forgive me?'

'Very well.' She dipped her head, smiling. 'Since, in truth, I have some knowledge about you too, now I know your name.'

He smiled in a most attractive way and started that fluttering again in her stomach.

It was an uncommonly mild night for early spring. Anna stole glances at Mr. Cowan whenever she bent to smell a flower. He was quite magnificent to look at, with ebony hair, a straight nose, and a strong jaw line. His broad shoulders tapered to narrow hips, and the fine material of his trousers didn't disguise the well-muscled thighs. The rumours of him working alongside his workers must be true.

They came across a small alcove in a grove of dense rhododendron bushes. Inside, a perfectly placed bench sheltered visitors from any cool breeze. Anna shivered as she sat, more from the close proximity of Mr. Cowan and the suddenly strange effect he evoked than because of the night air.

'Here, take my coat.' He shrugged off his coat and laid it around her shoulders.

'Oh—there's no need, really.' His musky, manly scent lingered on his coat, filling her senses. Again, the quivering started in her stomach, as well as a tightness in her chest. *What is the matter with me?* The strong physical feelings that beleaguered her body just by being near him confused her. Having never felt this way about anyone before, she wasn't sure what to do. It was as though her body had taken possession of her mind and it was experiencing unknown, but welcoming sensations.

'Is your wrist better?'

Anna blinked. In his presence everything that happened before his arrival faded from thought. She wriggled her hand and felt no pain. 'It's completely well, thank you.'

'Good.'

She strove for some semblance of intelligence. 'I have heard you travel the world seeking gemstones. What makes you do that?'

Cowan sighed. 'Well, I have a passion for adventure, and I admire beauty. So, by mining gemstones, I've the thrill of pitting my skill against hazardous conditions, and hopefully, at the end, I get a priceless gem.'

'How fascinating.' She stared openly, no longer coy about admiring him. It was as though he was an exhibit at a museum. He totally captivated her.

'Have you travelled, Miss Thornton?'

She snuggled further into his coat. 'Once. My father took me to Paris for my eighteenth birthday.' Anna laughed. Compared to Cowan's travels, it was nothing.

She gazed up at the velvet night sky. 'Tell me about your travels. It must be so intriguing to explore foreign countries.'

He chuckled. 'I wouldn't say every day was delightful. There were times when all I wanted was a comfortable bed and plenty of hot water to bathe in, which in some countries is a rare thing indeed.'

'You must relish what you do, to put up with those kinds of conditions. What is it like?'

Cowan stared at her as though puzzled.

Anna lowered her lashes, for once annoyed with herself for being too informal. Thankfully, the diffused light from the house hid her blush. 'I do apologize for my forwardness, Mr. Cowan.'

'Don't be sorry. I find it hard to believe you're interested in such details.' His face brightened. 'Most women don't really care for the particulars of my journeys. They usually ask about the gems.'

'I should tell you, Mr. Cowan, I am not like most women. Anyone who knows me will confirm this. I am very much a forward-thinking woman. An independent.'

'How refreshing.'

'Really?' Her eyes widened in disbelief. 'My mother and sister see me as an oddity, an embarrassment. I think they avoid me whenever possible.' She frowned as his expression changed. 'You see, now you are doubting me too.'

'No, I'm not. I'm just surprised by your frankness.' He grinned. 'But I do like to be surprised.'

Her whole body ached with something she didn't understand. She simply knew that she wanted to sit beside him until time stopped. It was madness really. They were strangers, having just met. In the past, she never cared about the conservative judgments of others, and usually did or said whatever she wanted, but this situation was all so new and different for her. She didn't want to make a mistake. It was suddenly vital she didn't turn this man away with her unique way of doing things. No man had ever affected her the way this fine, extraordinary man did.

Approaching footsteps broke the seductive spell woven around them. A gentleman marched past. A garden torch lit his profile. Anna straightened. 'Edwin?'

He turned. 'There you are, Anna. I've been looking for you everywhere'

She stood, frowning at him. 'What is the matter?'

Edwin glanced from Cowan to Anna. 'It's your mother. She has taken ill and wants to go home. I believe it's one of her headaches. Your father has ordered the carriage and asked me to find you and your sister.'

Anna reluctantly handed Mr. Cowan his coat. 'I must go,' she said, though her tone belied her wish to do so. To walk away from him after such a brief time together seemed wrong. She hesitated.

'May I call on you tomorrow?' He took her hand and bowed over it, smiling. 'Perhaps we could go riding?'

She felt dizzy with excitement and relief. 'Yes. I would like that very much. Good night.'

A discreet cough came from Edwin. 'I will see you to the carriage now, Anna.'

She stared at him, not liking his high-handed manner. Childhood friend or not, he didn't control her. With a last lingering look at Mr. Cowan, she walked away.

***

Matt watched her leave. His heartbeat quickened as he recalled every detail of Miss Thornton's lovely heart-shaped face. She made his breath catch in his throat and the blood race through his body, making him feel very much alive. Taking a deep breath, he tried to slow his frantic pulse rate. It was absurd. He could not fathom why she should affect him so strongly. A few hours ago, he didn't know she existed. Now he wanted to know everything about her. Feeling such a reaction, and not only physical, was not common for him. His customary dealings with women consisted of polite conversation or bodily fulfilment. Marriage and children, he knew, would interfere with his way of life. He needed the freedom to come and go as he pleased. Therefore, he always made sure not to let a woman become too hopeful of him.

However, when he least expected, here was this splendid creature, and for the first time in his life, he wondered what it would be like to have someone to love and for that person to love him in return.

This inner torment couldn't have happened at a worst time, when he was so busy collecting investors for the mine and with the hope of leaving the country again by the summer.

He strolled back towards the house. He'd call on her tomorrow and then never see her again. He could do that. Nodding at his strategy, he relaxed. Nothing would change his plans.

Chapter 3

Twin rays of sun streamed through the tall sash windows of Anna's bedroom when she awoke the following morning. In her large, warm bed, she lay thinking of the night before and of the man whose face swam in front of her eyes. Today, she would see him again. She bit her lip to stop a smile from spreading. Something had happened to her last night. For the first time ever, a man had grabbed her attention and held it, no mean feat for anyone. Yet, Matt Cowan had done it with ease, and she was glad. Perhaps it was time for her to spread her wings and feel the giddiness of being the centre of attention. Arabella did it all the time and kept a string of beaus hanging on her every word.

She frowned. Could she do it? Could she keep Mr. Cowan's interest? She'd had no practice, having spent her adult life shying away from entering the marriage market. Did she have the skills to capture a husband? Did she want one?

Slowly she sat up, deep in thought. A husband? The idea wasn't new, but neither had it been a pressing concern. Secretly, she had assumed she'd be content becoming a spinster, riding her horse and being a lovable aunt to her siblings' offspring. She hadn't expected to be swept away by the idea of some romantic hero coming into her life. That was until Mr.

Cowan looked at her with his smoky eyes. Mr. Cowan as a husband? The thought gave her a thrill, made her heart thump. Would he be the kind to let her remain herself?

Maisie breezed into the room carrying fresh towels and a jug of warm water. 'Good morning, Miss. Did you enjoy your evenin'? I didn't want to ask last night with the Mistress feeling so poorly. I hope she's better this mornin'.'

Anna threw back the bedcovers and then went into her dressing room. She stripped as Maisie poured warm water into the basin.

'It was interesting,' she said as she lathered the scented soap on her arms. The aroma of lavender filled the room.

'That's grand.' Maisie pulled open the doors of the double wardrobe. 'What do you wish to wear today, Miss?'

Donning a clean chemise, Anna observed her clothes. 'My green riding habit. I met a gentleman last night. He is calling today and we're going riding.'

Maisie's mouth gaped.

'There is no need to look like that, Maisie.'

'Eh, I'm sorry, Miss,' Maisie mumbled, helping her with the dress. 'I'm surprised, that's all.'

'Well, to be honest, I am surprised too.' Anna grinned. Anticipation bubbled up inside her. If this was the feeling when one went courting, then she could kick herself for waiting so long to begin.

* * *

The breakfast room situated on the east side of the house caught the warmth of the rising sun. Decorated in pale shades to reflect the light, its mahogany furniture gleamed in polished perfection. This less impersonal and more cosy setting was the dining area favoured by the family.

Entering the room, Anna smiled at her parents and Arabella, already seated at the table. 'Good morning all. You look a little better, Mother.'

Louise nodded and dabbed her mouth with a napkin. 'Yes, I feel slightly improved.'

Anna took note of her wan face and the bruised skin beneath her eyes but said nothing of it. She stepped to the sideboard laden with covered silver platters containing hot food. After filling her plate with bacon, eggs, kippers, and toast she sat down at the table and smiled at Arabella. Not even she could spoil her happiness this morning.

Arabella scowled from across the table. 'Why are you in such a fine mood?'

'Do not start, Arabella,' Thomas warned from his place at the head of the table. He folded his newspaper. 'I'm to go into York on business. I'll be gone most of the morning.'

'You are going to York?' Arabella became instantly alert. 'Oh, Papa, may I go with you? Could you leave me at the Conways' and collect me this evening?'

'No. I want you to stay home and help your mother. I shall call at the Conways' myself.'

Louise sipped her tea. 'Do apologize on my behalf again, Thomas. Tell Harriet I will see her during the week.'

Arabella pushed back her chair and stood. 'But Papa why can't I go? Mama has her maid, and Anna is here. I want to see Violet and—'

'I will be busy today.' Anna buttered her toast. 'I have a visitor calling to see me.' She smiled at Arabella's shocked expression.

'What? You have a visitor?' Arabella sat down with a disgruntled thump. 'Oh, I should have guessed. It's dreary old Edwin.'

Anna smiled sweetly. 'It's not Edwin at all. Mr. Matthew Cowan is coming.' A blaze of triumph warmed her as she glanced at her mother and sister's stunned faces.

'Is he really?' Louise sounded amazed.

Anna looked at her father. 'Does that surprise you too, Papa?'

'No, no, my dear. It's just I was going to meet with him later in the week, but if he is still here when I return, I might as well discuss a bit of business with him today. That is, if it's all right with you?'

'Yes, of course.' Anna turned to Nancy the parlour maid, who entered to clear away. 'Has Miss Maggie had her breakfast?'

'Yes, Miss. Had her tray early she did, Miss. She wanted to go for a ride, I think, Miss.'

Nodding her thanks, Anna began to read her father's newspaper and finish her breakfast but when Evans stood in the doorway to announce Mr. Cowan had arrived, her nerves jingled with excitement.

He strode into the breakfast room, and at the sight of him, Anna's heart trembled, and her stomach flipped against the breakfast she'd just eaten. He looked magnificent. The riding clothes he wore clung to his lean taut body, showing the classic figure of a man in the prime of his life.

Anna's senses heightened as her pulse sped up. She was amazed to find herself aware of little things like the light shining on his dark hair and the heavy aroma of bacon and kippers mixed with the delightful perfume of hothouse orchids and jonquils placed in a vase in the middle of the table.

Cowan flashed everyone a boyish grin and apologized for interrupting the meal.

'Nonsense, my good fellow.' Thomas waved to Nancy to set another place. 'Sit down and have something to eat.'

'No, thank you, Thomas. I've already eaten, but I will have coffee, please.' He gave Nancy a smile and looked across at Anna as he sat beside Arabella. 'I've developed the taste for it.'

Arabella scowled at him and Anna knew her sister well enough to know she was remembering his slight of her at the Conway's ball.

Louise refilled her teacup from the silver teapot. 'Are your aunt and uncle well, Mr. Cowan?'

'Indeed, they are, Mrs. Thornton, though a little tired after last night. They send their regards to you.'

Louise nodded in acknowledgement.

Thomas folded his napkin. 'I know you are here to go riding with Anna, Matt, but maybe later we could have the discussion we talked about at the club?'

'Certainly.' Glancing over at Louise, he asked if she'd recovered from her recent ill health.

'Yes, thank you. I am well recovered,' Louise's priggish reply accompanied the haughty raising of her chin. 'What are your plans for today, Anna?'

Anna stared at her mother. Louise rarely took any interest in her daily activities. 'Mr. Cowan and I are to go riding. I thought I might show Mr. Cowan the estate.'

Thomas nodded. 'You must ride one of our horses, Matt, and save your own beast for the journey back to York.'

'Thank you.' Matt inclined his head.

'Why was I not informed of Mr. Cowan's visit?' Louise suddenly demanded.

Anna looked at her father who flushed at Louise's outburst. 'Last night you were not well enough to be disturbed.'

Louise turned to her husband. 'Did you know about it, Thomas? Are you all hiding things from me? I would like to know what is happening in my own house.'

'No, I didn't know about it until this morning, but what of it? And I wouldn't hide anything from you, you know that.'

Matt stood. 'If you will excuse me, Mrs. Thornton. I shall wait at the stables for Miss Thornton.' He strode from the room before Louise uttered another word.

Arabella choked on her tea. 'How rude!'

'Be quiet,' Anna hissed, watching their mother hold her head and screw up her face in pain.

Bleached of all colour, Louise dismissed the maids with a wave of her hand and then addressed Anna. 'Arabella will…will go with you. It's not suitable for you to…to gallop around the countryside on your own with a stranger.'

Arabella gaped. 'Mama, I have no wish to go riding with *them*. I intend to go visiting now I cannot go to York. I left my card with Florence Moorhouse last week and I—'

'You may go and see your friend, Arabella.' Thomas nodded at her, overriding Louise's order.

Arabella quickly left her place without looking back.

Anna rose, swishing the skirt of her riding habit out behind her. 'We will be home around noon.' She looked at her father, darted a glance at her mother and stepped from the room. Out in the hall, she paused, as her father's words reached her. The urge to run to the stables and Matt Cowan was strong, yet something made her stay and listen.

'We should encourage this new friendship of Anna's,' Thomas said. 'It's time she was married, and he is the first to interest her. She is in need of a husband, Louise. At twenty-one she should have children by now.'

'She gazes at him like a bitch in heat.'

'Louise!'

Anna closed her eyes, mortified by her mother's words. Her heart wanted her to run but her head told her to wait.

'It's wrong for her to be with a man unchaperoned,' Louise spat. 'You let her run wild.'

'As you did?'

Louise's gasp was loud in the stillness. 'How dare you, Thomas.' Her cold voice sent a shiver down Anna's spine. 'But if you insist on degrading me by flinging the past in my face then yes, I don't want her to repeat my mistakes. Lord knows I've paid dearly for them.'

'Being married to me for all these years is so painful is it?'

'No, of course not. Don't twist my words.'

'I shall encourage Anna's relationship with Matt Cowan. I'd have thought you to be eager to have her wed?'

'I am, but—'

'But what?'

Anna held her breath and leaned against the red silk-papered wall of the hall.

'It doesn't matter.' Suddenly, her mother sounded very tired.

'Louise, Matthew Cowan is of good character. He is a gentleman,' Thomas said quietly. 'He is our dearest friends' nephew. I like him, and I would not do business with someone I didn't trust, now would I?'

'Do business with?' Louise sounded puzzled. 'I do not remember you doing business with him.'

Frozen to the spot in the hall, Anna heard the rustle of movement, a chair scraping across the highly polished breakfast room floor. Her father's voice now came from a different direction. 'I mentioned it on the way to the Conways' and again this morning, remember?'

'Everything…everything is all very vague.' Louise's tone sounded strained. 'I have a blinding light flashing behind my eyes, Thomas. I cannot bear another headache so soon. The pain is torture.'

'Come, my dearest. I'll take you upstairs to rest.'

The noise of rustling skirts and moving chairs indicated her parents were leaving the table. Anna crossed the hall into her father's study. She left the door ajar and peeked through the gap like a naughty child. Her parents emerged into the hall, her father cradling his wife against him. 'Let me call the doctor, Louise, I beg you.'

Louise halted; her expression etched in pain. 'No. It will pass.'

'But it comes back, dear heart. You cannot go on like this.'

She held on to his arm. Her lips became a thin blue line in her pale face. 'What is happening to me, Thomas?' Her voice trembled.

'I don't know, but I'm going to find out. I insist you see some doctors.'

'I am frightened.'

'Don't be, my love, for I am always here for you.' He placed a small kiss on her forehead. They continued on and Thomas called to Evans. Anna turned away from the door and nibbled her fingertips.

What were her mother's mistakes?

The thought of her righteous mother having made errors in her past intrigued her, but Mr. Cowan was waiting. *Matt.*

* * *

Jasper pranced sideways, pulling at the bit in his mouth and impatient to be away. Already alarmed by her mother's outburst, Anna felt like giving him a slap for his shenanigans. She knew her tension relayed to him. 'You can have your way in a minute,' she muttered to him. The horse turned and Anna had to twist in the saddle to speak. 'Do I shock you, Mr. Cowan by riding astride?'

He adjusted his grip on the reins and grinned. 'Not at all.'

'Good.'

'If you want to be truly daring, you could call me by my first name. That would be even more shocking.' He sat back in the saddle with laughter in his eyes. 'How audacious are you, Miss Thornton?'

'Very.' She laughed. 'As you shall soon find out.' Jasper broke into a trot as she spoke.

'Is he always such a handful?' Matt indicated her horse. He rode Tom's horse, so as to rest his own mount.

She patted Jasper's neck. 'No, he isn't. Only, I usually let him have his head at the beginning. He longs to be thundering over the fields and racing through the woods.'

'Well, don't let me stop you.' He scanned the fields spreading beyond the stable block. 'How about a race?'

'You aren't familiar with the area. It wouldn't be fair.'

Matt grinned. 'The horse is, though.'

She stood in the stirrups and pointed to a craggy outcrop high on the hill, her favourite spot. 'Up there. Do you think you can do it?'

'You watch me,' Matt shouted, and with a loud whoop, he urged the horse into a gallop.

Anna screamed with laughter. 'You cheat!'

It took a fair distance for her to catch him, but once they were out of a small belt of trees at the bottom of the hill, they rode neck and neck. The many rabbit holes and walking ruts, from the sheep and cows, as well as outcrops of rock dotting the hillside, made for a perilous climb. Halfway up, Matt went the wrong way. Anna, knowing exactly where to go, raced ahead and arrived at the top first.

She was sitting on a long flat rock with a smile on her face when Matt bounded over the rise.

At the sight of her, he laughed. Dismounting, he came and flopped himself down beside her, puffing. 'You were right, it was unfair.'

'You should not have cheated.'

Matt reclined back on the rock. 'I cannot remember the last time I rode like that. What a delight.'

After a moment of indecision, Anna lay down alongside of him. His presence stimulated her, but she also felt secure with him. They were silent for some time, happy just being together. They stared up at the clear blue sky, watching the birds fly overhead and listening to the sounds of nature.

Matt smiled. 'What a magical place.'

'I come here all the time. When I was younger, I would escape my governess, beg our cook, Mrs. Wilson, to pack me some food and I'd spend all day up here with my dog.'

'I can imagine you doing that. What was your dog called?'

'Shep.'

'I always wanted a dog.'

'You never had a dog?'

'No.'

Anna sat up and gazed down at him. His face was
unreadable. The laughter had left his grey eyes as
though replaced by a mask. From her own childhood,
she knew not everyone was happy during those
seemingly innocent years. She remembered Sir Hugh
once telling her his brother had died, and his only
nephew was overseas. 'Did you have a happy
childhood?'

'No. My father died when I was young. When my
mother remarried, my stepfather and I didn't become
friends. I was sent away to a boarding school, which
meant leaving my mother.' He sat up, pulling his legs
up to rest his arms on his knees. 'I hated my
stepfather from that moment on and vowed never to
return home to live under his rules or use his money.'
He reached to pick at a patch of moss growing on the
rock's grey surface.

'You never went home?'

'A few times. To visit Mother, but I never slept
under *his* roof again.'

'Your mother must have been awfully sad about
this?'

Matt shrugged. 'Perhaps. Later she had another
son. So, after finishing school I went overseas
searching for some purpose to my life and hopefully
some happiness. I met up with a good friend of my
father's, and he took me under his wing. I stayed with
him until I received my inheritance, and then we
became partners in business.'

Anna felt his pain. She could see the lines it etched
into his face. He spoke without emotion, as though
reading from a verse. They shared something in
common, rejection. Being a man, he was able to cover

his rejection by roaming the world, losing himself in new countries, immersing himself in his work. However, it was much harder for a woman. Rejection in the family, by all its members or by just one, might mean the home became a prison and one room a cell.

'What about you?' He glanced at her. 'What were your years as a young child like?' 'I cannot honestly say I was unhappy all the time, because I wasn't. My brother and I, and sometimes our friend Edwin, enjoyed playing and riding. My father has always been my knight, to listen to me and love me. Still, for all of that, I felt the undercurrent of my mother's…dislike. She hid it well and still does most times. I know how she feels about me, but I don't know why. Ever since I can remember, I have had to call her Mother, not Mama, like Tom and Arabella could. When Maggie was little, she was told to call her Mother also. To me that makes it perfectly clear how she feels. And dear Papa never mentions it.'

She gazed out over rolling fields. A swift soared in front of them. It glided for a minute on a warm air current. 'I guess he is torn both ways. That is why I found this place. My sanctuary.' Anna swept her arms out wide, taking in the top of the hill. Her chest swelled with love and pride over this land of her forefathers. 'Up here I can think. Here I can sing, scream, and shout. I can pretend I'm happy and content. No eyes watch me, and no ears hear my voice. I can say what I like and know there is no one waiting for me to make mistakes, no one ready to criticize all I believe in. Nobody gossiping about how strange I am.'

'Gossip about you?' Matt frowned, puzzled. 'What is there to gossip about?'

'People talk about how different I am. I have no friends, except my maid. I don't go visiting. Rarely do I shop for frivolous things. Embroidery and sewing bore me. I am not interested in the piano or painting, and I talk to people of all classes instead of staying amongst my own. I ride astride, instead of side-saddle. Oh, the list is endless,' she declared, exasperated.

Matt moved closer and took hold of her hand. 'Don't be ashamed, and never change. Yes, you're a little unusual, but wonderfully so. It would be a happier world if everyone behaved differently than the next person, instead of everyone trying to mimic each other. Why do you think some men make lives away from their families? Because they want something new and refreshing. Whether it be a mistress or their work, it doesn't matter, and I'm sure women are just the same. We all want our lives to be stimulating, for they are too short to let them go stale.' He frowned and his voice lowered as he turned away. 'We must do what it takes to makes us happy, even if others don't understand us.'

Anna gazed at him in wonder.

'Forgive me, I was too forward, my words too bitter.' He smiled. 'I've spent too much time alone with my thoughts.'

'There is no need to apologize.' She reached out to touch his sleeve but pulled her hand back just in time. 'I find it amazing to believe you feel the same as I do. I thought I was a bit mad.'

His gaze locked with hers. 'No, you're not mad.'

Her heart thumped hard against her ribs. He understood. At last, she was not alone in her outlandish thinking. This man thought the same as she did. She would treasure this moment for the rest of her life. The urge to reach out and make sure he was real made her tremble. She desperately wanted him to kiss her. Her mother's nasty words flashed through her mind, but she didn't care. She wanted his touch and didn't have the will to resist the need. 'Will you…will you kiss me?' She whispered, unashamedly bold.

His eyes lit up as a lazy smile creased his face. 'I've been wanting to since I met you, but are you sure?'

'I know I shouldn't want to, but then that makes me want it all the more. Am I very wanton?'

He chuckled and lifted a tendril of her hair with his finger. 'Some people would believe that a man and woman should never touch unless it's in their marriage bed, but I've been to countries where women and men love as nature intended, without constraint, without the blessings of a priest beforehand. I admire them for such freedom.'

Such intimate talk took her breath away. 'But…but men do have freedom unlike women.'

'True.' He wound the tendril around his finger. 'However, I know of some women who enjoy the same liberties, only they hide it very well.'

'Yet when they are found out, they are scorned, unlike men.'

He leaned closer. 'I can't change the ways of the world.'

She swallowed and whispered, 'No, but I think you'll change mine.'

Leisurely he lowered his head, blocking out the sun. Feather-light kisses rained over her face. The whispery sensation tingled every nerve. After what seemed forever, their lips met. An intensity of emotions engulfed and overwhelmed her. She curled her fingers into the cloth of his riding jacket, and he pulled her closer. The hardness of his chest tantalized as well as frightened her.

Matt gently pulled away and took a shaky breath. 'Nice.'

'Yes, and worth waiting for.'

He frowned. 'Are you telling me that someone as adventurous as you has never tasted the delights of a man's kiss before?'

'No one has ever tempted me.'

A wry smile lifted the corners of his mouth. 'Can I tempt you again?'

'Yes, I'd like to, but...' Confused, Anna lowered her head to hide her face. 'A lot of men are put off by such forwardness. It's very unladylike. Only, I cannot help being what I am.' She shrugged, wondering if she'd done the right or wrong thing by asking him to kiss her. In the end, she did what felt right to her and ignored the tug of guilt. 'Mother is correct to think badly of me.'

Matt lifted her face with a fingertip and stared into her eyes. 'Life makes it terribly hard to be perfect. Your station makes it twice as difficult.'

'If I was a village maid working in a mill would it be easier?' Anna shook her head. 'No.'

Sadness flickered across his face. 'I don't have the answers, Anna.'

'Neither do I, but I should try harder. I know what the family expects of me. Only, I don't think I'm able to deliver it. I fail them all.' She hurriedly scrambled to her feet and moved away. 'I apologize. You don't wish to hear my concerns. I'm ashamed of myself. Forgive me.'

As agile as a jaguar, he jumped to his feet. 'Forgive what? Do you know how honoured I feel to receive such honesty and openness?' In two steps, he was inches from her. The naked emotion on his face shocked and thrilled her. 'I feel as if I've known you all my life. I've told you things I've never mentioned to anyone before. Astonishingly, it seems quite natural discussing my thoughts with you. It's as though you were waiting here for me to find you.' He touched his forehead to hers and sighed. 'Maybe I needed to find you.'

Anna reached up, cupping his handsome face in her hands. 'I too, think I was waiting here for you.' Passion filled her like a bursting dam, violent and terrifying. Her senses whirled with bewilderment and awareness. She didn't know whether to laugh or cry at this unexpected miracle.

'Promise me,' he said.

'Promise you what?' She gazed up at him. Knowing she would promise him the world if she could.

'That for the rest of the day I will receive nothing but smiles and laughter from you.' He winked and held out his arm to escort her back to the horses.

They returned to the house at midday. As they entered the hall, Evans told them a small luncheon awaited them on the terrace where the table was laid with cold meats and delicacies. Matt held Anna's chair for her and, as she sat, Thomas and Maggie came out to join them. Anna grinned at Maggie. Louise's absence from the meal had allowed Thomas to send for his youngest daughter.

As the meal progressed, Matt told wonderful tales of his adventures in the countries of Africa and South America. Anna forgot to eat as she listened and laughed.

'I would adore travelling.' Maggie sighed dreamily. 'It would be so splendid to cross oceans and see the dolphins swimming along the side of the ship, and whales, too.'

'And sea monsters,' Matt teased her, making them all laugh.

'There are no such things,' Maggie retorted, though she didn't look completely sure of her statement.

'I shall bring you one back, from my next trip,' he joked. Then, as though realizing what he'd said, he looked over at Anna.

She forced a smile to her lips, but it felt wooden. *So, soon you'll have to leave me.* She averted her gaze and took a sip of tea. This morning they had talked plenty and when Matt mentioned his work, she heard the fervour in his voice.

Placing her teacup back on its saucer, she risked another glance at him. He ate thoughtfully, temporarily lost to the conversation at the table. Anna wondered if he struggled too with this sudden relationship. Their meeting must have come as a surprise to him as well as her.

'Well, if you are finished Matt, shall we go talk some business? We shan't be too long, Anna dear.' Thomas rose from his chair. 'Oh, maybe you can check on your mother? Tell her I will be up in a while.'

Anna nodded and summoned a smile. *Please, Lord, don't let Mother read my face.*

'I like Mr. Cowan, Anna,'' Maggie said, interrupting her thoughts.

Before Anna could reply, Miss Foster came to whisk Maggie away to the gardens to paint the new spring flowers.

Anna sat and fiddled with her silver teaspoon. 'Yes, Maggie, I like Mr. Cowan too,' she mumbled to herself. She'd only known him for such a very short time. Was it only physical attraction she felt, or was it more? Never having been in love, she didn't know what to think, and there was no one to confide in. Her mother rejected any intimate discussions and talking to Arabella was certainly out of the question. Maisie wouldn't really understand, for she'd never been in love either.

Nancy and Edith startled her as they came bustling in to clear away the debris of the meal. 'Oh, beg your pardon, Miss. We thought everyone had gone.' Nancy hastily backed away.

'It's quite all right.' Anna rose. 'And how is your grandmother?'

'She's much better, thank you, Miss. Your food baskets were very welcomed.'

'Let me know if you need anything else.'

Anna lingered while going up the plush, red-carpeted staircase to look at the familiar paintings of country scenes hanging along the wall. At the top, portraits of family members and ancestors filled the long gallery that ran the length of the first-floor landing. The latest addition was her very own portrait. She studied the painting of herself. The artist had done an excellent piece of work. The background of dark navy contrasted favourably with the lemon of her dress and highlighted her hair to nearly white-blonde. Her eyes twinkled with mischief, and her smile taunted the viewer. She remembered, at the time of the sitting, how Tom stood behind the painter and made faces at her, making her laugh.

Taking a step back, Anna surveyed the rest of the paintings and compared them to hers. The austere appearance of the dignified and solemn faces of her ancestors made her portrait seem overly bright and gaudy, definitely the cuckoo in the pigeons' nest. Well, she was used to that feeling. No wonder her mother said Anna's portrait looked common. Her father argued it wasn't bad at all and hung the portrait personally, to soften the effect of Louise's stinging words.

Anna walked along the gallery until she reached her mother's bedroom door, and after tapping gently, was bidden to enter. Louise reclined on a dark green velvet chaise pulled up close to the fire. 'How are you, Mother?' The room was uncomfortably hot.

Louise paused from the fine stitching she worked onto a new handkerchief. 'Why do you ask?' she asked, without looking up. 'I am perfectly well.'

'Papa asked me to see how you fared.'

'I cannot think why. Where is your father? He told me he would come straight up after he had eaten.' Louise's stare was glacial. Her hair hung in loose strands having escaped the bun at the nape of her neck. A tea stain blotted her blouse.

Anna frowned. She never saw her mother in anything less than impeccable attire. Astonished, she noticed Louise stitched the initials on the handkerchief upside down. A quiver of alarm tingled down her spine. 'P—Papa is in his study. He is discussing business with Matt Cowan.'

'*Mr. Cowan*? That man again?' Louise left the chaise and faced Anna. 'The one you lust after?' Spittle sprayed Anna's face as her mother leaned forward. 'I thought he had gone, and now I hear he is in the study. I do not want that man in this house, do you hear me?' Louise gripped Anna's arm painfully. 'Nor do I want you near him.'

'Mother, calm down.' Anna unfastened her mother's cruel fingers. 'Matt Cowan is a nice man, a good person. Why are you acting this way?' The outburst startled her. Her mother's ire over Matt didn't make sense.

'Listen to me. I am your mother, mistress of this house and what I say is—' Louise suddenly bent over, moaning in pain. She held her head with one hand, while the other groped around feeling for something to grasp.

Anna helped her, forcing her back on the chaise. 'Lie back. Yes, that's right.' She lifted her mother's feet and placing them under a woollen blanket. 'I will ring for Papa.'

'No.' Louise clasped Anna's arm as she made to leave. 'Tell your papa nothing.' She spoke through clenched teeth. 'He worries too much.'

'A doctor should be called—'

'It's easing now. I will be all right soon. It will pass.' Louise closed her eyes and slowly relaxed her body. 'It always does.'

Watching her mother, Anna resisted offering any comfort. She never willingly touched her mother for fear of the rejection she knew she would receive. 'How many of these attacks do you suffer? More than you let us know about?'

'I'll not tell you,' Louise snapped, but then she opened her eyes and peered at her suspiciously. 'Yes, I have these attacks often.'

'What about the doctor? You should see someone about this.'

'There is no need. I just need to take some laudanum to help with the pain and then I am better. Get it for me, will you? It's in the top drawer near the bed.'

Anna retrieved the small brown bottle and gave her mother a dose. The drug reduced the pain enough for her to fall asleep. The bedroom door opened and Maude, Louise's personal maid, entered. 'My mother is unwell, Maude. I have given her a dose of laudanum, and she is asleep. Don't let anything disturb her. My father will be up shortly.'

After a final check that her mother slept comfortably, Anne left the room and went downstairs.

* * *

Matt stood as Anna came into the study. She looked worried but managed to smile at him. His chest tightened and the sensation stunned him in its strength. He didn't want to feel anything for a woman, not now, not when he was all set to go abroad again.

'I'm sorry to interrupt, Papa,' she said. 'Mother had another headache attack a short time ago.'

Thomas immediately made for the door; his face strained.

'Papa, she is sleeping now. She is all right,' Anna assured him.

'I'll go up and make certain. Can we finish this another time, Matt?'

Matt nodded. 'Yes. Yes, of course, Thomas.'

Once her father left the room, Anna seemed to wilt. Matt crossed to her. 'Sit down. Shall I pour you a brandy?' He glanced over to the array of bottles and glasses in a cabinet.

'No, thank you.'

'Is your mother terribly ill?'

'I don't know.' She gazed up at him. Her blue-green eyes showed doubt. 'Have you ever met my mother before?'

'No, I haven't. Why do you ask?'

'Oh—it's nothing.' She waved her hand in dismissal. 'Um...do you care for a walk in the gardens?'

'No. I want to know why you asked that question.' He studied her. 'What is the matter, Anna?'

She turned from him and fiddled with her sleeve. 'My mother has taken a dislike to you. I cannot think why. She became terribly upset when she learned you were still here.' Her voice dropped to a whisper. 'I believe she is aware of our…friendship. She said some nasty things to me.'

Matt knelt on one knee in front of her, wanting to offer comfort. 'Maybe she doesn't like the thought of her daughter growing up.'

Anna shook her head. 'That wouldn't concern her at all. She is not herself. The mere mention of your name sends her into fits of rage. Something is wrong.'

'I'm sorry she feels this way.' He cupped her face in one hand and gazed deeply into her eyes. 'I know you must abide by your mother's wishes. If she forbids my calling, then I shan't. As much as it would pain me not to see you, I'd rather that than have you being in strife.'

She lowered her head. 'I don't want to stop seeing you, but neither do I want to be responsible for my mother having these attacks.'

'Have you been the cause before?'

'I have always been a disappointment to my mother. But recently I have been well-behaved. So no, at least, I think I'm not the cause.'

'There is your answer.'

'It's not so easy. She doesn't approve of me, of anything I do, and now she doesn't approve of you because we have become friends. I don't understand it.'

Matt stood and went to the window. He was torn between his duty as a gentleman and the desire to be with Anna at every opportunity. Only, he would be away soon and dare not tempt fate.

'So, what are we going to do?'

'We—We could meet in secret? If you want to, that is.'

He heard her unease. She was in conflict. He turned to her. 'I'll not be here for very much longer, Anna. Do you want to take the risk?'

'I honestly don't know.'

Chapter 4

Anna woke early. While Maisie prepared a hot bath, Anna stared out of the window and ate from the breakfast tray. She hoped it would not rain. A streak of cerulean on the horizon promised relief from the grey and overcast sky.

After bathing, she agonized over which dress to wear, lifting different ones out to Maisie. 'I think the duck-egg blue skirt and jacket, with the white blouse.'

Maisie looked sceptical as she helped her to dress. 'Never have I known you to be fussy on decidin' what to wear, Miss, and as for a bath and hair washin' again? It were only done three days back.'

'I wish to look my best,' Anna said, while Maisie finished buckling her kidskin boots for her. 'I'm spending the day in York. If anyone asks, I didn't take you because you are suffering from a cough. Understood?'

'But I don't have a cough, Miss.' Maisie frowned before a cunning expression crossed her face. 'Why can't I go with you like I allus do?'

Pinning on her small hat dyed the same colour as the outfit, Anna sighed. 'Today I need to go by myself. Can you please pretend to be unwell?'

'I don't like it.'

'There's no other way. Mother insists on my taking you when I go to York. You know I'm not supposed to go on my own.' Anna crossed the room and stood in front of the mirror. The pale blue suited her. She looked elegant and refined, every inch a lady—a stark contrast to the devilish thoughts that ran through her mind at times. The small hat was tilted at an angle over her forehead and at the back, its brim turned up to show the array of ringlets and curls Maisie had struggled to make perfect.

Adjusting the short-waisted jacket with lace under cuffs matching the frothy lace of the blouse, she gazed at Maisie's anxious face. 'Don't worry. I'll leave a message for Papa downstairs. You might not be bothered by anyone at all.' Anna picked up a silver silk reticule and put some money into it from her top drawer.

'I don't like lyin' to the Mistress. She can see straight through me,' Maisie moaned. 'Like last time, when I 'ad to lie about you and Master Tom. She knew you both hadn't gone ridin' but instead went to Holtby village and watched a prize fight. I were beside meself with worry.'

'That was two years ago.' Anna laughed, filled with excitement. 'Tom and I paid dearly for doing it. He was sent back to school early for taking me, and I was confined to this room for a week.'

Still, attending her first fight was worth the trouble it caused. She begged Tom for hours before he gave in and took her. An old barn held the fight with bales of straw for seating, not that anyone sat. She'd stood on a bale so she could see over the heads of the men who jostled each other for the best view of the ring. Tom became so nervous, hoping no one would see her there, that he gave her his old coat to wear and a hat to pull down low over her eyes. It was very thrilling, and Anna won three pounds on the winner.

'All will be well, dearest Maisie, just keep to this room.' Leaving the bedroom, Anna stole down the servants' steep and narrow staircase at the end of the first floor, the quickest way to reach the back entrance of the house.

She paused in the service corridor to listen for anyone coming before turning left towards the kitchen. As she opened the large green door, a blast of warm air enveloped her. The servants' chatter stopped as they nodded to her and said good morning. Evans stood to attention at once, and Mrs. Wilson, enjoying a cup of tea before the breakfast rush got underway, slowly rose from her chair.

'Please, sit down again, Mrs. Wilson.' Anna knew it was hard for her to walk in the mornings because of her arthritic knees. She enjoyed a quick respite once the cooking got underway and her girls went about their morning jobs. 'I'm sorry to disturb you all so early.' She turned her gaze to the butler. 'Could you give my father a message, please, once he is down to breakfast?'

'Yes, of course, Miss Anna,' Evans replied with a stiff, short bow.

'Inform him I am spending the day in York. I don't know what time I shall return.'

'Very good, Miss.' Evans bowed again.

Mrs. Wilson smiled as Anna also thanked her for the lovely breakfast tray.

On leaving the kitchen, she stepped out into the cobbled yard. It was a hive of activity as maids came and went carrying bundles of laundry and buckets of ash or slops, efficiently going about their mundane chores as they did no matter what the weather or day. A cart rumbled into the yard to deliver produce from the home farm. The driver dipped his cap in greeting, and Anna nodded in reply. She strode through one of the archways in the six-foot high stonewall bordering the yard and headed down the path to the stables.

The hubbub continued in the stable yard, as men and boys toiled beneath the rising sun. They were highly experienced and skilled in equine care and were proud to be associated with the Thornton Estate's magnificent horses. As young lads mucked out the horse stalls, piles of fouled straw grew and steamed in the morning air. Two grooms carried bales of clean straw and hay, while others rolled heavy barrels of molasses, oats and corn to the large stockroom. All the horses were tied to their stable doors in readiness for their brush down. The noise of their hooves striking on the stone flags of the yard sounded like a dozen blacksmiths at work.

Anna noticed Watson checking the family transports for damage. At his feet, stood a small can of black grease to coat the axle and working parts of the undercarriage. She loved the sight and smell of the stables. As a child, she spent many hours here watching the men work, listening to the talk about the yard.

'You're up and about early, Miss.' Bert frowned. He came toward her, wiping his hands on an old rag.

'I'm going to York, Bert. Can you have Jasper put in the trap, please?'

'You'll be there before shops open, Miss,' he joked, and then he called out to one of the men to bring the trap out and harness Jasper to it. 'Are you waitin' for young Maisie, Miss?'

'No. She is unwell and will stay home.'

'I'll be gettin' one of the men to drive you in then, Miss,' replied Bert, already turning away searching for a groom.

Anna smiled with indulgence at this kindly man, who had known her since she was a baby. 'There is no need, thank you. I'm quite capable of driving to York on my own as you well know.'

'Nay Miss, Master'll not like it. 'Appen it's best if I—'

'No, thank you, Bert.' Jasper whinnied to her, and she walked over to pet him.

Bert scowled. 'Miss, I don't like the thought of you travellin' all that way on your own.'

'Don't fuss. Besides, I will be on a well-used road in broad daylight. I'll be perfectly safe.'

Assisted up onto the seat and gathering up the reins, Anna smiled down at him. With a click of her tongue, she rattled out of the yard.

As she drove along, the morning mist lingering in the hollows drifted away. The rising sun brought the countryside to life. Rabbits scattered through the long grass by the side of the road. Their bobbing white tails played peek-a-boo with her as she watched them dive for cover. Birds called out their morning greetings from high in the trees. The crisp fresh air caused energy to soar through her body. She turned her face up towards the sky to smile at the sun that seemed to shine down especially for her on this beautiful spring morning.

A small number of travellers walked along the York road. Anna waved to some individuals she recognized from the villages situated around the estate. Most of the people didn't look up as she passed. The homeless—many out of work because the local mills were unable to obtain cotton since the war in America started—walked with bowed heads and slumped shoulders, concentrating only on putting one weary foot in front of the other. They were cold and hungry; most probably having spent the night in a roadside ditch or under a hedge. Their spirits eroded as, day after day, they tramped the roads looking for work and food.

Close to the city walls traffic became dense. She slowed Jasper along Monkgate, and they passed through Monk Bar, one of the many impressive, stone-arch entrances of the old city walls. She hurriedly found a suitable stable where, for a small fee, she was able to house Jasper and the trap for the day.

Numerous church bells around the city struck the hour as Anna left the stables. She groaned and quickened her pace. The crush of people shopping along the thoroughfares impeded her way, as did the filth that coated the cobbles and ran freely down the open drains. The Gothic architecture of the Minster Church loomed up before her when she walked into Minster Yard. To Anna, the two hundred-fifty years it took to build the immense cathedral was well worth it. It held an unsurpassed grandeur and was famous for its one hundred and more stained-glass windows.

Quiet serenity surrounded the church. She felt her rapid heartbeat slow and return to its usual rate in the tranquil sanctity that shrouded the area, blocking out the harsh realities of the everyday grind of living. Here, in the vicinity of the Minster's cold stone-walls, one could put one's life into perspective. For a brief time, the world could stop, and one could look for the answers of their life, either from God or from the inner self. For a moment she let herself feel guilty at meeting a man in a cathedral before she squashed the uneasy thoughts. Later, there would be time enough for soul searching.

'Good morning, fair beauty.'

Anna whirled about in a flurry of skirts. 'Matt.'

He held her hand to his lips. 'I'm glad you came.'

She blushed. Her guilt intensified, but she ignored it once more. 'I said I would, even though others will believe it's wrong.'

'I worried you might have changed your mind.'

'I did. A number of times during the night.' She smiled.

'I imagined you had decided I was not worth the effort, what with one thing or another.' He shrugged.

'Meaning my mother?'

'Yes.' He offered his arm and they strolled out of the Minster's grounds.

Being so close to him sent shivers of pleasure over her body, and Anna had to take a moment to order her thoughts.

'I cannot be what Mother wishes. I must answer to my own conscience.' She stopped and gripped Matt's hands. 'Do you not see? I've come to York unchaperoned to meet a man. Something a lady should never do, but I've done it because it felt right.'

'Then how can it be wrong?'

'Exactly.' She dropped his hands, suddenly feeling less confident than before. 'Lately, I have been so unhappy, worrying about the future and where my life is heading. Then yesterday, talking to you, made me realize I should just be myself, and what happens, happens.'

'I do not want to see you unhappy nor ask you to do anything that makes you uncomfortable.'

She nodded, understanding. The image of her father came to mind. Her mother would be horrified if she knew, but it was her Papa and his disappointment, which would hurt her the most. Her steps faltered, and when Matt gazed down at her with his smoky eyes, she trembled.

'Let us spend the day without a serious thought in our minds.' Matt grinned. 'I want us to smile and laugh and nothing more, agreed?'

'Very well.' She titled her head, shutting out the doubts. 'What shall we do then?'

'Go shopping, I wish to buy you things.'

Anna rested her hand on his arm. If she was seen by family acquaintances, she knew her reputation would be lost, but her mind and heart were concerned only for Matt. He felt strong and warm under her hand. How could an innocent day shopping be wrong?

For the next couple of hours, they strolled through the labyrinth of streets and alleys, tactfully keeping away from the more expensive shops in case they ran into family friends. They purchased gifts for each other in total happiness. Anna saw a lovely dove-grey, silk necktie in a tailor's window display and insisted on buying it for Matt. In a small tobacconist, she also bought cigars for him. He lingered over his choosing until she laughingly told him she could no longer tolerate the thick aroma of musty snuff and tobacco that hung perpetually in the airless shop. In another shop, Matt bought Anna a delicate hand-painted ivory fan in a beautifully carved rosewood box.

Then, getting her own back on Matt for making her wait in the tobacconist shop, she entered a bookshop crowded from floor to ceiling with reading material and became totally absorbed leafing through enormous dusty volumes of Shakespeare, Walter Scott, Defoe, the Bronte sisters and more. Finally, a playfully groaning Matt bought her the Charles Dickens's novel, *Great Expectations.* After that purchase, he steered her down the street, swearing never to enter another bookshop with her.

They delighted in being close, to be able to touch and to laugh at foolish trivial things. After lunching at a little café in a side street, they toured the Museum and its surrounding gardens. Anna felt as though they had known each other forever as they sauntered along one of the many walkways near the River Ouse.

The afternoon drew to a close and reluctantly they strolled towards the stables. An overwhelming stench of raw meat filled the air as they passed the entrance to the Shambles, a long narrow street consisting mainly of butchers. Meat of every description hung from hooks or was displayed on benches outside the many butcher shops. Mangy dogs and cats prowled the street waiting for a chance to seize a scrap and be away before the whack of a shopkeeper's broom descended upon their heads.

Anna sighed. 'This has been the best day of my life.' The apprehension of the morning had faded like a summer's mist.

'For me too, my beauty.'

'Look.' She pointed to a street artist, who began to quickly draw her likeness.

Matt nodded. 'He is making a splendid job of that.'

They stopped to watch his progress. When the artist finished, Matt paid him well.

'He must do one of you, Matt.'

Matt shook his head. 'I don't think so.'

'Yes, you must. For me, please,' she pleaded. Unbidden, the artist began a drawing of Matt. Anna grinned in satisfaction as Matt's likeness came alive on the paper.

'You little minx.' Matt laughed, his eyes sending her subtle, sensual messages of their own.

At the stables their merriment died. Their special day would forever remain in her memory, but sadness at parting from Matt squeezed her chest. For the first time in her life, she wanted to wallow in a man's attentiveness— not just any man's, but Matt Cowan's. When he looked at her, her heart seemed to flip against her ribs. She ached for his kiss, but more than that, she simply wanted to be near him, listen to him, touch him.

With a ragged sigh, she watched the stable lad harness Jasper to the trap. 'When will I see you again?' she asked Matt.

Matt paused from checking the tightness of Jasper's harness. 'I've business meetings for the next two days.' He gazed over the horse's rump to smile at her. 'Why don't you come to Conway House on Friday? Hugh has a small boat, and we can go rowing on the river.'

For an instant, her mother's acid words sprung to her mind, but Anna shoved the thought away. The very devil himself couldn't stop her from seeing Matt again. 'Wonderful. I would like that very much.'

He came up to her as the youth led Jasper out into the lane. 'I'll arrange for both sketches to be framed tomorrow. I can give it back to you on Friday.'

'Oh, yes.' She reached up and cupped his face. Her stomach clenched in anticipation as he lowered his mouth to hers in a tender farewell.

'Until Friday,' he whispered, kissing her nose, her eyes.

After one last kiss, which heated her blood and made her body beg for more, she walked out into the lane where Matt helped her up onto the seat.

Smiling, feeling like she'd tasted heaven, she drove away, knowing it had been the best day of her life.

***

Twilight reached the estate before Anna did. She'd driven home slowly, pondering the day. So many conflicting emotions surged throughout her mind and body when she was with Matt—delight and joy mixed with the trepidation of her family's disapproval.

Why should she have to hide her new happiness? Matt admired her. He wanted to know her as much as she did him. Oh, how she longed to be openly courted by him, but her mother's reaction urged caution.

'Dash it all,' She growled to the growing dusk. Why did her mother have to ruin her one chance for true happiness? Wasn't it enough that the woman had been cold and hateful toward Anna all her life? Did she have to destroy Anna's future, too?

Driving into the stable yard, she saw her father talking to Bert. Thomas helped her down in silence and collected her parcels from the seat.

It wasn't until they were walking the path towards the house that he spoke. 'You have been gone a fair time, Anna.'

The fact he'd called her Anna, and not 'my dear,' gave her an indication of his mood.

'I'm sorry, Papa. I did not realize the time.'

'Why did you not take Maisie? You know how we dislike you going to York alone.'

'I—'

'Sometimes your mother is right. I give you too much freedom.'

Frowning, she glanced at him. 'Papa—'

Thomas paused and turned to her; his eyes clouded with concern. 'I don't want you to do it again. Promise me you'll not.'

Anna could not make the promise for she knew she would break it. 'Papa, I have always gone everywhere on my own or with Tom.'

'Yes, well, your mother has been acting strangely ever since she found out you were gone. She has said all sorts of silly things, even suggesting you had run off with Matt Cowan.' He looked at the parcels as they entered the house. 'She is in a state. She is adamant you had arranged to meet Matt Cowan today. Did you?'

Guilt reared its head again. She straightened her shoulders and raised her chin. 'What if I did?'

He sighed heavily.

'I think very highly of Matt, Papa.'

'I do, too, but sneaking around isn't the way, Anna. It's wrong.'

'I have no choice.' She halted by the staircase. 'Oh, Papa, why is Mother so against him? She hardly knows him; yet she speaks so terribly of him. He hasn't done anything to deserve that. You know he is a good man. Can you not explain this to her?'

'I have tried, my dear. Really, I have, but it does no good. Why she is acting like this I don't know. I've sent for some specialists from London to come and examine her. Hopefully, she will be better soon.' Obviously weary, he wiped a hand over his face. 'It's all to do with these headaches I'm sure, but until she has seen the doctors, I do not want her upset.'

Anna's defiant stance wilted. 'I cannot stop seeing him.'

'Your mother has taken a dislike to Matt. His name cannot be mentioned. I cannot have you distressing her and making her more ill. For once you must do as asked. Please. Your mother's health comes before Matt Cowan.'

'This isn't fair.'

'No, it isn't, and I am sorry.'

Anna turned away and charged up the stairs to her room. Her mother would *not* stop her from seeing Matt. If they had to continue to meet in secret, they would. Why should she consider her mother's feelings when her mother had never cared about Anna or her needs and desires?

Opening her bedroom door, she jumped. Her mother sat on the window seat staring out towards the ridge of hills in the distance.

Hiding her surprise, Anna placed her parcels down on a small table, summoned a smile and glided over to her mother. 'Good evening, Mother.' She pretended it was a usual practice for her to be sitting here.

Louise stared blankly; eyes unfocused. Without saying a word, she rose and calmly left the room.

The dressing room door opened slightly, and Maisie popped her head out, sighing with relief when she saw Anna. 'Eh, Miss, I'm that glad you're home.' She groaned dramatically. 'It's been a day and half, I can tell you.'

'How long has Mother sat there?'

'An hour at least.'

'Did she say anything to you?'

'No, Miss.' Maisie helped Anna to change. 'I were hangin' up some gowns, and when I came out, she were sittin' there on the window seat, just starin' out over the fields. I jumped a foot in fright, I did.'

'She didn't speak?' Her mother's recent behaviour was totally bewildering.

'Nay, Miss. I was ready for a tirade, but nowt.' Maisie shrugged. 'I thought for sure she'd give me a tongue lashin' for lettin' you go to York on your own, but she said nowt to me. Though, there was some carrying on downstairs earlier.'

Anna slowly sat on the vacated seat. She wondered what her mother was up to. Was she losing her mind or playing games?

* * *

Dinner was a quiet affair, talking subdued. Louise rarely took part in any conversation anymore. She ate little, a vast contrast to her normal appetite. The wife and mother they all knew was a good eater who had dominated the conversation around the table. With her keen wit, she'd been able to talk to one person while listening to discussions elsewhere and still keep a sharp eye on the maids.

After the meal, the family retired to the green sitting room. Thomas settled himself with the newspaper, and every now and then, read aloud any interesting snippets. Arabella quietly played the piano, her fingers nimble, the piece simple.

Anna and Maggie sat at the round ivory-inlaid card table. Dealing the cards, Anna kept an eye on her mother. Silent, Louise perched on her gold Louis XIV rosewood chair and watched the dancing flames of the fire. Her embroidery sample lay untouched on her lap.

'Thomas, we must go visit Aunt Mary,' Louise said suddenly.

The girls looked up from their game, and Arabella's fingers paused ever so slightly over the keys.

'My dear.' Thomas glanced over the top of his paper. 'Aunt Mary died last Christmas.'

Louise blinked rapidly for a few seconds. 'Yes, yes of course. I forgot. Silly of me.'

Thomas smiled at her. 'Easily done, darling, it being so recent.'

Louise shifted slightly in her chair. Firelight painted her pale skin with golden hues. 'When will Tom arrive? I miss him so.'

'Soon, dearest, soon. I'm sure he will make haste the minute he is free from Oxford.' Thomas's gaze reflected the worry in Anna's mind. Where had their forthright Louise gone?

The Yorkshire Longcase clock in the hallway chimed nine o'clock, drowning out the little silver mantelpiece clock's gentle ring. Maggie, always sent to bed at that time, tensed, obviously waiting for her mother to say so. When Louise made no comment, Maggie looked at Anna who in turn indicated they continue on with their game.

Having finished playing her tune, Arabella looked up, her eyes narrowing. 'Mama, Miss Foster has neglected her duties. It's of the hour Maggie should be upstairs.' She quirked an eyebrow at her sisters, her smile devious as she fingered the keys.

'I hate her,' Maggie whispered under her breath, pulling a face at Arabella. She rose, gave Thomas a kiss, and then stopped in front of Louise. 'Good night, Mother.'

Louise dismissed her with an absent wave. 'Good night, Magdalene.'

Anna placed the cards away in a drawer of the chiffonier. 'I will take you up, if you want.'

Upstairs, Miss Foster helped Maggie dress for bed and then left the two sisters alone, closing the door quietly as she departed the room.

Maggie snuggled deeply into the bed. 'It's my birthday in three weeks,' she confided. Her child's innocent face glowed with anticipation.

Anna tickled her. 'Yes, I know. You're not going to let me forget. So, what would you like for a present?'

Maggie sat up; her face serious. 'I'd adore a new saddle. I've seen the one I want in a book. It's *American.*'

'Really? Did you tell Papa?'

'Yes, I dropped some hints.' Maggie laughed. 'But could you remind him?'

'I shall see what I can do,' Anna promised. 'Now off to sleep. Good night, Scamp.'

'I love you, Anna. Good night.'

'I love you too. Sleep tight.' She lowered the lamp's wick and went downstairs.

When she returned to the sitting room, only her father remained, the others having retired for the night.

Thomas smiled. 'Louise needs her rest, and Arabella has an early start in the morning because she is going with Violet Conway to Luke Hammond's estate near Haworth.'

'Luke Hammond? I thought he was not good enough for her, at least in Arabella's opinion.' She poured a glass of wine from the tray Evans brought in.

Thomas lit his pipe. 'Well, I think she has realized how wealthy and influential his family is. I hope nothing happens between them. Arabella needs a strong hand to keep her…selfishness in line, and I don't think that Hammond fellow is made of the right stuff to take on the job. She would walk all over him, and the marriage would be an empty shell before too long and should Arabella become unhappy, your mother will blame me.'

She raised an eyebrow. 'What about me? What kind of man do I need?'

He tapped his finger against his chin in thought. 'That is hard to say. You need someone who will understand your independence and that you've a will of your own. He would have to put up with your temper too.'

'I don't have a temper.' She tutted then laughed. They sat in silence for a while, and then she asked her father if he remembered Maggie's birthday was in three weeks.

'Yes, I know. I have ordered her a new saddle, designed like an American one. That is what she hinted when I saw her looking at pictures of them.'

'She asked me to find out if you had bought her one.'

Thomas smiled. 'She is a cheeky monkey. Well, I should retire as well. I have a big day ahead of me tomorrow. As you know, in March, I visit all the tenants. Do you wish to come with me again?'

'I would, yes. I forgot all about it. I enjoyed going last year and hearing their problems and helping to fix them. I can sympathize with most of the women. They feel they can talk to me about some things a little easier than they can to you.'

Sucking his pipe, Thomas gave her an odd look. 'They should be happy I'm not like most landlords and let them live in squalor. At least I provide decent cottages, and the rents are reasonable.'

'Everyone knows that, Papa. Your cottages are well sought after by many people around here, but that does not mean it wipes out all other problems. We need to know and understand their conditions so we can help them live better.'

'I'm aware of that. I'm a fair and understanding man.'

Anna rose and kissed her father's forehead. 'Yes, that you are, Papa.'

Chapter 5

Anna sat in the library. A book lay unread on her lap as she remembered the wonderful day yesterday.

She had trailed her hand in the cool water as Matt rowed the boat away from the Conway's small jetty, away from the town, away from the heavy flow of water vehicles that plied the Ouse and the River Foss and, most importantly, away from prying eyes.

In contented peace, they had rowed in the sunshine until they found a pleasant place to stop for their picnic; a secluded, shady bank covered in knee high grass.

Under large canopied trees, they lunched on salads, chicken, ham, bread, cheese, and fruit. While they ate, Matt spoke of his frustration at not being able to find many investors for his new mine. He informed her that a trip to London might be necessary in order for him to meet with some bankers and businessmen he knew.

She frowned now, thinking of his mounting irritation. She rose and replaced the book on the shelf. He had very definite plans—plans that at one time had not included her, but did they now? Had he considered a future with her? Did he lie awake at night as she did, agonizing over what might be?

A knock on the door interrupted her tortured thoughts. She turned as Evans came to her and bowed. 'Excuse me, Miss. Mr. Turnbull is here to see you. I've put him in the drawing room.'

'Thank you, Evans. Arrange for some tea, please.' She walked to the drawing room, glad that Edwin had come to divert her from contemplating the uncertainties of her future.

He stood as she entered the room. 'Anna, you look lovely, as always.'

'It's nice to see you, Edwin.' He kissed her cheek before she sat. 'So, how have you been?' she asked.

'Quite well, thank you.' He fidgeted with his right sleeve cuff, sat down, and then stood again. 'And you? Are you well?'

Anna felt oddly uncomfortable and wondered why. Edwin was like a brother to her. 'I am in great health.'

'Good. Good.'

'Is something wrong, Edwin?'

He jerked. 'No. Yes. Did-did you have a pleasant day in York?'

She rose and went to the fire. 'You saw me?' Heat flooded her cheeks that had nothing to do with the warmth from the fire.

'Yes, and who you were with.'

'Does it concern you what I do?' Turning to face him, she raised her chin a fraction higher. 'I believe it doesn't.'

'You were alone with him all day.' Edwin paced the length of the room. 'It's wrong! Where was your mother, or sister, or maid? Have you no thought to your reputation?'

'Did you follow us?' Her temper rose. 'You spied on me?'

He put his hands up. 'No, not intentionally. I was out and I saw you, that is all.'

'But you continued to follow us,' she snapped.

'I didn't want to leave you alone with that man. You hardly know him.'

'It is none of your business.' She paused as a tap on the door preceded Nancy who carried a silver tea service, which she placed on a small table by the sofa.

With the door closed once more, Anna rounded on him. 'How dare you decide what is good for me. Do you think me stupid and unable to make my own decisions?'

'No, but—'

'I can do what I like, when I like, with whom I like.'

'You only just met this man. I had to make certain you were safe with him.'

'I know enough to realize he's warm and kind and generous. So far I've had immense pleasure from our time together.' She folded her arms and stared at him, barely concealing her contempt. 'We also spent Friday together boating up the river. It was marvellous. Or did you already know that too?'

Edwin blanched a shade whiter than his normal pale colour. 'Are your parents happy about this?'

'Mr. Cowan is Sir and Lady Conway's nephew.'

'I know who he is, but are your parents aware you spend time with him alone?'

'Edwin—'

'Do they approve, Anna?'

'I've told you it's none of your business.'

'Obviously they are ignorant of this liaison then.'

'No, I mean yes...' Such was her torment, she sat gently on the sofa as though fragile as glass. 'I—I must keep it a secret from Mother. She has taken a dislike to him, but only because she is ill and not herself.' Anna squirmed under his gaze. 'Papa likes him though and is even investing in his business.' Only such a long-standing friend would have received even this much explanation from her.

Edwin didn't seem to fully appreciate the exception she made in his case. 'Maybe you should heed your mother's words.' His hands shook ever so slightly as he poured himself a cup of tea. 'Think of your reputation. I know you were wild when we were younger, but I had hoped you may have gained a little more decorum with your coming of age.'

Her patience could not survive his narrow-minded response and her hand itched to slap his pert face. 'Oh, be quiet Edwin. I don't have to take this from you. I am an adult. I can make my own decisions. As for my reputation, I was only on an outing with a friend, not down some alley with my skirts up around my legs.'

He choked on his tea and spluttered. 'Anna!'

'What is the matter? Did I shock you? Did I speak in a way no lady should? Well, you should know by now that I'm no lady.'

'I'm concerned for you. I don't want you to be hurt,' Edwin whined. 'Please don't be angry with me.'

She gazed at him and could not help comparing him to Matt, sadly finding that Edwin lacked all she admired in a man. Oh, he was nice, in a gentle sort of a way, but he was missing the strength of character as well as the strength of body that Matt possessed.

'Are you…will you meet him again?'

Anna poured herself a cup of tea before she answered. 'You are straining the boundaries of our friendship, Edwin.'

'If you do, eventually you'll be seen. How will you keep it from your mother?'

She flashed him a tight smile. 'That is for me to worry about, not you. Please don't interfere.'

'I cannot remain silent.'

Alarmed, she glared at him. 'If you speak out about this, I will never acknowledge you again. To me you will be dead.'

Edwin blinked, his eyes widening. 'I'm thinking only of you.'

'Then don't. Forget what you saw and remember instead that I have been your friend since childhood. How many more can claim the same?'

Defeated, he nodded. 'I must go.'

Thankful his interrogation and threat was at an end, she walked with him to the front door and waited while Evans helped him with his hat and coat.

'When will Tom be home?' inquired Edwin, pulling on his gloves.

'Papa received a letter yesterday. Tom hopes to be home in two weeks. He has one more exam to do next week.'

'It will be good to see him.' He hesitated, and then gave her a peck on the cheek. 'Well, goodbye, Anna.'

* * *

Anna and Matt devised an arrangement to meet regularly in the dense wood at the far southern boundary of the estate. Apart from the gamekeeper, checking once a week for poachers' traps, the grove was virtually abandoned. It was not only secluded, but also touchingly beautiful with a wide, meandering stream running through it.

Under the shelter of enormous old chestnut trees, the ground was moist and spongy from fallen vegetation. The pungent aroma of dampness and earth filled the air. In one area, near a small trickling waterfall, a cleared grassy stretch provided an ideal spot for fishing or sitting quietly and daydreaming in the dappled sun that managed to filter through the trees and warm the cool shade. Anna remembered the place from her childhood. She had played here as a child with Tom and Edwin. Now, it had become a haven for her to meet Matt, unnoticed by others.

On their third meeting in the wood, Anna brought along a fishing line and some scraps from the kitchen for bait. At times, their sudden bursts of laughter shattered the quiet and caused the birds to fly away in alarm. With much cursing on Matt's part, he eventually caught a small fish no bigger than Anna's hand. Getting the fish off the hook, however, proved to be an even larger problem. It wiggled and squirmed in their hands until it jumped off the hook and with a plonk landed back in the water.

'The famous one that got away.' Matt laughed, hugging her to him. His smile faded as he realized her hilarity didn't match his own. 'Anna? What is it?'

'Nothing.' She forced a smile, but it faltered, and she returned to the old log they used as a seat.

'All this secrecy is troubling you, isn't it?'

Anna watched a kingfisher swoop low over the water. A dragonfly hovered near the edge of the bank before it darted away. Her heart ached with growing love, yet her mind told her she was dishonouring her family. 'It doesn't bother you all this sneaking about?'

'Indeed, yes, but what is the alternative?' He came closer. 'You said yourself that your mother mustn't know about us.'

'This isn't suitable. I've pushed the boundaries of behaviour before, but not like this. For once I want to do the right thing.' She searched his face for answers. 'I am torn.'

'Anna, I will be gone soon. So, I'll understand if you don't want us to continue as we are.'

Despair filled her at the thought of never seeing him again. 'Is that your wish?'

He gently pulled her up from the log. 'No, of course it isn't. I want us to grow stronger together so that we'll survive our times apart.'

She frowned. 'Times apart? What do you mean?'

'I am rarely in England for long periods. If we married, we would spend lengthy periods away from each other.'

'Marriage?' Her heart banged against her ribs; she felt her legs weaken.

Matt sighed and drew her to him. 'Yes, marriage. I'd like us to be wed on my return to England.'

'But how long will you be gone? You have yet to give me a definite answer.'

'I cannot stay for certain, but a year or two, perhaps more.'

'Two years…' The happiness drained from her. How could she cope with such a separation?

'Knowing that you are waiting for me will make my trips much shorter.' He grinned and kissed the tip of her nose. 'What man could stay away from such a woman as you?'

She closed her eyes as he kissed her, but for the first time she didn't fully respond. Her mind whirled. He wanted marriage yet was content to leave her quite often. As he left a sensual trail of kisses down her throat, she arched her head back and smiled. If he thought she'd meekly wait for him year after year, he'd have to rethink his opinions of her. She'd be no wife that waited by the hearth for her man to return when he felt like it.

* * *

March merged with April, and everyone was busy with the Easter celebrations. Tom's arrival was anxiously anticipated, more with each passing day, until finally at the end of the second week in April, with much fuss and excitement, he came. In the three and a half months since his last visit home, his shoulders had broadened. An air of maturity surrounded him. His family felt hesitant in greeting him until he smiled and called out for his kisses. Taller than his father but with the same grey eyes and boyish grin, he charmed the household effortlessly.

His sandy-coloured hair touched his collar making Louise tut. Tom was devilishly good-looking and not totally ignorant of it. He was one of the most eligible bachelors in the district, and Anna teased him about it as they slipped easily back into the fond companionship they always shared.

The day after his homecoming, Tom and Anna rode over the fields and splashed across becks, urging their horses to jump higher walls and wider ditches in challenges against each other. The warmer weather heightened their spirits as they raced under the cloudless sky.

Resting their horses in the shade of an old oak some miles from the estate, they sat at ease on the grass near a stonewall boundary.

'Golly, I needed that.' Tom took off his riding jacket and rested his back against the wall. 'It was tremendous fun.'

'Oh, why did you need that? Is studying architecture becoming too hard, little brother?' she teased, spreading out her skirts. They both were breathing heavily from their exertions. Anna's hair had come loose from its pins and was wild about her head.

'Ha-ha,' he joked back at her. 'No, I am coping all right. It's just that sometimes I feel as though I am chained to the damn desk. I feel the urge at times to just leave and go for a fast gallop.'

Anna picked at the grass. 'There are plenty of open spaces at Oxford. In your leisure time, why do you not ride?'

'Because I'm usually catching up on study.'

'Poor boy.'

'Get away with you.' Tom pushed her playfully. 'Though, I will tell you, it's not all work and no play. I've gone to a few little soirees.' He peeped at her from under the long hair that fell over his eyes. 'I've been introduced to someone.'

She frowned. 'What do you mean?'

'I have fallen in love with a wonderful girl, Anna.'

'Fallen in love? Are you mad?'

Instantly defensive, Tom sat straighter. 'What is so mad about it? People do it all the time, you know.'

'Don't be so foolish, Tom.' She gathered her skirts and stood to glare down at him. 'I thought you would have more sense than to fall for the first girl who flutters her eyelashes at you. You must know of your responsibilities—'

'I'm not a complete fool.' Tom scrambled to his feet and faced her angrily. 'Besides, you know nothing about it.'

She walked over to the horses and putting her boot into the stirrup she mounted.

Tom picked up his jacket and followed her. Once mounted, he shook his head, disillusionment etching his features. 'I told you because I thought you'd understand. I guess I was wrong.' With that last remark, he spurred his horse into a canter, leaving her behind.

The last thing Anna wanted was to fight with him. He had confided something important to her. It was unfair of her to criticize him when she too felt the same way about someone she'd only met some months ago. She realized it was a privilege that he confessed to her.

It took her half a nearly a mile to catch him. Tom's horse was slowing, and Jasper, much fitter, covered the distance easily. When Tom finally stopped, Anna brought Jasper close until both horses were flank to flank.

'I'm sorry.' She gazed at him as he stared out over the lush fields.

'I didn't mean to be cruel, Tom. I just don't want you to be hurt.'

'Who said I would be?'

Anna gave him an understanding smile. 'You are only twenty. You have years of hard study before you. You are of the age where you should be unshackled, sowing your wild oats and all that nonsense.' She grinned at him. 'Then there is travelling. All of Europe and beyond is waiting for you to explore. Papa wants you to experience so much before you marry.'

'I don't want to travel, at least not for some time.'

'But why? Papa has said you can spend a year on the continent.'

'I want to come home, Anna.' Tom sighed. 'After Oxford I want to come home.'

'And forgo Europe?' She sat puzzled, relaxing the reins so Jasper could crop at the grass. 'I don't understand. It would be a wonderful adventure.'

He fiddled with his horse's mane. 'I was sent to a boarding school at age ten. I've been living away from home since then and I'm tired of it. You girls don't know what it's like and how lucky you are to stay home.'

'We all thought you were fond of school. You did so well there.'

He shrugged. 'I had no choice but to do well. The alternative was to be so miserable you'd die from it.'

His deep sigh spoke more than his words did. 'All I wanted was to come home.'

'Oh Tom, why didn't you tell us, or me at least.'

'What good would it have done? Mama was always so proud of my achievements. I couldn't come home.' He took a deep breath. 'But the minute I'm free from Oxford I'll be coming home for good, and I'm bringing Cecilia with me.'

Anna reached out and grasped his hand. 'You must do whatever makes you happy.'

'Cecilia makes me happy. Oh, I cannot explain it. I just know I want to be with her always.' Tom looked flustered at the enormity of his feelings.

'I understand how you feel.'

'No, you don't. Not until you're in love will you know how it feels.'

'I am.'

Tom swiftly turned in his saddle. 'You never said. Why did you not write and tell me?'

Laughing at his expression, Anna reminded him that he'd not written and told her about Cecilia.

'Well, who is he?'

She recalled Matt's handsome face, his smiling mouth, and intense dark grey eyes. Anna understood how Tom felt. It was agony hiding her love for Matt from everyone. She longed to tell someone how she felt. 'Mr. Matthew Cowan. Though, Mother is against him, and so I must keep it a secret for a while.'

'Why does Mama not approve?' Tom asked, perplexed. 'Is he of ill repute?

'No, of course he isn't.' She rubbed her forehead. 'Mother has not been very well lately, and it has affected her way of thinking to some extent. Did Papa write to tell you she has been unwell?'

'No.'

'He wants her to visit some doctors in London, but she refuses. At times she is quite unreasonable. We are worried.'

Tom's eyes widened. 'Gosh, why did you not write and tell me?'

'I never thought it was serious until lately. Mother has always been distant with me…' She shifted in the saddle. 'With you home for a short time perhaps you can persuade her to meet the doctors? She always listens to you.'

'Well, I will try. Absolutely.'

'Good. It'll ease Papa's worries.' Anna smiled with love at her dear brother. Then, to break the strained atmosphere, she dared him to a race. They thundered off with the wind in their hair and laughing like young children again.

* * *

Dusk sketched fine lines about the countryside as Anna cantered around a bend, urging Jasper to go faster. She was awfully late. Her head spun with the events of the day and Matt's behaviour. The day in York with Matt had been a disaster. He'd been remote, with pressing matters on his mind. She knew his business needed him and that becoming acquainted with her had thrown him into a situation he hadn't anticipated, but then neither of them had expected to find love. They'd talked little of the future and she was becoming frustrated with his vague ideas of getting married once he returned from his next voyage to South America. They hadn't been able to repeat the glorious day of their previous time in York, and now Anna wondered if it had been worth the risk. The clearing in the wood provided a more private location of their meetings.

Ahead she saw a rider coming, peering into the dim light she recognized Tom as he neared.

'Where have you been?' he demanded, reigning in beside her as she slowed Jasper.

'Is Father worried?' Guilt, her old friend, made her hands grip the reins tighter.

'It's Maggie's birthday tea. Everyone is waiting for you.'

'Yes, I know, I am late. I told Maggie this morning that I'd be back for her celebratory tea and I am.' She nudged Jasper into a trot.

'There have been numerous visitors calling all day and Mama is tiring. Why did you have to go into town today of all days?'

'It was important and I'm only half an hour late. Stop fussing.'

Tom's expression hardened. 'He isn't more important than Maggie. This cannot continue Anna. Your reputation will be ruined.'

Anna snorted and tossed her head. 'I care nothing about my reputation.'

'This fellow should show his hand. He has no right to compromise you this way.'

'He is not asking me to do anything I don't wish to, Tom. Matt wants to talk to Papa, but Mother's illness prevents me from letting him.'

Her thoughts turned again to Matt's sudden detachment from her. Perhaps she should let him talk to Papa, but if such a move added to her mother's illness, her father would never forgive her. Anna's shoulders slumped. Remorse and the uncertainty of the future sickened her.

'I don't want you to be made unhappy,' Tom broke the silence.

Sighing, Anna drew Jasper to a walk. Staring down at her gloved hands holding the reins, she was surprised to find a teardrop splash onto the leather.

'Why do you cry?' Tom steered his horse closer. 'Are you hurt?'

'No.' She took a deep breath. 'But I think I'm about to be.'

'Why? Talk to me.'

She bit her lip, willing the tears to go away. 'Matt is to sail away soon. He may be gone for two years and he asks me to wait for him.'

'A couple of years isn't so bad.'

'You don't understand. That wouldn't be the end of it. He told me that he lives a nomadic existence, travelling from country to country with his business, looking for new opportunities and while he does that I'm expected to stay in England and wait.'

'Lots of women manage it. Look at sailor's wives. They do it all their lives.'

'If that is what I wanted to do then I'd marry a sailor,' she snapped. 'Don't you see? I'll grow old alone, forever watching the door, waiting for him to appear and then dreading the moment he walked out of it again. I couldn't live like that. I'd rather not marry him at all.'

'Then don't.'

She laughed without humour. 'Easy to say. Could you walk away from Cecilia?'

Tom paled. 'No, I guess not.'

'Matt once said that he admired my uniqueness, but underneath the words, he's shown that he doesn't respect it. He treats me the same as any other woman, as though I'm as fragile as spun glass. Despite my pleading that I'm nothing like the other women of our class, he rejects my pleas to join him on his travels.' She paused as they entered the estate's drive. 'Matt says the places he visits, the mine sites and villages, aren't suitable for a lady. No matter how hard I argue that I could and would live as he did and not complain, he still won't consider the option.'

'Perhaps it's for the best? You have not known him awfully long after all.'

'How is love measured? By time? By how many conversations you have?' She shrugged. 'Meeting Matt has changed my life and how I want to live it. Nothing is the same anymore and never will be again. Before I met him, I existed in a daze, content not to really feel any deep emotions. Now I've tasted the alternative, I cannot go back to what I once was.'

At the bottom of the front steps, they dismounted and allowed the groom to take the horses around to the stables. Evans opened the door for them, but Tom laid his hand on her arm, halting her. 'What will you do?'

She shrugged and her chin wobbled as fresh tears welled. 'He won't take me with him, and I cannot spend my life waiting for him.'

Chapter 6

The horseracing season began the weekend after Maggie's birthday. The family attended the races to cheer on Thomas's thoroughbreds entered in the three-day meet.

Each morning, Anna pretended to feel unwell and stayed at home. At least, that was until the family departed, and then she rode into the wood and to Matt. Luckily, the weather was kind to them and remained warm. They sat in the cool shadows of the tall trees on a rug Anna brought with the hamper she asked Mrs. Wilson to make up for her. She told her she would have a picnic in the sun and for sure that would fix her ailment. Mrs. Wilson agreed being outdoors in the fresh air was the best medicine, but sometimes her knowing gaze followed Anna out of the kitchen.

An ache grew in the pit of Anna's stomach as Matt's changing moods became more frequent. At times he was loving and attentive, and then he suddenly became inaccessible, detached. The future was never discussed, no promises given. Urgency crept into their time together, and Anna felt a desperate need to keep Matt close to her for as long as possible. She hated saying good-bye to him, knowing it was another day gone, bringing the date he was to leave ever closer.

Each time she came close to speaking to her parents about Matt's offer of marriage, her mother illness resurfaced, forcing her to reconsider the announcement. During Easter, the festivities at Thornton House were scaled down to just a few small dinner parties as Louise's headaches worsened.

Anna thought she would explode if something wasn't resolved soon. Time was running out. Soon Matt would be gone, leaving her behind to spend a year or more trapped in a house that no longer felt like a home but a prison. Her life no longer made sense. Nights were spent tossing and dreaming. Her appetite faded and so did her spirit.

Finally, doctors came to treat her mother, creating a gloom of despondency over the house. Their opinions varied as to what ailed her, from her diet being too rich to a brain canker of some sort. Thomas, fed up with their evasiveness, told them to get out and learn how to be real doctors before they killed someone. After receiving permission from his university, Tom delayed returning to Oxford.

'Will you not miss too many lectures, Tom?' asked Anna, as they sat eating dinner one evening in May. The meal was the first Louise had attended for a fortnight and she eyed everyone and everything with suspicion.

'Oh, I will soon catch up.' Tom poured some wine into his glass. 'My tutor wrote me that notes would be put aside for me.'

Father nodded. 'How exceptionally good of him. I will write to show my appreciation.'

'Yes, the old boy is not such a bad stick.' Tom grinned.

'Why do we not have a garden party this weekend, to celebrate Mama leaving her bed for the first time in weeks?' Arabella suggested eyes bright with anticipation.

Thomas frowned. 'Not a good idea, Arabella. A party will tire your mother.'

'But, Papa, we have hardly entertained this spring. It's causing comment.'

'Am I supposed to care about that?'

'It's all right, Thomas.' Louise regarded him like a regal duchess. 'I'm sure a small garden party would not hurt. Besides, I've not seen my friends for some weeks now. Although it's short notice for them, I'm sure they would want to come and see how well I am. It will benefit me to have something else to think about.'

It was agreed a small garden party should be held for Sunday. Anna and Arabella wrote the invitations out that night, so they could be sent first thing in the morning. Anna made sure she was the one who wrote the Conway's invitation to include Matt.

It rained periodically for the next three days, but by Sunday the sun shone. After their gentle soaking, the flowerbeds bloomed in a profusion of colour. The morning's work started early as estate workmen put up the large white canvas marquee and set up the tables and chairs. At sunrise, the maids started their long and exhausting day as they ran back and forth from the kitchen to the marquee with linen tablecloths and napkins, crockery, cutlery, fragile glassware, and all the other trappings needed for the fine dining accorded to the Thornton's guests.

Mrs. Wilson prepared a kitchen full of food. There were tureens of cold soups, trays of salmon, cod, haddock, and trout, accompanied with sauces of plum, brandy and apple. In addition, were pickles, chutneys, bread and cheese, savoury pies and boiled chicken, platters of cold meat, and salad vegetables of every description. Then, to keep the thirty guests from feeling peckish in the afternoon, tiered stands were filled with fancy pastries, tarts, cakes, puddings, biscuits and sweet pies of peach and strawberry. A table was set aside for beverages; tea, coffee, lemon cordial, cider, fruit punch, ale, wine, and spirits.

Sid, the head gardener, cut enough flowers to fill the large vases on the food tables in the marquee and throughout the house. Every room in the house was to have at least two vases or bowls of perfectly arranged flowers.

Anna had made perfumed garlands to hang in the marquee. She had become skilled in flower decoration and thoroughly enjoyed the challenge of merging the varying colours into attractive arrangements that brightened the house.

Guests began arriving by eleven-thirty. Louise and Thomas greeted them at the door. Anna had sent a note to Matt telling him to delay the Conway's departure for as long as possible. That way, by the time they arrived, there would be enough people to distract Louise from noticing his presence.

At breakfast, Louise seemed to be her normal self, and Anna hoped she would not want to cause embarrassment to herself and her guests by making a scene if she saw her and Matt together. Nevertheless, she planned for them to stay out of Louise's way. The excuse of showing Matt the lake and Thomas's fine racing horses would surely give them a chance to be alone without too much comment.

'Why, Anna. You look very fetching in that gown.'

With a sigh, Anna turned away from checking the table displays and faced the woman who addressed her. Mrs. Eileen Longbottom stood a few feet away with a smug expression on her face. Anna detested the woman. She was a small, plump, nosy old windbag who had nothing nice to say about anyone if she could help it. Even so, as her mother's friend and also a guest, she had to be acknowledged.

Summoning a smile, Anna thanked her and was ready to move away when Mrs. Longbottom, put her half-rimmed glasses up to her eyes and spoke again. 'Yes, I must say the stripe suits you.' She gestured at Anna's simple-but-stylish lime green dress in lightweight linen with matching wide brimmed straw hat dyed the same colour as the dress. 'Frills and fussy bits are not you at all. You're not delicate enough to do them justice. You must agree. I always find that one's manner reflects one's dress. Are you of the same opinion?'

Anna breathed deeply. The woman was hateful. 'I suppose that is true, Mrs. Longbottom. I prefer classic designs for my clothes. I do tend to shy away from layers of frills and froth, as they make one appear rather larger than one actually is.' Anna purposely eyed the older woman's over-pretentious, burnt orange taffeta dress with its array of beads, pearls, ribbons and multiple rows of lace. It made up an unappealing outfit that strained at the seams on the fleshy woman.

Mrs. Longbottom blushed and quickly changed the subject. 'I understand you're still not close to marrying?' she queried, with a hint of conceited arrogance.

Anna gave a false, dainty laugh, her irritation mounting. 'You are quite correct.' She smiled sweetly at the woman who had been married and widowed three times. Her fortune had accumulated immensely with each marriage, and she spent her self-centred life going from one social gathering to another.

'Well, I've always said that there's nothing to be ashamed about being a spinster.'

'Really?' Anna tilted her head in thought. 'I think I remember you once stating that remaining a spinster was social death and you'd not wish it on your worst enemy.'

Mrs. Longbottom appeared flustered. 'I…You—'

'If you'll excuse me, there is someone I must speak to.' Anna heard Mrs. Longbottom mutter her outrage as she walked away.

* * *

At the edge of the crowd, Matt stood under a silver birch tree, its leaves rustling in the whisper of the breeze. He watched Anna as she stopped and talked to new guests. Every now and then, she would lift her head and search the crowd. He was sure she looked for him.

His heart constricted at the sight of her. On the slight breeze, her tinkling laugh reached him. He ached to hold her close. How had she come to mean so much to him in such a brief time? Lately, their meetings in the woods had become more passionate, as though the time for restraint was coming to an end. He sensed the need in her as they kissed, and by God, he could barely control himself when she touched him. He held no doubt that, should he forget he was a gentleman and wish to take the next step in their relationship, Anna would be very willing, but what damage would that do? There was no time to marry before he sailed. Anna's arguments for him to take her along when he left England showed a side of her that startled him. Her determination was so strong, he had the suspicion that he couldn't easily put her to one side when he felt like it. But how could he possibly take her to countries were his own safety was always under threat?

Running a hand through his hair, he swore softly. He'd recently acquired a substantial investment for his mining company, and there now was no reason to stay in England. Except for Anna. If he were truthful, he would admit he longed to go back to South America. The man he left in charge to keep an eye on his mining equipment had written, inquiring about when he was returning to Columbia. Matt was impatient to begin work on the new mine, to tackle the inevitable government paperwork, and to see old friends. A lot of people depended on him. Responsibilities awaited him.

A young man came to his side bearing two tall glasses. 'Care for a drink?'

'I'm much obliged.' Matt accepted the drink, wanting to shut out his worries.

The fellow held out his hand, smiling. 'Tom Thornton.'

Matt nodded and shook his hand. 'Matt Cowan.'

'Sir Hugh Conway's nephew?'

'Yes.'

'He is my godfather, and yet you and I've never met.'

'I spend most of my time abroad.' Matt studied Anna's brother, trying to work out whether Tom knew anything about Anna and himself.

'Are you back in England for long?'

'For a while.'

'Interesting.'

They both regarded each other as they drank.

'Here comes Anna.' Tom indicated as she made her way to them. He turned slightly towards Matt. 'If you think you may soon disappoint her, then I suggest you disengage yourself from this…association as soon as possible.'

Matt blinked in surprise at the whispered warning.

'What are you two whispering about?' She smiled.

Before either Matt or Tom could reply, a young maid sidled up beside Anna and bobbed a short curtsy.

'Yes, Florrie, what is it?'

'Er…well...it's...it's to do with Maisie, Miss.'

'Maisie?' Anna frowned.

Florrie nervously twisted her apron in her hands. 'Well...she did say I weren't to bother you, Miss. She didn't want to disturb you.'

'Tell me, Florrie.'

'It's her Mam. She's taken poorly, and Maisie's upset. Doctor 'as been called for.'

The doctor? Anna looked at Tom. 'It must be serious for Maisie to call the doctor. Will you make up some excuse if Mother should comment on my absence? Mother wouldn't understand my wanting to see if Sylvia is all right.'

Tom waved her away. 'You go, and I shall keep Mother occupied.'

'I'll come with you, Anna.' Matt gave Tom a pointed look and then took her elbow.

When they reached Sylvia's cottage, a group of servants hovered in front her door, but quickly made way for Anna and Matt. Inside the small house, Anna went straight into the tiny bedroom where Maisie knelt on the floor beside Sylvia's bed.

'I think it's her heart,' Maisie whispered, her face pale.

'Florrie said the doctor has been called.'

'Aye.' In times of need, their formal relationship of mistress and servant diminished under their close bond of friendship.

'I'll bring in some chairs,' Matt said from the doorway. He brought in two straight-backed, wooden table chairs and helped Anna to seat a dazed Maisie on one of them.

Anna went out to the waiting servants. 'Someone go and meet the doctor from at the road and bring him along the service drive away from the party.'

'I'll go, Miss.' A young lad ran off. Next, Anna arranged for a cot bed and blankets to be brought to the cottage for Maisie to sleep on, plus extra food to be sent down from the kitchen.

Returning to the bedside, Anna smiled as Sylvia's eyes opened. Her shallow breathing hardly moved her thin chest. She tried to lift her head, but the effort was too much.

'Doctor is on his way, Mam. You'll be fine then, I promise,' Maisie murmured, continually stroking her mother's hand.

Although the sun shone brightly outside, the room, with only one small window, was dim. Anna lit the lamp to give more light then sat down next to Maisie.

Sylvia closed her eyes for a second before opening them to focus on Anna. 'I...I want...to thank...you...for giving...us...a...good...life.' Her face became grey with the effort of talking.

Anna blinked back tears. 'You mustn't thank me. I was repaid far more than I can ever say with your friendship and by having Maisie as my very special friend.' Anna bent and kissed the older woman's forehead.

Sylvia turned her gaze to her daughter. 'Lass—'

'Don't talk Mam, save you strength.'

'Nay...listen to...me.' Sylvia struggled to breathe and grimaced in pain.

'Mam, please rest.' A tear rolled down Maisie's cheek and landed on her mother's hand. 'Don't leave me, I beg you.'

'There are...troubled...times...ahead.'

'Shush, Mam, don't talk.'

'God...bless...lass.' Sylvia's eyes gently closed. She let go of her last breath just as the doctor came into the room.

'Mam? Mam?' Maisie shook her mother's arm and looked at Anna in disbelief. 'She...she...'

'Oh, Maisie. I'm so sorry.' The words were inadequate, Anna didn't know what to say or do for her. She turned to the doctor, and he indicated they should all go into the other room. Slowly, with Matt's help, Anna drew Maisie away from her mother's bedside.

Anna held Maisie in her arms as she sobbed and recalled the day she'd first bumped into Maisie as the girl ran from a fruit stall owner she'd stolen from. After paying for the fruit and saving Maisie from a constable's hold, Anna listened to her tearful story. She'd told the girl to lead her back to her lodgings where she found Sylvia sick and wrapped in rags in the back-street slums of Walmgate. She'd rescued them from the slums and had been repaid by their friendship.

Anna thought of the fun times she, Maisie, and Sylvia had spent in the cottage, playing cards and drinking wine 'acquired' from her father's cellar. She remembered the nights of making coloured paper Christmas decorations in front of the fire, of warm days when they gone on walks together to pick wildflowers and taken drives through the countryside.

Matt touched her arm. 'I'll go now, Anna. You're needed here.'

She nodded. 'I am sorry the day didn't turn out as we had planned.'

He smiled tenderly. 'I'll send you a note tomorrow.'

'Yes.' She ached for him to hold her, to kiss away her sadness. Instead, she watched him walk away out of the cottage.

Maisie raised her head. 'I'm sorry to have spoilt your day.'

'What nonsense you do talk, Maisie Shipley.' She kissed her friend's tear stained cheek. 'Come, let us sit by Sylvia, she would like that.'

Later, as the setting sun threw long shadows, Anna left the cottage and headed for the house. On the lawns the workmen were in the process of pulling down the marquee, the guests had gone. Anna hoped the party had been a success.

Upon entering the back entrance to the house, she was quite unprepared for the hostile glare she received from Arabella, who was obviously waiting for her.

'Must you always be an embarrassment to us?' An ugly sneer contorted Arabella's face.

'I beg your pardon?'

'What makes you think you can behave the way you do?'

'Now wait—'

'No.' Arabella stamped her foot. 'For once you shall listen to me. All my life I have tried to be the *good* daughter and where have my pains got me?'

'Please...'

'I am so very tired of being jealous of you, Anna.' Misery blanched Arabella's face. 'You are the eldest, the prettiest, the better rider, and so on. You are Papa's special child, his princess. You have his love-'

'As do you,' Anna cried, desperately not wanting this argument now.

'I deplore being your sister. I wish you would go away and never come back. Mama feels the same as I do.'

Anna reeled. She put her hands behind her, needing the wall's support.

Obviously satisfied she'd caused Anna pain, Arabella's expression turned smug. 'Mama awaits you in her sitting room. I've done my best to paint the blackest picture of you. Your *attachment* to that Cowan man is well known now. You were seen leaving the garden together and didn't return for hours. Mrs. Longbottom wasted no time is spreading rumours to all and sundry. Edwin knows something and was whispering in Tom's ear about you. Mama is furious.'

Arabella led the way upstairs to Louise's sitting room adjacent to her bedroom. Entering the room, Anna felt extremely weary at the thought of another confrontation with her mother. Louise sat rigid in a red velvet-buttoned chair placed in front of an intricately carved rosewood secretary. Anna watched her replace her pen before turning to her with a cold stare.

Haughty, Arabella sat opposite their mother at a small tea table made of the same rosewood and waited for the tirade to begin.

'Well, it is nice of you to finally join us, Anna. The party has been over for an hour or more.' Her mother carefully folded her hands in her lap.

Anna's gaze didn't waver from her mother's. 'There is a reason, Mother.'

'I care naught for your reasons,' she snapped. 'It is extremely hard to find your good points, Anna, when your behaviour constantly humiliates this family.'

'If you'll let me explain.'

'I do not want to hear it. First, you insult Eileen Longbottom, my friend—'

'I insulted *her*? She insulted me! The silly overdressed old—'

'Enough.' Louise slapped the desk.

Anna raised her chin. She noted the blood vessels throbbing at her mother's temple. A vein stood out on her neck. She would suffer another headache.

Her mother stood. 'You have ways of making me incensed beyond reason. You always have. The garden party was a disaster. Eileen has not stopped talking about you and your rudeness.'

'Mother—'

'But there is not only that little episode, is there? Oh no, you must take it one step further by inviting Cowan. How dare you, when you know I detest the man?' Her mother's lips twisted into a tight line. 'You both disappear from the party and are gone all afternoon. I can hardly believe it. Your reputation is severely damaged, likely beyond repair. I cannot begin to tell you of the disgrace you have caused. One minute, you are talking to guests and showing a presence that is required. Then the next, you are gone. Of course, people would wonder and think it strange. Even your father asked where you had vanished to.'

'I didn't spend the afternoon with Mr. Cowan.' Anna gripped the skirts of her of her crinoline but spoke calmly. 'He was included on the invitation because he is your best friend's nephew and happens to be their guest. It would have been impolite not to invite him.' She took a breath. 'I wish to know why you dislike him so, Mother.' She heard the misery in her voice but was too tired to hide it. 'There has to be an explanation, and although I try, for the life of me I cannot think of one.'

'I do not have to clarify myself to you.' Louise blinked. A look of confusion crossed her face. 'Nevertheless, I will tell you this. I have made arrangements for you to go and stay with Great Aunt Prudence. Maybe some time spent with her will teach you some manners, ones I have obviously missed instilling in you.' Louise picked up the letter she'd written.

'I will not go.' Anna stood frozen at her mother's suggestion. Great Aunt Prudence, her own mother's aunt, became Louise's guardian when her parents died in a boating accident off the Isle of Man. Her great aunt was an old woman now but would make sure Anna followed a strict routine while staying with her—a routine that, if Anna could remember rightly, involved a lot of church attendance, praying, and many boring nights reading passages from the Bible.

'You *must* go.' Arabella leapt to her feet, her face crimson with rage.

'Sit down, Arabella,' Louise hissed. 'I will handle this.'

'Mama, something has to be done. She will ruin any chance I have of a marriage to Mr. Hammond. Her antics have caused whispers for years. Everyone knows she's wild and impulsive and consorts with the lower classes. The never-ending scandals she causes will make Mr. Hammond rethink about marrying into this family.'

'I will not be sent away like a naughty child just because Luke Hammond lacks enthusiasm to marry you.' Anna glared at her sister. 'He has most likely realized what a cold-hearted and soulless witch you are!'

The sitting-room door banged open drowning out Arabella's gasp. Thomas stood inside the doorframe. His livid face showed the tight grip he held on his anger. 'What in God's name is going on? The entire estate can hear the racket from this room.'

'Close the door, Thomas,' pleaded Louise, holding her head.

'Why? What difference would it make now?' Nevertheless, he closed the door and none too gently. 'Right. Now tell me what has happened.' He looked sternly at Anna and, much to everyone's surprise, she ran out of the room crying.

* * *

Thomas knocked gently and entered Anna's room. She sat on the window seat staring out over the grounds. Quietly, he took the place beside her. 'Anna?' He clasped her hand. 'I'm sorry. I only just found out about Sylvia Shipley. Your Mother was also unaware.'

'Mother did not want to know.' Her voice was flat. 'She preferred to draw her own conclusions instead of listening to the truth. Though, that is hardly surprising is it? She has always thought the worst of me.'

'Your mother is not well. You know that.'

'And I suppose that is my fault too?'

'No, of course not, but we do have to make allowances.'

'I will not go away,' she said, a determined tone creeping into her voice.

Thomas repressed a shiver and patted her hand. It was Great Aunt Prudence's rigid control of Louise's life that had made Louise fall for the exciting and reckless charms of his elder brother, Richard. In Louise's mind, she was still paying for that mistake. 'You don't have to. It was a misunderstanding. It's forgotten.'

'Not by me.'

'Anna.'

'Why does she hate me?'

Thomas sighed. The relationship between Louise and Anna was not getting any better, and he was tired of playing the peacemaker. 'She doesn't hate you.'

She turned to him with blue-green eyes so like his mother's. 'I no longer believe you, Papa. I used to when I was little, but no more.'

He felt her pain. Louise's lack of love towards Anna always reminded Thomas that Louise picked him on the rebound from Richard. He sighed heavily. The moment had come for him to stop pretending that his wife would ever care for her eldest daughter. 'Are you very fond of Matt Cowan?'

'Yes, Papa.' Her gaze didn't waver. 'I love him.'

'You haven't known him long.'

'What does that matter?'

He nodded and sighed. 'I only want your happiness.'

She took his hand. 'I know.'

'So, when is the funeral?'

'Tuesday.'

'Is everything sorted?'

'Yes, I believe so. Maisie is still in shock. It happened so suddenly. From what I know, Sylvia was in recent good health. Maisie is taking it hard.'

'I'll attend the funeral with you.'

'There is no need, Papa. I know you're busy at Knavesmire this week.'

'I don't have any horses racing on Tuesday as Tom returns to Oxford and I wanted to be home to say goodbye. Friday is our big race day, with Thornton's Lass running in the cup.' He gave her a little smile, and she returned it. 'We will attend the funeral together.'

'Thank you, Papa.'

* * *

On the evening after Sylvia's funeral, Anna and Maisie sat on large cushions in front of Anna's bedroom fire, sipping hot cocoa. Darkness had come early, and rain lashed against the window. They were both dressed in their nightgowns, silently watching the flames leaping and dancing, so comfortable in each other's presence that words were not needed. However, Anna did want to talk about something that had played about on the edge of her mind.

She regarded Maisie over the rim of her cup, her friend looked tired and desperately sad. 'Maisie?'

'Aye, Miss?'

'Do you remember what your mother said as she was...as she was...' Anna could not say dying.

'Aye, I remember.'

'She said there were troubled times ahead. What do you think she meant?'

'Sometimes, she could see what was goin' to happen in't future. She never let on to anyone about it, except to me, and even then, she'd only tell me a few things.'

Anna stared at Maisie. 'She could see things? The future?'

Maisie shrugged her shoulders. 'Aye, at odd times. She didn't make a fuss though. She didn't want no one to know.'

'Why didn't you tell me?'

'Mam never wanted it known, not even to you.'

'Can you? I mean, do you have the second sight?'

'Nay, not at all, nor do I want it.' Maisie glanced down into her cup. 'It's not allus pleasant, Mam said.'

'Amazing.' Anna turned back and watched the flames. 'I wonder what Sylvia meant?'

'Best not to know, Miss.' Maisie got to her feet and put more coal on the fire.

Anna pulled her dressing gown down tightly over her knees as a tremor ran under her skin. Tomorrow she was meeting Matt in the wood. She couldn't help feeling a little apprehensive about their future. She knew he had stayed in England longer than necessary because of her and she sensed his edginess. In unguarded moments his eyes reflected his longing to be away. He was torn, she knew, between her and his other life, which meant such a great deal to him. She loved him and would soon lose him. It was indeed a day of mourning.

Chapter 7

Clear water tinkled as it flowed over the rocks in the stream. Jasper's hoofs crunched the undergrowth. The overcast day made the woods gloomy and damp. A pheasant erupted from beside the path, sending out its frightened call, and the big horse shied away nervously. Smoothing his neck, Anna urged him on, winding through the beech and chestnut trees until they came to the clearing. She loosely tethered Jasper to a tree and then stood for a moment watching Matt. He stood close to the bank, throwing pebbles into the water. He paused for a moment, head bowed, and shoulders hunched, as though he carried a great weight.

Her stomach churned and her heart suspended its beating for a moment. She gazed lovingly at the profile of his strong handsome face. She memorized the clear grey eyes and straight nose, the curving lips that could send her into another world from just the smallest kiss. She felt certain that today he would tell her something she didn't want to hear. *Be strong*, a silent voice told her. *Be strong.*

Matt turned and smiled. He came to her with open arms. She fitted so well against his body, as though they were made from two halves of the same mould. For a few sweet minutes, they held each other with their lips touching tenderly, reaffirming the link between them.

'Come and sit down.' Matt led her to the fallen tree they always sat on. 'How is Maisie? Are you managing?'

'Yes, we are, slowly. It'll take a long time for her to come to terms with it. I'm all she has now.' Anna smiled up at him, tracing the line of his jaw with her finger. 'What have you been doing these last few days?'

Matt shifted uncomfortably on the log. 'I went to Liverpool. I came home late yesterday evening.'

'Liverpool?'

'Yes.'

'Was the trip successful?'

'It was. I secured a vessel and freight in readiness for the voyage to South America. It's important I take a large cargo of equipment. I must carry all that I need for the mine.' He lowered his head to study his boots. 'Columbia is not the best place in the world to acquire mining provisions. It's a very primitive kind of place. In England, I can buy new mining inventions that are not yet even heard of in Columbia.'

'Take me with you.'

Matt pulled away to stared incredulously at her. 'I cannot take you. It's impossible.'

'Why is it? We could marry quickly and go together and—'

'No, Anna. I will not take you there, not to Columbia. But we can still be married, and you can set up a home for us for when I return.'

She jerked to her feet and glared at him. 'I shan't stay behind. I want to go with you and share your life.'

Matt sprang up and gripped her arms. 'Columbia is no place for you to live. It's primitive and dangerous. The natives rebel and start skirmishes. Even my men and I are targeted sometimes. The government can be unstable. Ten years ago, the military seized power but were later overturned. There are so many dangerous animals to contend with that we must kill everything that moves before it kills us. Do you think I would risk you in such a place?'

She pulled out of his grasp. 'You know I'm not a fragile, empty-headed miss who would scream and swoon at the slightest unpleasant thing. I can cope with anything, and we would be together. Don't you want that?'

Matt ran his fingers through his hair, a clear sign he was agitated. 'I will have enough to worry about, without the added concern of you. I couldn't concentrate on the mine from worrying that some poisonous snake might bite you or that a burly native had taken a fancy to you and wants to contest me over the rights to you. No, I'm sorry. I won't take you with me.'

'Please, Matt. We would be together always.' She would do anything to make him take her with him, including begging on her knees. She couldn't stay home without him—couldn't endure years of living a non-existence.

'That is just it. We shan't be together always. I must take a hundred or so men into virgin jungle. We must carve out our path the entire journey. Then, when we do reach the mine site, we must build a complete village. We will need basic shacks for the men and their families to live in, plus a hospital for the doctor. Crops have to be planted and pens made for the animals. So much has to be done before we even start the excavation of the mine. I will be working non-stop to get this up and running. Too many people are relying on its success for it not to have my total dedication. I've responsibilities to the shareholders.'

She raised her chin. 'You put the mine before me?'

'Mining is what I do, who I am, Anna. I cannot sit around a house all day or a gentleman's club and do nothing. It would drive me insane before long. Can you understand that I'm not a normal gentleman, idling away his days on his estate?'

'And I am not a normal lady either.'

The tension in the air about them was impenetrable. Tears blurred Anna's vision of Matt's back as he walked away towards the river. Minutes passed endlessly by, while she tried to control her emotions. She had to make him see the benefits of taking her.

Slowly, she walked to where he stood, took his hand, and held it to her lips. She felt him shudder, and the tension eased a little.

'Imagine the warm nights of us lying in each other's arms,' she whispered. 'Will you promise at least to think it over?'

A misty drizzle began to fall, and she shivered, feeling desperately cold and afraid. He *had* to take her. She could bear no other option.

Matt sighed, sounding miserable. 'I've done nothing but think this through.'

'Kiss me,'' she whispered, reaching up to cup his face, postponing the words she didn't want to hear.

He brought her in, tight against his chest, and kissed her with a deep longing until the rain became heavier, forcing them to part. Matt helped Anna to mount Jasper, and after a final kiss and plans to meet on Friday at the races, she rode away through the trees.

* * *

Friday morning dawned bright and sunny, with a brisk breeze that chased the clouds across the sky. Excitement gripped the house as the family prepared for the finest day of York's racing season at Knavesmire.

In the kitchen, Mrs. Wilson filled huge hampers with cold meats, savoury pies, cheeses, bread and pickles, cakes and fruit. Casks of wine, bottles of ale, cider, plus chairs and tables were loaded onto the wagon that went ahead of the family carriage. Once at the racecourse, Nancy and Edith would set up the tables in the Thorntons' personal marquee. All would be in readiness for the family's arrival.

'Will you please hurry your daughter, Louise?' Thomas paced the drawing room. 'She will be to blame if we miss the first race. Why she must take longer than everyone else is beyond me. She starts getting ready at dawn and is still late.'

'We will be there in plenty of time, Papa,' Anna soothed, as Arabella entered the room.

'Thank the Lord.' Thomas quirked his eyebrow at his errant daughter. 'Now that Arabella is here, we shall go.'

Louise scrutinized them as though she doubted any of them could possibly be allowed in public without having an inspection from her first. She peered at both Anna and Maggie. 'Behave yourselves.'

'I do hope there isn't a strong wind blowing.' Arabella straightened her voluminous skirts. 'Knavesmire is always terribly windy. Keeping one's dignity in the wind is so difficult. My new dress shall not be seen to its advantage in a gale.'

'We are going there to watch the horses, Arabella, not you,' remarked Thomas.

'May I place a bet, Papa?' Maggie's brown eyes danced with gaiety.

'Certainly not.' Louise glared. 'Be thankful you're going at all.'

Thomas eagerly ushered his daughters out into the carriage and instructed Watkins to make the journey to the far side of York quick.

At Knavesmire the crowds were large, but orderly. Anna groaned at the thought of finding Matt here, but hoped he'd stay in the Conway's marquee until she arrived. Thomas ushered his family to the enclosure for the gentry. The marquees of the wealthy, influential families of the surrounding counties were spread over a large area

In the Thorntons' own tent, Nancy and Edith waited behind the beautifully laid-out tables, ready to be of assistance to anyone who might ask for refreshments. Friends and acquaintances of the family soon filed inside, asking Thomas on his opinions about different races.

Anna used the opportunity to make her escape.

Maggie caught up with her at the entrance. 'Can I come with you?'

Anna longed to be alone with Matt, but Maggie looked so beguiling that she gave in. 'Very well, then.'

They walked to the Conway's marquee and inside Anna searched for Matt, but after conversing with Sir Hugh, she found out he'd been and gone.

Disappointed, Anna agreed to take Maggie to the parade ring. They spent some time watching the fine thoroughbreds with their shining coats and rippling muscles. Clapping and laughing, they watched the first race. Although they didn't bet, Anna and Maggie picked out a horse each and cheered them past the finishing line.

Anna scanned the crowds for Matt as she and Maggie headed for the saddling area. She shielded her eyes from the sun, but such was the throng she saw nothing but a mass of moving colour.

The mad hustle and bustle of horses, jockeys, and owners milling about the stables made it unpleasant. The morning grew hotter and the pungent aroma from the stables and hundreds of horses became thick in the air. Matt couldn't be found, so Anna suggested they return to the marquee for refreshments. She groaned on seeing their tent overflowing with people.

Maggie spotted a young girl she knew from another family and went to talk to her. Abandoning the idea of obtaining a drink and keen to find Matt, Anna slipped out again.

For nearly two hours she walked around the noisy gathering unable to find him. Tiredness strained her shoulders, her feet ached, and her head throbbed from fighting the crush of the crowds. Spying an unoccupied bench seat, she sat down to rest. Predictably, the breeze had grown stronger, which didn't help her headache. She tried to control her hair, which had come loose, as the wind blew uninhibited across the wide expanse of common land that held the racecourse. Not so many years ago, this land had been the site of the public gallows and in her current mood, Anna thought it a fitting place.

Putting her parasol down, in fear of the lace on it being torn by the wind, she longed to slip off the dainty shoes she wore to match her pale-yellow linen dress. For a while she watched the people pass by. A young lad caught her attention. He was successfully applying his trade as a pickpocket.

'You're more beautiful every time I see you,' a familiar voice whispered softly in her ear.

Spinning around, she was only inches from Matt's smiling face as he bent over the back over the bench. 'Where have you been? I have looked everywhere for you.' She complained, brushing away a fly hovering near her face.

He smiled with lazy appeal. 'I've been looking for you, too, my beautiful.'

Anna felt the familiar fluttering of her stomach as she stared into his grey eyes, but alcohol fumes radiated from him and irritated her. 'Where did you look? The wine tent?'

Matt laughed and stepped around to join her on the seat. 'Don't be angry. An old acquaintance offered me a drink. I could hardly refuse now, could I?'

His silly grin annoyed her further. 'Just one drink? I doubt that.'

He shrugged. 'It could have been more.'

'Well, while you were enjoying yourself, I was going around in circles looking for you.'

'Let me apologize.' He reached for her but frowned when she shifted back.

'You have insulted me enough. I'll return to my family.'

'Don't be foolish, please, Anna. I'm here now, so let us—'

'No, don't bother. You are drunk. Go back to your friends.' Anna twirled away from him. Her head pounded. She was thirsty, dusty, and hadn't eaten since early morning and it was now after one o'clock. She even missed the cup race, although she heard through people's excited talk that her father's horse, Thornton's Lass, came in second.

Matt grabbed her arm. 'Why are you acting like this? I'm sorry.'

'How dare you spend hours drinking, when you knew I'd be waiting for you?' She glared, not understanding him. 'We arranged to meet at ten o'clock. We have things to discuss. We have our future to talk about. Or am I the only one who thinks we have such a thing?'

'Now listen, Anna.' Matt ran his fingers through his hair. 'This is all exceedingly difficult for me. I didn't expect any of this to happen. I needed to think. Falling in love was not something I expected.'

'I'm sincerely sorry for inadvertently thwarting your plans.' Haughtiness straightened her spine.

'Oh, for God's sake. Don't start behaving like that. It doesn't suit you.'

'I'm beginning to think you know nothing about me at all.'

'You want what I can't give.'

'I thought we wanted the same thing, each other…' Emotion tightened her throat, she felt ill, wounded.

'We do, but on different terms. Why can you not wait for me? Most women would wait for their men to return. I've heard of engagements lasting years.'

She trembled with rage and despair. 'I'll not waste away my life waiting for you, Matt Cowan. I'd have thought you'd want to treat me better than that.'

'Anna—'

'I'm going back to my father.' She strode stiffly away before she screamed out her misery for the whole of York to hear.

* * *

Streaks of pink clouds littered the sky the next morning, and a gusty wind blew. Anna stood at the window fully dressed in a riding habit of deep green, banded with black velvet around the hem of the jacket and divided skirt. She watched the sun come over the horizon and banish the gloom. She loved this time of the morning. It was early, barely gone six o'clock.

Her bedroom window looked over the back of the house, the cobbled yard, and service gardens. Further away, she could just make out the rooftops of the stables. They were easier to see in the wintertime when the tall trees lost their leaves. As yet, not many servants worked outside, though she fancied she saw one of the under-gardeners walking through the rows of vegetables. The busy day would start all too soon for them.

Anna stared into the distance, watching the dark blue sky turn slowly into dusky pink then pale yellow as the sun's rays climbed higher. Her heart thumped loudly in her chest. She'd woken around three o'clock in the morning and ever since had sat on the window seat and stared into the blackness of the night. At first, her mind remained shuttered, and she liked that, but after a while she started to ponder. She loved Matt and believed he loved her in return. Yet he wanted to leave her for some years. Had he made that decision lightly? Did he think of ways they could be together in the wilds of South America? With a sigh, she shook her head, letting the anger build again. He was taking the easy option and she hated him for it.

Grabbing her gloves, she hurriedly left the room and went downstairs.

Phyllis, a young housemaid, shuffled down the hallway, her arms straining under the weight of a bucket full of ash from the recently cleaned hearth in the drawing room. The maid bobbed a curtsy and said good morning. Anna nodded in reply. She could not bring herself to say good morning, for she felt she would never have a good morning again. Why wake up to greet the sun only to realize your life had changed in the most unkind way, forever? Her future was uncertain, and it plagued her mind like a fly on an open sore.

Fury ate away at her and demanded release. She must get away—away from Maisie, who smothered her with good intentions, away from the house and her mother, whose strange antics were beginning to scare everyone, and finally she had to get away from her own thoughts. Fast riding usually helped. To ride so swiftly that all her efforts were concentrated on staying on Jasper's back, leaving no room for self-doubt.

She headed for the stables. Grooms, making their way down from their rooms above the stables to wash at the yard pump, called out greetings.

Anna sent a hesitant stable boy away as she drew Jasper out of his stall and rubbed his nose, whispering her greeting to him. He waited patiently as she went to the tack room and collected his saddle, cloth, and bridle. She was aware the men stared but she didn't care. Let them talk and whisper. It only fuelled the insatiable, raging fire tearing at her insides.

In a few minutes, she had saddled Jasper and was up on his back. She wore no hat and had not tied up her hair. The men, stripped to the waist and lathered in soap, watched, mesmerized, as Anna, her face set in cold determination, urged Jasper into a trot out of the stable yard.

Once clear of the outer buildings and fences, Anna sent Jasper into a gallop. Her hair flying out behind her, she bent down low over his neck, gripping the reins tightly, forcing him to go faster than he'd ever done before. Being a strong and fit horse, he relished the challenge. Sailing high over stonewalls and jumping long over ditches, he galloped as though sensing this was what Anna wanted. She didn't direct him, only clung to the reins with the blood pumping through her veins, tasting the wind in her face.

Eventually, reluctantly, she slowed Jasper and turned him back for home. The sun held warmth as it rose higher and the countryside basked in its hazy glory. In the distance was the track leading into the wood. Anna stared at it and then on impulse, she nudged Jasper in that direction. Matt wasn't meeting her today, but at their secret place she felt close to him. Perhaps she could think there in the quiet and decide once and for all what was the best course to take.

At the clearing she dismounted and let Jasper tug at the sweet grass while she strolled to the water's edge.

'I'm glad you came.'

Anna jumped at Matt's voice coming out of the shadows. She turned and waited for him to join her on the shallow bank.

He took her hand and kissed it. 'I'm sorry for yesterday. It was unpardonable.'

She remained silent. His words were easily said. It was his actions she wanted.

'You haven't forgiven me.' Matt sighed and dropped her hand. 'Anna, I haven't the time to play games. I'm to sail in three days.'

Birds sang in the trees, rabbits rustled the undergrowth nearby, and the water trickled contentedly over the rocks as the condemning words hung suspended between them.

'Anna, will you talk to me?'

Her gaze didn't falter as she stared out over the sun-dazzled river. 'Will you take me with you?'

'I cannot.' Anguish rang in his voice. 'I've told you that.'

'Then, there is nothing to talk about.'

Matt bent, picked up a stone and flung it into the water. 'We can be married when I return. In the meantime, we can become engaged. I'll leave money at your disposal for you to buy our house and make it comfortable for my home coming.'

'How presumptuous.' She stared at him, hating and loving him all at the same time.

He frowned. 'I love you. You love me. It's as simple as that. The rest can be sorted out later.'

'No.'

His expression hardened. 'You do want us to be married, don't you?'

'No, I don't think I do.'

'Why not, for heaven's sake?' He stepped back in amazement. 'You just asked me to take you. Have you changed your mind?'

She stood as rigid as a statue. 'I asked you to take me away, not to marry me and leave me alone.'

'We won't marry then, simply be engaged. We can wait until I return and have a large wedding, whatever you want.'

'And that should satisfy me?'

'What do you mean?' He raised his hands in the air as though in appeal. 'Why would it not satisfy you? Every woman wants marriage, children, and a home to organize.'

'Not me!' She blazed at him. 'I don't want those things unless you are there to share them.'

His eyes softened. 'Anna, I adore you. I wish to make you my wife—'

'A*nd* you want me to stay in England,' she cried.

'I've explained that to you.'

Her chin quivered as tears filled her eyes and tripped over her lashes. 'Why can't you understand? Why is it so hard for you to realize that I want to be with you all the time, not just when it fits into your business routine? I cannot be the wife you want, Matt, the kind that patiently sits alone for months on end, content to embroider and receive your letters. I cannot be that woman. It would slowly kill me.'

'You could if you loved me enough.'

She suddenly smiled and even chuckled at the bizarre situation. It was a useless argument. Neither of them would give ground. Tears ran faster down her cheeks. It was over. The window of happiness closed.

'Anna...' Matt winced, his eyes mirroring her distress.

'It's been an honour knowing you, Matthew Cowan.' She ran her hand down his cheek. 'I'll never regret becoming involved with you.'

Pain flashed across his features. 'Don't you dare walk away from me, Anna.'

'I have to,' she whispered. 'It's all I can do.'

'No.' He grabbed her hard against him, holding her so tight she couldn't breathe but she didn't care. 'I love you. Say you'll wait for me, please?'

She traced her fingertip across his forehead, down his cheek and across his lips that parted in a shuddering sigh. His tongue flicked out and licked her finger. The sadness left his eyes as desire darkened them. Heat circled her belly, throbbed through her loins. When he kissed her, she welcomed it readily, needing his touch, his passion, his strength to banish her heartache.

As one they walked hand in hand out of the sunshine and under the umbrella of deep shade cast by the trees. In mutual consent, they knelt and slowly undressed each other in silence. The time for talking was done. All they had was today and it had to last them a lifetime.

He gently pressed her down on their bed of clothes and kissed away her tears. His hands explored her body, creating a fire within. She wanted release, ached for it, as his hands and kisses burned her skin like a branding iron.

Nothing had prepared her for this moment when she finally became a woman in the truest sense. Her body knew what it was meant for and had driven her mad with its urges for weeks, and now her mind claimed the knowledge of the act as Matt parted her legs and slid into her.

Slowly, gently they moved as one. Anna gripped his buttocks, her eyes wide with wonder as he smiled down at her and kissed away all thought. Her world dimmed and narrowed on the sensations coursing through her body until Matt suddenly shuddered and strained. Blinking in confusion, she held him as he gave a small groan and collapsed against her.

Lifting himself on his elbow, he kissed the tip of her nose. 'I didn't hurt you?'

'N—no.' She bit her lip. Was that it? There'd been no pain, but neither did she feel fulfilled. She frowned and berated herself for wanting more.

'Anna.' He lifted her chin up and stared into her eyes. Beads of sweat dotted his brow. 'You did not enjoy it?'

'Of course…'

Realization dawned on him and he swore. 'I'm sorry. I was too impatient. I couldn't hold back any longer. I've wanted you for too long.'

She leaned forward and kissed his lips. 'Let us swim,' she whispered, and before he could take her in his arms, she spun away and ran into the river.

She shrieked playfully as the cold invigorating water lapped her bare skin and laughed loudly as Matt ran in after her.

For half an hour they played and splashed and made love in the water. Then, becoming chilled, they scrambled out and lay on the grass, letting the warm sun dry them. Leisurely, they again discovered each other's body, recording in their minds the details of every line and curve of the beloved other. As Matt entered her for the last time, he made sure that her cries of delight would echo through the wood.

Chapter 8

As the quiet of the night stole across the countryside, Anna sat on the window seat in her bedroom, staring out into the darkness. Her chin rested on her drawn-up knees and her nightgown was pulled down over her toes. She was waiting for dawn and to say a final goodbye to Matt. She sighed deeply. Sleep had eluded her as she knew it would.

The silence afforded her the time to think properly, clearly. Without a doubt her decision to set Matt free was the correct one, and he knew it, too. It would've been impossible to her nature to marry a man she'd hardly ever see. To spend every night like this one, staring out of a window, waiting for dawn and the hope of his return, would drive her insane.

How would she have filled in the time? How could he think it fair for her to waste her life away, waiting for him to walk through the door? *He* would have a life overflowing with excitement and purpose while she paced the house each day, hoping and praying a letter would arrive from him. She couldn't live a life studded with his homecomings and departures.

Irritation seeped through her like water through a piece of chalk, slow and menacing. Why was he so damn stubborn? A little voice whispered, wasn't she just the same? She frowned. Was she being unreasonable? Perhaps she should wait for him. Wasn't loving someone all about sacrifices?

A tear rolled down her cheek. *Why did he not love me enough to stay in England?*

Anna woke to someone shaking her shoulder.

'Wake up, Miss.' Maisie's anxious face hovered near.

She rubbed her eyes and stifled a yawn. 'I must have fallen asleep. I didn't think I would.' She gasped as she stretched out her cramped legs.

'Aye, well, 'tis a wonder you can stand.' With a sniff of annoyance, Maisie folded her arms across her chest. 'Fancy sleeping on that while a good bed goes wastin'.'

'Yes, silly me.'

Maisie peered closer. 'You're all right then?'

Matt flashed through her mind. The day had arrived. 'Yes.'

'You haven't changed your mind then?'

'I'm so confused...' She sighed and knew she couldn't abandon him or a promise of a future together completely. She loved him and they'd shared such a beautiful day of loving in the wood. How could she turn her back on that? 'Everything keeps going around in my head and none of it helps or makes sense.'

'I thought you were givin' him his marchin' orders.'

'So did I.' She shrugged, uncertain. 'Try as I might, I just cannot cut him off entirely.'

'Right, well, 'appen you've done the best thing.' Maisie nodded and bustled around the room tidying. 'You have a wash and then I'll help you dress. I've got everything ready. The mistress had a bad night again I was told in't kitchens.'

While Maisie chatted and relayed the servant's gossip, Anna washed and dressed, her mind occupied with her swaying decisions. Despite all her tortured thoughts, sleepless nights, and common sense, she simply knew that Matt meant everything to her and, if she could, she would wait for him. Nearly two years…It seemed like a prison sentence, but what was the alternative?

Near the bedroom door, Anna hesitated, not wanting to leave the sanctuary of her room and face the day. 'Will I do?'

Maisie looked up from collecting the clothes needing to go down to the laundry. She smiled and sighed lovingly. 'Aye, Miss, you're a painting, you are.'

Anna smoothed down the pale lilac dress made of linen, with fine cream lace on the collar and cuffs and six inches of lace along the hem. Maisie had trimmed her hair at the ends and then curled it up onto her head, securing it with mother-of-pearl combs.

'Thank you. I need to look my best to give me courage.' Her bottom lip quivered.

'Nay,' Maisie quickly came to her side and fussed with her dress to cover her emotions. 'I'll not have you talkin' like that. You're the bravest person I know. You're strong, and I know you can do this. An' when it's all over, come back up here, and I'll be waitin' to help you get through it.'

Anna kissed her cheek. 'What would I do without you?'

'Well, if I get me way, Miss, you'll never have to find out.'

Smiling and swallowing back tears, Anna squeezed Maisie hand and left the room.

At the breakfast table, everyone listened to Arabella chatting happily. Her cheerfulness resulted from Luke Hammond being allowed to court her. A tentative wedding date was set for June the following year with an engagement to be announced soon. She excitedly told her two sisters she was put out a little by the year-long engagement, but both sets of parents had insisted on it.

Sipping her tea, Anna longed to be away from her inane babble.

'Can I be a bridesmaid, Arabella?' Maggie gushed, all caught up in the thrill of wedding talk.

'Why of course, Maggie. You can have a beautiful dress made in a pastel shade, not white of course, for I shall be in white, or maybe ivory with silver lace. I have not yet made up my mind. I am going to see Violet today to help me decide. You may come if you wish.' Arabella smiled. 'I think I may have at least eight bridesmaids.'

Anna leaned over to her father. 'How is Mother this morning?'

'A little better, apparently. At least that is what she tells me.' Thomas sighed. 'She left her bed and dressed this morning, which is a good sign. I asked if she wanted to accompany me to York, but she declined. She refuses to leave the house.' He dabbed at his mouth with his napkin and rose. 'Is Matt coming today?'

'Yes, this morning.'

'I didn't think I would get the chance to see him today, so I sent him a note wishing him a good journey. He sails tomorrow?'

'Yes, on the morning tide. He leaves for Liverpool this afternoon.'

'He will be missed, hmm?' Thomas raised his eyebrows.

'Very.'

'Chin up, dear. It will not be forever.' Thomas patted her on the shoulder as he walked past. 'He might be home before you know it.'

I hope you're right, Papa.

'I'll join you in a moment, Papa,' Arabella called after him, rising from her chair. She suddenly leant across the table, gripped Anna's hand in a cruel vice. 'I'm glad Cowan is going because if you do anything to bring further scandal to this family before, I'm married, I'll not be responsible for my actions.'

Recoiling from the attack, Anna spilt her tea.

'Oh,' Maggie jumped back as the tea stain spread towards the edge of the table and her.

There was a flurry of activity as maids hurried to sop up the mess and replace the teacup with another, but Arabella sailed out of the room without a backward glance.

'I'm sorry I asked to be a bridesmaid,' Maggie whispered. 'For a moment I forgot she was hateful.'

Anna forced a smile. 'No, you must be a bridesmaid, Maggie, because I won't be and if the both of us aren't there, then it will cause comment.'

'You won't go at all?' Maggie's eyes widened in admiration at her daring.

'I believe I will be violently ill that day.' She winked.

Maggie giggled but stopped when Nancy entered the room and came to the table. 'The Conway carriage has just arrived, Miss Anna.'

Anna felt the warmth drain from her face, but she straightened her shoulders as though ready for battle. She must manage to get through this with her pride intact. She could do this. She had to.

With a smile to Maggie, she made her shaky legs walk out into the hall, only to stop short as Evans opened the doors to admit Lady Harriet Conway.

'Good morning, Anna.'

Anna fixed a smile on her face. Her stomach churned and hands shook. 'How are you, Lady Harriet?'

'I am well, my dear, quite well.' Lady Harriet nodded. 'You are the very person I wanted to see before I go up to your dear mother.'

'You wish to see me?' Anna asked, as they stepped into the drawing room. 'Do you need another person for your charity committees?'

'No, my dear, although volunteers are always welcome.' She patted her hair into place. 'Are you waiting for Matt?' She smiled knowingly. 'You and he have become good friends.'

Anna nodded.

'Yes, well, he'll be along shortly. He had a few last-minute things to attend to this morning.' Harriet chuckled. 'The poor boy is in such a hurry to get back to the jungle, though only the good Lord knows why. Imagine living in huts with such uncivilized people.'

'He—he seems in a great hurry?' Anna squeaked. She should not have asked such a question. It would only cause more pain to know he was in a hurry to leave England, to leave her.

'Oh, yes. He told Hugh only last night that he would enjoy being back in Colombia again. It is a huge task setting up a mine, as well as a village for the people who work in it. Not every company would do such an honourable thing as that. Mind you, Matt does have a certain interest in those people beyond their just working for him.'

'Oh?' Anna felt an ice-cold shiver trickle down her neck. She abruptly sat on the cream sofa. 'Why is that?'

'Well, we like to keep it a secret, but since you and he are good friends, I'm certain he won't mind you knowing.' Her voice lowered. 'You see, he is sort of married to one of them, you know.' Harriet gave a snort of disgust as she sat on the matching sofa opposite. 'Such a disgrace if you ask me. The news of it killed his poor mother. It's really quite appalling to be connected with such low-class *native* people. We are all quite disgusted really. Both Matt and Adam...'

Anna heard very little from then on. An enormous weight sat on her chest threatening to suffocate her. Her mind reeled from the devastating news. Filtering through the dull void of her mind came Lady Harriet's voice. 'When we heard that Adam had died...well, naturally we were grieved—'

'A—Adam?'

'His half-brother, my dear.' Harriet waved a dismissive hand. 'Did Matt not tell you of Adam?

136

You know Matt's father died and his mother remarried?'

With her throat constricting as though to choke her, Anna could only nod.

'Well, the poor boy hardly knew his half-brother really, being away at school for so long and then travelling, but during a rare visit home, Matt grew to know and like Adam.' Harriet paused, as though selecting the right words to say. 'Against the wishes of his parents, Adam decided to join Matt on his first journey to South America. His stepfather blamed Matt for filling the boy's head with nonsense. Their parting was acrimonious, and Matt vowed never to return to his stepfather's house again.'

'I...see.'

Harriet flicked at a speck of fluff on her skirt. 'But then, to hear that Adam co-habited— is that the word? —with a *native* woman was completely scandalous. Then poor Adam died of fever and Matt, on his brother's death, had to virtually marry and take care of her, as by right of her tribe's law or some such. I can tell you it was such a shock indeed. His mother never recovered from it. We all have to carry this shameful secret.'

Anna stared, unable to believe a word.

Harriet pulled a white handkerchief from her reticule to dab her nose. 'Matt didn't seem too concerned at the time. In fact, he wrote and told us the woman was very pleasant and it would be no hardship to take care of her. Her name is quite pleasant too, I believe, um...what is it?' Harriet frowned. 'Oh yes, Nanita or something similar, and then there is the boy. He is called, Carlos. Yes, that is it.'

Anna felt her blood turn to ice. 'A boy?' She croaked.

'Matt has plans to bring his son to England for schooling eventually, but we must talk him out of that. He must be about four now, but he'll never be accepted of course. Matt is ridiculous to think he ever will be.' Harriet stood gracefully. 'Dear me, look at the time. I must go up now and see your dear mother. How is she this morning? Better? I do hope so. It's all rather worrying, do you not agree?'

Numb, Anna stared after Harriet's departing figure and wondered how she could stand the pain consuming her. Harriet's words repeatedly stabbed deep into her heart. She was slowly dying, fading away. No tears came. Anger surfaced, only to be denied an outlet, so it, too, withered away. To be angry meant experiencing an emotion, and that meant pain. Anna could not cope with any more pain. It was easier to be frozen, to accept the black emptiness. To feel nothing.

Sometime later, she watched Matt frown when he saw her sitting so still. He quickly tossed the parcels he carried onto a nearby chair, knelt in front of her, picked up her hands, and kissed them. 'Darling? Is something wrong?'

Anna lowered her gaze to him. Her eyes searched his, trying to find some reassurance that it was all a ridiculous mistake. He loved *her*. She had given her heart and body to *him*. 'Are you married?'

Matt rocked back on his heels, his eyes wide and staring. 'Who told you?'

'So, it's true.'

'No! It means nothing. It's not a proper marriage. Not an English marriage. My only obligation is to provide for her.' He spoke fast as if his haste might make her understand. 'She has no close family, and the village elder insisted she became my responsibility after Adam died, that is all. No man in her village wanted her after she'd been with Adam and she didn't want them...'

Matt gathered her stiff body into his arms, talking all the time. 'Adam should not have been with her in the first place. I told him not to, but would he listen?' He tried to break her cool gaze by kissing her cheeks. 'It does not stop us from marrying here in England. My marriage to Nanita is not a real one. It's not even a marriage, just a simple ceremony that showed everyone that she is in my care, that is all. She has only an old uncle and his family, and they could not provide for her. They are poor people. I could not break my promise to Adam. He begged me to take care of her. What could I say?'

She rose serenely and walked to the hearth, feeling as cold as ice and as old as time. 'Tell me about your son.'

Matt swore and ran his fingers through his hair. 'They are not as important to me as you.'

'As long as we are kept in different countries,' she spat, trying not to lose control. 'How could you not tell me you had a son?'

'Anna, please—'

'Is that why you were so adamant I stay here? So I'd not come face to face with your other family?'

'Anna, listen to me. I love you—'

'And them?'

'I promised Adam, as he was dying in my arms, that I'd take care of Nanita. Carlos…the boy was conceived at a time when we were both very lonely and grieving. It was a mistake that will not happen again. I wasn't thinking straight and felt responsible for Adam's death. He should have stayed in England.'

She stood rigid, her chin a fraction higher than normal. This was a nightmare she couldn't wake from. 'Why didn't you tell me?'

Matt bowed his head. 'I don't know. Perhaps I was frightened you wouldn't understand.'

'Then you don't know me,' she whispered. 'I don't want to see you ever again.'

'No.' He jerked towards her, but she ignored him.

Head held high she walked to the door, trying desperately not to fall in a screaming heap at his feet. Everything was out of focus and the blood pounded in her ears.

Matt dashed across the room, grabbed her arm and swung her around to face him. 'We love each other. We made love.'

She slapped his cheek hard. The noise rang like a gunshot in the room. 'That day in the wood is to be forgotten. You should have told me everything at the beginning. Now it's too late. You lied to me. You kept something particularly important hidden from me when I was baring my soul to you.'

'Please listen to me, let me explain—'

'You have had months to explain,' she screamed and then clapped her hand over her mouth. How would she survive this? She wanted to laugh hysterically. She had been tearing herself apart about whether she should wait two years for him and all the time he had another family. Humiliation clawed at her. She couldn't breathe.

'I promised Adam.' He groaned in throat. 'Anna, I'm not married, I promise you.'

'You have a woman and a son, and you never mentioned a word about them. How could you do that to me?' She bowed her head and a tear fell to the floor. She watched as another joined it. The anguish she suffered would kill her she was sure of it. He had shattered the beauty of what they shared. She felt sullied, dirty.

Abruptly, she seemed detached from herself and the scene. It was as if she was no longer blood and bone. 'What a fool I've been.'

'This doesn't change anything.'

She lifted her gaze to his. 'I never want to see you again. Get out.'

Anna heard him calling her name as she ran up the staircase to her room and hoped to God he wouldn't follow her. Her control was slipping, and if she was not careful, she would become hysterical with grief. She slammed the bedroom door on his yelling.

Evans, coming into the hall at the sound of the raised voices, stared in bewilderment.

'Anna! Anna, come back. We must talk, *please.*' Matt stood at the bottom of the stairs, ignoring Evans attempts to pull him away.

Above, a door opened and then Louise appeared on the landing, her eyes wide and glaring. '*You!* How dare you,' she snarled down at Matt. 'Leave this house at once.'

'I need to speak to Anna.' Matt's attention shifted to his Aunt standing behind Louise. 'Aunt Harriet, can you please go to Anna and tell her I need to see her? Please?'

Louise marched to the top of the staircase. Her face reddened and she put a hand out to grip the banister. 'Get out. You have ruined my life enough, Richard!'

Harriet's eyes widened. 'Louise? Louise dear, you're confused, ill.' She tentatively reached for her. 'Come back and sit down.'

Shrugging off Harriet's restraining hand, Louise took another step, leaning heavily on the banister. 'I said get out,' she yelled at Matt. She put a hand to her head and winced, but her hate-filled gaze never left his face. 'You are evil, Richard. You need to be destroyed.'

'I'm not Richard. Please let me speak to Anna.' Matt murmured, aware something strange was happening to Louise, which he'd no control over.

'I should have killed you years ago, when I had the chance.' Louise's breath came in short gasps. 'How many times did we go grouse shooting together? I could have shot you then and claimed it to be a mistake, an accident.' She let go of the banister and rocked gently. 'Where is Thomas? He will help get rid of this evil that threatens us.'

'Louise, it's Matt, not Richard,' Harriet said quietly. 'Let us return to our tea.'

'Thomas knew Richard cared nothing for me, used me.' Louise twisted to her friend. She opened her mouth to speak again when without warning she swayed backwards and overbalanced. Her eyes grew wide in fright. Her screams mingled with Harriet's as she fell and rolled down the stairs to land in a tangled mess at Matt's feet.

Chapter 9

Maisie arranged the flowers in a vase and placed them on the mantle in Anna's bedroom. She turned to Anna who sat on the window seat, as she had done every day for weeks since Matt's departure. 'Florrie picked these. Aren't they lovely, Miss?'

Receiving no answer, Maisie sighed and tried to think of something else to say. Anna's grave despondency frightened her. She'd run out of ideas to bring Anna out of the gloom she dwelt in.

'The Master said the Mistress's broken leg is gettin' better every day. She'll allus have a limp, but she can walk about with a stick.'

Anna continued to stare out of the window.

'Master Tom will be home shortly for summer. Won't it be good to see him again?' Maisie fiddled with the petals on one of the roses. 'The weather's warmin' up now. July's allus lovely, don't you think?'

A nod was her answer.

Maisie worried her bottom lip with her teeth, wondering if her darling Anna would ever be the same again. In the weeks since the incident with Matt, Anna's depression had deepened. She sat on the window seat all day and watched the clouds drift across the sky. If only she'd take an interest in the people working below in the gardens or the maids as they came and went, she might begin to recover, but she simply sat with a blank expression, seldom speaking a word. It concerned Maisie how little Anna ate. Her already slender frame became gaunt. Her once beautiful glossy hair hung limp and lifeless. She never left the bedroom and didn't show any curiosity when her father or Maggie came to talk to her.

It seemed as though her wound was so deep and severe, she no longer cared whether she lived or died. Never did she think Anna would be the kind of person to give up and fade away. Maisie sniffed in disgust. If loving a man did this to you then she was happy to remain without one.

'Do you want to walk in't gardens?' Maisie walked over to adjust the curtains.

Anna continued to stare.

'I can have Jasper saddled for you?'

'No.'

'That horse misses you.'

'Please…go away.'

A knock on the door saved Maisie from acting on the urge to shake some sense into her.

Maggie inched into the room but, hesitant to come too close, she stopped. 'H—how are you, Anna?'

'She's fine, Miss Maggie.' Maisie answered, knowing Anna wouldn't. 'Have you come to sit a while?'

'Yes, if you want.' Maggie looked from Maisie to Anna and back again. 'Does Anna wish me to?'

'Aye, pet, course she does.' Maisie was quick to reassure the child. Anna's past rebuffs obviously still hurt the girl. 'Don't you, Miss Anna?'

Maggie edged onto the window seat at the opposite end to Anna. 'P—Papa told me that Tom is to marry.'

Anna blinked.

Maisie rushed to the seat. 'That's wonderful news, Miss Maggie.'

Maggie smiled. 'Yes, and her name is Cecile. Papa is going to visit her family in Oxford.' Her smile faded a little. 'Only, Tom is not coming home for the summer now. He is travelling to Cornwall with Cecile's family instead. They have a house there, near the water.'

'Aww, that's a shame.' Maisie turned to Anna. 'Isn't it, Miss? The house is full of laughter when Master Tom's home.'

Anna slowly rose, her gaze vacant. 'I am tired.'

Maisie watched Anna tread wearily over to the bed and lay down.

'I must go back to Miss Foster,' Maggie flung over her shoulder as she ran from the room.

Shaking her head in despair, Maisie glanced at the ruin of her darling friend. If she ever saw that Matt Cowan again, she'd give him what for and no mistake. His lies had smashed Anna's heart into pieces. It was bad enough that she'd been willing to let him go, thinking he had business to contend with, but to learn he had some kind of a wife and child was just cruel. Her trust had been shattered.

* * *

In the last week of August, Maisie sat down at the large pine table in the silent kitchen. A wild summer storm had lashed the house and grounds all evening, keeping everyone inside. Not that it mattered much as the family had not entertained for many weeks due to Louise's accident and bouts of illness. A solemn air pervaded the house, affecting everyone in it.

Mrs. Wilson poured out two cups of tea, passed one over to Maisie and then sat her large bulk down opposite. 'You look all in, lass.'

'Aye, Mrs. Wilson, I am.' Maisie gazed around the warm tidy kitchen. Shiny copper pots and pans hung from hooks above their heads, reflecting the flames of the fire in the hearth, one that was never allowed to die out. The big cooking range shone from the constant black-leading it received. Everything ever needed in a busy kitchen such as this was in its proper place.

'Tis been a bad lot and that's putting it mildly. Ever since the accident, the whole house has changed. The master looks fit for the grave, and the mistress never leaves her room.'

'Aye, well besides her broken leg, she got her headaches.'

'Headaches my backside, lass.' Mrs. Wilson's expression became secretive, her voice lowered. 'She has something more wrong with her than headaches, I can tell you. More like madness.'

Maisie stared in horror. 'Nay, that can't be true.'

'What else could it be? She's always in her room and one minute she's normal and the next she's screaming her head off fit for bedlam.'

'Aye, I've heard her rantin' from Miss Anna's room. Lord knows how that Maude puts up with it.'

'She came down here yesterday sporting a nice cut on her forehead from where the Mistress threw something at her.' The cook shook her head sadly. 'Poor Master, he's got a rough deal of it that's for sure.'

'Well, he married her, and apparently she's allus been a handful. Still, I'll never like her for the way she treats my Anna.'

'How's the Miss been t'day?' Mrs. Wilson sipped her tea. 'I miss seeing her face.'

'No change. She's the same every day. I long for her to do or say summat that'll show she's gettin' better, but nowt happens. All day, every day, she sits and stares out the window.' Maisie sighed.

'Nay, I can't believe she's taken it so bad.' The older woman sighed, too, clearly mystified. 'I've never seen anyone pine away before.' She sniffed. 'I can't imagine doing anything so daft.'

'I wish she'd never met him. In the end nowt good came of it. She loved him so much, and I thought he did the same. What kind of man hides such things from a decent young woman like Miss Anna?'

'Nay, lass, those gents think they're God's gift and answerable to no one.' Mrs. Wilson sat back in the chair and folded her arms across her wide stomach. 'What do you think will happen? I mean, she can't stay in her room forever, can she?'

'I don't know, Mrs. Wilson. At least she's no trouble to anyone. The Mistress said she doesn't want to see her ever again. She blames Anna for her fall as well as for bringin' Mr. Cowan in't house. Miss Arabella said she no longer has an older sister

148

because of all the gossip about what happened that day.'

'Well, that's hardly fair, is it?'

'No.' Maisie shrugged and rose. 'Anyway, I best be off back up. I'm ready for me bed.' She took her cup to the sideboard to wash it.

'Nay lass, leave it there. It'll wait 'til morning.'

'Goodnight, then.'

'Before you go, lass,' Mrs. Wilson became grave. 'I want to bring something to your attention.'

'What's that?'

She shifted uneasily in her chair. 'As you know, I'm no gossip. Oh, I don't mind a joke and a laugh with rest of them, but I put me lasses in their place if they start brandying nasty talk about. Even so, this is different and serious about Miss Anna.' Mrs. Wilson paused and took a deep breath. 'You know I'm fond of the lass?'

Maisie nodded.

'I heard some of the lasses whispering in the scullery this morning. They don't know I heard them. Anyway, it's about young Miss, and I think you should know what being said.'

Maisie stiffened. 'Oh, aye?'

'I think it started in the laundry, the gossip, I mean. Somebody mentioned the Miss hasn't had her monthly cloths sent down for soaking and washing for some time now.' She frowned. 'Have you been doing them?'

'No, I haven't.' Maisie sat down again, for her legs could no longer hold her up. 'I haven't done her monthly washin', because there hasn't been owt to wash.'

'Nothing at all?'

'What were them girls sayin'?'

'That she could be havin' a bairn.'

Maisie snorted. 'Don't be daft. She'd never have lain with him.'

Mrs. Wilson raised her eyebrows knowingly. 'Aye, well, it's been known to happen. As you said, she did love him.'

Maisie sprang from the chair. 'I don't believe it. I want such talk to stop. How'd you think she'd cope if she heard that? It's bad enough people talk about her outside the house, but for the rumours and gossip to spread inside is...is…'

'All right, lass.' Mrs. Wilson raised her hands in protest at the barrage. 'I'll see that there's no more talk.'

A burning fury gripped Maisie as she left the kitchen. She ascended the steep servants' stairs at the back of the house and strode along the gallery.

In Anna's room, she stopped by the bed and looked down on her. Even in sleep, Anna looked sad. Dark circles shadowed under her eyes highlighting her pale face.

Had she lain with Matt Cowan?

Maisie agonized. If they had—she did a quick calculation. Could Anna be nearly three months pregnant? Maisie swallowed and tried to dismiss the crazy thoughts that flew around her head. Anna wouldn't have been foolish enough to lay with him before marriage. But then, she'd allus been different…

* * *

The long slow strokes of the brush lulled Anna into a serene state. She enjoyed Maisie's attention to her hair. Sleepiness washed over her in slow waves. She liked to sleep, for in slumber she need not think or feel. Glancing at Maisie's reflection in the dressing table mirror, she frowned at the sight of such dejection. Was Maisie ill? The thought shocked her. What would she ever do without her Maisie?

Suddenly, her mind snapped into wakefulness. She jerked away from the brush and Maisie jumped. They stared at each other in the mirror.

Blurry images played on the edge of Anna's mind. Her breathing became rapid. She blinked rapidly, impatient for her slow mind to work. 'Maisie?'

'Aye Miss?'

'Are...are you well?'

'Me?' Maisie stared at her in the mirror. 'Aye, Miss.'

'You look ill, tired.' It was the longest she'd spoken for some time. It felt strange, as though her tongue was too big for her mouth.

'I'm right as rain.'

'Oh—' Anna's mind returned to blankness and she welcomed it. She didn't have the strength to think. Her breathing slowed.

'Don't you dare.' Maisie's face flushed in anger, and she slammed the brush down on the dressing table. 'Don't you dare retreat back into that shell of yours, I ain't havin' it.'

'Maisie—'

'No, Miss Anna, no more. I'll not watch you waste your life away because of that useless man who stole your heart.'

'I cannot—'

'Yes, you can.' Then Maisie's sternness crumpled, and she hugged Anna tight. 'I'm here to help you, my lass. I'll not let anything hurt you again, I promise, but please start livin' again. I hate seein' you like this.'

Anna rubbed her eyes and face. Her mind was fuzzy, like waking up after a deep dreamless sleep. Her heart raced. Memories of Matt whirled through her endlessly, making her giddy. She heard his laughter and cringed. She'd no wish to go to that painful part of her brain and relive what only brought her unhappiness. She took a shuddering gulp of air.

'I want my old Anna back.' Tears filled Maisie's eyes. 'I want the lass back who'd not let life beat her down no matter what.'

Anna faltered. Was she brave enough to step out of the void, to think and feel again?

Rising slowly, she realized she wore her nightgown. Again, haziness came over her. She tried to think. She gazed around the bedroom as though seeing it for the first time after being away for a long while. A low fire burned in the grate, meaning the day must have been cool, though she had no memory of being either cold or warm. In fact, she'd no recollection of feeling anything for some time. Spying a tall vase full of yellow and red Dahlias on the mantelpiece, she scowled, slowly remembering the last time she walked through the garden the Dahlias were not in flower. A small groan sounded in her throat.

Maisie, noticing the direction of her gaze, nodded. 'Sid gave them to me for your room. He said they were your favourites and you always waited for them to flower. They're late this year, he said.'

'They are usually in full flower by August.'

'Aye, well, 'tis now the end of August.'

'It is? I didn't realize…'

They stared at each other for a long moment, knowing things had changed between them. The last few months had not been kind to either of them, and it showed in their faces.

She nibbled her lip. 'I'm sorry, Maisie, so sorry.'

Maisie smiled. 'Things will be better now, I promise.'

Anna took a deep breath and recognized that she'd turned a corner. The pain was still there but duller now. 'I couldn't believe I could be so hurt, Maisie. After all, I've lived all my life knowing my mother doesn't care for me. I thought nothing could be worse than that, but I was wrong. Matt…Matt wounded me beyond my imagination.' She paused, shivering with an inner coldness. 'I gave him everything, my heart, my soul, my body and he threw it all back at me. Our relationship was built on lies, deceit. Oh, I know I was setting him free to pursue his concerns in South America, but in the back of my mind I think I always knew I'd wait for him to return to me. Wasn't I stupid?'

Maisie had paled, her eyes large in her face. Silently she opened her arms and Anna gladly stepped into them.

* * *

Anna paused in the doorway of the breakfast room. The maids saw her first and Nancy smiled in welcome. With a shaky sigh of relief, Anna smiled back.

Thomas, Arabella, and Maggie suspended their eating to stare at her as if she were an apparition.

'Oh, Anna. I am so happy to see you well again,' Maggie gushed, unable to contain her delight.

'Thank you, Maggie. I am indeed better.' In truth, she felt a little out of place, which was rather silly considering this was her home and family. The effects of her numbing grief still lingered. It took significant effort to wash and dress this morning, and then leave the sanctuary of her room. Maisie encouraged her all the way, saying she must begin her life again and she might as well start with breakfast. Very practical was her Maisie.

Thomas stood and held out a chair for her. 'Nothing pleases me more than to see you sitting here beside me, dearest.' His eyes became moist and he swallowed convulsively. 'You have done my sore heart an unbelievable amount of good.'

Feeling guilty for causing him anxiety, Anna reached for his hand and squeezed it gently. 'Everything will be fine from now on, Papa, I promise.'

Breakfast proved to be lively as news and gossip flew around the table as they regaled Anna on what she'd missed. Tom, she was told, was besotted with his fiancée, Cecile and incredibly happy.

'Thankfully,' Arabella said, replacing her teacup on its saucer, 'she is from a good family.'

Anna didn't mention she'd a vague memory of Tom telling her about his new love. It seemed to have happened an awfully long time ago, not only just this year. Blinking, she concentrated on her sister as Arabella changed the subject to her favourite topic, her wedding plans.

'I made Tom promise not to marry before me.' Arabella snorted with humour, but her eyes flashed dangerously.

Maggie rose. 'Anna, can you come to the stables and see my new horse which Papa bought me? Old Snowy died two weeks ago.'

'Really? I'm deeply sorry, Maggie. Of course, I shall come.' Anna folded her napkin and prepared to rise. Hesitating a moment, she turned to her father. No one had spoken of Louise, but Anna felt her unspoken presence. 'Is Mother well, Papa?'

Thomas looked uncomfortable. His gaze flittered from Anna to Maggie and back. 'She is still abed.' He lowered his voice. 'Her leg is mending slowly, and her head causes her pain still.'

Anna nodded. She had not seen her mother since the accident and had no wish to now. The house and grounds were big enough for them to stay clear of each other.

Maggie took Anna's hand and pulled her out of the house and along the path to the stables. As they passed through the gardens, a young under-gardener, prompted by old Sid, ran to give Anna a bunch of colourful carnations. She waved to Sid in thanks and asked the lad to take the flowers to the kitchen. She would collect them later. Overwhelmed by the good wishes received from the staff inside and outside the house, she swallowed back threatening tears and raised her chin. The worst was over.

* * *

Lightning flashed across the steel-grey sky. Anna knelt on the window seat in her room and watched the black angry clouds roll closer. Energy cursed through her veins. She longed to run through the rain when it came. She remembered doing that with Tom when they were children. Their governess had a difficult job keeping them clean and respectable.

Everyone in the house was hot and testy. Summer held the land in a vice-like grip even though August was done. Servants grumbled going about their work. Horses and many of the other animals on the estate refused to cooperate with their handlers. Mrs. Wilson complained to the manager of the home farm that the cream had gone sour and the milk was too warm. Louise shouted at anyone passing the door of her rooms. Maude, Louise's maid, became red faced and flustered at having to run up and down the stairs a dozen times on one errand or another. They all hoped the storm would break soon and offer some relief from the heat.

Picking up her hated, crumpled embroidery, Anna considered the day. It hadn't started well. This morning she woke to a sick sensation in her stomach, causing Maisie to silently fetch some tea. Deciding not to go riding, Anna then asked Maisie if she felt like a picnic down by the stream. She was sure Mrs.

Wilson would make up a wonderful hamper for them. Once the queasiness passed, Anna felt quite hungry. Maisie, giving her a sharp look, pleaded too much work to do and added she wasn't particularly in the mood for a picnic. Anna suggested the two of them spend the day in York but again Maisie declined.

In the end, Anna spent the day reading and walking in the gardens with Maggie and Miss Foster. She even endured Arabella boring her with honeymoon destinations.

The change in Maisie's attitude perplexed Anna. She could find no exact cause of the shift, yet it was there, shimmering under the surface of her polite manner. Never one for having an enormous amount of patience, she tried to encourage Maisie to confide in her, to no avail.

Now, as the storm rumbled overhead, Anna turned to engage her in conversation. 'I have not seen Edwin for some time, not since the garden party, though he didn't speak to me then. He hasn't forgiven me for our quarrel.' She paused as a sharp pain of remembrance hit her, they'd quarrelled about Matt. Thrusting it from her mind, she stabbed the needle into the sample. 'I wonder if he has called lately.'

Maisie sat quietly in a chair, darning a stocking. 'I've no idea, Miss.' She didn't look up.

'It's your birthday soon. What would you like for a present?'

'I'm sure I don't know, Miss.'

'I can buy you a new dress?'

'If you like, Miss.'

Anna gazed out of the window as the first fat drops of rain fell from the sky. 'Sid will be glad of the rain.

He told me this morning we'd get a storm this afternoon. It's amazing how men like Sid, so in tune with the earth, know just what the weather is going to do.'

'Yes, Miss.'

Anna threw down her sample.

Maisie's lack of worthwhile responses frustrated her, and she was trying so hard to be normal. 'Is something the matter?'

'No, Miss.'

Her patience came to an end. 'Oh, for heaven's sake. Will you stop answering me like some tedious fool?'

'I wasn't aware I was, Miss.'

Anna marched over and stood directly in front of her. 'Have I done or said something to upset you? Though I cannot think what I've done lately to cause anyone any upset at all. In fact, my behaviour has been exceptional.' She tilted her head slightly as she studied Maisie. 'You have been acting strangely for some weeks. I'm not used to you being quiet. Is something wrong? You can tell me whatever it is.' She waited to hear a confession or some slight upset.

'Everythin' is fine, Miss.'

'I thought things were becoming easier now I am…well again.' Anna sighed. 'You aren't the same anymore. Why?'

'A lot of things aren't the same anymore, Miss.' Maisie stood and stepped towards the dressing room.

'Dash it, Maisie. I want you to tell me what is going on.' Thunder clapped loudly overhead. 'I've never seen you behave this way before.'

Maisie spun back. Fury heated her cheeks and narrowed her eyes. 'What way would that be, *Miss*?'

Anna faltered at the display of defiance. Lifting her chin, she glared. 'Out with it. I demand to know what it's.'

'Very well, today is me Mam's birthday.'

Anna's stance slumped, and her voice became softer. 'Oh, Maisie. I'm so sorry I forgot. Why did you not mention it earlier? We could have gone to put flowers on her grave.'

At the gentleness of Anna's concern, the strung tightness seeped from Maisie body. 'Aye, I should've said summat to you. I wanted to go and visit her grave but didn't.' Maisie sniffed. 'What kind of daughter am I not to go and visit her grave on her birthday? But it was so hot, and with the storm buildin' up and...and oh, there's no excuse, is there?'

Anna turned back to the window. The rain pitter-pattered against the glass as the storm continued heading east on its way out to sea. 'Come on. We shall go now.'

'Now?'

'Yes. We will go and collect some flowers from Sid and take them to place on Sylvia's grave.'

'We can't go now. It's bucketin' down.' Maisie frowned, looking out at the sodden view.

'Nonsense. The storm is passing. We can take the carriage and be there in no time.'

The storm gave an encore and sent a thundering applause as the rain beat a last tempo on the windowpane.

Anna collected her gloves from the dressing table but paused in putting them on to look at Maisie. It was so unlike Maisie to stand and dither. In fact, her whole countenance made Anna feel queer. Since Maisie became her personal maid, she knew she could rely on her in all matters. Only this year, events changed that relationship. Their special friendship had altered. Anna knew her involvement with Matt Cowan and the subsequent incidents that left her so devastated were the cause.

Now, as she watched emotions flitter across Maisie's face, an odd feeling shivered down her spine. Once again, Anna felt the need to run away, to hide from the unease and apprehension that filled the room. 'Maisie?'

The room grew cold. The rain had left a chill in the air. Across the space of the bedroom two pairs of eyes locked and pleaded with each other, one begging the other not to hurt her and the other pair already apologizing.

'Come and sit down,' Maisie began quietly but firmly, and for a moment their roles were reversed. 'We need to talk.'

Anna sat. 'Do I want to hear this?'

'Not likely.' Maisie reached for her hands and held them tight. 'You see, Miss, there's summat you should know.' Maisie wet her lips and took a deep breath before continuing. 'The thing is, there's been some talk about you.'

'What kind of talk?' Anna asked, unconcerned. 'I'm used to people whispering about me.'

''Tis hard for me to say, because it's to do with Mr. Cowan.'

Anna's chin rose, but she indicated for Maisie to continue.

''Tis the women in't laundry who started it, well, mainly a new lass who's just started earlier this year. Sue Brewer her name is. A real troublemaker and all. Nobody thinks much of her—'

'But they listen to her gossip?'

'Aye well, everyone listens to gossip.'

'So, what has she said, this person whom I don't even know?' Anna raised an eyebrow in annoyance, the initial dread leaving her.

Maisie blushed. 'She's brought to everyone's attention that…that your monthly cloths haven't been sent down for boilin'.'

'My monthly cloths?' Anna scowled in puzzlement. 'Lord, I cannot even remember when I last had my monthlies. Why is she talking about them for? I don't understand.'

'Oh, Miss. Do I've to spell it out for you? What happens when women don't get their monthlies? What does that usually mean?' Maisie sighed at Anna's expressionless face. 'It means they're havin' a babby. That's what that Brewer woman been sayin' to all and sundry.'

'How dare she. I will not have a snip of a laundry girl spreading such rumours about me. I shall make sure she is off the estate first thing.'

Maisie sighed with obvious relief. 'I knew it were rubbish talk. Only, I knew how much you loved him, but I knew you wouldn't allow him liberties—'

'What?'

'Well…you know…'

'Oh my.' Anna felt the tiny hairs on the back of her neck rise. She rose and took a step. 'It could be true,' she admitted, more to herself than to Maisie.

Maisie whimpered. 'You mean…No, Miss, say it can't be.'

Shame scorched her brain. 'I'm...not sure.' Her stomach flipped. A baby. *Matt's baby.*

Maisie blinked rapidly and held her hands together as if in prayer. 'I—I took the liberty of talkin' to Mrs. Wilson about it and—'

'You have discussed this gossip with Mrs. Wilson?' Anna's temper flared like a flame put to gunpowder. 'Well, thank you very much, Maisie, for keeping me in the dark. So much for your loyalty.'

Springing to her feet, Maisie faced her with a rebellious glare. 'Loyalty? Keepin' you in't dark? That's a laugh. You were already in the dark by you own makin', if you remember. I had to deal with everythin' on me own. You shut yourself off in your own world, half mad with grief at losing him. I didn't know what was goin' to happen to you.'

Tears ran down Anna's cheeks. 'I'm so sorry, Maisie. You must know that you're the last person I'd want to hurt.'

'Well, I'm hurtin'. I've lost me mam and you've been a broken shell of the person you once were since the business with *him*.' Maisie's own tears fell. 'It felt like I'd lost the two people most important to me within months.'

Anna rushed to enfold Maisie in her arms. 'I'm sorry.'

Sometime later, they dried their eyes and gave each other a watery smile.

'Shall I order us some tea, Miss?' Maisie said, after rinsing her face.

'What about visiting your mother's grave?'

'No, Miss. We'll leave it for today. Mam won't mind I'm sure.'

Anna stood in front of the dressing table mirror and studied her reflection. 'What did Mrs. Wilson say exactly, about all of this?' she asked as she ran her hands down the front of her flat stomach. Could it be true?

Maisie opened the bedroom door, her hand on the door handle, ready to go down for a tray of tea. 'Nowt much.' She let out a deep sigh. 'We...wondered whether you'd lain with Mr. Cowan. I know you're a good lass, and not man mad, but still, you did love him, and you didn't have your monthly curse...'

A small glow spread throughout Anna. She smiled slowly, if not a little painfully, as she remembered that magical day in the wood. It would live forever in her memory despite the awful aftermath. 'Yes, I loved Matt in the full sense you mean. It was not long before he sailed.'

Maisie shook her head and her shoulders sagged. 'Aye, I thought so.'

Anna gazed out of the window wondering if it all could be possible. Could Matt's baby be growing inside her? How could she bear it?

'What am I to do?' She put a hand to her forehead. 'What will Papa say?'

Chapter 10

The slow September days brought with them cooler breezes. Foliage turned from green to amber and red. Instead of riding, Anna now took long walks. Strolling through the gardens, she walked on a carpet of dry leaves and watched them float on the lake. Sometimes, Maisie or Maggie accompanied her, or she would go alone, enjoying the peacefulness it brought her. Morning sickness reminded her each day of the miracle that grew inside her, changing her life forever. Plans needed to be made.

Anna threw the last of the bread to the black swans gliding at the edge of the lake. For a second, Matt's image clouded her mind, but she shoved it away. He was no longer important, no longer of use to her. Fate had chosen her path and she must follow it.

She dusted her gloved hands and turned away to head for the house just as Maggie ran lightly down the slope. 'Are you running young lady?' she joked.

Maggie slowed, giggling. 'I hope Miss Foster wasn't watching.'

Anna looked back at the lake glistening in the evening sunlight. 'It's so beautiful.'

'Did you feed the swans?'

Anna glanced at her. 'Yes.'

'Are the babies grown?'

'Yes, they have, but I think we lost one to Mr. Fox.'

'Bad Mr. Fox.' Maggie scowled. 'I shall tell Papa.'

A breeze rippled the water before gently touching Anna's face and lifting the hair from her brow. She took Maggie's hand and tucked it over her arm. 'Come, it's becoming cool. Let us go in. I've been walking for hours.'

They headed towards the house, admiring the swallows diving across the gardens.

'Can we picnic tomorrow before it's too cold to do so?' Maggie asked.

'We will see.'

Maisie waited on the steps at the back of the house. At once, Anna knew there was a problem. Maisie's cheeks glowed red, and not just from the weather.

'What is it?' Anna asked, walking ahead of her sister.

Maisie looked at Maggie and then back to Anna. 'You can't go in. *She knows.*' She indicated, with a small lift of her head, the upstairs window of Louise's room.

Anna's heart leapt in distress. A small groan escaped before she could stop it.

'What is the matter, Anna?' Maggie came to stand beside them.

'Nothing, pet. You go on up and I'll be in shortly.' She gave Maggie a little push towards the doors.

Grabbing Maisie's arm, Anna strode across the gardens and through an ivy-covered archway into the service gardens. 'Tell me.'

'Not long after you left, an unholy row erupted in the mistress's room.' Maisie's eyes were wide. 'I could hear it as I went about me work. The mistress was shoutin' and throwin' things. I know, because I heard things smashin' against walls.'

'Was Papa there?'

'No, he'd already left. I'd seen him cross the yard through one of the windows as I went down to the kitchen.'

'Go on.'

'I were goin' about me work when suddenly the Mistress came bargin' into your room. She were leanin' heavily on one of her walkin' sticks and she started wavin' the other one around as though she wanted t'brain me with it.' Maisie lowered her voice. 'I tell you, she frightened me. She ranted and raved, askin' me where you were. She told me she wanted to strike you down. She said some horrible things.'

'Good Lord.' Anna tried not to sound alarmed. Louise's lack of control worried her. Her mother's strange behaviour made it impossible to know what she would say or do next. Anna knew she must talk with Papa about the doctors returning to examine Louise once more.

Maisie reached for Anna's hand. 'It don't matter what she said, except for one thing. She said she'll make sure you'll get rid of your bastard.'

Anna swayed. 'How did she find out?'

'I don't know. Staff gossip I expect.'

She took a shuddering breath. 'I'm not ready for this.'

'You've got no choice, my lass.'

Anna straightened and tried to quell her trembling. She'd no option but to confront her mother. It was time to stop daydreaming and make a future for her child and herself.

Slowly, but surely, her old self was re-emerging from the broken spirit she'd been for the last several months. The mental strength, always a big part of her character, returned and she was thankful. 'Let us prepare for battle then.'

It felt like a small victory to them when they reached Anna's bedroom unnoticed. Unfortunately, it was short lived, as Louise stood in the doorway a few minutes later. Anna and Maisie remained perfectly still not wanting to trigger off any outburst of rage.

'Can I help you, Mother?' Anna asked cautiously.

'Yes, you can.' The words were as bitter as the iciness reflected in Louise's eyes. 'You can pack, you little whore. Your bastard will not be born in this house!'

Anna gasped and Maisie moved closer for support.

Louise held herself taut. She'd left the walking sticks behind. She stood with her hands clasped in front of her waist and her head tilted in a superior way so she could look down at them. 'All morning I have rehearsed what I needed to say. Now, the time has finally arrived for me to be rid of you, my lifelong curse.'

'Mother—'

'You and whatever belongs to you are to be out of this house by this evening. I have already summoned ordered for your horse to be put in the cart and for it to be brought to the front of the house. Evans will organize some men from the yard to take your belongings out. I advise you to pack absolutely everything you own because whatever is left will be burnt.' Her mother spoke without emotion, and no sentiment showed in her features.

'I will not pack one item until I've spoken to Papa.' Anna suddenly didn't care whether her mother loved her or not. She'd come to terms with that now. Nevertheless, she loved her father and would speak with him.

'Your *father?*' A sinister smile spread across Louise's face. '*He* is not a part of this. *He* has been dead and buried for many a year.'

'What are you talking about?' Anna whispered, not wanting to know what her mother implied, but already suspecting the truth.

Louise's laughter was harsh and awful, a fleeting glint of madness lit her eyes. 'Your loving Papa? Thomas is not your real father. Richard Thornton, his brother, is the man who put you in my womb, and I have hated you every moment since then. You have been a living torment from the moment you took your first breath, and you would never have taken it if I had been granted my wish.'

'You lie.' Anna reached back to find Maisie's hand and clasped it tight.

'I have waited years for an excuse to get you out of my life, and it is you who now gives me that excuse. Oh, the joy of it.' Her evil laughter filled the room.

'Why do you do this to me?'

'Because you remind me of my mistake. Richard used me for his amusement. He promised me everything and all I received was you. Just like that Cowan man did to you.'

168

'No.'

'Yes. Thomas saved me and my reputation and declared you to be his, but you won't be as lucky as me. You have no one and I'm glad. I hope you and your brat die in the gutter.'

'Why do you hate me so much?' Anna winced at the desperation in her voice.

'Simply because you live and each day you are proof of what Richard did to me. Now get out and never come back.' Louise's loathing glare took in the entire room before she quietly limped out.

Maisie and put an arm around her. 'Don't listen to her, my lass, she's sick. Her mind's not right at the moment. You know that.'

Trembling, Anna bit her lip to stop the tears. 'No, Maisie. For once her mind is clear. She speaks the truth. I can feel it here.' She jabbed her chest with a finger. 'In my heart, and I think I've always known something was not quite correct.'

'Aww, lass.'

Anna shrugged, trying desperately to be brave. 'All my life I've known there must be some awful reason why Mother does not like me, and now I know.'

'What are you goin' t'do?'

She looked into her dear friend's face and managed a shaky smile. 'First, I must find Papa. While I'm doing that, will you start to pack?'

'We're leavin' here then, tonight?' Maisie's face reflected the shock at the suddenness of it all.

'Of course, I cannot stay here under this roof with my mother. Besides, I want to go now, today. I need to get away from here and all the memories. I shall start a new life. I was also hoping that you'd want to come with me.'

'As if I'd stay here without you, you daft sod.' Maisie shook her head. 'Go on, go find the Master while I start packin'.'

'I will send up some of the girls from downstairs,' Anna added on her way out.

Anna spent longer in the kitchen than she planned, for once Mrs. Wilson found out she was leaving she became upset, as did the kitchen maids. Not wanting to cry herself, Anna asked Mrs. Wilson to fill a hamper for her to take on her journey. Luckily, this proved to be a smart tactic as the cook dried her eyes and busily organized the girls into action.

On leaving the kitchen, Anna made her way to the stables, only to stop as her father walked up the path. She studied the man she'd always loved as her dear papa. The stress of the last couple of months had aged him. Yet he was still a handsome man, and it was quite uncanny how much she looked like him. But then, she remembered, he was her uncle after all. A tremor ran through her.

'Are you waiting for me?'

A lump came to her throat, and tears welled in her eyes. 'Can—can I speak with you?'

He took her hands. 'What is it?'

'Something has happened.' Anna closed her eyes. It was all too much really, and her strength was failing. 'I—Can we talk in private?'

They walked through the gardens to a bench beneath a beech tree, sat, and faced each other. Anna didn't want to hurt him, but in the end, she knew she would. She must leave here. The very thought made an ache spread throughout her body. She tried not to think of it. Tried not to think of saying good-bye to Maggie and everyone. Leaving this wonderful house and its beauty hurt her heart as easily as a knife piercing it.

'I must leave,' she began. 'I've got to go away.'

'Go away?' Thomas frowned, puzzled. 'Why?'

'I am having a baby. Matt's baby. I'm sorry.'

'A baby?'

'Yes. Please forgive me.'

'I cannot believe it. A baby?' Thomas ran a hand over his face. 'Are you going to find Matt?'

'No.' Anna's stomach constricted. 'That is all done with. There is no going back.'

'Lord, a baby.' He shook his head, bewildered. 'We must find Matt.'

'No.'

'We must. He has to marry you now.'

She stiffened. 'No. I'm sorry, Papa, but I wouldn't have him, not now. I much prefer to go away. I can manage.'

'You don't need to leave.' He stood and paced. 'We will go on a trip, and then when we come home, after the baby is born, we shall say—'

'There is more to it than that,' Anna said quietly.

'Oh?'

'Mother knows about the baby and has disowned me. Her instructions are that I am to leave here and never come back.' She winced at the thought.

'No.'

Taking a deep breath, she braced herself to impart the next bit. 'She also told me that my...my real father was Richard, your brother.' Anna heard his gasp. His face blanched. She went to him and gripped his arm. 'Please, Papa, don't take it badly. I don't care if Richard is my true father. He means nothing to me. I love you. You are my papa. Please, believe me.'

Thomas hugged her tightly, murmuring into her hair words she couldn't understand. For a few minutes they held each other and cried together. Then, he led her back to the seat.

'I made Louise promise never to tell you that you were Richard's child. She gave me her promise, but lately her illness has made her a different person.' He sighed. 'She carries so much hate.'

'Oh, Papa. We both know Mother has never loved me. Don't make excuses for her.'

'I know, and I am most sorry. I've tried to make up for her lack of love by giving you extra of my own. Louise was never fair to you, and it was the one thing I didn't like or understand about her. I tried to pretend it didn't happen.' He closed his eyes. 'I failed you.'

She kissed his cheek. 'You have nothing to apologize for. If you had not loved me as much as you did, I'd never have survived my childhood.'

They sat in silence for some minutes and watched the sun begin to make its descent over the trees. Anna wondered if she'd ever sit here like this again. She had to be strong and face the future, whatever it brought. 'Papa?'

'Yes?'

'How did it feel knowing that Mother had loved another before she married you?'

Thomas looked at his hands as they hung loosely between his knees. 'I don't think Louise truly loved

Richard. I think she thought of the security a marriage to him would bring. Remember, all she'd had was a strict old aunt looking after her. Marriage to Richard meant all of this.' He swept his hands out wide, encompassing the house and gardens. 'Only, Richard had other ideas, and not one of them involved marriage, at least, not for some years. Louise thought he would change his mind if she surrendered to him. He didn't. He didn't care at all for her, whereas I—' Thomas smiled. 'I loved her unconditionally. So, I asked her to marry me.'

'And me?'

'When you were born, we told everyone you were early. You were fair like me. No one thought there was anything unusual. Actually, you are the very image of my mother. I adored you from the very first moment, and I still do.' He took her hand and kissed it. 'That is why you aren't leaving here.'

Anna rose, mentally composing the words she'd to say. 'I must go. Mother is adamant. Even so, I feel I need to get away for a while. I cannot stay here with Mother.'

'Where will you go? Abroad?'

'I may travel for a while, yes.' Actually, the thought of travelling delighted her. Maybe it was just what she needed to do.

Thomas frowned, his fingers tapping against his thigh as he thought. 'Once you find a place to stay, send me the details and I'll pay for everything. Then when the child is born, we'll make arrangements.'

She twisted to stare at him. 'Arrangements?'

'Adoption.'

'No.' The very idea of giving her baby away horrified her. 'Oh no, Papa. My baby stays with me.'

He jerked back in surprise. 'Don't talk nonsense, Anna. We'll find a good home for it and—'

She backed away. 'That is not going to happen. I know other families of our class do it, but not me, never me. This is my baby. Mine.' She spun around and made for the house, eager now to be away from any threat.

'Anna.' Thomas hurried after her. 'Anna wait.'

Ignoring him, she gathered up her skirts and broke into a run. It was beginning to grow dark, and she wanted to be on her way.

When Anna entered her room, it was completely bare of all her possessions. Maisie and two maids had packed travelling cases as fast as they could. They'd cleared everything from Anna's bedroom and dressing room. All that remained was the furniture. Even the bed sheets and curtains had been packed.

'I don't think it was necessary to take the sheets and curtains, Maisie.' Anna's heart thumped in her chest.

Maisie stood with her hands on her hips, her face flushed from exertion. 'The Mistress came back and made sure I packed everythin'. She said the furniture is goin' to be burnt.'

A small shiver ran through Anna. She would miss so many things here, but she would be glad to be away from such hatred.

'Well, well, well.' Arabella came into the room and looked about. She smiled with false brightness, her eyes steel cold and hard. 'So, now I know why I didn't like you. You are a bastard. A bastard carrying a bastard,' she gloated.

'Get out, Arabella.' Anna hid her trembling hands behind her back.

'No, no. It's *you* who is leaving. I am incredibly happy about it, too,' she sneered. 'We can all forget you ever existed. My whole life I've contended with being second best in Papa's eyes, when all the time you were not even his true daughter as I am.' Loathing etched her every feature. 'When we were children, people would always say how pretty *you* were, never me. I began to make it my full-time hobby showing people how odd you were. When visitors came and commented on your absence, I'd point out that you were climbing a tree with your skirts up around your waist. As we got older, I told people you liked to mix with the lower classes, and you felt an affinity with them and not us.'

Arabella stepped closer to glare. 'Oh, you would not believe the stories I told and how many people believed them. Did you ever wonder why certain people ignored you at functions? Everything you did was unladylike, and it helped my tales a great deal.'

'Get out,' Anna shouted. It took a great amount of effort not to hit her sister and keep on hitting her.

'Before I go, I want to tell you that I detest you, and you'll never be welcome in this house again. I'll make certain of that.' She left in a flounce of skirts with her perfume lingering in the air.

'Nasty piece of work is that one.' Maisie gathered up a small case and a material bag. 'Like her mother.'

'Yes.' Anna blinked back tears.

'I'll take this downstairs and say goodbye to Mrs. Wilson. Don't be long.'

'I shan't.' Anna took a final look around the room, which had been her sanctuary for many years. She walked into the dressing room. From the floor, she picked up a stray ribbon. For the last time she strolled to the window seat. She would miss looking out at the view she knew as intimately as her own face. Sighing, she went to the dressing table, and checked that the drawers were empty. With a final look about the room, she moved to stand by the door. Anna realized that without her belongings it was just a simple room full of memories.

Softly closing the door, she also closed a Chapter of her life.

'Papa said you're going on a holiday.' Maggie stood at the foot of the narrow stairs leading up to the nursery. 'Why do you have to go? Will you be gone long?'

Anna rushed to Maggie and hugged her tight. 'I don't know how long I will be gone, but I promise to write.'

'I shall miss you.'

'And I you, very much. Always remember that I love you. I will be thinking of you every day.' Anna promised, swallowing her tears. 'Now, go back upstairs. I don't want you to come down to see me go, understand?' Anna spoke more harshly than she meant, and Maggie's chin trembled. 'Listen to me. Are you listening?'

'Yes.' Maggie nodded.

'You are very special to me. Whatever you hear in the future, remember we are sisters and I love you.'

Quickly, Anna kissed her and then walked away, not trusting herself to stay any longer.

Outside, Anna was shocked at how much luggage was piled onto the farm wagon. To help pull such a load, Jasper had been joined by Misty, the home farm's old mare.

Members of the staff stood on the gravel drive unable to believe their eyes that the Master's daughter, the lovely Miss Anna, was leaving in a cart for who knew where.

Thomas waited at the bottom of the steps, looking pained. 'I've sent for Armitage to drive you to York. I'll come in the morning and see to all the arrangements for your trip.'

'No, Papa.' Resolve stiffened her spine and straightened her shoulders. 'I want a clean break. I do not want you to come to York tomorrow. I can handle everything myself.'

'Nonsense,' he thundered. 'Now listen, if this is about my comments regarding the child—'

She held up her hand, aware all the servants were listening with mouths agape. 'Papa, I want to do this alone. I need to be responsible for myself, and I cannot do that if I let you take control.'

'What about money?' he asked in anguish. 'How will I know where to send you money?'

'I don't need any money. I have my own in the bank. I'll be fine.' Anna assured him, taking his hand and holding it to her cheek.

'I don't like this at all. Tomorrow I will visit, and we can talk this through. Which hotel will you stay at? Or perhaps you can go to—'

'No, Papa, no details. I have decided to just see what each day brings. This is it.' She kissed him lightly on the cheek. 'When I am settled, I'll write to you.'

'How will you manage? You are a lady. You cannot simply travel the country alone.'

Anna tilted her head in thought. A feeling of lightness overcame her. The weight of sorrow and unhappiness lifted. In a way, it was a kind of release, a release from the past, from Louise, Arabella, and especially the memories of Matt. 'You know, Papa, I can do anything I set my mind to.'

'Take one of the men.'

'I've got Maisie, she's all I need.'

'This is madness.' He paced back and forth, looking frustrated, angry, and scared. 'I won't stand for this. Go back inside, we'll sort something out.'

Laying a hand on his arm, she stilled him. 'I love you and I'll be perfectly fine. I have money, intelligence, good health, and Maisie. Nothing will happen to me. Now, wish me well and fret no more.'

'You promise to write?'

'When I am settled, yes.' With his help, she climbed up onto the seat next to Maisie and gathered in the reins. She looked down at him. 'Remember to fuss over Maggie. She'll feel quite alone now.'

With a last wave and goodbyes to all, Anna slapped the reins against the horses' backs. The animals walked down the drive and out onto the road that would take them to their new lives.

'What on earth are we goin' to do?' Maisie whispered.

Bone-weary, Anna gave the matter some thought. 'We'll go to York tonight and find somewhere to stay. Then, in the morning I'll visit the bank before we make for the open road.'

'The open road? I thought we were to travel abroad?'

'Not at first. I'd like to stay somewhere quiet first. Perhaps rent a little cottage on the moors somewhere away from everyone.'

Maisie rolled her eyes. 'You can't be serious?'

'Deadly. I like the thought of being free and at peace.'

'Are you not frightened?'

'Yes, very much, but we'll be all right. I know it.' She reached out to grip Maisie's hand. 'Some things are meant to be and, as scary as it is, this feels right.'

Chapter 11

Anna put a hand to her throat, staring at the solicitor. 'I do not believe it.'

'I'm most sorry, Miss Thornton. As I said when you came in, I was just about to arrange for an appointment with you. I've been putting it off, hoping the situation would recover, but it does not seem to be.' Mr. Smythe rubbed two fingers across his forehead. 'The Civil War in America has affected many things.' He grimaced. 'Had I known you were making plans to leave your father's home, then naturally, I'd have informed you sooner.'

Anna took a deep breath to clear her head and ignore the panic that threatened to overwhelm her. She smoothed out the skirt of her dark green and navy blue checked dress. Her clothes were becoming tight and she needed to buy new ones. 'So, Mr. Smythe, you are telling me that I'm without income?' she asked him, her voice steady.

Viewing the sheets of papers in front of him, Colin Smythe frowned. 'No, not completely. There is a regular, if only small, return on your shares in the coalmine in Castleford. Also, you receive a small annuity from the candle-making factory in Bolton. For the time being, they are doing well.'

'And the rest?'

Smythe removed his glasses and rubbed them with a cloth from his desk drawer. 'I'll be honest with you, Miss Thornton. The small percentage of shares you own in the two cotton mills in Manchester are, at the moment, worth very little. With the halt of cotton importation from the Southern States of America, the textile industry is in upheaval. The naval blockade of all their ports is highly effective. Cotton hasn't been coming in from America for quite some time. The owners of cotton mills are finding it difficult and your share returns prove this. It won't change until either the war stops, or excellent quality cotton can be imported from elsewhere.' He leaned back in his chair with a remorseful expression.

'I've shares in a shipping company in Liverpool,' Anna said hopefully.

'Indeed, you have, but what was their major cargo? Cotton. Of course, the ships will be sent to other ports now, and that too is causing concern because there will be too many ships and not enough cargo in some ports. Until the new trade routes become stabilized and profitable, I'm afraid there will be a wait for your share of returns in regards to that company as well.'

Anna thought hard. She must become self-sufficient. To ask her father for money now would be going backwards and not forwards. It was a bitter blow this morning to realize the amount of money in the bank would be all she could count on for some time. The eventual travel plans she made with Maisie last night in their little room in the inn would have to be scrapped. Instead, she must find a way to make an income and build a life somewhere away from York for her child, Maisie, and herself.

'Well, Mr. Smythe, it seems I shall have to make some drastic changes.'

'Ah, Miss Thornton.' He smiled in a slightly patronizing tone. 'I'm sure that if you return home to your father, your life may go on as before.'

'I'll not be doing as you suggest, Mr. Smythe.' Anna gave him a sharp look that had him sitting straight in his chair. 'Please listen carefully. I want you to sell my shares in the cotton mills and also the shares in the shipping company. I need the money they will bring. Next, I want—'

'Wait.' Smythe nearly launched out of his chair. 'Good heavens above, Miss Thornton, you can't simply sell everything off. Besides, they have dropped in value. They are worth half of what your grandfather paid. No, you're much better to hold on to everything.'

'Shall I take my custom elsewhere?' Anna glared at him. In twenty-four hours, her life had been turned upside down. She possessed less money than she thought and had nowhere to live, but she was damned if she would let some scrawny little man tell her what to do.

'No, of course not, Miss Thornton.' Smythe rubbed his brow with his handkerchief. 'I just don't want you making a mistake.'

'Very well, then. Let us get down to business.' She smiled and inclined her head graciously.

* * *

Anna walked along Clifford Street towards a little tearoom, which she knew sold refreshing cups of tea and tasty tarts. The two hours with Mr. Smythe had given her a headache in more ways than one. In such a short period of time everything that had been safe and familiar to her was now unstable and alien. The open hatred from her mother and the news about her parentage shook her more than she cared to admit. She also knew how terribly she would miss her father, Maggie, and Tom.

Now, on top of all that, her finances were not as affluent as she first thought. For her to be independent she must make new plans. If she could not live in comfort on the income from the investments she and Papa had made with her inheritance, she must earn a living. The odds were against her, being a woman born to wealth and privilege, but she was young, strong and, most importantly, determined. Besides, there was no other choice for her. She would be successful.

'Anna? Anna!'

Hearing her name called, she paused, but then hurried on. She'd no wish to make polite conversation with some family friend right now. The caller's footsteps approached rapidly. Reluctantly, Anna slowed and turned to see Edwin striding towards her, his coat flapping out wildly behind him like some hideous bird.

'Good day, Edwin. It's nice to see you.' In truth, she would rather not see him at all. He was bound to tell her father of their encounter and upset him even more.

'I only just heard…' he said, out of breath. 'I went to visit you this morning, and Arabella told me you had been ordered to leave the house by your mother. What have you done?'

'Why do you assume I've done something wrong? Though I suppose Arabella has told a fantastic tale?' Anna raised her eyebrow at him.

'No.' He flushed. 'Well, I'm sure she'd not mention it to another soul outside of the family.'

'You always try to see the good in people, Edwin. However, there is very little good in Arabella.'

'She did tell me something, something that I really cannot quite believe,' he whispered, his cheeks staining red.

'That I'm with child? It's true.' Anna didn't feel guilty and wondered fleetingly whether she would burn in Hell.

Edwin's head jerked at the admission. 'I had hoped Arabella lied.'

'Not in this instance.'

'I hate to think of you in this way. You're better than that, Anna.'

She smiled and touched his arm. 'I'm not worthy of your high opinion.'

'Will you marry me?' Edwin gushed.

'Pardon?' Anna stepped away as though he'd struck her.

He glanced around at the passing strangers. 'I'm sorry,' he mumbled into his chest. 'I—I didn't mean to embarrass you.'

Her shoulders slumped at the kindness of her dear friend. She'd been hard on him in the past, and now it shamed her.

'Oh, Edwin.'

She sighed with regret. How easy it would be if she could suddenly fall in love with him and live happily ever after. Only her heart was still in fragments over Matt, and she knew a long time would pass before she could even try to put the pieces together again.

On hearing the pity in her voice, Edwin held himself erect and looked directly into her eyes. 'I have been in love with you for as long as I can remember. I know you don't love me, but I promise you I will give you a good life, if not here, then somewhere else. I will love your child as though it were mine.'

He meant every word, she knew, and it pained her to hurt him. 'I cannot marry you, Edwin. You are very dear to me—'

'No, Anna.' He gripped her shoulders. 'Don't fob me off. Think about it. You—'

Her tender kiss on his cheek stopped his flow of words. 'Don't do this to yourself. Don't waste your love on me,' she whispered. Seeing a passing hansom cab, she quickly hailed it to stop and climbed in. Edwin's cry of anguish was lost in the rumble of wheels. The tears that ran down Anna's cheeks went unchecked as the cab sped her back to the inn and Maisie.

* * *

'A farm? Eh, Miss, why in God's name do you want to buy a farm?' Maisie asked, astounded to learn of Anna's most recent plan for their future.

'Don't be alarmed, Maisie. I've worked it all out.'
This morning she awoke with a sound resolution that,
from now on, there would be no more tears. Today
was a new day. Therefore, they would be confident
and positive about their future.

'Don't be alarmed? Of course, I'm alarmed.
You're an unmarried lady carryin' a babby, I'm as I
am and neither of us have a great deal of money.
Now, you're sayin' you're buyin' a farm.' Maisie
huffed, holding onto the seat as the cart's wheels
rattled over a rut. 'Here we are at dawn, drivin' this
silly bloody cart away from York and out into the
countryside, and you suddenly announce you're to
buy a farm?'

'Yes.'

'God in Heaven help us. For we'll die on't side of
t'road or in this bloody cart.'

'Stuff and nonsense.'

'We can't buy a farm, Miss.'

'Of course, we can,' argued Anna. 'I've enough
money to at least put a deposit on a small holding.
With a lot of hard work, we can build it up into
something grand. I'm determined to make it a
success.'

'Why can't you buy a little tea shop or summat?'

She grinned. 'Because I know nothing about
running a shop, but I do know a bit about farming.'

'You're mad, Miss.' Maisie crossed her arms to
show she wasn't happy with the idea.

Anna winked. Since leaving the estate, Maisie
occasionally dropped the 'Miss' when talking to her.
By rights, she shouldn't, and they both knew that, but
somehow things were no longer the same. They were

186

in this together, whether they sank or swam, and together they were equal, just the two of them on the open road.

Maisie frowned, giving her a sidelong glance. 'So, where do you want to buy this farm?'

'Anywhere really, it does not matter, but I think we will head towards Leeds. Mr. Smythe has a cousin who is a land agent there. I have his address. We'll call on him to see if there is anything available.'

'You talked it over with Mr. Smythe, then?'

Anna glanced at her. 'Yes. I told him I didn't want to stay in York, and he suggested Leeds. This cousin of his may know of a farm we can buy. If not, then we shall move on. We can come and go wherever we please.'

Anna gazed at a herd of cows grazing in a nearby field. To roam as free as a bird was wonderfully relaxing. The past few days could be forgotten. The events of this year could be forgotten. The peaceful countryside and fresh air had an amazingly calming effect that soothed her strung nerves.

'I've never been to Leeds,' commented Maisie as the horses plodded on sending up puffs of dust with each lift of their hooves. 'How long will it take us to get there?'

'Well, if we drive hard, we could be there sometime this evening. However, the cart is full, and I don't want to push Jasper and old Misty too much. We don't know how far we will be travelling in the future, and I don't want either of them to go lame. Also, I want to stay off the main roads. I would hate to pass someone we knew. If Papa knew that we travelled the roads, he would never rest from worrying. Taking the smaller roads will add a day or two to our trip, but we have all the time in the world.' Anna grinned. 'In fact, we may pass through a nice little village and choose to stay for a week or two and explore it. There is no hurry.'

'I should think there is. You don't fancy havin' that bairn in't back of this cart, do you?' Maisie face was a picture of affronted self-respect.

'Oh, Maisie. I've five months or so to go before I have this baby.'

'Aye, but have you thought about the weather? 'Tis October now, and winter is just around the corner. The nights are drawin' in. Have you even thought about tonight? Where'll we sleep, in't cart? An' what if it starts rainin'?'

'We will come across an inn before nightfall. They are dotted all over the place.'

''Tis surprisin' how scarce they are when you're cold and tired,' Maisie warned, obviously unable to find any joy at being on the open road. She'd already spent most of her life homeless and hungry, and probably didn't look forward ever to finding herself in that situation again. Anna also knew Maisie didn't want them roaming the countryside, at risk of been done in by any villain lurking in the hedgerow.

Near midday, when the sun was at its highest, they crossed over a narrow stone bridge and stopped near a clear, meandering stream for a rest and to eat. The weather had turned rather pleasant again after the last few days of coolness and Anna hoped it would be a good omen. The cloudless sky showed no signs of rain. The hamper Mrs. Wilson had tearfully packed, was well stocked, and even though they ate out of it yesterday, it was still crammed with food.

Piling two plates high with sliced ham, pickles, cheese, and crusty bread, Maisie took them down to the bank of the stream. With a rug and a bottle of cider tucked under her arm, she made a comfortable picnic spot.

Anna gave the horses their feed in nosebags, before joining Maisie by the water.

'This is lovely.' Anna gazed around. A mixture of forest and green open fields surrounded them. Although the going seemed slow, it pleased her they had come so far in such a brief time. With the city streets of York now behind them, the air smelled better, the colours brighter.

Contented, they ate their food while watching the minute fish dart in the water. A gentle breeze lifted the hair on Anna's forehead. She turned as a faint sound carried to them. Biting into her ham, she munched slowly as the noise came again.

Anna glanced at Maisie who frowned. Sipping her cider, Anna nearly choked as a long moan reached her across the open space. She shivered despite the warmth of the day.

Maisie's cheese was poised halfway to her mouth. 'What the hell is that?' she whispered.

'An animal I think.'

Instantly, Maisie collected their things together. ''Tis time we were off.'

As long as Anna had known her, the unknown outdoors always made Maisie nervous, obviously even more so with the two of them being totally defenceless out here in the open.

'Shhh, Maisie.' Anna spoke low, pulling Maisie down again when she tried to rise.

The noise came again, softer this time, more of a whimper. They only just heard it above the trickling water.

'Let's go,' Maisie urged.

'It might be injured.' Anna stood and looked towards the bushes further up the stream.

Maisie hovered. 'I don't want to know. 'And no, I'm not goin' to help find it,' she said, warding off what she apparently knew would be Anna's next question.

The moan sounded again, louder this time. 'It's coming from near the bridge, I think,' Anna said, walking in that direction.

Maisie looked uncertain whether to run to the cart or follow. Finally, she put the plates back down and crept with Anna towards the bridge. 'We'll get eaten alive,' she muttered.

Twenty yards separated the picnic spot from the bridge. The stream widened as it ambled under the construction. Bushes and brambles tangled into a wall of foliage by the water's edge, making it harder to find a direct path. Filtered shade covered them from the branches of a mammoth oak tree. Picking up a stick, Anna whacked the undergrowth to make a path. She searched through the bushes, trying to see the animal.

'This is silly, Miss Anna.' Maisie reverted back to calling Anna Miss in her fright. 'You'll end up hurtin' yourself,' she grumbled, and then jumped when a weak but clearly human voice called for help.

Anna, with her heart in her mouth, peered over the bushes and into the gloom under the stone bridge supports. She was able to make out an object halfway up the bank. Stepping closer, she could just see what looked like a clump of dark clothing. 'Who is there?'

'Can you...help...me...please?' called a faint female voice.

Taking courage when she recognized the voice as that of only a woman or young girl, Anna pushed her way through the tangled growth. She bent down and scrambled up under the supports, with Maisie following. What she found made her pause. The woman had her knees drawn up to her chest. Even in the diffused light, Anna saw the swollen stomach, and a small amount of blood soaking through the centre of the woman's skirt. The young woman's mouth worked but no words came. Her panic-stricken eyes pleaded with them to help her. Anna and Maisie quickly knelt on either side of her.

'The—baby is coming,' the woman said between pants.

'It will be all right. We will help you,' Anna assured her.

Maisie took control. Apparently, now that she knew she wasn't going to be attacked by a wild animal her compassion had returned. Anna knew she'd grown up in the city, in the middle of the slums, where babies were born with regularity. Many times, she'd been present when her mother helped a labouring neighbour. Often, she assisted, taking over some small job such as fetching fresh towels or more warm water. Because of this, she obviously knew more about childbirth than Anna did.

'How long have you been havin' your pains, lass?'
she asked.

'Since first light—dawn.'

'Are they regular?'

'No. They come and go. A short time ago I got a
show of blood.'

'We'll have to move you, all right?' Maisie spoke
a slow steady tone. 'We'll get you out into the open.
That'll be easier than bein' cramped up under here.'

The woman cried out when she moved her legs.
They had stiffened from sitting so long in one place.

Anna and Maisie half-carried and half-dragged her
as gently as they could back to their picnic spot.
Straightening the rug out, they placed her down on it.
Anna ran up to the cart to look for another blanket
and her pillows, which Maisie had put into a chest.
She was thankful indeed her mother insisted Maisie
pack absolutely everything from her bedroom.

Returning, Anna noticed Maisie removing the
lower part of the woman's clothing. Spying the empty
cider bottle, Anna took it down to the stream and
filled it. She brought it back and put it to the
stranger's lips. The woman thanked her and closed
her eyes.

'What else shall I do?' Anna asked.

Maisie leant back on her heels. 'There's nowt we
can do at the moment. 'Tis up to the babby.'

'Shall we take her back to the last village we came
through? Or find a farm nearby?' asked Anna.
'Tadcaster is not too far away.'

'No.' The woman's answer was vehement. 'I don't
want to go anywhere, please. Let me stay here.'

Anna knelt beside her. 'There should be a doctor or midwife close that can help you. I have a cart, we can—'

'No, please.' The woman moaned from deep in her chest. She grabbed Anna's hand and squeezed it hard. Some minutes later, when the pain receded from her, the woman apologized.

'There is no need,' Anna told her with a smile. 'What is your name?'

'Emma, Emma Webster.'

'We are Anna Thornton and Maisie Shipley,' Anna replied, indicating first herself and then Maisie. 'Are you a local?'

'No, I'm from Selby. I've been on the road looking for work the last few months.' Emma wearily closed her eyes.

The next hour trickled by as slowly as a bitter cold winter. Exhausted from the pains, Emma weakened. She was petite in build and lack of food had drawn the skin tightly over her bones. Dressed in rags with dirt under her nails, she spoke a little of her journey, of sleeping rough and searching for work. Large frightened eyes dominated her tiny heart-shaped face. With long dark brown hair flowing down her back, she looked like a nymph from deep within a dark forest rather than someone who roamed the roads.

'I wish we had taken her on to Leeds or back to Tadcaster,' Anna whispered to Maisie as they watched Emma doze between her pains. 'She would have seen a doctor or midwife by now.'

'Well, 'tis too late. I dare not move her. I think it might be a clever idea to light a fire. There's safety matches in the hamper.' Maisie wiped her hands over her eyes then looked up at the sky. In the last hour, clouds had scattered across the sun cooling the afternoon. 'We may have to stay here all night.'

Anna worried her bottom lip. 'I shall go find a farmhouse.'

'Nay, you're not leavin' me here alone.'

'What if something goes wrong?'

'Let's just hope it doesn't.' Maisie walked off to gather some wood for the fire.

Tired and cold Anna went to the cart for a warm coat.

* * *

'Good. You're doing so well.' Anna sat beside Emma, holding her hand and wiping the sweat from her brow. It sent shivers up her spine to think soon she would be going through the same experience. She watched as Emma's face screwed up in pain, her suffering clearly apparent in her gentle hazel eyes.

Emma groaned. 'I think death would be a blessing right now.'

'No, you don't mean that.'

'I—I can't do it,' she cried.

'Of course, you can,' urged Anna. 'Squeeze my hand.'

'Come on, Emma. You nearly there,' Maisie shouted. 'The head is out. Steady now. Slowly…'

Anna moved down the blanket a little to see the tiny little head and stared in astonishment. 'It has hair.'

In fascination, she watched as Emma strained once more to expel the rest of the baby.

The baby's cry shattered the still air.

'You've done it.' Maisie tied off the baby's cord with ribbon and cut it with Anna's sewing scissors. She then wrapped the baby in a bed sheet that Anna herself had slept on a few nights ago. 'Hold the baby, Miss Anna. There's still the afterbirth to deliver yet.'

Gingerly, Anna held the tiny baby. She smiled at Emma and nestled the baby beside her on the blanket. 'Your beautiful daughter.'

Emma wept. Her arms were full, so Anna wiped away the tears. She watched the afterbirth come away with no mishap and sighed with great relief.

Maisie washed Emma and changed her into a clean dress borrowed from Anna, because Emma had no other clothes of her own. As darkness fell around them, Maisie helped Emma put the tiny baby girl to her breast, while Anna filled three plates with food and built up the fire.

'What will you call her?' asked Anna as they ate.

Emma smiled at her new daughter. 'Sophie, after my mother.'

'Would you like us to take you back to Selby, now the baby is born?' she asked tentatively.

'There is nothing for me in Selby. I've no wish to go back,' Emma murmured as she looked from Anna to Maisie. 'I'm sorry for putting you to so much trouble. Please, don't feel obliged to do anything more for me. You have done so much already.'

'That wasn't any trouble to us,' Maisie assured her. 'We were happy to help, and we'll be happy to take you anywhere you want to go, isn't that right, Miss Anna?'

'Yes. Of course, we will. Is there any family you wish to visit?'

'I've no family. My mother died long ago when I was a child. I became an orphan and then I went into service. The only person who made me feel as if I had someone to care for me is now dead. That is why I'm on the road. I was on my way to York to see if I could get work.'

'The father…' Maisie began. 'Is he the one who died?'

'No.' Emma shifted position and winced. 'Sophie has no father, nor will she ever have one.'

'Sorry.' Maisie glanced at Anna. 'I didn't mean t'be nosey.'

'It's fine, Maisie. I shouldn't have snapped at you, not after all you've done for me today.' Emma gave a small smile and put her plate down. 'I think I might have a little sleep. I'm dreadfully tired.'

'Yes, yes you must be.' Anna gathered up their plates. 'It's getting late. I think we should make for the next village and find an inn. We can't stay out here in the open with a new baby.'

Going to the horses, she gave each a friendly pat before securing the load again after they'd searched through it during the day.

Maisie joined her, carrying the hamper and placing it on the cart. She glanced back to where Emma lay curled up on the blanket with her baby. They both slept soundly. 'What do you think of her?' She nodded in Emma's direction.

Anna followed her gaze and frowned. 'I like her so far. I think she has endured a lot lately. I noticed her clothes were once of decent quality, except now they are torn and very worn. She looks the least like a vagabond of any I've seen, and she speaks well too. I'd guess she has been educated.'

'How? She said she's no family and was an orphan.'

'She could have educated herself.' Anna shrugged then turned to the cart and took out the lantern. 'Do *you* like Emma?'

'Aye, she's nice.'

'Good, because how would you feel if I asked Emma to come with us and, once we have a house, to live with us?'

'Live with us?'

'Yes, what do you think? I believe she needs us.'

'It's a bit sudden.' Maisie frowned. 'We don't know her.'

'She has nowhere to go.'

'But why take her with us?'

'Why not?' Anna sighed and leaned against the cart. 'She is alone with a baby, no money, no home, no family. Can we walk away from her and leave her with nothing again?'

'What are you saying then? You want her to work for you?'

'Work with us.' Anna corrected.

'She has a babby. Are you sure you want to be lumbered with the pair if 'em?'

'Only if you do.'

'Umm—ye, all right then.' Maisie helped to repack the cart. 'I suppose we'll need help to run a house and the farm.'

'Are you certain you don't mind?'

'Nay, it'll be fine, I'm sure. Besides, I think she could do with us takin' care of her. She's so thin and pale, but she's quite a looker and wouldn't last two minutes on her own with a new babby.'

'True.'

Maisie winked. 'Saved another one, 'aven't you?'

* * *

Emma sat holding Sophie as the three women drove away from the inn early the next morning.

'Of course, it's up to you to choose,' Anna said. 'You may not want to live on a farm with us.'

Emma gazed at the two women fate had sent across her path. How kind and generous they were, complete strangers helping her and now taking her in. Tears filled her eyes. It had been such a long time since anyone showed her kindness, let alone offer her a home. 'Thank you, Anna, and you, Maisie. I cannot tell you how happy I am. I'd dearly love to come with you both. I promise you'll not regret asking me. I'll work hard for you.'

'Oh Emma, I don't want you to work for me, but with me,' Anna corrected. 'Together, the three of us, striving to give our children and ourselves a wonderful home. Three women showing the men that we can do whatever they can do and better.'

Emma laughed for the first time in many months. 'I don't know what kind of farmer I'll be, but I'll try.'

'That's all right, Emma. I don't even like animals.' Maisie grimaced, and they laughed.

Once on their way, Anna confessed to Emma about her own pregnancy.

'I didn't realize,' admitted Emma. 'Your coat disguises it well.'

'Good. For the moment I don't want anyone to think I'm with child. I'm without a husband, and in the eyes of businessmen that alone is a hindrance. If they knew about my fall from grace, they'd shut their doors in my face. I'll pretend to be a widow.'

The annoyance Anna felt was clearly evident in her voice and Emma smiled ruefully.

'Well, speaking from experience, I suggest you become used to such attitudes. Nobody wants anything to do with a lone, expectant woman.'

'You have had a difficult time?'

Emma nodded. 'It was awful. I couldn't get much work, and when I did, as soon as the employers found out I was having a baby they sent me on my way. They called me dreadful names. I'm not a whore—'

'Couldn't you have stayed in Selby?' Maisie questioned from behind them, perched on top of a trunk.

'No, after my employer died, I had to move on. The house was left to his son.'

'You weren't asked to stay on by the son?'

Emma shivered. 'That man should be hanged.'

Chapter 12

Anna flicked the reins over the horses' rumps, and they left the grime of Leeds behind. The weak October sun shone, though it didn't warm them. Birds chorused in the trees. Happiness spread through Anna. She should be frightened by the prospect ahead, but only joy filled her. At last she'd have a home of her own. Her heart lifted at the thought of it.

She smiled, thinking of the last weeks living in lodges in the heart of Leeds. After scouring agents' offices, she'd come across a listing for a property some thirteen miles from Leeds. Intense bargaining reduced the price and, as of yesterday, she became the proud owner of a run-down farm situated on forty-five acres.

Most of her funds had gone on the deposit for the farm, and after a day purchasing goods, the rest was dwindling fast. On checking with the bank today, she learned that a small amount of money had been deposited from the returns of her other investments. It was not enough for her grand dreams for the farm, but it was a start. Therefore, the farm needed to start making a profit very quickly in order for them to live well. Common sense—with which she was blessed even if she did ignore its warnings from time to time—told her the farm would most likely eat up all her money faster than it would bring any in, but at least it was hers.

They passed several small holdings and received a wave from a passing farmer sitting high on his cart filled with produce. Apart from another man, walking along the side of the road, they saw very few people at all.

On reaching the gate and driveway to the farm, Anna halted the horses for a moment to gaze up at the house. All at once, her chest tightened as she silently gazed at the property. The house nestled in the side of a low valley with gentle wooded hills rolling away behind it. Built of grey stone, it contained three stories, with the top floor having three dormer attic windows that gave the house a quaint appearance. In her mind's eye, she could see the house as she wanted it to be, with clean sparkling windows and snow-white lace curtains blowing in the breeze, surrounded by flowerbeds in brilliant colour—

'Good Lord, we've our work cut out for us,' Maisie groaned, breaking into Anna's dreams with her more practical observation of the scene.

Starting the horses up the drive, Anna noticed the flowerbeds were just tangles of overgrown weeds and bramble bushes. Nevertheless, they could wait before being transformed. Winter fast approached and more important things needed attention.

Suddenly, her baby fluttered. She rubbed the spot with one hand. Lately the baby had started to make its presence felt. It was a constant reminder she would soon be a mother for the first and maybe the only time. It also reminded her of the struggle she had ahead. She carried a bastard and both of them could easily be shunned by people in the area. Buying a farm and acreage miles from the nearest village had been a good decision. The isolation suited her.

'Are you all right?' Emma asked.

'Yes, the baby moved. I think it approves of its new home.' Anna grinned, overwhelmed with feelings as the baby moved inside her.

Maisie poked her head in between Emma and Anna's shoulders. She shook her finger in disapproval at Anna. 'The first thing we do is light a fire in't kitchen, and Miss Anna, you're goin' to sit still for five minutes. You've done nowt for the past weeks but run from one thing to another and it's time you 'ad a rest.'

In the yard behind the house, Anna reined the horses to a stop and gazed around at the sheds, yard and house. All this was hers. Well, hers and the banks.

She climbed down from the cart and stepped down a path that led from the yard through the middle of a small courtyard, where an herb garden nestled inside, to one of the two aged, dark oak doors.

Anna unlocked the door on the right. The day had come. She was entering her own house. Tears blocked her vision. She turned to Maisie and Emma. 'Our new home.'

Maisie rolled her eyes. 'You're soft in't head. Now, get the kettle on, you daft happ'orth.' She pushed them inside.

The three women stood in the dimness of the kitchen. Directly opposite was an open doorway that led into the hallway. The kitchen gave evidence that the outside neglect continued inside. Cobwebs hung from every conceivable place. Dust coated surfaces and a strong smell of dampness hit them.

A large oak dresser stood along the back wall, and a big square table covered the centre of the room. The only light came from a wide window overlooking the yard, but it was so dirty Anna could not see out of it. Under the window was a stone sink and bench.

Anna and Maisie walked into the hall. On their left was the dining room with an enormous table that could seat up to twelve people, and when polished, Anna knew it would shine beautifully.

A pair of doors faced them from the opposite side of the hall. The first opened into a parlour or sitting room and the next a small study. Beside the study, a staircase took them to the next floor. To Anna's dismay, out of the four bedrooms, three had damp patches on the ceiling and walls, indicating problems with a leaky roof. At the end of the narrow landing was a steep set of stairs leading up into the attics. She and Maisie took the opportunity to inspect them.

'There's holes in't roof.' Maisie pointed up where they could see the sky.

Anna scowled. 'That is how the weather has damaged the bedroom ceilings below.'

'We can only fix one thing at a time.'

'Yes.' She sighed but refused to get downhearted. 'We'll make it right, Maisie, I know we will.'

Downstairs once more they began making plans.

'Right.' Maisie rubbed her hands together, looking in distaste at the filthy fire grate in the oven range. 'Let's get this place warm. I'll find some firewood.'

Emma gave Sophie to Anna. 'I'll see if I can get some water out of the pump in the scullery. The table will need wiping down before we dare put any food on it.'

It was forty minutes later before any spark showed in the fire grate, much to Anna's amusement. The fire, even after the grate had been thoroughly cleaned out, showed no signs of burning. 'You're covered in soot and ash, Maisie.' Anna laughed as she placed Sophie in her new perambulator. 'Do you admit defeat?'

'Never!'

Grinning, Anna helped Emma scrub the table as best they could for now.

At last, Maisie achieved a very welcome blaze that instantly transformed the kitchen into a much cheerier room. She gave a triumphant look at Anna. 'I'll go unpack the cart.'

As Emma set out a meal, Anna found a rag and cleaned the window so she could see out into the yard. It was then she saw the man.

He wore no hat. The gentle breeze whispering about the hillside blew his overlong chestnut-coloured hair into his eyes. Thoughtlessly, his hand came up to toss it back in a movement that was nearly sensual. He wore chestnut brown cord trousers and a black long coat, left open to reveal a cream woollen shirt. His boots were worn and dusty and over his shoulder hung a canvas bag, not unlike the ones sailors carry.

For a timeless moment, Anna watched, fascinated, as he stopped beside Maisie and gave her a most disarming grin. Unable to hear what was being said, she walked down the path towards them. Nearing the cart, she saw the man lift his head and stare at her with undisguised interest.

'It's a beautiful day.' His voice was musical and pleasant to the ear, like most Irish tones are. The small lines at the corners of his blue eyes crinkled when he smiled, as though smiling was something he did a lot.

So, he is Irish. Anna's first thought about him came unbidden.

'This fella is lookin' for work, Miss Anna,' said Maisie.

Anna stared at him. An odd sensation stirred in the pit of her stomach, one she instantly recognized. It made her angry even to think she could find any man attractive again after all that had happened to her, especially a tramp off the roads. What on earth was the matter with her? Annoyed, she stiffened her shoulders.

'There is no work here.' She dismissed him with a frown. The harshness in her tone made Maisie's eyes widen.

'I'd have thought there is plenty to be done here,' the Irishman commented with a lazy smile.

'That may be—' Anna faltered as Maisie, tugging at her arm, pulled her away.

'We need help. We can't fix this place on our own.'

'I know, but I do *not* want just anyone coming off the road,' Anna whispered back defiantly. 'Besides, as yet I don't know whether I can afford to hire a man.'

'Excuse me, ladies.' The Irishman strolled over to them. He looked at Anna. 'Is your husband around? Maybe I should talk to him?'

Lifting her chin a fraction, Anna stared coldly. 'I have no husband.'

He shrugged with only a touch of arrogance and, again, the lazy smile. 'All the more reason, then, to hire me.'

'Miss Anna, please, just until we get on our feet,' pleaded Maisie.

Anna tried to think clearly about the situation and ignore the rapid heartbeat this man's smile created. True, they did need someone, but preferably not this fellow. He was too good looking, too sure of himself. Anna felt apprehensive just from his mere appraisal of her. She didn't like it at all, but, at the same time, the convenience of him being on hand and willing to work outweighed her doubts.

Sighing, she glanced at Maisie and then at the Irishman. 'Very well, I will give you a two-week trial at fourteen shillings a week. Agreed?'

His smiled widened. 'Agreed.' He winked at Maisie.

'You can start by unloading this cart and stacking everything in the front parlour. Maisie will show you where.'

'Right you are, Ma'am. By the way, the name is Brenton O'Mara.' He grinned.

Anna blushed. How foolish to forget to ask his name. 'Mrs. Thornton,' she said woodenly. The man irritated her, and she instantly regretted hiring him. Something was there when their eyes met that made her question her very sanity. Turning on her heel, she went back inside.

'Don't take much notice of her, Brenton,' Anna heard Maisie say, as if in defence of Anna's abruptness. 'She's had it hard this past year, and she's a little touchy. I'm Maisie, and inside is Emma and her baby, Sophie.'

'I'm very pleased to meet you, Maisie.' He nodded towards the cart. 'I'd best get on.'

As Brenton unloaded the cart, Maisie and Emma scrubbed the kitchen. Anna toured the bedrooms and again inspected the water damage. With paper and pencil, she wrote down the furniture needed for each room, though it would be some time before decorating could begin. Two of the bedrooms had large iron beds in them, but no mattresses. One room boasted a huge carved mahogany wardrobe, and Anna wondered how on earth someone had managed to get it in the room. She added up the cost of making the house comfortable and found it a little depressing.

Downstairs, she started in the dining room. Apart from the table and chairs, there was little else in the room. A beautiful long sideboard would look lovely under the two windows, as well as two ornate sideboards. With a sigh, she added them to the list.

Crossing the hall, she noticed the threadbare carpet on the staircase, it, too, was added to the list. Next, she entered the parlour, which was slowly filling up with the contents of the cart. Here, she inspected the wood panels along the walls and found them to be in good condition, which pleased her immensely.

She sat on the wide window seat and gazed around the room. An elaborately carved mantelpiece with two shelves to display ornaments topped the fireplace. The tiles around the hearth featured little pictures of country scenes in shades of green and cream. She pictured dark green velvet curtains hanging on either

side of flimsy white lace at the window and brown
and green rugs on the highly polished floor. In her
mind, she saw occasional tables and chairs, a sofa and
tall plant stands with glossy dark green leafed plants.

'Anna, it's time to eat.' Emma stood at the door.
'It's getting dark in here.'

When Anna rose, her back ached. She rubbed it.
'I'm coming now, but we have to sleep in here
tonight. The bedrooms need airing.'

'We could light a fire in here and put the
mattresses on the floor.'

Anna tapped the pencil against her skirts. 'I should
have thought to organize a lot more than I have.'

'Nonsense.' Emma tucked Anna's hand over her
arm. 'You've had so much to think about. It's a
wonder you've managed to remember your name.'

'Still, I should have sent someone on ahead to air
the house. I've never done this before.' Anna entered
the kitchen to find it shining brightly in the firelight.
All surfaces were clean and free of cobwebs and dust.
The floor tiles had been swept and washed.

'My, you two have been busy.' She hugged them
both. 'It looks wonderful.'

'I found all sorts of stuff in't cellar,' Maisie told
her excitedly. 'A kettle, a few pots, two buckets,
some rags, and a couple of candles in their holders.'

Anna chuckled as she sat down at the table and
hungrily eyed the spread. 'You were game to go
down there.'

'That boiler in't scullery will need a good clean
before we do any washin'. I'll see to it in't mornin','
Maisie said as she poured out the tea.

'Mr. O'Mara took his plate over to the barn,' Emma picked up Sophie from the perambulator. 'He said he wants to find a place to sleep before it got too dark.'

'I believe there are sleeping quarters upstairs in the barn. I didn't go up to look the first time I came here with the land agent because the ladder didn't seem safe.' Anna took a bite of bread.

'Mr. O'Mara said he'll start on the barn in the mornin'. He's put Jasper and Misty in the holding yard behind the barn.' Maisie looked vague. 'Apparently, the stable has bad straw in't stalls and would make them sick or summat.'

After they had eaten, Maisie lit a fire in the front sitting room and made up a makeshift bed while Anna went out to check on the horses.

Entering the barn, she found it swept and the stove in the tack room lit. On the left a large storage area stood empty and on the right were the horse stalls. Along the back wall two large doors opened out into a holding yard. She went through these doors and found Mr. O'Mara brushing down Jasper.

'I can do that.' Anna indicated the brush he held.

'It's no bother. I enjoy it. He's a nice fellow.' Brenton O'Mara smiled; his blue eyes tender. His face was shadowed in a honey glow cast from the lantern where it sat atop the fence rail.

Anna patted Jasper's neck and kept her gaze averted so as not to stare at him.

'This place is going to take a great deal of arduous work.' He moved to the other side of the horse.

'That does not deter me. I take pleasure in challenges.' Her gaze dared him to argue.

'It will not be easy though, without a man to help you.'

She stared across Jasper's back at him. 'That is why I'm paying you. Unless, of course, you've changed your mind and decided to leave.'

Blue eyes held hers. He spoke ever so gently. 'I'll be here for as long as you need me.'

Anna stepped away. Without a word, she turned and walked back to the house. She cursed herself for letting him unnerve her. The last thing she needed was a man who thought he could charm the birds out of the trees. It had been a mistake to employ him—a silly, blind mistake. She didn't require a man. She couldn't cope with an attractive male in her presence, not now, not ever. Tomorrow, she would tell him to go. She'd no wish to play any games with some penniless Irishman.

* * *

Hammering woke the women of the house. When Maisie and Emma entered the kitchen, they found hot water waiting for them. O'Mara had risen early, re-lit the fire in the kitchen, and put a pot of water and the kettle on the range to heat before the women had even awakened.

Maisie praised him for over ten minutes while she ate her breakfast.

Anna sighed. The man was making it impossible for her to get rid of him. Still, it was nice to have the extra help and his thoughtfulness said much.

After piling wood in the corner, O'Mara came in through the scullery. 'Good morning, ladies. Do you need more water?'

'Yes, thank you.' Emma smiled at him. 'And thank you for what you did this morning, having things ready for us. It was good of you.' She indicated a chair. 'Please, sit down. I'll pour you a cup of tea and get you some breakfast.'

'There's no rush.' His smile disarmed them all. 'Though in truth, I'm starving. I've been up before the sun and there is still so much more to do.'

Anna stood and carried her plate to the sink, making a conscious effort to ignore his presence. However, soon she was sitting with the others listening to him as he talked of his mother and grandfather, whom he'd left behind in Ireland some five years ago. He told the women that, for those years, he worked his way around England, as well as spending some time in France and Austria. His funny stories about his travels made them laugh. He had a natural way of being at ease, of making people feel relaxed.

'Lord, look at the time.' Emma stood and placed Sophie in the perambulator. 'I'll bake some bread and a currant cake as well.'

'That would be wonderful, Emma.' Anna pulled on her coat. 'You're the only one with any talent in that area.'

'Are you going outside?' O'Mara asked Anna.

'Yes. I want to take notes on the state of the buildings.'

'I'll join you.' He scooped the last of his breakfast into his mouth and then stood and grabbed his coat.

Anna wanted to dissuade him, not wanting him by her side when she had to concentrate, but if he was to work here, even for a brief time his opinion would need to be considered.

Together they did the rounds of the outer buildings, discussing the good and bad points of each barn and any pieces of equipment left behind by the previous owner.

'Only the door needed fixing on the chicken pen, and I've done that,' O'Mara said, testing the strength of the pen's wooden frame. 'The rest of the pen is sound and should last for a while yet, so hens can be bought straight away.'

He carried himself well and could pass himself off as a gentleman. His voice had a cultured lilt, with none of the harsh Irish brogue. His tone belied a working-class upbringing. Anna liked the sound of it as he talked. The admission frightened her, and she quickly put it from her mind. What did it matter how he spoke?

She scowled. She disliked how he easily he'd won over Maisie and Emma. She couldn't let her guard down and depend on him. It was safer to depend only on herself.

'Mrs. Thornton?'

'Pardon? I'm sorry—I was—' She fussed with the skirt of her brown striped dress to cover her embarrassment.

A smile tugged the corners of his mouth, as he repeated his question. 'Have you thought what kind of farm this is to be? I mean, are you going to specialize in any one thing?'

Frowning, she gave it some thought. 'No, I don't think so. I just want it to pay its way and give us all a comfortable life.' She strolled over to what was once the pigpen and studied the number of animal pens next to the holding yard, at the back of the barn.

'I'd like a mixture of animals and crops,' she said, as he came to stand beside her.

'Crops? I'm afraid I only know about animals,' he admitted.

'Vegetables.' Anna tapped her chin with her fingertips. 'That is what we will grow, and all surplus vegetables, fruit, and animals will go to the markets. What do you think?'

He shrugged. 'Sounds sensible.'

'Over there,' she said, pointing toward the two-acre orchard located on the west side of the house, 'are a variety of fruit trees, apples, pears, figs, plums, besides the ones I don't recognize. We will be able to make pickles and jams to sell.'

Turning to the one-acre vegetable garden nearer to them, she told him they could start straight away and plant winter vegetables.

He nodded as they eagerly entered the barn. 'There is a plough in the last horse bay. Do you think the old mare can pull it?'

Anna smiled. Both were taken up with the challenge of turning the neglected farm into something to make them proud. 'Yes, she is strong. She was a plough horse back home.'

* * *

O'Mara cleaned the rusty plough with rags dipped in oil before he harnessed it to Misty. Together, Anna, Maisie, and Emma watched as he walked behind

Misty turning up the first row in ground made hard from many years of lying fallow. However, after the first difficult strip, Misty settled down to her task, and O'Mara understood the essence of what he was required to do at his end. The girls applauded them as they passed.

Brenton looked up, grinning at Anna, only to find she already turned away towards the house.

Chapter 13

Storms raged outside for a third evening. Anna sat at the kitchen table re-reading the letter she received from Mr. Smythe with the news her shares in the cotton mill and the shipping company had finally sold. It was much more than she hoped for, but the extra money was sorely needed. Each day brought her another list of items she needed to buy and additional expenses. Her worry increased as the amount of money in her bank account dwindled a little more as trips to nearby villages for supplies become more frequent.

Sighing, she laid the letter down and thought of the past month. The weeks of November had passed with great speed as they had tackled the numerous jobs, including planting many seed rows of onions, turnips, silver beets, cabbages, and cauliflower.

In pleasant weather, they worked in the orchard cutting down the old fruit trees past their best productive years, pruning the rest and bundling the branches, which were then stacked in the barn to dry out for fragrant firewood. At the markets they bought four geese, a crate of chickens and one handsome rooster that Emma immediately named Casanova because of his attentions to all the hens he lorded over.

As the days shortened and cooled, O'Mara spent most of his time in the woods, sawing fallen timber.

For now, Anna decided they would only use the front parlour room and the kitchen to save on heating. She didn't want him cutting firewood all the time when so many more jobs needed his attention. His two-week trial came and went in a flurry of long, exhausting days. Despite the subtle attraction she felt existed between them, they got along well enough, and he never did anything that was beyond politeness.

O'Mara proved to be a man of many talents with a keen eye for shooting wildlife. After he borrowed a gun from a nearby elderly farmer, Henry Hobbs, pheasants and rabbits became their regular meals.

Anna smiled at the thought of Henry. The dear old man lived a mile or two down the road. He freely gave them advice plus the loan of tools. A small, thin man in his late sixties, he possessed a weather-beaten face that looked like worn leather. He and O'Mara struck up a friendship, and Henry could be seen most days helping O'Mara with one job or another. Since he was on his own and his farm was quite small, Henry admitted he'd plenty of time on his hands, and was only too pleased to help his new neighbours.

A clap of thunder startled her, bringing her back to the present. Something hit the kitchen window.

'It's still wild out there.' Emma stood, kneading dough, but kept glancing at Sophie who lay in the perambulator crying and fussing.

Anna peered out the window at the grey clouds racing the wind. Night was falling. 'I've never seen such a storm. We have had no let up for days. Mr. O'Mara and Henry have endured a constant battle trying to keep the water from coming into the attics.

The temporary timber boards are continually ripped off the roof as soon as they are nailed on.'

'I don't like the thought of the men on the roof,' said Emma. 'Yesterday, I was sure Henry would be swept off the ladder. He's too old to help Brenton.' She turned to Sophie as the baby wailed.

'What's matter with the babby?' Maisie asked, coming in from the scullery, where she'd been hanging wet clothes to dry.

'I don't know,' Emma grumbled. 'She's been fed. She should be asleep.' Tired, she wiped a flour-covered hand over her eyes.

Anna looked at her with sympathy. Sophie seemed unable to sleep for more than an hour at a time. Emma spent most of her time going between Sophie and the range as she tried to cook enough food for them all. Her cooking skills were limited, and having a crying baby distracting her didn't help.

'Little madam,' Maisie said, adding more wood to the fire.

'I shall try to rock her to sleep.' Anna put down her letter and scooped up the baby just as O'Mara came in through the scullery.

'Take your wet things off in there,' Maisie shouted to him over the roar of wind. 'I've no wish to be washin' the floor at this time of the day, Brenton O'Mara.'

He stopped, took off his boots, and then hung up his wet coat. His silence made the three women turn to stare at him, for they were used to his easy banter and good-natured company. Brenton smiled as he sat down, but sadness shadowed his eyes as he looked at Anna.

'What is it?' she asked him.

'The bottom field is flooded, but that's the least of our concerns.' He nodded his thanks when Emma put a steaming cup of tea down in front of him. 'Most of the vegetable rows have been washed away at the bottom end of the plot, and two apple trees have blown down. They were ripped right out of the ground.'

'Dash it.' Anna paced the floor rocking Sophie. 'It might not be too late to re-seed.'

Brenton took a sip of his tea. 'Also, the rain is coming in through the barn over Jasper's stall, and I didn't notice it until just now. I've moved him over to another stall. I hope he doesn't get a chill. He's playing up a bit with the storm and won't settle.' He sighed.

Anna considered him. The last few days had been difficult. Exhaustion lined his face. He had worked hard with very little sleep. Handing Sophie to Maisie, she went into the scullery and put on her coat and boots.

'What you doin', Miss Anna?' Maisie demanded, following her. 'You're not goin' out there.'

'I must check on Jasper.'

'Nay, you're not.' Maisie stood poised to pull Anna back into the kitchen.

'I will take care, Maisie. Don't fuss.'

Maisie puffed her chest out as though ready to speak her mind, but Brenton left his chair and stepped between them

'Wait, Mrs. Thornton, you'll need help to get across the yard.' He donned his wet coat and boots again. 'The wind is strong enough to have you on your back.'

'I will be all right.' Anna held up a hand to stop him. 'Stay and have your tea.'

'I can have it when we return.'

The wind took her breath as they faced it head on crossing the yard. She'd not been out in it before and it was much stronger than she thought. O'Mara gripped her elbow as they battered the onslaught. His strength surprised Anna. A tall man with wide shoulders and narrow hips, he was built lean but strong. She realized he'd never touched her before and despite the elements, she felt a tremor run through her body. The wildness of the day fired the blood in her veins, alerting her senses to the raw energy around her.

O'Mara virtually pushed her through the barn doorway as the wind whipped at the door, nearly wrenching it out of his hands. Inside, Anna stood for a moment to get her breath. She noticed how much work had been done since she last entered it. When wet weather forced O'Mara to stay indoors, he obviously spent his time wisely. All the loose timbers were secured and the harnesses polished. The floor was swept and the tack room neat and tidy. Shelves now lined the walls and the smell of fresh paint, probably from upstairs, lingered.

'Are you all right?' He asked, bolting the door, his chest heaving from the battle against the elements.

'Yes. Of course.' She felt she couldn't look at him, at his hard body that made her think of things better left alone. She quickly entered Jasper's stall and ran her hand over his coat. Something was amiss. He breathed rapidly, blowing through his nostrils in great gusts. Looking at his sides, Anna saw they heaved with each breath. Her heart flipped in alarm. She turned to O'Mara. 'He is sick.'

'He might have caught a chill. I'll get a blanket.'

Suddenly, Jasper tried to kick at his stomach. Anna jumped out of the way.

'Stay back, Mrs. Thornton.'

'He is in pain.'

'I'd say its colic.' He took Jasper's bridle and walked him out of his stall and around in a circle. 'We must keep him walking. He can't lie down.'

Anna and O'Mara took turns circling Jasper, trading off when one of them tired. As the evening wore on, Jasper became weaker, while outside the storm grew wilder. Finally, O'Mara bought fresh straw into the box and made a thick bed for Jasper when his legs gave out from under him.

'What shall we do?' Anna cried as Jasper attempted to roll. He snorted in pain at the effort. She gripped O'Mara's sleeve. 'We must do something. Do you know of a cure? Is there someone we can bring here to help him?'

Tenderly, O'Mara took her hand, his eyes full of concern, but before he could answer, a loud crash sounded outside. They raced to open the barn door and saw the chicken pen roof blow across the yard. Torn off in one piece, it lay close to the small wall of the courtyard. The chickens ran around their pen cackling and squawking in terror.

'If the wind blows that up again, it'll be blown onto the house,' O'Mara warned, closing the door against the gale.

'I will help you.'

'No, it's too dangerous.'

Anna looked back at Jasper then to O'Mara. Her hands clenched into fists. 'I feel so useless.'

'Just stay here.' He inched the door open again and slipped out.

Terrified for his safety, Anna watched him struggled with the roof. A sudden gust tore it out of his hands and up into the air. With one huge bang it thumped against the house roof. What remained of the chicken pen's cover, whirled off over the house.

Maisie and Emma looked frightened as they stared out of the kitchen window. Anna waved letting them know she was all right. She held the door open as O'Mara staggered back into the barn. A cut bled on his forehead.

'Go to the house and let Maisie clean that cut.'

'No, it's fine.' He took out his handkerchief and held it tightly against the small wound. 'I think it would be best, though, if you went back.'

'No.' She held up her hand to stop him. 'I'm staying here to help Jasper. He means too much to me.' She walked into the stall.

'I'll take care him. You should be in the house where it's warm.'

'He is my horse, and I shall stay.'

'Mrs. Thornton—'

'Mr. O'Mara, I'm remaining here for as long as it takes. Now, you can either go back to the house or up to your quarters.' Anna stroked Jasper's neck. Wild eyed and trembling, the horse tossed his head and laboured to breathe. His coat glistened with sweat.

'Shall I go and get Henry? He may know what to do with him,' suggested O'Mara.

'No. It's too treacherous. I don't want to be responsible for you getting hurt out there. We will have to wait until the weather settles.' Anna sat on the straw beside her treasured horse and whispered to him.

It pained her to see him struck down. Closing her eyes, she willed him to get better. Should she pray? Would God listen to her when she doubted she held any faith? She heard O'Mara moving around doing little jobs to keep himself occupied. Whenever he turned his blue-eyed gaze on her, he made her nervous and tongue-tied.

Night descended and more lanterns were lit. Even with the small stove in the tack room lit, it was chilly in the huge barn. The wind found every crack in the walls and whistled through them eerily. For hours, Anna and O'Mara tried to coax Jasper to stand. She flinched each time he took a rasping breath.

Anna lost all track of time. The wind continued to howl and batter against the barn. Tiredness overcame her, even though she struggled against it. For a few moments, she rested her head against Jasper's hot shoulder. Hitching her coat closely around her, she prayed.

* * *

The silence woke Anna. Dreamless sleep drugged her mind. For a moment she didn't know where she was. A cramp in her leg caused her to gasp in pain and made her movements slow and careful. She sat up to rub it. Beside her, Jasper lay on the straw his eyes open in the stillness of death.

Stifling a moan, she crawled on her hands and knees to lift his head and place it on her lap. Somewhere in the far reaches of her mind, she understood he was gone, but refused to accept it just yet. For a little while longer, she wanted to pretend he was alive, to remember the times they galloped madly across the lush green fields of the estate. She closed her eyes and a tear escaped as she recalled them racing wildly, jumping fences and brooks, beating Tom to some tree in the distance, and sending the groomsmen running for cover when they came tearing into the stable yard. It tore her heart to say goodbye to him. Another link to her home, her old life, was lost.

'Mrs. Thornton,' O'Mara whispered. He squatted down beside her. 'Let me help you up, *acushla*.' His distress made the lilt in his voice stronger. Gently, he helped her to stand, and with his arm about her, led her away.

She relaxed against him and for a moment allowed someone else to hold her and shoulder the burden. The feel of his strong arms banding around her was so pleasant, so reassuring that she felt she wasn't completely alone. It seemed like forever since—

Swiftly, she leapt from him. Her heart pounded in her chest. 'Get away from me. I don't need your help.' Ignoring his startled look and with a last glance at her beloved horse, she ran from the barn.

The rain had stopped, and the wind had eased to a mere whisper of a breeze. The sun rose in the east dispelling the gloom of a grey dawn, but Anna cared little of it as she ran into the house. At the kitchen table, she stopped and sucked in a deep breath. The small clock above the range showed it was just past six.

Maisie came down the hallway. 'My heavens. Tell me you've not stayed all night in't barn, me lass?' she asked, shaking her head. Going to the fire grate, she stoked it up. 'Come over here and get warm. Honestly, sometimes I don't think you've got a brain in your head.'

Anna stood frozen. An ache spread throughout her body. 'Jasper died.'

Maisie straightened. 'Eh, I'm that sorry. I didn't know he were so sick. It took him quick.'

'Yes. I…Maybe colic…Damp straw…'

'Aww, lass.'

Anna lifted one shoulder in defeat, unable to speak.

'The storm was so wild, it's all we 'ad on our minds.' Maisie crossed the kitchen and put her arms around Anna. 'We were worried the roof would come off just like it did on the chicken pen.'

'I'm awfully tired, Maisie.' She moved towards the hallway. 'I think I might go to bed for a while.'

'Aye, you do that.' Maisie patted her hand. 'You need your rest.'

Henry came to see how they fared. He told them the storm damage was widespread. He stayed to help O'Mara bury Jasper in a deep pit by the wood. It took them all day.

Anna kept inside until they finished the dismal job. When the men came into the kitchen for their meal, she couldn't suffer to be in the same room as O'Mara.

224

His tender looks nearly brought her undone, and she was glad to wander up the hill behind the house to the woods and the spot where Jasper lay.

The ugly mound of overturned soil blotted the landscape. She hated the sight of it. Hurrying back to the barn, she found a shovel and carried it back into the woods. It took some time before she found what she wanted, but at last she spied a small sapling, no taller than her waist. From the fallen leaves on the ground, it looked to be an elm or beech. Within a short time, she had replanted the tiny tree on top of Jasper's grave. To cover the freshly dug dirt, she spread leaves gathered from the forest floor. It was not a significant improvement, but anything was better than a heap of dirt constantly reminding her of Jasper's absence. Before long nature would cover the soil again and improve even more on her efforts.

'Why didn't you ask for my help?' O'Mara asked gently, coming up behind. 'I'd have done that for you.'

'I wanted to do it myself.' Averting her eyes, she swept her skirts aside and walked down the slope and back to the house. She didn't want his kindness. She didn't want to allow herself to feel again.

In the days that followed, Anna refused to go near the barn and hid away in the study. She spent hours reading books concerning farming and kept precise accounts on the expenditures of both the house and farm. She needed to keep busy to banish the pain of losing Jasper. She cleaned the study and set it up for its intended purpose. When the room was ready for furniture, Anna hitched Misty to the cart and went to Halifax. She bought a solid mahogany desk, some books, a small bookcase, and thick red curtains. On impulse, she added a watercolour landscape to her purchases to hang above the small fireplace. With determined bargaining, she bought all the items at a decent price.

Using the money from her shares, she purchased a few other things for the house to make it more comfortable. The front parlour finally received dark green velvet drapes and snow-white lace curtains, plus two throw rugs for the floor that Maisie painstakingly polished every week. A pair of easy chairs and a sofa, all in rich apple green velvet, as well as a lovely dome clock for the mantelpiece. She could ill afford to spend the money, but the indulgence was like a salvation and eased her loss.

* * *

Brenton swung the axe. It sliced through the timber with ease. He stooped down and picked up the fallen piece and threw it onto the ever-growing woodpile. Sweat trickled inside his collar even though the day was cold. His back ached but he continued swinging the axe into the log, slowly eating away at its length.

His thoughts turned to the woman who haunted his dreams and shadowed his waking hours. Only, she barely spoke to him, and since the storm had hardly looked his way. Brenton blamed himself for the horse's death, and he knew Anna blamed him, too. He was sorry for letting Jasper become ill and had tried to apologize, but she refused him the chance.

He couldn't stop criticizing himself for losing her horse. He should have seen the water seeping in. He should have smelt the damp straw, but then everything smelt damp in the rain. Why didn't he see the mould in the hay? It didn't matter that for those few days of the storm he worked nearly non-stop, trying to keep the place from falling down around their heads. It wasn't an issue that he'd stolen only four hours of sleep a night in that dank and musty room above the stalls.

Every day, he did the work of six men, but the farm needed the work of a dozen more to keep it from declining back into ruin. He had tried desperately to turn the farm into a successful business for her. For a whole month, he'd given his all to his work and the women of the house. Worn out and exhausted, knowing Anna had limited finances to spend on improvements, he tried to make do with his own restricted skills. Yet, not once had she thanked him or even looked at him with kindness.

Wearily, he bent to adjust the angle of the log. Straightening, he swung the axe high and brought it down in one smooth action. He cursed when it missed the mark and heaved a sigh of frustration as his jumbled thoughts distracted him from his work.

A small black spider crawled out from a tiny hole in the log. Brenton watched it for a moment before it scarpered into the grass. Groaning, he sat down on a stump. He let the axe drop and rubbed his hands over his face. *Why in God's name did I come to this farm?* The last thing he wanted was to tie himself to one place. However, his usual wandering ways were lax in moving him on. Each morning, he rose before dawn, cold and shivery, starting another day of endless demanding work, all for her.

He hung his head and closed his eyes. Suddenly, Anna's face imprinted itself before him. His mouth curled into a smile as he pictured her joking with Maisie or gurgling nonsense to baby Sophie. Brenton imagined unpinning her hair, letting it flow free down her back like a golden waterfall. His body responded with male urges he'd not released in many a month. He ached for her to smile at him, to laugh with him like Maisie and Emma did.

Opening his eyes, he stared down at the weeds and earth trampled underfoot. A tightness in his chest frightened him. 'I'm attracted to a penniless, pregnant, English widow.' He shook his head at his foolishness.

He thought fleetingly of Ireland, of home, of the green hills surrounding his grandfather's cottage and the warmth of his mammy's fireside.

Why do I stay? He asked himself the same question numerous times every day.

The answer was there, buzzing around in his head, but it went unacknowledged. He had no wish to torment himself more than he already had—better to let the matter rest and try not to think about what held him here so firmly.

Chapter 14

'Henry, I know nothing about pigs,' Anna admitted, grinning at her friendly neighbour as he and O'Mara released a sow and her ten piglets into the pigpen behind the barn.

A piglet's high-pitched squeal rent the air.

O'Mara grimaced. 'Neither do I.'

'There's nowt to it. Feed 'em up and sell 'em off. Easy.' Henry laughed at their doubtful expression. He pulled his pipe from his coat pocket. 'She's a young sow, and you can put her to me boar for nowt. In return, you give me two piglets from her litters.'

Anna sighed at his generosity. 'But I cannot pay you now for her and this litter.'

'Listen, I told you. You're doin' me a favour for taking her off me hands. I've got more than enough to cope with at the minnit.'

'Yes, but at the butchers you could get good money for her,' she argued.

'Then call it an early Christmas present,' he teased with a grin, while stuffing tobacco into the pipe's bowl.

For the moment, Anna let it lie, but she silently vowed she would repay him one day.

Emma and Maisie came from the house to see the new additions to the farm. 'Oh, look at them,' cried Emma. 'Aren't they simply darlings?'

'I think they're ugly.' Maisie sniffed, wrinkling her nose. 'And they smell.'

Henry scowled and waved his pipe at her. 'Nay, they don't.'

'What's the mother's name?' Emma asked Henry.

'She's a sow and she don't have a name. She ain't a pet.'

'Anna, we have to call her something,' protested Emma.

'Well, you seem to be the one who names all the animals. I will leave it to you.'

Emma leaned over the wall of the pigpen. She rubbed the coarse hair on the sow's back. 'Very well then, we'll call her...Maisie.'

'What?' Maisie spluttered, while everyone laughed. 'Why you cheeky—'

'I'm only jesting.' Emma chuckled. 'Her name will be Polly, Polly Pig.'

As they strolled back to the house, Anna gazed around her. Only two weeks until Christmas and the farm was, at last, starting to take shape. Apart from the pigs, Henry had purchased two milch cows for them, at a fair price, making an enormous difference to their diet. The winter vegetables grew slowly, due to the season, but the chickens were still laying.

Ambling down the path towards the kitchen door, she glanced at the newly weeded herb beds. It was a pleasure to smell the fragrant aromas of the herbs as her skirts brushed by them.

Entering the kitchen, Anna listened contentedly to the flow of talk around her. She watched Maisie cut slices of currant cake and Emma pour cups of tea after checking that Sophie still slept. A regular visitor now, Henry sat relaxed at the table joking with O'Mara. It was comforting to see these wonderful people around her. They were all pieces of her new life.

At times, it was easy to forget she'd had another family and had lived in another way than she did now. Naturally, she thought of her Papa, Maggie, and Tom and yes, she missed them, but not as much as she had thought she would. Her days were busy, crammed with the demands of the house and the farm, but she thrived on the challenge of making it work. Of course, at times doubt and insecurity surfaced. However, that only made her want to try harder. She awoke each day aware she was solely responsible for all that surrounded her, but instead of it frightening her, the knowledge filled her with purpose. For once in her life she had direction. When she walked around her fields, she felt content and at peace. Slowly, the restlessness inside her seemed to be dissipating. Her mind was putting the past in its place. She could see a future for herself. The pain of Matt's deceit lessened even as his baby grew larger under her heart.

* * *

The morning sun rose higher and Anna despaired of ever leaving for Halifax to do their Christmas shopping. She wanted time to visit the bank and post letters to her father and Maggie describing her new home.

As a precaution, Anna sealed the letters without issuing an invitation for them to visit. Their dear faces would only remind her of what she left behind. She was not ready to see her beloved father and sister; she needed more time to settle in and heal. She hoped they would forgive her and understand. Soon she would feel strong enough to close the gap her departure created in their relationship, but not yet.

'For heaven's sake, Maisie, will you hurry up?' Anna called, tapping her fingers on the staircase banister. 'It has gone nine o'clock already.'

Tired of waiting, Anna went through the kitchen and outside, where Emma, with Sophie, sat in the cart.

'I really do think it would be better if I came with you, Mrs. Thornton,' O'Mara said, assisting Anna up onto the seat.

'No, thank you, Mr. O'Mara. There is no need for us all to go. Besides, someone has to stay here with the animals.' Anna adjusted her coat over her swollen stomach. From the corner of her eye she noticed his gaze resting on her before he moved away. She couldn't stop herself from wondering what he thought. She often sensed he watched her when he believed she wasn't looking. He never asked about her so-called husband, which she marvelled at. She was curious about his opinion of her and that annoyed her—she didn't need to know his thoughts.

Nevertheless, she wanted a day away from his unnerving presence and penetrating gaze. She purposely maintained a cool reserve towards him, so he never saw the real her. She didn't understand why she behaved this way. She only knew it kept her focused on the more important issues. Brenton O'Mara brought out emotions in her she would rather ignore, *had* to ignore. He made her want to be pretty and feminine, smart and witty. Her desire for his approval irritated her. O'Mara could not, must not, become significant to her in any other way than as a helper in achieving the farm's success. She would not let it happen.

Emma leaned forward. 'Brenton, there's plenty of food in the larder for your midday meal.'

Anna rolled her eyes. Emma was conscious of her role as the cook of the household, but both she and Maisie treated O'Mara like a helpless child. 'I'm sure Mr. O'Mara will survive without us for a few hours, Emma.'

'I will savour every mouthful, sweet Emma.' His handsome face broke into a grin and he gave Emma a wink.

Catching it, Anna felt her heart miss a beat. He was so damned compelling. He hooked people into liking him, wanting to be with him. Thoughts of that nature aggravated her. She detested being constantly aware of him. She had a farm to manage and plans to make for herself and her child. Nothing must distract her from that, especially not a farmhand, even if he was charming.

Upset by her wayward thoughts of O'Mara and fed up with waiting, Anna swore in a most unladylike manner. 'Maisie we are leaving without you,' she yelled.

Instantly, Maisie came running from the house and scuttled up into the back of the cart. 'I'm sure I don't know why there's such a rush.'

'Because I have things to do,' Anna snapped.

* * *

As the cart rolled and jerked down the rutted drive, Brenton watched it go. The thought of Anna driving a loaded cart back from town made him frown with unease. Sighing, he turned away in frustration. The more he wanted to get close to her, the more she drew away.

An hour later, Brenton paused in swinging the axe as Henry rounded the barn.

'Hey there, lad.' The older man sat on a stump beside the woodpile. 'It's quiet around here. Where is everybody?' He gazed around the empty yard, his pipe hanging out the corner of his mouth.

'They've gone to Halifax to do the shopping for Christmas.' Brenton swung the axe down hard.

'Women and shoppin'. They're a queer lot and no mistake.'

'Don't ask me, Henry, about women's logic, I'll end up with a thumping head.'

'Do you want to come down the road with me and have a pint?'

'Thanks, but no. I've too much to do.'

'Nay, lad, the lasses'll not mind, and one pint won't hurt.'

Brenton tossed the small log he just halved onto a pile. He stared out towards the orchard and beyond. 'You know, Henry, I feel like just walking away, walking so very far away from here. Even as far as Ireland and back to my mammy's fireside.'

Henry took his pipe out of his mouth and stared at it for a moment. 'I thought you liked it here, lad. You couldn't ask for better women than the ones here. Some women are nagging old crows, but not them.

I'd have thought a man couldn't ask for anything more than living with three lovely lasses.'

'It's not them, well, not really anyway. It's just that for years I've roamed about not really caring what happened to me. Now, suddenly, I've got this need in me to settle, to have a place of my own and a family.'

'There's nowt wrong with wantin' that, lad.'

'You see, it's my birthday today. Thirty years of age, with nothing to show for it.' He was spending his birthday alone yet again, and for some reason it mattered more this year than ever before.

'Nay, lad, you should've said.' Henry creaked up from his seat and grinned. 'A cause for celebration, no doubt.'

Brenton smiled but shook his head. 'Another time, Henry, I promise.'

'Aw, come on, lad.'

'Have one for me.' They shook hands on it. Brenton watched the old man walk out of the yard and over the hill behind the barn. An ache weighed heavily on his chest as he turned back to the logs and the deep thinking that plagued him night and day.

* * *

Anna smiled and nodded her head to various sales girls standing behind low timber counters as she made her way through the haberdashery store to Maisie and Emma. Winding her way between large bins and tables crowded with bolts of black and grey cloth, reels of ribbons and lace, she reached them and stared at the considerable number of parcels piled on the counter. 'Good gracious, Maisie. I leave you for five minutes to post some letters, and you buy up the store.'

'Well, 'tis Christmas and what else would I spend me money on?' Maisie chuckled.

'I didn't know you possessed such money,' Anna whispered with a raised eyebrow.

Maisie gave a wink. 'All those years back at Thornton House you gave me everythin' I needed. So, I was able to put me wages away for a rainy day.' A shadow crossed Maisie's face, and her smile slipped. 'When Mam died, she had a small amount of money saved for me. Nowt much mind, just a few bob.'

Anna gave Maisie's hand a squeeze. 'We have to make this Christmas especially good in memory of your Mam. She would like to know you're happy.'

'Aye, it'll be me first without her. I'll have to have a nip of sherry for her. She allus liked a drop of sherry on Christmas mornin'.' Maisie's cheeky grin returned.

It had gone two o'clock when Anna protested that she was tired, and they must go home. After enjoying a simple meal at a teahouse and more shopping, Anna's back and feet ached. Leaving the marketplace and heading for the stable where Misty and the cart waited, they noticed with alarm how much the weather had changed. A dense fog blanketed the town, reducing visibility to mere yards.

'I hate fog. It's ruddy useless,' Maisie grumbled, hitching the parcels up in her arms.

With Sophie wrapped up well against the damp, they kept close to one another and made slow progress through the vapor-shrouded streets. Many

236

times, they nearly bumped into someone as the people around them hurried to get home to a warm fire. The noise of the town grew quieter, subdued by the weather. Cabbies were content to stay in one spot, resting the horses. Most of the hawkers packed up their goods and headed inside the nearest public house.

Passing a narrow alley, the muffled sounds of groaning, and the undertone of another's softer voice filtered to them. Anna paused, making Emma and Maisie stop and look at her.

'What's up, lass?' Maisie asked, peering into the gloom.

'I heard something.' Anna stepped forward into the alley. 'Is anyone there?'

Maisie pulled on her arm. 'Nay, Miss, come away.'

Suddenly a shuffling shape loomed out of the murkiness at them. All three women gasped and stumbled back, but Anna, the first to recover, shook off Maisie restraint. The shape altered into an older woman straining to keep a giant of a man upright. Anna instantly went to assist.

'Let me help you.' She eased the woman's burden by taking the fellow's other side and holding him up. Looking into his bleeding face, she realized the fellow was young about eighteen or so, but immensely large in stature.

'Thank you kindly, madam.' The older woman puffed, allowing her son to lean against the wall while she placed a large bag at her feet and examined the cuts on his forehead. 'My son was set upon by a gang of ruffians.'

'I'm all right, Ma.' The fellow hung his head, wincing as he drew in breath.

'Perhaps we should send for the doctor?' Anna looked at Maisie and Emma for confirmation.

'Nay, we'll be fine.' The woman nodded with a crooked smile. 'We're used to being set on and can't afford any doctor's bills. My Ned here has lost his job and I'm not working neither.'

Anna studied the woman, who appeared to be in her late fifties or early sixties. Her clothes were worn, patched in places and basic, as were the lad's. 'We could aid you in getting home if you need it? Do you live far?'

'Thanks all the same, but we'll be right. Ned'll come good, he allus does.'

'I insist on paying for a cab for you both.' Anna opened her reticule and retrieved some coins. 'Here, have this. What's your name?'

'My name's Agnes McCarthy and this is my son Ned.' Agnes's eyes lingered hungrily on the coins, but she shook her head. 'Nay, I don't want your money, Madam. You've been more than helpful. Besides, we can walk, it ain't far and Ned's fine, aren't you, lad?'

Raising his bloodied head, his eyes dazed, he nodded. 'I'm all right, Ma.'

'That's my good lad.' She turned back to her large canvas bag and fetched out a square piece of material, which she used to wipe the blood from Ned's face.

Maisie, staring at the opened bag, nudged Anna and nodded to the bag's contents. A dented frying pan rolled up bedding and a battered tin teapot stuck out.

Anna touched Agnes's arm. 'Are you homeless?'

238

AnneMarie Brear

Agnes paled. 'I—We—' She swallowed and tried again. 'It's only temporary like, until we get some more work.'

'What work did you do?' Maisie asked.

'I was a cook for a big house near Bolton. Ned was a knockabout there. He did all the filthy jobs no one else wanted to do. We were turned out without references when the house changed owners. The new owners treated Ned as if he was an idiot that should be put in an asylum.' Agnes folded her arms across her ample chest. 'I wasn't having that, and I told them, so they gave us our marching orders. Forty years I worked in that house. I started when I was fifteen, but it wasn't like it used to be when the old family were there. I don't regret leaving,' she finished proudly.

'It must have been a terrible experience for you,' Emma murmured.

'I can't say it's been easy since. I'm getting on now, and me legs won't take me far to search for work and then there's Ned—' Her expression became loving as she gazed her large son. 'He's a good lad and a hard worker...'

Helping someone who was in a desperate situation swelled Anna's heart. She looked at Maisie, and Maisie winked back. 'We live on a farm not far from here,' Anna explained. 'We need a cook and another labourer to help the man we have. I cannot pay you at the moment, but you'll have bread and board. Would you and your son be interested in the positions?'

Agnes reared back as though struck, two identical spots of colour shading her cheeks. 'We're not beggars, mind. I wasn't after charity.'

'But you do need a place to stay, don't you?'
'Aye, but—'
Anna smiled. 'That settles it then.'

* * *

The slow journey home in the dark exhausted
Anna. She listened to Maisie telling Agnes and Ned
about the farm and a little bit about each person who
inhabited it. The fog lifted, but no moon illuminated
the black night. The lantern on the cart provided little
light, making Anna strain her eyes to see the road
ahead. She hid a yawn with the back of her hand. Her
neck and shoulders were stiff from concentration. As
they neared the farm's drive, they saw a lantern
swinging head high. O'Mara walked towards them.

'Where in God's name have you been?' he fumed
as the cart drew near. 'I've been worried to near
illness.'

Worn out, Anna sighed. 'We didn't mean to be so
late.'

'Did you not think I'd be concerned?' O'Mara
strode along the cart, throwing her angry glares.
Looking over his shoulder, he made out the two
strangers sitting with Maisie. 'Who are they?'

Maisie made the introductions as they drove
behind the house.

In the yard, he helped Maisie and Agnes down,
still too angry to make polite conversation. Spinning
back to Anna, he continued his tirade his Irish accent
growing thicker with every word. 'What possessed
you to travel in the dark? Anything could have

happened. Sure, and why didn't you leave in plenty of time?'

Anna, desperately tired, longed for her bed. She ached in every part of her body and felt in no state to tell the story of their day. Even so, O'Mara's anger fuelled her own, resurrecting the smouldering flame of resentment she'd held since Jasper's death. She lifted her chin and glowered at him. 'I'm *so* sorry we worried you, Mr. O'Mara. I can assure you it was unintentional.'

He reached up to help her down, but she ignored his hand. She climbed down from the cart and felt the strain on her back as she straightened. The baby kicked. 'Mrs. McCarthy and her son needed our help,' she tossed over her shoulder, striding past him. 'That is why we are late.'

'And what about me?' His words had her spinning back.

He stood with his hands on his hips and his feet apart. 'I was here all day, wondering how you fared. Why you wouldn't let me accompany you is beyond me. You're in no fit state to be travelling the countryside.'

'Have you finished?'

'Finished?' His handsome face whitened. Rage flared in his blue eyes. 'Oh, yes I've finished right enough. I'll be gone by morning.'

'No!' Maisie and Emma cried as one.

Maisie stared at him. 'You aren't leavin', Brenton, tell us you aren't.' She spun to Anna. 'Stop this carryin' on. What's the point of it?'

'The point is, Maisie,' Anna ground out between tightly clenched teeth. 'That I won't be spoken to like

241

that by anyone, especially someone I employ.'
O'Mara's anxiety for her safety fanned the blaze even
further. She didn't want him worrying about her. It
was a responsibility she couldn't handle right now.

His hands clenched at his sides as a muscle
worked along his jaw. 'Well, I sincerely apologize for
having *you* at the forefront of my mind. After all, it's
not my place is it?' He shook his head and gave a wry
smile. 'I'm sorry, *Mrs. Thornton*. I will make sure
that in future I don't concern myself about you. I will
see to Misty and the cart now.' He bowed arrogantly.

His conceited manner infuriated Anna to a point of
wanting to run her fingernails down his face, but the
wave of exhaustion consuming her won over the
anger, and she simply wanted to crawl into bed. She
took a step closer to him, not allowing him the last
word. 'Never, ever, patronize me again*, Mr.
O'Mara*,' she whispered bitterly. Turning swiftly on
her heel, she then marched into the house.

Maisie followed her, tutting at such a performance.

In the scullery, as they took off their outdoor
clothes, Anna apologized. 'I'm sorry, Mrs. McCarthy,
that was unforgivable of me.' She turned to Maisie.
'Can you settle them in? I'm going to bed.'

'Aye, go on up. I'll see to it.'

'Please, don't give us another thought, Mrs.
Thornton.' Agnes smiled as Anna left them. She
stepped into the kitchen. Her eyes roamed about the
room, taking everything in. 'My, this is right cosy
isn't it?' She ran her fingers over the table. 'It'll be
grand working in a lovely kitchen again.'

Ned hesitated on the doorstep holding Agnes's bag
containing their few possessions.

'I'll show you to your room, Agnes,' Maisie said. 'I bet you're done in as we are.'

'Isn't it through here somewhere?' Agnes asked, pointing to the scullery door when she saw Maisie heading into the hallway.

'No, upstairs.'

'Upstairs? Nay, but I can't. I can't go upstairs with my legs like they are. They'd never take it.'

'But there isn't anywhere to sleep downstairs,' Emma said, as Sophie cried.

'I just can't make the stairs, lass.' The glow faded from Agnes's face. 'Some days I can barely stand.'

'Well, we will have to make do.' Emma stifled a yawn and placed Sophie in the perambulator. 'Maybe you could sleep on the sofa in the front room for tonight, and we'll see what we can arrange in the morning. Ned can sleep in the barn with Brenton.'

Maisie smiled. 'Go on through, Agnes, while I get some bedding.'

Emma waited until the older woman was up the hallway before sidling over to Maisie. 'What was all that fighting about between Anna and Brenton? He was only concerned for her and us. You could see in his face how worried he was.'

Maisie sighed. 'Aye I know, and that's the problem. She don't want him caring for her for it might stir up a response in her and she's not ready, not ready at all.'

'But he's a good man.'

'It don't matter, he's a *man* and in her book all men are lying, cheating buggers.'

* * *

Agnes woke at five o'clock. She folded the blankets and placed them and the pillow she used on the edge of the sofa. Going into the kitchen, she lit the lamp in the middle of the table before stirring the embers in the range. Once it was ablaze, she filled the kettle and three large pots with water from the two buckets left by the door. Only then, did she let herself sit down at the table.

She gazed about the kitchen, taking in the shining copper pots and pans and the vase of dried flowers and herbs on the windowsill. She rose and crossed to the dresser, opening each drawer and cupboard to familiarize herself with all the contents. This was to be her domain, and for the first time in a long while she felt alive. Cooking was what she did best.

Agnes took the buckets into the scullery and filled them up from the pump. After that, she opened the larder door and counted the stock. On a marble slab lay strips of bacon, and in a muslin bag hung a leg of ham. She found a dozen eggs in a basket and jars of currants, prunes, and dates. Above her head hung string bags of onions, garlic, and wild mushrooms. Sacks of flour, oats, and potatoes, plus five-pound bags each of sugar, tea, coffee and salt lined the floor. Last night Ned had stacked the crates of vegetables and the other ingredients bought in Halifax. Agnes's mouth watered. She hadn't eaten this well for many a long day.

Loading herself up from the larder, she made trips back and forth to the table. She cooked until the kitchen filled with the mouth-watering aromas of sizzling bacon, mushrooms, and eggs frying.

The tea brewed in its pot and porridge was bubbling on the stove when O'Mara came in. Recently washed and shaved, his wet hair glistened in the lamplight. Although in her fifties, Agnes still acknowledged a handsome man when she saw one, and Brenton O'Mara was certainly that.

'So, Mr. O'Mara, I hope you don't mind us just appearing in the middle of the night like that,' she said, heaping food high on his plate.

He smiled up at her as he sat down at the table. 'No, of course not. I'm sorry you received the reception you did, but I was out of my mind with worry. And please, call me Brenton.'

'Maisie told me last night you all have only been here a few months.'

'Yes, that's right. I arrived here the same day the ladies moved in.'

Agnes poured them each a cup of tea. 'Was it that same day you fell in love with her?' She nodded her head in the direction of the staircase. They both knew which of the three women sleeping up there she meant.

Brenton spluttered and nearly choked on a mouthful of food. 'What?' he gasped.

Agnes shrugged. 'Well, it looked that way to me last night.'

'I...I... You see, I…'

'Lost for words? Surprised that a stranger has seen something you didn't?'

He groaned deep within his chest.

'Nay, lad, don't take on so.' Agnes comforted him, patting his hand in a motherly fashion. 'I'll not be telling anyone. You can count on that.'

Chapter 15

Anna sat in the study the day before Christmas Eve. A low fire shifted and settled in the grate. She meant to work on the accounts, but instead gazed out the window while rubbing her rounded stomach. She no longer wore her crinoline cage and her skirt flowed out around her like a collapsed tent.

As the days had sped towards Christmas, she and Maisie had sorted out the goods bought in Halifax, wrapped Christmas gifts and piled them on a side table in the front room. There they waited to be placed under the tree O'Mara and Ned were to cut down today and bring in to be decorated.

Last week, Agnes had started on the season's baking, and with Emma's help, the larder quickly filled with mince pies, tarts, and puddings for Christmas. Freshly baked bread and cakes tempted everyone to hover around the table for little titbits. Henry arrived every day and enjoyed sitting down with a cup of tea in one hand and a jam tart in the other. He and Agnes chatted happily away together like a couple of lifelong friends.

The weather had become colder and sharp frosts swathed the fields in the mornings. The bare trees were etched starkly against the backdrop of the ice-blue sky as winter's long fingers changed the landscape and the days grew short. Red-breasted robins hopped about the herb garden looking for the crumbs Agnes threw out to them to supplement their meagre pickings. The land was slowing down and she felt she was doing the same as she prepared for the final months of her confinement.

Maisie startled her from her daydreaming as she came in carrying a tea tray. 'Emma's been very quiet of late,' she said, placing the tray to one side of the desk. Out of habit she tidied Anna's papers into a pile and weighted them down with the bone-handled letter opener.

'Oh, do you know why?' Anna sugared her tea.

'No, but summat is wrong.'

'She's extremely tired.' She picked up her teacup. 'Sophie barely sleeps.'

Maisie frowned and moved to the fire to add another log to it. 'Aye—'

'Well, why do you not just ask Emma?' Anna shrugged as her attention was caught by the account figures before her. She needed to find extra money from somewhere to buy more livestock.

'Aye, all right, I will.' Maisie nodded, walking to the window that looked out over the vegetable garden and the orchard beyond.

'What else?' Anna inquired, watching Maisie, who thoughtfully stared out of the window.

'What makes you think there's owt else?' Maisie asked defensively. 'I was just lookin' out the window.'

Anna gave a short laugh. 'Because I know you, and you never have time, in the middle of the day, to gaze out of a window. So out with it.'

''Ave you spoken to Brenton?'

Anna glanced back at her books and studied the neat row of figures she'd written. She didn't want to think about the argument with O'Mara and had purposely kept herself busy to keep it from her mind. She stayed out of his way, thinking it easier for them both. However, the tense atmosphere that existed between them when they did meet only damaged the fragile existence of their working relationship.

'Well?' Maisie persisted.

'You know I haven't, so why ask?' She muttered, forcing her mind to add the numbers on the page.

'Don't you think you should?'

Anna put the account book in the desk drawer and rose. 'No, I don't.'

'For heaven's sake, he were upset because we were late comin' home. He was concerned.'

'He had no right to speak to me like that.'

'You'd have been in't same state if any of us 'ad been gone that long. Brenton didn't mean any disrespect and you know it,' Maisie argued, hands on hips. 'An' I found out it was his birthday the same day. It was a terrible day for him.'

'I didn't know it was his birthday,' Anna said, suddenly deflated. 'Why did he not tell us?'

'We didn't give him a chance.'

'Nonsense. He could have told us the day before.' Anna tapped the desktop with her fingernails. 'I don't want to talk to him right now. He infuriates me.'

'Lord, Miss Anna, there's times when you remind me of your mother,' Maisie threw over her shoulder as she flounced out of the room.

Her mother! Crossing over to the window, Anna leaned her head against the cold pane. Never did she want to be like her mother. Only, she *was* Louise *and* Richard Thornton's daughter. Good God, what a dreadful combination of blood to have running through one's veins. Anna raised her head and prepared to face Brenton O'Mara. She wasn't one to back away from anything, but for the sake of her sanity, it had just seemed more prudent to stay away from him.

The muffled sound of swishing skirts and slippers tapping on the polished floorboards made Anna turn as Maisie came rushing back in.

'I'm on my way to see O'Mara now, Maisie,' Anna said, quickly forestalling her.

''Tis not that, 'tis Emma.'

'Emma? Why, what has happened?'

Maisie pulled Anna out of the study and towards the staircase. 'She's upstairs, and she's packin'.'

Anna stopped at the first step. 'Packing? Whatever for?'

'She thinks she's not wanted anymore, because Agnes is here to cook.'

'Not wanted anymore?'

'Oh, don't let her go, Miss Anna,' Maisie begged. 'I've grown right fond of her.'

'It'll be all right. She will *not* be going anywhere.' Anna lifted her skirts and mounted the steps. 'Go and make us some tea. I will have her down for it in a minute.'

Emma was in her bedroom, placing clothes into a carpetbag.

'Had enough of us, have you?' Anna asked lightly, entering the room.

Tears shone silver on Emma's cheeks. 'No.'

'Then why are you going? Nobody wants you to leave. You and Sophie are family now.' Sitting down on the bed, she took both of Emma's hands in her own. 'Are you not happy here?'

'Of course, I'm happy here,' Emma cried. 'It's just that now, with Agnes doing all that I did...Well, it makes me feel useless. I know she asks me to help her just out of kindness, because she doesn't really need me. In fact, I only get in her way.'

Anna slipped her arm around Emma's shoulders. 'We needed a cook because I don't want you slaving away at that range when you have a far more significant role as mother to Sophie.'

'Yes, but at least I was doing something worthwhile. At least, I earned my keep.'

'I didn't hire you, Emma, I befriended you,' she corrected with a smile. 'You're a part of this family, and you're my friend. I want you and Sophie in my life. You don't have to prove your worth to any of us. Agnes may be the cook now, but I can assure you that you'll have plenty of work to do. Every pair of hands is needed. All of us together can make this farm work. One big family is what we are going to be, with everyone sharing the workload.'

'But—'

'No buts.' Anna grinned.

'I was so troubled.' Emma sagged in relief. 'I thought you'd ask me to go now Agnes is here.'

Anna leaned back in surprise. 'Do you believe I'm the kind of person to do that?'

Emma shook her head. 'No, but with money being scarce—'

'Never doubt your role here. You are a part of us and this farm for better or worse,' she joked. 'Come along, now. Maisie has a cup of tea waiting for us downstairs and I never want to hear of you leaving us again, understand?'

'Completely.' Emma wiped her eyes with the back of her hands. 'I'm sorry, Anna.'

'There is no need.' She linked her arm through Emma's. 'I suppose we all want to know where we fit occasionally.'

Later, Anna plucked up her courage and went outside to speak with O'Mara, only to learn from Ned he'd gone to the village to have Misty shod at the blacksmiths.

She watched Ned busily digging the soil between the rows of vegetables. He worked at his jobs with great care and efficiency. He and his mother had happily settled down to the work and life on the farm, and each task he was given received his complete and undivided attention.

'Did Mr. O'Mara say what time he will be back?' Anna asked.

'Nay, Mrs. Thornton, he didn't. He did say come dusk, we'll be goin' out to check the traps and then maybe go and have a pint.' Ned grinned like a mischievous child as he leaned on the spade handle.

'Very well then.' She lifted her skirts up and stepped over a neat row. 'The vegetables are coming on a treat, don't you think?'

Ned nodded. 'Aye, Mrs. Thornton, doin' well they are.' He watched as Anna carefully treaded her way back to the top of the plot. He shook his head and returned to his digging. Imagine a lady like the mistress asking his opinion on vegetables? Until he came to this farm, he was hardly even looked at, let alone asked an opinion. It was the best day of his life when he and his mam met her and no mistake.

* * *

Christmas Eve day dawned bright, but cold. A hoar frost blanketed every surface. Agnes had baked fresh bread before breakfast, and the tantalizing aroma filled the house. Everyone complained their clothes were tight from all the tasty food Agnes piled onto their plates.

The older woman beamed at the compliments. 'As I see it, you all needed a good feed. Look at Emma there, all skin and bones she is.' Agnes wagged a wooden spoon in Emma's direction.

Emma sighed heavily, pushing a strand of hair behind her ear. 'Yes, well, my daughter has me running after her twenty-four hours a day.'

Something in her manner made the three women in the kitchen study her. They noticed the tired lines around her mouth and the dark circles beneath her eyes. As if knowing the conversation was about her, Sophie started to cry, and immediately Emma hurried up the staircase to see to her.

'That little 'un is a handful for Emma,' Agnes said, taking a suet pudding off the boil. 'She is getting more frail by the day.'

Anna sipped her tea. 'Do babies cry like that all the time?'

'They shouldn't, unless there is somethin' wrong with them.' Agnes pouted thoughtfully.

'Like what?' Since she was to have her own baby soon, Anna wanted to learn all she could.

'It might be just wind. Some babies suffer greatly from it. My Ned never did, but I've heard of other babies who have a dreadful time. Giving them warm water helps.'

Maisie turned from where she washed the dishes. 'Do you think Emma's milk is good?'

'I can't say, but Sophie might sleep a bit better if Emma was to try goat's milk or cow's.'

'Do you think that might work?' Emma's voice came from the doorway, where she stood holding Sophie in her arms and caught them unawares. 'I'm at my wit's end trying to get her to sleep longer than two hours.'

'Come sit down, love,' Agnes invited.

'Here, give this little madam to me.' Maisie plucked Sophie from her mother.

'I need to go to Halifax for a few more things. Do you want to come with me?' Anna asked Emma.

'Yes, you go with Mrs. Thornton.' Agnes decided for them all. 'Maisie and me will look after Sophie.'

'I cannot leave her for the entire day. She'll need feeding.'

'Exactly.' Agnes nodded. 'And we'll see how she goes with something else in her tummy while you're not here. She may actually sleep.'

Anna left the kitchen and went outside. She found Ned by the barn door. 'Ned, could you attach Misty to the cart for me, please?'

'Mrs. Thornton,' Ned said loudly. He glanced inside the barn and back to Anna again with a guilty expression on his face.

Anna frowned at him. 'What is the matter?'

Ned hopped from foot to foot.

'Where is Mr. O'Mara?'

'Er, he's...'

'I'm here, Mrs. Thornton,' O'Mara called, coming through the barn. With him was a woman, who smoothed down her hair and smiled like a contented cat.

Anna's head jerked in shock and the blood drained from her face. She couldn't have been more surprised if the very devil himself strolled out. Staring from the woman to O'Mara, she felt something shrivel and die inside her. She looked at him as though he'd committed the most heinous of crimes, which her fragile heart was already accusing him of.

Swallowing a lump of emotion, her throat constricting, she stepped back, distancing herself from all association. For him to have a woman here, in her home, was something she would not tolerate. She'd an overwhelming desire to hit something or someone, preferably O'Mara. The dormant anger she still held from their last argument bubbled up like a volcano in her chest smothering or perhaps feeding from her ridiculous hurt.

Anna lifted her chin and stared with interest at the woman. 'A guest at the farm? How lovely.' Her comment was over-polite, the scorn she felt thinly veiled. 'I'm Mrs. Thornton. Pleased to meet you?'

'Flora Jones, Mrs. Thornton.' O'Mara introduced the two women cautiously, as though sensing her mood. His face was pale, strained. 'Flora works at the Pig and Spit Inn. Flora, this is Mrs. Anna Thornton, the owner.'

The two women studied one another. For a split second, they saw in each other what the other one wanted. It was gone in an instant, and Flora was the first to recover. Turning to O'Mara, she reached up on her toes and planted a sensual kiss on his lips.

'If you should need anything else, Brenton, you know where to find me.' With a secret grin she walked away, swinging her hips as she went and making Ned's eyes nearly pop out of his head.

O'Mara watched her go with a stupid smile on his face, but that soon disappeared when he saw the savage look on Anna's face. 'Mrs. Thornton, it's not what you think.'

'What *I* think? You have no idea what I think, Mr. O'Mara, but I shall tell you this. Should you ever bring one of your doxies here to my house again, you'll find yourself back on the road faster than you can blink. Is that perfectly understood?' She had an intense urge to scratch his eyes out.

'Now wait just a minute.' O'Mara just as fiercely defended himself. 'Flora isn't like that. She's a good woman. She came here to do me a favour, that's all.'

'Oh, I bet she did,' scoffed Anna.

'I'm telling you the truth.'

'Save your lies. I don't want to hear.' She shook with rage and disappointment. 'Just remember not to bring her, or anyone else, back here to my home ever again.'

His eyes narrowed and his fists clenched by his side. 'Your home? Is it not my home, too?' He growled. 'Even if it's just a bloody damp room above the stables?'

'Dear me, I'm sorry,' sneered Anna, taking a step towards him. 'Maybe you'd like me to build you a fifteen-room guest wing? Or maybe you'd prefer to sleep in the house, and I will sleep with the pigs. Would that do you?'

'Yes, maybe it would,' O'Mara threatened, advancing.

'Of course, it would,' she bawled at him, hating him for making her feel again. 'Because then you'd think that things were in their natural order, the man in the house as it should be, not a group of women. Is that not right?'

'Anna. Brenton. Stop this,' Emma and Maisie cried at them in one voice as they came racing across the yard.

Taking a deep breath, Anna turned away, ashamed at herself for behaving in such a way yet again. She sounded like a mad woman. Why did Brenton O'Mara have the power to bring out her emotions like that? Never had she lost control of herself so wildly and so often as she did with him. She knew she had a temper, but it seemed as if she could not control it at all whenever *he* was nearby. Sometimes his tenderness toward the animals or the others made her catch her breath, yet most times his presence only irritated her. *Oh Lord, am I suffering like Mother? Am I losing my mind?*

'Do you still want the cart, Mrs. Thornton?' Ned asked, coming to her side.

'No, thank you.' She was too upset to go shopping now.

He hovered anxiously for a moment then left to go about his work.

Emma and Maisie reached her side. 'Are you all right?'

'Yes, just embarrassed.'

'Brenton has gone, Anna.'

Anna's head snapped up so fast it hurt her neck. 'He is leaving?'

'Not for good, no,' Emma quickly replied. 'I think he's going to Henry's.'

'I don't know what came over me.' She shrugged, bewildered at the enormity of her reactions to O'Mara and the woman from the inn. Her hands trembled. She clasped them together to stop their shaking.

Maisie glowered. 'It was wrong of Brenton to bring a woman here.'

'No, he was right,' Anna reasoned with a sigh, despite the ache that squeezed her heart like a vice. 'This is his home too. If he wishes to have…visitors, then he should feel free to do so. I—I overreacted.'

'Is he courting?' Emma asked.

'Nay, he'd have said summat if he was.' Maisie sniffed.

'Let us not talk about it now.' Anna walked away. *O'Mara courting?* She didn't want to acknowledge such a notion now or ever. She was ashamed of her behaviour and confused at her feelings. No, that was a lie. She wasn't confused. She knew what she felt. Desire, attraction, and worst of all, perhaps love. Was it to happen all again? Was she to want someone totally unsuitable, a liar, and a cheat? She stuck her fist in her mouth to smother a moan. No, she couldn't do it again. Never again…

Later, Anna watched as Maisie and Emma put the final changes to the tree decorations and arranged the gifts underneath. The drawing room looked welcoming and festive. Emma and Maisie had gone to a great deal of trouble during the day, making paper chains to hang from the mantelpiece shelves and across the tree and the presents. Henry came at dinnertime bearing a large goose for Agnes to cook the following day for Christmas dinner. He had then whisked O'Mara and Ned away to the inn for a Christmas drink. Anna was glad they were gone.

The tension-filled day had drained her. To clear her mind from agonizing thoughts, she dug in the front garden until she could barely stand. Until now the front gardens had been neglected due to other more important work needing attention. The animals and produce demanded all the immediate consideration, but she was determined to tidy up the front. Come spring she wanted to see beautiful flowers in full bloom.

For hours, she dug and weeded. The rambling roses received a harsh pruning, and last summer's dead wildflowers were pulled out and burnt. Her toil transformed the four long rectangle gardens that formed a large square in front of the house, into some semblance of their former selves.

Towards late afternoon, when Anna tired, Maisie and Emma came out to help her. Once all the weeds were gone, they found hundreds of bulbs buried deep in the soil. Daffodils, jonquils, bluebells, hyacinths, and many other varieties filled the beds, nestled in amongst the rosebushes, azaleas, camellias and rhododendrons. It was with a great deal of satisfaction that they came into the kitchen at dusk to devour the excellent meal Agnes cooked.

Now, as the clock chimed nine o'clock, a tide of weariness coupled with a little melancholy descended over Anna. In the stillness of the night she missed her Papa and Maggie.

They heard Sophie cry from upstairs and Emma went to see to her, leaving Maisie and Anna staring into the fire.

'Our first Christmas here,' Maisie stated, putting another log on the fire.

'Yes.'

'Who'd have thought last year that this is where we'd be this Christmas.'

Anna shifted in her chair to find a more comfortable position. She'd paid for her day's labour with an aching back and swollen ankles. 'It could be worse,' she mused. 'We could be alone in a poky little room in some foreign country as we first planned. At least this way, we have a lovely home and good friends around us. Still, it has been an exceedingly difficult year, and I'm glad it's nearly over.'

'I agree. 'Tis me first Christmas without me Mam, and I miss her,' Maisie murmured.

Anna reached out her hand to clasp Maisie's. 'I'm sorry, Maisie. I've been so selfish. I worry about the farm, the future, and everything else. I've been so wrapped up in my own concerns that I never thought about how you've been missing your mother. Please forgive me.'

'Don't be daft, Miss. There's nowt to forgive. You had enough to see to here, with the farm. I know you care without you havin' to say owt.' Maisie took up the sock she'd been knitting. 'Only, there is one thing…'

'What is it? Tell me.'

Maisie hesitated. 'Well, I don't want a row with you…'

'I promise not to argue.' Anna pulled a funny face at her.

'It's just that we can all have a nice Christmas, or we can have an awful one, and you'll be the one to determine which we'll have.'

'Of course, I want you all to have a lovely day tomorrow.'

'Aye, we know,' Maisie quickly butted in. 'But with Brenton and yourself at logger heads all the time, it makes everyone tense. Why can't you both get on?'

Rising awkwardly, Anna ambled over to the Christmas tree and fondled the pine needles. 'We seem to rub each other the wrong way. I cannot explain it. We are better off staying at a distance, if that is possible. Maybe I should send him away.'

'But he's a lovely man, lass.' Maisie frowned. 'A nicer one you couldn't find. Look at the way he's taken to runnin' the farm and seein' to it for us. We wouldn't have come this far, in such a short time, if it weren't for him.'

'I know.'

'An' he genuinely likes us too. He once said to me that he feels responsible for us. He thinks of us as his family. Isn't that lovely?'

Anna turned away from Maisie's earnest expression. 'Perhaps that is the problem? He is too nice,' she whispered. 'How can we be certain? We've not known him long. What if he hasn't been honest with us? He might be someone who in the past was not a good person.'

'You don't believe that do you?' Maisie asked, incredulously.

'I don't know what to believe. I cannot trust my instincts like I once did.' Anna gazed down at the collection of Christmas presents. 'I feel…that he is not what he seems.' She gazed at Maisie. 'There is more to him than he tells us. I cannot quite believe he is the humble man he appears. He's intelligent—knows things a working man wouldn't know.'

'He's not Matt Cowan, you know. He has nowt to hide, and you can't paint him with the same brush as Cowan. It ain't fair.'

Anna was saved from answering by a commotion outside. 'What is that?'

Going to the window and moving the heavy curtains aside, Maisie and Anna saw, in the dim light of a swaying lantern, Ned and O'Mara trying to hold up a drunken Henry, who was singing carols at the top of his voice.

'Quickly, let's get him inside and quiet before he disturbs Sophie.' Maisie ran to unbolt and open the front door, which normally they never used.

Agnes came through the hallway wiping her hands on her ever-present apron. 'What's going on?'

'They have brought Henry back, and he is drunk.' Anna shook her head at the foolishness of men.

'Why didn't they take him home?' Agnes glanced up at the stairs. 'We've a baby in the house.'

'He's makin' enough noise to wake the dead,' Maisie muttered just as Ned and O'Mara stumbled in with a laughing and singing Henry.

'Shush,' Maisie and Anna said together.

'Ahh, Maisie lass, lovely Maisie girl,' Henry cooed. Alcohol fumes radiated from him. Looking up at Anna he smiled like a circus fool. 'An' b— beautiful Mrs. Thornton, sweet, sweet Anna. Such…good friends they are…to me.' Henry turned to O'Mara, swaying dangerously. 'Isn't she beautiful, Bren…Brenton?'

O'Mara looked at Anna. For the first time in a long while, there was no animosity in his eyes, just tenderness. Gazing at her, a slow sensuous smile curved his mouth. 'Yes, Henry, she is beautiful.'

Those few words started Anna's heart beating like a drum, and she bent her head to hide the hot flush that touched her face. Oh heaven, how was she to cope when he looked at her like that.

'Come now, let's get him up to the spare room and into bed,' tutted Maisie, going ahead of Ned and Brenton as they heaved a very tired and heavy Henry up the staircase. 'Why you had to bring him here, I don't know.'

'He'll have a head on him in the morning.' Agnes laughed as she and Anna went into the kitchen.

They heard a thump overhead and both chuckled, as muffled voices come through the ceiling.

'It's good to see you smile, Mrs. Thornton. You don't do it often enough,' commented Agnes, making hot chocolate.

'I've not had a lot to be smiling about.'

'You have good health, a roof over your head, food in your belly, and good friends.' Agnes handed her a cup of the sweet drink. 'To me, I'd say you had much more than most.'

Anna sighed and felt selfish. 'True, but it has been a particularly difficult time for me, Agnes. I've only just come to realize that. I was naive enough to think I could leave a sheltered home and start a new life and business without any problems at all. Stupidly, I believed I could do it all my own way.' Anna placed extra cups and saucers on the table. 'I suddenly acknowledged, not long ago, that I do miss my family and my home. I thought I'd not, you see.'

'You're bound to miss them. You made an enormous decision, Mrs. Thornton, to live a life you're not accustomed to. You have courage.'

'At the time, I didn't think I had a choice.' She took the glass jar of Agnes's shortbread from the dresser. 'All at once, so much was taken from me.' She paused. 'I didn't help matters…I know my faults. I did things along the way that I should not have done.'

'But you've made a lovely home here, and you've helped Emma, and me and Ned. That's something in itself. You should be proud of what you've done.'

'Yes, I suppose so. But every now and then, I feel a little insecure. I miss my father, but when I sent him a letter, I didn't put my address on. Now I wish I had.'

'It's never too late, Mrs. Thornton. Send them a telegram after Christmas.'

'Yes, I shall.' Anna grimaced at the mention of her name. Being called *Mrs.* Thornton made her uncomfortable. 'Agnes, since we all live and work together closely, would it be possible for you to call me, something other than Mrs. Thornton?'

'Oh?' Agnes paused by the oven to look at her oddly. 'Like what?'

'I'm not sure…'

'You're not married, are you?'

'What makes you say that?'

Agnes smiled sadly. 'You never mention your husband.'

Anna held her breath and then let it out slowly. 'You're correct.'

'Don't worry, I'll not say a word. It happened to me sister, so I'll not be throwing any stones.'

'Thank you.'

'How about I call you Mrs. Anna?'

Anna felt the weight on her shoulders lighten. 'That would be lovely.'

'And maybe you shouldn't worry about everything so much, love,' Agnes added gently. 'Maybe you should just let things happen. It's Christmas and a time to be happy. Tell me, what would make you happy right now?'

Anna stared at the cup in her hand. 'I'd like to see my father, Maggie and Tom. Also, I really would like to have my horse, Jasper, back. I know that can never happen, but I'm awfully sad without him. I miss riding him.' Looking up, she saw O'Mara standing in the doorway with a sorrowful and guilty expression on his face.

'I'm sorry, Anna, deeply sorry.' He had used her first name without permission. His gaze held hers.

AnneMarie Brear

'I don't blame you, not now. It happened, and that is an end to it.' Anna tried to smile at him but felt tears rise instead. 'I'm tired. Goodnight,' she said in a rush. With her head bent so they would not see her face, she quickly left the kitchen.

265

Chapter 16

The sun's rays peeping between the gap in the curtains awoke Anna to the morning. She lay in her bed for a short while, gazing at her belongings. Her bedroom was still rather sparse in its furnishings and decoration, but that didn't unduly worry her. The empty cot sat in the corner of the room, and as Anna stared at it, she rubbed her hand over her swollen stomach. Eight weeks was all she'd to wait until her baby arrived—her and Matt's baby.

The pain of their illicit affair had waned since her arrival at the farm. The money problems and all the work needed to be done helped in that respect. In fact, lately, she rarely thought of Matt. All she felt now for him was pity. He had lost her love and their baby.

Anna turned over onto her side and thought of her family and the estate. She made a silent vow to invite her father and Maggie once the winter was over. It was selfish to not let them visit her new home. Her father would be worried about her and Maggie would be missing her company. The haunting memories of the scenes with her mother and Arabella were easing. It was time to move on.

Having made that decision, she felt better. As Agnes said, she should be grateful for having good health, a new family, a home, and soon her baby would be born. Boredom and restlessness never bothered her now like it had back home. Every day brought something to keep her occupied. Her old way of life seemed so long ago.

The bedroom door opened, and Emma and Maisie stuck their heads around it.

'What you doin' lyin' in bed? 'Tis Christmas,' Maisie cried, sweeping into the room with a jug of hot water and a white towel. 'Here, Miss, get washed and hurry up. We want to open our presents.' She was like a child in her excitement.

Sitting up, Anna laughed at them. 'We cannot open the presents yet. I promised Agnes we would not open them until she and Ned came back from church.' The disappointed looks on Maisie and Emma's faces made Anna laugh harder.

Grumbling about churches and puffed-up overbearing vicars in general, Maisie and Emma helped Anna to wash and dress.

'Do you want to go to church, Emma?' Maisie asked afterwards, as they descended the staircase.

'No, not really. I used to go to church every Sunday with Marcus, but I lost all my faith in God this year with all that has happened to me. The only good thing this year was meeting you and Anna, and I don't think God had a hand in that.'

'An' havin' Sophie.'

Emma stopped at the bottom of the staircase. 'Yes, of course, and having Sophie. Only, she was not wanted for such a long time.'

'You do love her, though?' Maisie was anxious for Emma to confirm her undying love for the baby.

'Yes. Yes, I love her. Thankfully, she has nothing of her father in her, and she is all mine. No one can take her from me. I will love and protect her for the rest of my life, and if something should happen to me then I hope both you and Anna will take care of her.'

'You know we will,' Maisie assured her. 'Now come on, let's go and have breakfast. It's Christmas.'

It was a glorious day from beginning to end. They used the dining room for the first time. Christmas dinner was superb, seeming to be the best meal any of them had ever eaten. Maisie and Emma lit a fire in the dining room and put candles and decorations on the great table, which Maisie had polished until it shone. They sat for hours, eating, drinking, talking, and laughing in the warm, cheerful room.

When the time came to open the presents, they gathered in front of the fire in the parlour with wine and chocolates. Anna stood by the tree and watched everyone exchange small gifts until it was her turn to give out her presents, too. Watching as Emma hugged O'Mara her thanks for his gift, Anna was ashamed to feel strangely jealous. She countered that by wondering where O'Mara got the money to buy such expensive presents, certainly not on the wage she paid him.

As Anna handed him her gift their gazes locked, and she nearly dropped the present from the intensity of it.

Turning away, she prodded the fire with her back to him as he removed the paper wrapping. His silence made her swing around and she saw him tenderly touching the dark, tanned, leather-bound writing case.

'It's so you can write home to your mother,' Anna told him. She blushed, annoyed with herself for buying such an expensive gift. She should not have done so.

'She will think it's the Queen of England herself, writing to her with this,' he said, making them laugh. He nodded to Anna. 'Thank you.'

Finally, it was Anna's turn. She smiled as she opened gifts of books and perfume. Then came O'Mara's present. Her hands shook ever so slightly, and when she opened the velvet box to find a set of small diamond earrings glistening at her, she felt as though she would faint. Everyone bent to see their beauty, but Anna gazed over their heads into O'Mara's eyes.

'It's too much,' she breathed with a slight tremble.

'Not for you.'

For the first time Anna let down her guard. She smiled. 'Thank you.' Her tone was free from stinging words and hidden meanings, but inside her stomach coiled inward with suspicion. Where did he get the money to buy such gifts?

Maisie and Emma stood to put away their gifts and Agnes mentioned making some tea, but O'Mara stopped them all at the door. 'Wait. There is one more gift I have for Mrs. Thornton.'

'Oh no,' Anna protested. 'You've given me enough.'

He ignored her and with a wink to Ned left the room. Within a few minutes he returned with his hands behind him.

'Really, I...' Anna stopped talking when O'Mara brought his hands around in front and held them out to Anna. Curled up in a fluffy ball in his palms was the cutest puppy.

'He is all I ever got from Flora Jones,' he whispered.

To Gain What's Lost

* * *

During the long winter nights of eighteen sixty-five, Anna discussed her plans for the coming year with O'Mara and Ned. The sow had already been put back with Henry's boar, and come spring, O'Mara and Ned would put more acres under plough—a necessity if they were to grow enough vegetables to make a profit. Everyone was involved, as Anna wanted it to be, when decisions were being made. They supported O'Mara's suggestion that a herd of cows or a flock of sheep should be bought to fatten up over the summer and sold off next winter. Naturally, acting on the decisions would depend on money, of which at the present time there was very little.

Now, Anna sat at her desk in the study reviewing the month's budget. The cold February winds bashed against the house, rattling the windows. Her account books showed far more money was being spent than earned. Yesterday, O'Mara gave her a list of the additional tools and equipment needed for spring, when their work would start in earnest.

Awkwardly, he'd mentioned that another younger horse to replace Jasper would be beneficial. Misty was getting old and the need for two horses was paramount.

These problems desperately concerned her, but to buy everything on the list was nigh on impossible. Her limited financial resources, the little that remained in the bank and the small but regular return on her remaining investments, only provided enough to cover the mortgage payments and live frugally. Also, she wanted to pay Agnes and Ned a wage. Until now, they willingly worked for food and board, and, while Agnes was glad just to have a roof over her head, they deserved monetary compensation.

O'Mara had made Agnes a pallet bed and she slept on that in the kitchen each night, but Anna wanted her to have a room of her own since Agnes's swollen ankles and legs wouldn't let her climb the stairs. Agnes wouldn't hear of it, insisting she was quite all right in the kitchen. The solution was to build another room onto the scullery.

The money problems went around in Anna's head, making her fidgety. She slammed the account books into the desk drawer and heaved herself up. Her large stomach protruded out farther as she arched her throbbing back. Plodding into the kitchen she rubbed her back and scowled.

'You all right, my lass?' Maisie asked, ironing a petticoat.

'No.' Anna reached over and took a freshly baked jam tart from the tray. 'I'm fat and annoyed.'

'Poor pet.' Agnes pulled out a chair for her. 'Sit yourself down. Would you like some tea?'

Anna shook her head. The ache in her back made sitting uncomfortable. 'I might read for a while.'

'I'll bring you dinner on a tray,' Maisie called as Anna retreated along the hallway.

O'Mara and Ned noisily came into the scullery, placing armloads of wood in the corner.

'Don't say or do anythin' to annoy Mrs Anna,' Agnes warned them.

O'Mara looked up from taking off his boots. 'What's the matter with her?'

'She's close to her time, that's all,' Agnes said, with the superior look of someone who knows what she's talking about.

Anna shuffled back into the kitchen, chewing on her lip.

Maisie stopped folding the clothes. 'What's up? I were bringing you a tray.'

'I can't settle.' Anna rubbed her nape. She ached all over.

'Sit down and have your meal, love,' Agnes crooned, ladling out thick soup from a tureen into bowls.

Anna gave her a small smile. 'I'm not very hungry, Agnes. A little soup will be fine.'

'You'll eat the lot, my dear. You're eating for two,' Agnes reminded her with a glare.

O'Mara hesitated and then pulled out a chair and sat, his gaze lingered on her. 'Is everything all right?'

'Yes, of course.' Anna moved away a little. Increasingly his looks and words sent messages she wasn't ready to receive. She and O'Mara had grown a little closer during the frigid winter evenings as they discussed the welfare of the farm. However, Anna still felt the need to hold herself back. She looked fat and ugly in her last stage of pregnancy, and she was in no mood to try and pretend any differently. His sympathy only irritated her.

The talk flew freely and easily around the room as they ate their meal, but Anna found it of little of interest. With her soup only half eaten, she excused herself and went up to her room.

Standing in front of her small square dressing table, she fingered the letters she received from

Maggie and her father a few weeks ago. Shortly after Christmas, she wrote to them giving her address and inviting them to visit her in the spring. To her great delight, letters from both of them arrived within the same week.

Maggie's letter came first; she wrote of her enormous sadness after Anna's departure and how nothing was the same without her. On a more cheerful note, she went on to say she and Miss Foster had gone to Scarborough for a week last October and enjoyed collecting seashells. She told Anna Christmas had been cold and lonely and Father spent most of his time with Mother, who was terribly ill. Lastly, she declared her immense excitement at the prospect of visiting in the spring.

Anna picked up her father's letter to re-read it again.

January 17th 1865.

My Dearest Anna,
What a pleasure it was to receive your letter. It made my day instantly brighter. Maggie excitedly brought it in to me at breakfast and then disappeared to read her own. The news of your good heath brings me joy. I long to see you and hope that it will happen in the near future.

I'm writing with news that your brother Tom was wed on Christmas Eve to Cecilia Lord. They married in Oxford near her parents' home, apparently in the same church where her parents married. They shall live in Oxford until Tom finishes university then will come home to Thornton House to spend the rest of their lives here in happiness. Praise be to God.

Your mother and I didn't attend the wedding, as your mother is quite ill. I'm afraid she will not be long for this life. There is nothing that can be done for her. She has lost all sense of reason and suffers a great deal from the pains in her head. The only relief she receives is from the bottle of laudanum. It hurts me tremendously to see her reduced this way. There is nothing left of the beautiful and clever Louise I married. In a way, I long for her release from the agonizing distress she endures.

Arabella's wedding has been temporarily put off as Luke found it necessary to go abroad on some family business. Naturally, Arabella is upset at this and seems intent on making everyone else miserable as well. You know your sister well enough without me adding more.

I've promised Maggie that she may visit you come spring. I hope that meets with your approval. It depends entirely on your mother's health as to whether I may accompany her and Miss Foster.

My regards to Maisie, I pray she cares for you admirably, though I've no doubt she does. My thoughts are with you always, my dear daughter. It's with unconditional love, that I send you this letter,

Your father,

Thomas.

Anna had read the letter several times since it arrived. She was overjoyed at the thought of seeing them in the spring, but also a little sad at the news Tom married without her even knowing. It was her own fault. She should have written to him earlier, but she'd make amends and send him her congratulations. It was hard to fathom the mixed emotions she felt on reading her father's news. Her feelings careened between the joy of hearing from them and sadness that they carried on with their lives without her.

Her father sounded wearied by the great task of nursing her mother. Anna too prayed her mother's illness would not linger much longer, for everyone's sake. Earlier, Anna considered asking her father for money to help her build a room onto the house for Agnes. However, since the arrival of his letter such thoughts had disappeared. Her father endured enough without her adding to them. She'd vowed to make it on her own, and so she must. *I'm no coward. I've gotten this far.* Lifting her chin, she straightened her shoulders.

Her gaze wandered over the dressing table and rested on her large jewellery box. Opening it, she ran her fingers over the sparkling jewels. Selecting the smaller pieces, she studied them. Gently placing them back, she then picked up the velvet case that contained the sapphire and diamond necklace and earrings given to her by her parents on her twenty-first birthday. She remembered wearing them the night of the ball, the night Matt Cowan entered her life. If she had a daughter, she would give her the sapphires and diamonds one day and tell her the story of meeting her father. It brought a small ache to her heart to think of him. Indeed, sometimes she felt as though it was a lifetime ago since she was an independent woman bent on defying the rules.

A light knock on the door broke her reverie.

Maisie walked in carrying clean washing. 'What you doin', Miss?' she asked, placing the clothes on the bed.

'Looking through my jewellery.'

'Why?'

An idea came to Anna. 'I'm going to sell some of it. We need more money.'

'Are we that poor?'

'We need to build a room for Agnes. Furthermore, O'Mara has a list of equipment needed for the summer, including another horse. I don't have much money in the bank.'

'It's a shame to sell your beautiful things,' Maisie commiserated, picking up a small, sapphire, rose-shaped brooch.

'I never wear them. I'm not going to sell all of them, just enough to cover our immediate needs.'

They spent the next half hour sorting out the pieces Anna would take to Leeds to sell. In the end, they selected two rings, three gem brooches, a silver bracelet and a gold choker, leaving a few pieces left to sell at a later date, plus Anna's personal favourites that she would not sell at all, which now included the earrings O'Mara gave her.

'Do you think they'll sell for a good amount?' Maisie asked.

They walked out of the room and down the stairs. Anna paused in the hall to rub her throbbing back. 'They should, if we take them to the right kind of dealer. I don't know whether to take them to Leeds or to Manchester.'

'Manchester would be best, I think, but it's further away, and you're so close to your time. Why don't you wait until after the babby's born?' suggested Maisie as they went into the kitchen.

'What are you waiting to do after the baby is born?' O'Mara stood reading the newspaper by the window.

Emma sat in a chair embroidering.

'Take some of her jewellery to either Leeds or Manchester and sell it,' Maisie informed them.

O'Mara lowered the newspaper and stared at Anna. 'Is that necessary?'

'Yes. That is, if you want this farm to prosper.' Anna pulled out a chair and sat. 'We need money to build a room for Agnes. We need to buy another horse and everything else that is on the list. Jewellery is all I have to sell.'

'I don't think it's a clever idea to sell it all. You may need it for an emergency. We can get by with just one horse and—'

'It will take years for the farm to make a good profit at the rate we are going.' Anna stared at him. 'We require the money now to improve it, so we don't merely get by from one year to another.'

'I know of a good jeweller in London.' He paced the room, his brow furrowed deep in thought. 'He is a Jewish friend of my father's. I'm sure he will give you a fair price. Well, he would give me one.' He stopped pacing and stared at Anna. 'Would you trust me to take them to London?'

The silence in the room was deafening as they waited for Anna's answer.

His question ran over and over in her head. Did she trust him? Anna thought she did, but now he was putting her to the test. Together, the gems could sell for a lot of money, or at least Anna hoped it would.

She frowned. He had mentioned his father for the first time. He only ever talked of his mother and Grandfather. How would his father know a London Jew? Her skin prickled. What was he hiding? Where did he get the money to buy her Christmas present? She swallowed and then took a deep breath. Did she trust Brenton O'Mara to bring back her money?

Anna looked at his handsome face, into the gentle blue eyes. Her heartbeat against her ribs as though looking for a way out of her body. Trust. Could she? Could she trust a man again, and not just any man, but one that made the blood pound in her ears and who reduced her insides into a quivering mess from just one sensuous look?

She took a deep breath and prayed that the fates wouldn't dupe her twice.

Chapter 17

If Anna worried whether Brenton O'Mara would ever return, she kept it to herself. He had been gone six days before winter released its final grip on the land and the first full day of warm sunshine broke through the snow clouds and bathed the countryside. Icicles dripped from the eves in a monotonous tone.

After the long cold months Maisie and Emma started spring-cleaning. They brought down the curtains to wash them and dusted and polished every surface.

Anna tried to help but was constantly told to keep out of the way—only, doing nothing irritated her. Even her farming magazines and account books didn't hold her attention.

'Go for a walk and be out from under me feet.' Maisie shooed as Anna hovered.

Agnes heard her as she came in from hanging out the washing. 'Why don't you visit Henry? He's not been 'round for over a week.'

Anna grinned. 'I could take offence at how you three always wish to be rid of me.' She put on her cloak and boots and called Abe, the pup.

She strolled up behind the barn and over the hill, with the puppy galloping at her heels. On the rise, she paused and viewed the landscape in its late winter glory. Hues of grey and white conveyed a stark scene and suddenly Anna longed for the colours of summer.

She sniffed the freshness in the air. The recent rain and watery sun gave the signal to the wildflowers and the woodland animals that warmth and plenty would soon arrive.

Continuing, she headed west towards Henry's farm. Often Abe darted into the undergrowth and frightened a bird hiding there, then he'd look up at Anna with a puzzled expression. A beautiful collie with perfect markings of white and tan, he was her constant companion.

Before long, she passed through the gate of Henry's farm, which was no more than a small cottage with several outbuildings and a few acres of land.

When no one answered her knock, she went around to the back of the cottage and into the small yard. The pigs made a terrible noise and increased their grunting and squealing at the sight of her, pushing up against their pens demanding attention.

'Henry. Are you there?' Anna strolled to the pigpens. It was difficult to hear an answer above the noise. Thinking Henry might be slaughtering, she went into one of the outbuildings.

In the moment or two before her eyes adjusted to the dimness of the barn, she heard the sniffling noise of a sow in a holding pen over in the far corner. A strong and pungent odour assailed her nostrils on approaching the pen. Her stomach somersaulted with revulsion. The sow with her piglets lay on filthy straw with neither food nor water in the feeding troughs. The sow rose, sending her piglets off in all directions. Anna gasped as she saw two dead piglets in the straw where the sow had sat. It was obvious the piglets had been dead for some time. She frowned. Henry was quite vigilant where his pigs were concerned. A shiver ran along her skin.

Outside again, she paused to take a deep breath and then looked around the other pens. The animals, obviously hungry, rushed toward her making a deafening, demanding noise as she passed by. Heading towards the house, her fear increased. She stood on the back doorstep and banged hard on the door. While she waited, she rubbed her lower back. It pained her like a savage toothache.

'Henry,' she called through the door. 'Henry, are you there?'

Abe ran behind her heels as Anna circumnavigated the whole house and yard calling Henry. Banging on the back door once more, she winced as the movement caused her backache to worsen. Unexpectedly she heard a sound, maybe a voice but very faint. Panic rose in her.

'Henry, are you in there?' A crashing sound came from above. She stepped back to look up at the small window in one of the two attic bedrooms.

What if Henry lay injured and bleeding to death? Could he be sick, in need of a doctor? Sweat broke out beneath her coat. She tried to open the door again, but the lock worked against her. She dithered for a minute, trying to decide what to do. Should she run home for help? No, there was no time.

Next to the back door was the large kitchen window. Treading on the few plants that grew under it, Anna prayed it was unlocked then heaved the bottom half of the window up. It jammed a few times, but at last she succeeded. The task of actually climbing through would be more difficult, however. By the door, Anna found a crate to stand on. Then, she gathered her skirts, and lifting her leg, managed to place it on the windowsill.

'Mercy me,' she muttered. The ache in her back became a pounding drum. She was sure she would not fit with her stomach being so big, but there was just enough room for her to manoeuvre through the opening. Her feet found the floor and she whimpered in pain as she straightened.

Puffing, Anna stopped to rest, but Henry's call made her scramble up the staircase and into his bedroom. He lay in the bed, ghost-like. Drawn tightly over his bones, his skin was the colour of parchment. Beside his bed lay an over-turned small table and a smashed lamp.

Anna knelt beside the bed and held the hand he stretched toward her. 'Oh, Henry. I'm so sorry. We didn't know you were ill.'

'It's—all right—lass,' Henry whispered, his breathing harsh and strenuous.

'No, it's not. We should have realized something was wrong when you didn't come to the farm.' Anna's guilt knew no bounds. She staggered to her feet, trying not to flinch as a twinge stabbed her.

'I will go and get help.'

'Nay, lass—' Henry struggled to sit up, and Anna hastily helped him to get comfortable. 'A—drink.'

'Yes, yes.' She whirled around and saw an empty water jug. 'I will go down and bring you one.'

Holding her skirts high, she staggered downstairs and into the kitchen. In the larder she found a pitcher of water and grabbed a mug from a shelf. As quickly as she could, she made it back up the stairs. She paused beside the bed to catch her breath. Exhaustion sapped her strength. Her hands shook as she poured out the water. The pain spread around to her stomach. Clenching her teeth, she ignored it.

'The...animals,' wheezed Henry. 'They've...been...makin' a clamour.'

'I will have Ned see to them. Don't worry. Rest.'

'Go home, lass,' Henry mumbled.

'I will fetch the doctor from the village,' Anna told him. Weak and thirsty from her exertions she drank some water straight from the jug.

Henry lay back against the pillows. 'Go home and get...Brenton.'

'He is not back yet. Ned will take care of the animals. I'm going to fetch the doctor now.'

'You're too—tired. Get Ned first. I've been like this...for days. I'll...be all right for a few hours more.'

Henry's attempt to make light of his illness only worsened her guilt. 'I'm so sorry,' she repeated, patting his hand and then refilling the mug. She righted the table and placed the jug and cup on it. 'I will be back very soon.'

Abe jumped about her feet when Anna came out the front door. Twinges in her stomach caused her to stumble. She reached the road then hesitated. Should she go to the village or go home and get Ned? She wasn't sure if she could make the journey either way as tiredness overwhelmed her. The thrusting pain in her back left her dazed and unable to concentrate. Deciding to head for home was the best action, she focused on putting each foot in front of the other.

The day's events also took its toll of Abe. Being only a puppy, he was too tired to walk home and simply flopped down on the road, refusing to budge.

'Come on, I will carry you.' As she bent to pick him up a searing band of pain clamped her stomach, rending her to her knees with a cry. Abe yelped and jumped to one side.

Gasping for breath as the sting abated, Anna lurched to her feet again with Abe in her arms and began the slow shuffle home. A cloud passed over the sun, and in its shadow Anna shivered. Her coat weighed heavily, but she didn't have the energy to pull it off.

She bridged a small rise, saw the woods that formed the north boundary of the farm, and stopped. Crossing the field and travelling through the woods would be shorter than staying on the road and going around to the front of the house, which was over a mile longer. She headed for the woods and tried not to think of the pain.

Tall old trees blocked out all but the tiniest rays of sun in the cold, dim woods. She held Abe to her in desperation, but his weight seemed to intensify with each step until Anna was forced to sit down near a large oak tree and rest. The strong pains returned, hitting her alternately in the lower back and then in the stomach. Clutching at her swollen stomach, she heard herself moan as if from a distance. Fright mingled with the agony.

'I—I cannot take much more,' she whimpered, pulling herself up against the trunk. She walked with her back bent, which helped the aching. Abe plodded along behind her, too dejected to even raise his head.

AnneMarie Brear

* * *

Ned hammered nails into a wooden trough he'd
made from pieces of timber found in one of the
outbuildings. He planned to show it to Mrs. Anna
when she returned from her walk. He nearly
hammered a nail through his finger when she came
stumbling out of the woods and down the hill. It was
a good ten seconds before his mind realized she
needed help. The echo of the dropped hammer rang
through the yard.

He reached her side in time to catch her as she fell.

Ned carried her down to the house as though she
weighed no more than a newborn lamb. Kicking the
kitchen door wide, he frightened his mother half to
death where she sat with her back to him whipping
cream in a bowl.

'Ye Gods, lad, what do you think you're doing?'
Agnes hollered, turning to glare at him. She jerked at
the sight of Anna in her son's arms and lumbered to
his side. 'Oh, love, your pains have started, have
they?'

For a brief time, bedlam reigned as Agnes shouted
for Maisie and Emma. They were all at sixes and
sevens about what to do. They had been preparing for
this very event for weeks, but now it had begun they
were unsure of themselves.

'Stop. Stop and listen for a minute,' Anna
beseeched them. Ned had carried her to her bed and
was about to go for the doctor. Anna struggled to sit
up. 'Henry. He is ill—in bed. Ned has to get the
doctor for him first—'

285

She gripped the sheet and bent her head to battle the growing tide of agony.

* * *

'What is the date today, Maisie?' Anna whispered, not wanting to wake the precious baby in her arms.

'Um... it's the twenty-sixth, I think,' she replied, bundling up the stained sheets.

The door opened and Emma entered. 'How is everything?' she whispered.

'Everything in here is simply perfect.' Anna smiled at her and then down at her baby daughter.

Emma stood by the bed and gazed at the baby. 'I've finally managed to calm Agnes down. She was doing a jig on hearing the news, and you know what her legs are like. She'll not be able to walk in the morning.'

'How is Henry?'

'Better now he's safely installed down the hall. I've put him in the spare room. The doctor will be back again in the morning. He said he'll need to keep an eye on Henry for a while.' Emma picked up the basin of bloodied water.

'Aye, well, the doctor wasn't needed in this room, that's for sure,' Maisie gloated. 'I had it all under control, and he knew it. That's why he busied himself with seein' to Henry. He had to make it look as though he was doin' summat useful.' She left the room with a haughty sniff.

'Oh, Maisie.' Anna laughed. What a character she was.

'Do you want me to put her in the cradle?' Emma asked. 'You must be tired.'

'Yes. Yes, I am.' She kissed her daughter's head then handed her to Emma. Snuggling down into the blankets, Anna sleepily watched them, but before Emma had finished tucking in the blankets around the baby, she felt her eyelids close and could not stop them.

* * *

Downstairs they sat around the kitchen table and drank refreshing cups of tea.

''Tis been a grand day.' Agnes stirred her tea. 'The new baby born safe and well, and Mrs. Anna has come through it unscathed.'

'I hope the baby sleeps all night for her.' Emma said, giving Sophie a bottle of goat's milk from the newly acquired nanny.

As the clock struck eight o'clock, the back door opened. Brenton stood framed in the doorway. He brought a rush of chilly air in with him. The women rushed to hug him and greet him, all talking at once.

He laughed at such a wonderful homecoming. 'It feels good to be so wanted.'

'Anna's had the baby,' Maisie managed to tell him in the midst of all the talk.

Brenton's eyes widened. 'Is she all right?' He had wanted to be home when her time came.

'Aye, they're both fine. Aw, she's the most beautiful babby, Brenton,' Maisie told him.

Agnes poured him a cup of tea. 'How did it go in London?'

287

Sitting down, Brenton took a sip of his tea before answering. 'It went well. I think Mrs. Thornton will be pleased.'

Agnes nodded. 'That's grand. It makes a perfect ending to an eventful day.'

'Do you think I could go up and see her?' asked Brenton, draining his cup. He was eager to see for himself that Anna was safe.

'She is asleep,' Emma said, lifting Sophie over her shoulder. 'But Henry has been asking for you.'

'Henry?' Brenton scowled, puzzled.

'Henry has a bad chest. Anna found him in a terrible state earlier today,' Agnes said, giving him the additional news. 'We had Ned bring him here so we can look after him. The doctor's been and will be back again tomorrow.'

Upstairs, Brenton spent an hour chatting with Henry. When the old man fell asleep, Brenton went down the hall and peeped into Anna's room. A low burning lamp cast the room in a golden light. A fire glowed in the hearth. He silently crossed the floor to stand beside the cradle. The baby moved her arm out of the blanket. Brenton reached in and gently touched her hand. Tiny fingers clasped around his finger and held it tight. His chest constricted, overwhelmed to feel such strength in one so small. He knew he loved both mother and daughter.

'What do you think of her?' Anna murmured from her bed.

Brenton gazed up and smiled. 'I think she is as beautiful as her mother.' He grinned at the blush that spread across Anna's cheeks. 'What are you going to call her?' he asked, coming to stand at the end of her bed.

'I'm not sure. I do like Constance,' Anna said, sitting up.

She fussed with the bed sheets, trying to avoid looking at him.

He knew his eyes gave away his secret love and that she didn't want to know of it yet. 'May I make a suggestion?'

'Indeed do.'

'How about Clare? It's the county I come from, and a more beautiful place you'll not see, I promise you.'

Anna shifted, blushing deeper at his soft caress of words. 'I don't think you should be in my room, Mr. O'Mara.'

Brenton took a step back. 'No doubt you're correct, Mrs. Thornton.' Then, abruptly, he strode to the bed and sat down beside her. 'I've broken the rules all my life, Anna, so I shan't be stopping now.' He winked. 'Is Clare a good enough name for you?'

She raised a delicate eyebrow. 'It should be, since it's also my middle name.'

His gave her a wry grin. 'That settles it then.'

'The jewellery?'

'Ahh, the test you set me.'

'It was no test at all.' She defended, narrowing her eyes.

'Yes, it was. In any case, I think I did well.' He sighed and looked down at her hands clutching the sheets, hands that wore no rings, more importantly no wedding ring from another man. What was her story?

He wanted her to confide in him, to give him just a little of herself. 'Did you think I would come back?'

'Of course.' She sat straighter; chin raised. The gentleness left her to be replaced by the businesswoman she had become.

Brenton nodded and stood, forcing himself to smile. 'The money is downstairs on your desk. It's more than you expected.'

'Thank you.' Relieved, she looked away from him towards the baby and that glimpse of closeness between them vanished as though it had never been.

* * *

March and April, although wet, passed by without incident. The weather became a little better in May. The spring blossoms on the fruit trees were glorious in the sunshine, and the women often walked around the orchard sniffing at the fragrance floating on the air. Anna's garden beds sprang into bloom. The bulbs sent forth a profusion of scent and colour.

The sale of the jewellery was of enormous benefit to the farm. Anna engaged a carpenter to build the new room for Agnes. They purchased some Hereford calves and another work horse at a cheap price from a farmer immigrating to Canada.

They decorated the front parlour in shades of cream and bronze and bought good solid wood furniture to give the whole room a rich blend of style and homeliness. In readiness for Maggie's visit, Maisie gave the two spare bedrooms a thorough cleaning and Anna bought extra beds. In a letter Anna had received the previous day, Maggie wrote about her impatience to see Anna and baby Clare. Even Miss Foster was keen to visit.

As the days lengthened, the farm grew busier. Brenton and Ned worked incessantly. Not only did they have the general upkeep of their farm to manage, but they also cared for Henry's pigs.

Henry, although better, was still recovering from his bout of pneumonia, and seemed in no great hurry to return home. His illness had taken its toll. He easily became short of breath at times, and lost weight—a state that Agnes was determined to rectify by serving him enormous meals.

With the back door open to let in the sun, Anna sat at the kitchen table folding Clare and Sophie's baby clothes. 'It's such a beautiful day.'

Maisie stood at one end of the table ironing. 'Aye, too good to be workin'.'

Agnes hummed as she cut up vegetables for their dinner. They could see Emma through the open doorway, hoeing the weeds around the herbs in the walled garden. They laughed at her as she did battle with the flies and bees.

A series of knocks interrupted their laughter.

'Who is that?' Anna wondered, rising.

'Nobody knocks on't front door,' said Maisie, putting the iron back on the stove to heat. She went into the hall. Tradesmen and the occasional visiting neighbour always went around the back into the yard. She tutted. 'What's wrong with usin' the back door.'

Anna joined her as the knock sounded again. 'A minute, please,' she called, tiding her hair.

'It is I, Anna, Papa.'

'Papa,' Anna screamed, her fingers fumbling with the bolt.

Maisie moved her aside and did the job for her. Before the door was completely open, Anna was through it and into her father's arms. For several moments they were locked together. Then, slowly, they moved apart to stare at each other.

The change in her beloved Papa shocked Anna. The robust father she knew was gone and replaced by an old man, thin and gaunt. His hair was nearly white, and the lines on his face were trebled from what she remembered. The thick stubble covering his chin was new to her. She went weak at the knees when tears escaped from his tired-looking eyes and trickled down his cheeks.

'Oh, Papa.' It was all she could say as he hugged her to him again.

'Come away in, Sir, Miss Anna,' Maisie murmured. She, too, was teary at the sight of her old master. Maisie left them in the parlour to make some tea.

'I'm sorry to come unannounced, dearest, and in such a state,' Thomas whispered, looking at his crumpled attire. 'I'm ashamed of myself.'

'Nonsense, Papa. What does it matter? You're here.'

'I have news.' His voice thickened in his distress. Wiping the back of his hand over his eyes, he took a deep breath. 'Your mother died the night before last.'

Anna paused before she replied. 'I'm so sorry for you, Papa. I know you loved her very much.'

'Yes, I did. I always have, even when she did things I didn't agree with—especially how she treated you. Yet, I still loved her.' Thomas shook his head as if to clear it from certain images.

After a slight tap, Maisie came in carrying the tea tray. 'A nice cup of tea for you, Mr. Thornton,' she said, placing the tray down on a small oval table near the sofa. 'Emma's upstairs seein' to a room for you, sir. I'll have hot water for you presently.'

'I cannot stay. I must be back in York tonight. The funeral is tomorrow.'

Anna put her hand on Maisie's arm. 'Mother died the night before last.'

'Oh, I'm sorry, sir.' Maisie gave a small curtsy, and with a glance at Anna, she quietly left the room.

'Will you come back with me for the funeral, Anna?'

She hesitated while pouring out the tea to give the idea some thought. Indeed, she would love to go back with her father to see Maggie, Tom and everyone else, but she felt uneasy. Too many memories, yesterday's memories, were back there. Her mother's outburst about her true parentage and all the years of emotional neglect were still too raw and painful to deal with right now—especially since, for the first time in her life, she was finally finding contentment. She loved her new family and home with a passion that surprised her.

'I don't think it would be wise, Papa,' she answered as best she could.

'But, Anna—'

'Listen to me, Papa. Mother didn't like me. We both know that, and I don't think I can be a hypocrite and stand beside her grave to mourn her with the others. She would not have wanted it, and I'd feel like a fraud.'

'She was your mother, Anna, and I'd like to have you beside *me*.'

'I love you very much, Papa, but my place is here now. I'm needed here. I'm sorry.'

A slight knock announced Emma's entrance. She carried Clare. 'Sorry to disturb you, Anna, but she is hungry and will not settle.'

Thomas stood as Emma entered the room. His eyes rested on his grandchild. 'So, this is my beautiful grandchild?' He held out his arms for her.

It brought tears to Anna's eyes to see her dear Papa holding her darling daughter.

'My word, she is like you.' Pride shone from his eyes.

Anna beamed. 'Is she not too perfect?'

'And this must be Emma?' Thomas asked, looking up with a smile. 'How do you do?'

Anna nodded. 'Yes, Papa, this is my dear friend, Emma Webster. Emma, my father, Thomas Thornton.'

'Good day to you, Mr. Thornton.' Emma bobbed her head.

'Would you like to meet everyone else, Papa?'

'No. No, my dear, I must return home.' Thomas handed Clare carefully over to Anna. 'It will be nightfall by the time I arrive at the estate. I've many things still to arrange for...for…'

'How is Maggie? She was to come in the morning.'

'Oh Lord, I forgot all about that.' Thomas sighed heavily. 'She will be so extremely disappointed. She has talked of nothing else. I know her mother's passing was no real hardship for her. As with you, Louise could not seem to be a true mother to Maggie. Louise has done wrong by you both, as much as I'm ashamed to admit it.'

'Let Maggie come next week. It will do her good to take her mind off things,' Anna encouraged him, linking one hand through her father's arm as she walked with him to the front door.

'Yes, yes I will. I may even come too, if that is convenient with you?'

'Need you ask, Papa?' Anna grinned at him, glad to see a little colour back in his face. She would be here ready and waiting to bring some happiness and laughter back into both his and Maggie's lives.

Much later that afternoon, Anna walked to the woods. From the rise of the hill, she could see Ned a little way off, bringing the cows in for milking. When she reached Jasper's grave, she gazed at the little tree she'd planted. It boasted shiny new leaves, and grass grew, covering the soil around it. She wondered why she felt more upset over her horse's death than over her mother's. Surely that wasn't normal?

Stooping down, she picked up a handful of soil and let it sift through her fingers. She watched it fall and drift away as a slight breeze caught it. *Ashes to ashes, dust to dust.* Should she have gone back to York to stand at her mother's grave, as she was now standing at her horse's? Guilt tormented her.

'Anna?' She turned to find O'Mara standing a few feet away, a tender smile hovering on his lips. 'Maisie told me about your mother. I'm sorry for your loss.'

'I'm fine, thank you,' she assured him, turning away.

Lifting her head, she gazed out over her fields to the distant hills. Her heart hammered in her chest, but she did her best to ignore it. She knew of his feelings for her, he wore them openly, but she could not bring herself to examine her needs. For a little while longer she wanted to ignore the important questions in her mind and live quietly with her daughter.

He came to stand beside her. Together they watched the birds swooping and diving in their search for food.

'I've no feelings concerning my mother's death. I feel nothing at all,' Anna admitted into the silence between them. 'She didn't love me, and so I didn't love her. Is that not so dreadfully sad?' She blinked away sudden tears.

'Yes. Yes it's.'

She glanced at him, wondering if he thought her odd. It was vital to her that he didn't.

His eyes softened. 'I adore my mother. She is the most wonderful woman in the world.'

'That is how it should be. All my life I've pretended it didn't matter that my mother disliked me, but it does. Papa gave me extra love to compensate, even though I was another man's child, his own brother's child.' She waited for his reaction to her admission, but he didn't show any outward sign. 'Having Clare makes me understand what it's like to be a mother and to hold my very own creation of life. Yet my mother hated me simply because I existed. I was a constant reminder of the past she wanted to forget.'

'Different women react in different ways,' he told her gently. 'My mother had me out of wedlock. I'm a bastard, born to an English gentleman, and my dear mammy cared for me even more because of it.'

Shocked, Anna turned to look at him so swiftly that her neck cracked. Never did she think O'Mara came from such a background. It didn't matter to her at all, but it did help to understand him a little better. He, as Clare and Sophie would have to do, bore the bastard brand. Would the girls grow up to be strong and independent and have generous warm souls as this man had?

'Is it an awfully hard burden?' she whispered.

O'Mara sat on the grass, and Anna joined him before he answered. 'It isn't a greater load than some have to carry, though my father never denied me anything, not his love, not his money, nothing. He told my mother she could give me his last name, but she wouldn't. Instead, she gave it as my second name. Brenton Avery O'Mara.'

'Was it difficult for your mother?'

Giving the question some thought, Brenton shook his head. 'No, not as much as it could have been. You see, my mother and father love each other very much still to this day. Everyone understands that, even his wife.'

'Really? His *wife*?' Anna couldn't hide the surprise in her voice.

Brenton chuckled. 'To be sure, 'tis a strange set up where oi come from,' he mimicked a strong Irish accent.

'How interesting. I don't understand,' Anna confessed, frowning in bewilderment.

'My father was already married when he came to Ireland from England. His mother died shortly after his marriage to Esther.' O'Mara plucked a piece of grass and twirled it between his fingers. 'In her will, his mother left him a small estate in Ireland, so my father moved there. He is the second son in a large family, there was no way he would inherit his own childhood home in England.'

'You don't have to talk about it, if you'd rather not.'

'I don't mind talking about it, Anna. It's just that not everybody understands.'

'I will not judge, for I'm in no position to do so.'

'My mother's family had lived and worked on the estate since my grandfather was a young lad. My mother was a second assistant to the chef. To be brief, my father fell in love with my mother, and she him, soon after he arrived at the estate. They fought their feelings for over a year, but then my grandmother died in a fire that burnt down a small section of the staff quarters. In her grief, my mother turned to my father.'

'It must have been complicated for your mother, to love a man she knew was already married and also to work for him,' Anna said quietly, knowing how devastated she felt when she found out that Matt was married.

'Yes, at first it was, but father did something many people didn't comprehend. He told Esther about his feelings for my mother. Unbelievably, after a while, she accepted it. She'd recently given him his first son and was content to make mothering her main role. She knew my father loved both her and my mother and that he wasn't going to disregard either of them. He loved two women, but he could only be married to one. Still, he never denied Mother or me anything.'

'How extraordinary.'

'Yes, it is.' O'Mara smiled. 'The amusing thing is my mother and Esther are best of friends, despite their differing roles. Aunt Esther is often at the fireside in my mother's kitchen, drinking tea. Esther gave my father four sons, and I was treated equally to them in every way. I played in their nursery. I sat with them in the schoolroom and their tutor taught me the same as them. My father tells people he has five sons, not four.'

'And you never once felt it unfair?'

'No, never. I had a happy childhood. I've a loving grandfather, mother, father, and brothers. Even Aunt Esther loves me, and she didn't have to.'

'They must all be very—'

'Mad?' he teased.

Anna laughed. 'No, I wasn't going to say that.'

'Maybe madness is a key to it.' He chuckled. 'It was a success because of my mother. You see, she didn't want anything but my father's love and me. Esther didn't feel she was a threat to her happiness, because my mother didn't want the grand house. She didn't want the social life or the fancy clothes. She didn't want any of that. She was content living with grandfather and me in the gatekeeper's lodge at the bottom of the drive. She was content to see my father when he'd the time to come to her. She asked for no more, and that is why we all were very happy.'

'Then why did you leave?'

O'Mara paused, snapping off another blade of grass. 'I wanted to see the world, and not from a gentleman's carriage. I wanted to see if I could make it on my own, without my father's money.' O'Mara looked keenly at Anna. 'I think I made the right choice.'

'So, you're not the beggar man we all thought you were?' Her tone was sharp.

'Yes, I was. My father has always put money into a London bank for my allowance. I've never used it. In fact, I give most of it away to charities.'

Anna raised an eyebrow and tilted her head, ready to argue with him. 'Even so, it's there should you need it. Tell me, did you really sell my jewellery, or did you just take the money from your bank account?'

'Hey, that's not fair.' He turned to face her. 'I sold that jewellery just as I said I would. True, it was to someone I know, a family friend of my father's, but it was sold all the same. I wouldn't lie about something like that.' He shook his head. 'Come Anna, when will you realize I'll never do anything to hurt you? I will not lie to you, and I will not cheat you. Why do you think I would? You mean too much to me.'

Something in the way he beseeched her tugged at her heart. He had given her his total honesty and so much more. She held it all in the palms of her hands, and it terrified her.

She stood. Why did things have to change? It had been so sweet to sit with him, listen to his voice, and learn about him. However, it always ended with her feeling he asked for something she couldn't give him. Since the night of Clare's birth, they had spent little time together. Purposely, she wanted to distance herself from O'Mara and the emotions he stirred in her. She wasn't ready to openly acknowledge any feelings regarding him yet, perhaps she never would.

'How I hate it when you frown,' O'Mara muttered, rising.

'I will frown when I like and as much as I like, Mr. O'Mara,' Anna snapped.

'Oh, for God's sake, don't get all heated on me. I've never known someone who can become angry in a blink of an eye.'

'I don't.' She turned to go.

Catching her arm, O'Mara stopped her. 'Don't go yet, Anna. I hardly get the chance to talk to you lately.'

'I have to get back to Clare.'

'I enjoyed sitting here talking to you.' O'Mara stepped nearer, closing the distance between them. 'Why do you push me away? Do you still not trust me?'

Anna looked away and stared at the gathering clouds over his shoulder. She did trust him. That wasn't the problem. *She* was the problem. Matt had badly hurt her with his lies. He had loved her, she knew, but he also lied. O'Mara wouldn't do that to her, but she did it to him—everyday. She let him think she was a widow. She just accused him of not being what he said he was, and yet she'd been living a lie ever since leaving York.

'I've to go,' Anna murmured, her conscience weighing heavily on her.

'Call me Brenton.'

'P-pardon?'

'Say it. Say my name.' He pulled her closer. 'I'm not Mr. O'Mara. I'm Brenton. Say it, please.'

She swallowed. His gaze kept her mesmerized. She felt herself leaning towards him.

'Anna—' With his fingertips, Brenton lifted her chin. Slowly, agonizingly, he lowered his face until his lips merely brushed her eyes.

Like a gentle mist, he kissed her face. Her skin blushed and tingled. He trailed his lips over hers until she arched against him. Swiftly, he drew her close, crushing her against his body, his mouth hot and urgent. She clung to his shoulders, wanting more of him. It had been so long since she'd been held, kissed.

Brenton raised his head, and his gaze roamed over her face. A cheeky smile lifted the corners of his mouth. 'I've wanted to do that since the first moment I saw you, and even then, you were frowning.'

She blinked, trying to clear his spell, but when he lowered his head once more, she welcomed it. The tip of his tongue traced the outline of her lips. Gently he nibbled her bottom lip. Anna strained, wanting him to pull her close but this time he kept her apart from him, all that touched were their lips and his hands on her arms. It frustrated her.

'Say my name,' he whispered against her mouth. His tongue darted between her lips like a bird in a cuckoo clock.

Anna shook her head to clear it from his hypnotic effect. His kisses had been sent straight from heaven. She'd wanted them to go on and never stop, but to what end? He deserved the truth from her, and how would he feel then, when he knew the truth?

'No, I—I cannot do this.' Grabbing her skirts, she raised them high and ran off down the hill as though the very devil was chasing her.

Chapter 18

Maisie tutted as a knock sounded on the front door. Rain battered against the windows and the wind blew down the chimney. She returned to the warm kitchen to tell Anna she had a male visitor.

'A visitor at this time of the night?' Anna rose from the table where she had been discussing crop rotation with Brenton.

'Is it a neighbour, Maisie?' Brenton asked, concern etching his features.

'It if had been a neighbour I would've said, now wouldn't I?' Maisie gave him a look that spoke of his folly.

For some strange reason, Anna asked Brenton if he wouldn't mind coming with her to greet the man.

The little fellow, seated on a chair by the fire, jerked to his feet as Anna and Brenton entered the parlour. He looked nervous as he shook hands with Brenton and bowed to Anna. 'I'm most sorry to disturb you at such lateness of the day. I do sincerely apologize.'

'Please be seated, Mr...' Anna responded with a small smile, eyeing the man's open satchel and the paperwork spilling out of it.

The fellow had been about to sit down when he instantly jumped up again and bowed and apologized. 'Do forgive me. My name is Pinkerton, Mr. John

Pinkerton. I'm the temporary new local registrar for this parish. My predecessor, Mr. Perkins, unfortunately passed away last month. I was just appointed two weeks ago as his replacement, for the time being.'

His words washed over Anna. She'd not heard any of it after he said 'registrar.' She didn't need him sitting here in her home to remind her she'd not registered Clare. Indeed, it was something she always pushed to the back of her mind and hoped it would go away. The fact that Clare was illegitimate was something Anna didn't want to be made public, especially since Brenton still didn't know.

She poked at the small fire in the grate. She knew the Act of Parliament, passed in the eighteen thirties, made the registration of all births, deaths, and marriages compulsory. Fear of being sent to gaol gripped her.

'I can't begin to describe to you the state in which the parish registrations of births and deaths have been left in,' Pinkerton continued. 'I must confess that most of the paperwork there is quite beyond my capabilities.' He leaned over as if to impart a most damaging secret. 'It has come to my attention that my predecessor remained in a constant state of drunkenness. Consequently, all is not in order.'

A tap came at the door, and Maisie entered carrying a tea tray. After she left, the diminutive man shuffled some papers around in his satchel, looking for a particular sheet.

* * *

As Anna poured the tea, Brenton noticed how her normally steady hands shook, spilling the tea a little.

'Now, Mrs. Thornton,' Pinkerton said, accepting his cup and saucer. 'In conjunction with the good doctor's records, there it seems to me that a mistake has occurred, for I've no information on record of regarding the birth of your daughter.' He smiled before he added, 'She has, of course, been registered?'

Anna's cup rattled on her saucer.

Brenton frowned as her cheeks flushed. He sensed her turmoil and thinking quickly, stood and faced the man. 'Why, of course she has. Is it our fault your predecessor was incompetent?'

Pinkerton paled under in the face of Brenton's anger.

Anna gestured to him. 'Please, sit down. It's not Mr. Pinkerton's fault. Forgive us, Mr. Pinkerton.' She smiled her most winsome smile, and Brenton saw the poor man had no chance under the influence of such beauty.

Clumsily taking out a small bottle of ink and his pen, Pinkerton began to write on the necessary papers. 'If I'm nuisance, Madam, forgive me, but you see, I must do my job. I will need all the relevant details again to have the paperwork up to date.' The man shifted uneasily in his seat and shot a quick glance from under his lashes at Brenton.

'Very well,' Anna agreed. 'My daughter was born on the twenty-sixth of February, this the year of eighteen sixty-five. There were witnesses present. Do you wish for me to ask them to come in?'

'No, Madam, not at all. Your word, as a respectable lady, is enough. I will get their signatures or marks later.' He smiled. 'Now, your full name, if you please.'

Anna swallowed. Her eyes seemed to beg for Brenton's forgiveness. 'Anna Claire Thornton, Miss.'

Her words had Pinkerton dropping his pen and Brenton staring at her as if she were mad.

'Did you say Miss?' Pinkerton asked, swallowing hard.

Anna squared her shoulders. 'Yes, I did, Mr. Pinkerton. My daughter is illegitimate.'

Brenton felt her pain and suddenly was relieved— relieved that no man had married the woman he loved before him.

'And the father's name?' Pinkerton didn't look up from his papers.

'I'm her father,' Brenton spoke strong and clear. 'Brenton Avery O'Mara, from Avery Hall, County Clare, Ireland.'

Anna and Brenton sat in silence for some time after Pinkerton had gone. The only sound was the shifting of the logs in the fire.

Brenton sat with his head hanging low, his hands dangling between his knees. 'I'd not have thought any less of you if you had told me the truth.'

Anna stared into the glowing embers. 'I'm sorry.'

'Why didn't you tell me?' he asked. 'Do the others know?'

'Does it matter?' Anna looked away from his pain-filled gaze.

'I thought we...' Brenton sighed. 'I told you all about me.'

307

'I'm sorry, but please believe me when I say that I was going to tell you, really I was. I was simply waiting for the right time.' She hesitated, wanting to reach out to him, but shame held her back. 'Thank you for what you did, giving Clare your name. You didn't have to. I was going to give the father's name. I suppose I should have done so.'

'Do you've intentions of seeking out the father one day?'

'No.'

'Who is he?'

'A man with whom I fell in love. A man who, although he loved me too, still lied to me.' She stood and walked to the hearth, watching the flames leap around the wood, remembering her time with Matt. Sometimes, it seemed as though Matt was just a figment of her imagination and had never really existed. She felt so far removed from those months she spent with him. It was like another lifetime ago. Did she really used to spend her days as a carefree spirit, dreaming her dreams? When she met Matt, she'd never cleaned a dirty and neglected house, washed her own clothes, made her own bed, or worried whether she would have enough money to put food on the table. How easily life could change.

Anna heard Brenton rise from his seat and come to stand behind her. She trembled in anticipation of his touching her. She desperately wanted and needed him to do it. The tension was palpable between them, and she had caused it.

'Do you still love him?' he whispered from behind.

'No, not anymore. I did, very much so, at the time,' she answered truthfully. 'You see, it was all extremely exciting and secretive. I was in love with life and love itself, and he was the first man to make me feel alive in the way I had been wishing for.'

'So, what changed?' Brenton was very still.

'He had commitments elsewhere. He decided to go away abroad for two years, and he also had his brother's wife to care for—and the son she gave him.' Although she no longer loved Matt, his betrayal still held the power to cause her a little pain, for she'd trusted him completely. Now that she'd borne his child, she would always have a link with him.

Brenton put his hands on her shoulders and turned her to face him. For a moment, he gazed deeply into her eyes. 'Is he the reason you left your home?'

'Not directly, the main reason was my mother.' She took a deep breath to quell her quivering at his touch. 'We—we didn't get along, and she wanted me out of the house once she knew I carried a child. At the same time, she told me Papa was not really my father. It was exceedingly difficult. So much happened at once, and I needed to get away.'

'Maisie always changes the subject when I ask her questions about you and your husband.' Brenton smiled ruefully. 'Now I know why.'

'I owe Maisie more than I can ever repay her. Maisie kept me alive when all I wanted to do was die from heartache.'

Brenton took her hand and kissed her palm. 'You have a new life now with people who care for you, love you, and want to protect you.'

'I know—' Anna closed her eyes as he touched his lips to her wrist. Shivers of acute sensation tingled along her skin.

Inflamed desire made her catch her breath as he drew her close. He rubbed his thumb over her bottom lip. His simple act demanded a release of pent-up emotion. She sighed in longing as his hands pulled her tight against him. The scent of wood and lavender soap clung to his clothes and when he nibbled her ear, she leaned closer still. The barrier of clothes between them irritated her. She wanted to feel his hands on her skin, to hear his endearments meant only for her.

When finally they pulled apart, breathing fast yet yearning for more, Brenton leaned his forehead against hers. 'Do you think you could take the risk and fall in love again, *acushla*?' he asked, not taking his gaze from hers.

Anna smiled, acknowledging that her life would be greater with him in it. 'Yes, I think I could.'

* * *

'So, Papa, what do you think of my *farm*?' Anna teased.

She and Thomas had just walked the entire boundary of the farm. The brilliant sunshine hurt their eyes. It was a most glorious day, birds sang, and bees hummed. In the fields they heard the bellow of a cow calling her calf. From a distance, the enormous vegetable garden, with its long uniform straight rows, looked impressive. At the top of the hill near the wood, Anna slowly turned about and surveyed her domain as she'd done many times before, and always experienced the same pleasure from the view.

Giving her a wink, Thomas laughed. 'You don't need me to tell you that your farm is inspiring, my dear.'

Anna slipped her hand over his arm and grinned. 'Yes, but it's good to hear it from you, Papa.'

They strolled back to the house, listening to the high-pitched laughter coming from Miss Foster and Maggie as they played with Sophie and Clare on a rug under the trees in the orchard. It was the middle of July, and her guests had been at the farm for a week. After Louise's funeral, Maggie caught a bad cold and was in bed for nearly two weeks delaying their arrival. Now, though, as Anna and Thomas neared the little group on the rug, Maggie showed no sign of her recent illness, despite the black mourning she wore, and which never flattered the wearer. Her sister glowed with happiness at their reunion and had totally fallen in love with her new niece and everyone at the farm. Last night she spoke of never wanting to leave.

Anna was unprepared to see the change in Maggie. Her little sister had grown, not only in height, but also in maturity. That Miss Foster held an influence over her was evident, but thankfully, so far, it was all for the best. The two were inseparable, but then that was to be expected. After Anna left, Maggie would've had only Miss Foster to turn to for company and love.

'Anna. Papa. Come look at Clare grab after the insects,' Maggie called to them as they approached. 'Is she not the cleverest baby?'

Thomas leaned close to Anna. 'It has done Maggie a world of good coming here.'

She squeezed his hand gently. 'It has done me a great deal of good too, Papa.'

'I'm happy you're content. Until your letter arrived, I worried day and night while you were gone.'

'I regret I made you suffer.'

'I know.' Thomas nodded. 'As I know why you went.'

'Never think it was because I found out about my parentage. It changes nothing.' Anna kissed her father's cheek.

'I'm glad to hear it, my dear, for to me you're my daughter. You were never his.'

Anna paused, wondering whether she should say what was on her mind. 'Has—Has anything been mentioned of Matt by the Conway's?'

Thomas reached out to touch her cheek. 'Matt hasn't come back to England as far as I know. Have you heard from him at all?'

'No. We have nothing to say to each other. It is all at an end. My life is good, Papa. Matt had his chance and threw it away. He doesn't deserve my love when others may want it more. I pity him, for he has lost far more than I have.'

'Yes, only look ahead, never back.'

They turned at the sound of a pan being banged with a ladle, Agnes's way of announcing mealtime. Scooping up the babies, pillows and rugs, they walked through the trees laden with young fruit.

'Has Henry's tray been taken up?' Anna asked as they entered the kitchen.

'No, not yet, Mrs. Anna. I've got it set, though.' Agnes gave Maisie two plates full of food to take into the dining room. 'He's tried to leave his bed again, but this recent bout of illness has weakened him too much.'

'Maggie, will you put Clare to bed for me?' Anna asked. 'She has fallen asleep.' She gave the baby to Maggie and picked up the tray from the table. 'I will take Henry's tray up.'

Upstairs, Anna backed through Henry's door as she balanced the heavy tray.

'Nay, lass, I'll not eat all that,' Henry argued from the bed, eyeing the amount of food she carried.

'Well, you must,' she warned him and pretended to be stern. 'Otherwise you'll have Agnes to deal with, and that I'd not recommend.'

A racking cough shook Henry's body. When he finished, Anna helped him take a sip of tea. She worried about Henry and so did the doctor, who expressed his concern when he explained Henry's age was against him and the severity of his last attack had left him frail.

'I'm all right now, lass,' he gasped, short of breath.

'I will close this window,' she said, moving to the window that had been opened earlier that morning to let in fresh air.

'Sit here a minute, lass.' He patted the bed. 'I want to talk to you.'

'It can wait until you've eaten.'

'No, it can't.' He waited until she seated herself beside him before beginning. 'I've told the others and now, I'm tellin' you. I've made me Will, and your good father himself has written it out for me. He said he will take it with him to his own solicitors, so it's all done proper like,' Henry told her with a nod of his head.

Taking a deep breath, he continued, 'The important bit's this, I've left me farm and everythin' else I've got, to Brenton. I've no kin of me own, and he's been like a son to me, so it's all his. It's not grand, I know that, but he can make somethin' of it, and I've told him he can make a start on it now if he wishes. It's wastin' away over there, and I hate to think of it like that.' Henry paused to get his breath, his gaze not leaving her face.

Anna smiled with difficulty. The news that Brenton had been offered a farm of his own jolted her. It gave him a reason to go. Her heart thumped erratically against her ribs, and her mind went numb at the thought of his leaving. Henry was waiting for some comment, but she couldn't find her tongue. She stood and straightened the bed covers.

Henry frowned. 'What you think then?'

'Well, Henry, that is most generous of you, but surely it's all a bit premature? Who is to say you'll not be back there quite soon yourself?'

'Nay, I doubt it, lass.'

'Eat your meal before it grows cold,' she said and left him.

Downstairs, Anna sat with the others in the dining room and picked at her meal. For the first time the delicious food Agnes put before her went unnoticed. Brenton sat at the far end of the table, close to her father. The two men talked of farming and politics, amongst other things. It gave Anna a secret thrill that they got on so well. She watched Brenton as he spoke, and her stomach flipped as her gaze rested on his tanned face. He was handsome in a rugged sense. He held himself well—tall and straight. The strong muscles of his body tightened his clothes about him when he moved. His cheeky grin and flashing eyes always made her heart miss a beat. Would he leave her and go his own way? Sell Henry's farm and return to Ireland to pick up his old life once more? The thoughts flew around her mind, making her sick to her stomach.

As though he knew she watched him, Brenton slowly turned his head towards her and winked. Blushing at being caught out, Anna lowered her eyes and played with the food on her plate. When she raised her head again, she saw Miss Foster looking out of the corner of her eye at Brenton. Anna observed her for a time. It became obvious that Miss Foster was not listening to Maggie's chatter, but instead paid attention to everything Brenton said and did.

'Miss Foster, have you travelled at all?' Anna asked, a little louder than necessary.

Startled, Miss Foster blinked a few times and then shook her head. 'I'm afraid not, Miss Thornton. However, I'd dearly like to one day.'

'Maybe after you've finished your post as Maggie's governess, you'll be able to do so.'

Anna successfully prevented Miss Foster from studying Brenton again by asking her a barrage of questions about herself and then made a mental note to watch Miss Foster from now on. The woman was here as Maggie's companion, not to catch herself a husband.

In the afternoon, Anna took clean bed sheets across to Brenton and Ned's quarters above the barn. Entering the dim interior, she nearly bumped into Brenton coming out of the tack room.

'Hey there, do you want me to take them up?' he asked.

'No, I can manage.' The rhythm of her heart changed as she glanced at him.

'Have you spoken to Henry today?' he inquired in a quiet voice.

'Yes, when I took his tray up to him.' She fiddled with the sheets in her arms, avoiding his gaze. Her insides twisted at the thought of him leaving. He had no reason to remain here, now a farm awaited him, and she refused to beg him to stay. She'd left herself open again to pain. *I must have been mad*! It had cost her so much before that she could not do it for a second time. She had to build up the walls around her heart again. Fear of being rejected made her tone sharp. 'He told me about his will. I'm incredibly happy for you.'

'Are you?'

She lifted her head and met his eyes. 'Yes, I am. You must be pleased also. It's not an everyday thing to be left a farm.'

'I don't need it. I already have property in Ireland given to me by my father.'

'Henry does not know that though, does he?' She answered tartly. 'He thinks you're penniless.'

'He does know. I told him. I'd not lie to him.' His gaze held hers. 'Only you and he know about my family, about me.'

'Is it meant to be a secret?'

Brenton shook his head. 'No. I will tell the others in time, including your father.' He took a step closer to her. 'Anna—'

She stepped away frightened by the power of her own attraction to him and the risk of losing him. 'What are you going to do about the farm?'

'I haven't thought about it.'

'You should. It upsets Henry to think of the place going to ruin while he lies in bed unable to do anything.'

'I don't have the time to keep both places going. Ned and I've enough to do here.' He frowned. 'Why are you distancing yourself from me again?'

Anna forced herself to remain rigid, her face tight with control. 'Henry gave the farm to you. You should put that responsibility first. I can employ someone else to fill your place here.' The moment she spoke the words she regretted them, even more so when she saw the surprise in Brenton's eyes. She'd wounded him and ultimately herself, and she didn't know why.

No, she did know. She was scared he'd leave her, and so she was pushing him away first.

'Well, that certainly put me in my place. Thank you, Anna, for being honest.' Brenton strode away.

'Wait,' she called after him, following him outside.

He spun on his heel and faced her, the muscle along his jaw beating a rapid tattoo.

'I didn't mean what I said to sound unkind.' She reached out to touch him but snatched her hand back. 'I meant—'

'What you meant was I can pack my things and take Henry's few pigs and go.'

'No. You're wrong.'

'You might not have said it, Anna, but you meant exactly that.' He stood solid and unmoving, fixing her with a steel-hard glare.

'Don't speak for *me*.' Her temper rose. 'And don't raise your voice to me.'

'Raise my voice?' Brenton laughed harshly. 'The only thing I want to raise to you is my belt. No doubt you were spared too much of it as a child, a good thrashing is what you need.'

'How dare you!'

'Oh, I dare, Madam, I dare.' He took a step closer. 'I've bent over backwards to help you, and all you do is throw it back in my face.'

'Well, if I do, it's because you'll not leave me alone.' She stuck her chin out at him in full roar. 'Every minute of the day I see you, I hear you. I can't think with you around me. I can find no peace with you *here*.'

'Fine.' Brenton swung away, but quickly turned back for a parting shot. 'Find yourself another fool. I quit.'

'For pity's sake.' Thomas stood in amazement at the scullery door surrounded by the rest of the household. 'Anna. Brenton. What is going on?'

The air was thick with tension. Anna and Brenton went their separate ways without saying another word to each other, and it was left to Maisie and Emma to reassure a worried Thomas that arguments between the two were common.

In the kitchen, Agnes chuckled as she rubbed salt into a leg of pork. Standing at the table with the window open, she'd heard them arguing and grinned. Never had she known two people more right for each other.

* * *

Anna watched the sun go down from her bedroom window as she nursed Clare. While her daughter fed quietly, Anna relaxed slightly for the first time since Henry told her about his Will. She could not bear the strain downstairs. Everyone was edgy and nervous, waiting for the next round between her and Brenton to start.

After a slight tap on the door, Maisie opened it and popped her head in. 'All right?' she asked, coming into the room.

'Yes.'

Maisie sat on the bed. 'They're ready to eat. Are you comin' down?'

'In a little while, when Clare is asleep. Tell them to begin without me.'

'Brenton's gone to Henry's place.'

Anna remained silent and waited for Maisie to say more, which she knew she would.

Maisie crossed the room to stand at the window. Together they watched the golden globe of the sun as it slid into the horizon.

'Don't let him go, Anna.'

'He is a grown man, Maisie. He can do as he pleases.'

'We need him. Where'd we be without him?'

'Yes, I know all that. Of course, we need him, but I will not ask him to stay.' Anna moved away to lay Clare on the bed. 'He has been given a place of his own, his own farm to do with as he wishes. I've no right to ask him to ignore that and stay here to work for me.'

Maisie crossed to her. 'He'd stay if you asked,' she pleaded. 'Summat could be worked out so both farms were looked after. Brenton doesn't want to go, I'm sure of it. Please Anna, ask him to stay.'

'No, Maisie, I will not. It's not fair to make him decide between the two.' Anna turned her back to Maisie and began to change Clare's soiled cloth. Hopefully, Maisie would not ask any more questions. She didn't have to be reminded what they were losing. She knew that already.

Chapter 19

The slight drizzle of rain the following morning matched the spirits of the whole house. At breakfast, Thomas studied Anna over the rim of his newspaper. He didn't like the shadows under her eyes nor the way she played with her food. Obviously, something troubled her. He turned his attention to Emma as she came into the dining room carrying a plate of bacon that she put in the middle of the table. She too looked tired and, as the faint sound of Sophie's cries drifted down from the rooms above, he saw her eyes close in weariness.

Anna looked up. 'Did you've a bad night with her again, Emma?'

Emma sighed and pushed a stray strand of hair behind her ear. 'Yes, she is having enormous trouble with her teeth. I'm at my wits' end.' She tried to smile, but her eyes filled with tears and she quickly left the room.

Folding his paper, Thomas stood. 'Well, ladies, what I think is needed here is a shopping trip,' he suggested. 'Anna, go up and change and tell Emma to as well. I'm taking you all to Halifax, and you shall have a full day of shopping, my treat. You too, Maggie, and you, Miss Foster.' Thomas straightened his jacket. 'I shall inform Watson to get the carriage out. He has done nothing since we arrived other than eat Agnes's fine cooking. He needs some exercise.'

'But Papa—'

'There are no buts about it. Ahh…Maisie.' He smiled as she came into the room. 'Would you mind taking care of my granddaughter today, and little Sophie? I think their mothers need a rest from them.' Thomas rejoiced in taking control of a situation.

Agnes and Maisie were only too happy to have the babies to themselves for the entire day. Watson quickly whisked a polishing rag over the carriage, while the women readied themselves. Grinning, Thomas even wiped his own boots for the first time in his life.

Within the hour, they were away and travelling at a good speed towards Halifax. Anna relaxed and forgot about the demands of the farm and even tried to forget the fact that Brenton failed to return this morning. How would she cope, having him living down the road but as untouchable as if he'd gone back to Ireland? The situation was unbearable.

She watched the exhaustion slowly leave Emma's body the further away from the farm they travelled. Miss Foster, on the other hand, looked downright miserable, and she could see her father still keenly felt the ravages of grief over her mother's death. What a drab, sober party they made. Only Maggie chatted happily unaware of the dejection in the carriage.

The busy centre of Halifax soon swallowed them as they made their way towards the main shopping areas. After alighting from the carriage, Thomas led the way to the nearest dressmaker's shop. He waited on a plush yellow velvet chair and was given a cup of tea as the women chose materials and colours and were each individually measured. The middle-aged spinster who owned the shop was very proficient. She not only catered to the local ladies for dressmaking, but also ran a small millinery above the shop. Upstairs, the women spent another hour selecting the right hat for each of their dresses.

Afterwards, they made their way along the street to a shoe shop to complete their outfits. Anna cared little that as a family in mourning they should not be shopping for such frivolous things, but in her opinion, there were times when respectability needed a shove in the pants.

Long after the church bells chimed midday, they found a small eatery to rest in and recoup their spent energy. After a light meal was consumed, and many refreshing cups of tea drunk, Thomas rose to leave.

'Now ladies, if you'll excuse me. I've some business to attend and will meet you where Watson dropped us off at…say…three o'clock?'

Anna nodded. 'Very well, Papa.'

The women walked through the busy streets, gazing at goods on display in the shop's windows and sometimes entering to purchase something that took their fancy. They stopped to watch a busker play the accordion, and before strolling away, they threw some pennies in his hat on the ground.

As they passed the entrance to a hotel, three gentlemen stumbled out and bumped into Emma and Anna. Laughing and apologizing and evidently drunk, the men bowed and tipped their hats, making a spectacle of themselves.

With a raised eyebrow of annoyance and a stiff nod, Anna went to pass when she saw the horrified expression on Emma's face. Her stricken look of utter anguish made Anna grasp her arms. 'Emma? What is it?'

The tallest of the men stopped and stared in bewilderment at Emma. Then, slowly, his expression changed with recognition. 'My, my, my. Why, if it isn't little Emma. I didn't recognize you at first, so different you are,' he smirked. 'Tell me, how is it that you're now dressed as a lady?' His insult held laughter. His eyes seemed to undress Emma slowly as she stood there, shaking from fright.

'And just who are you, may I ask?' Anna's cutting tone hung in the strained atmosphere.

'Clive Atkins.' The tall man straightened to his full height to intimidate Anna. Contempt flashed across his face.

Her temper rose. 'Well, Mr. Atkins, you'll apologize to my friend for your insolent remarks and beg her forgiveness.'

'I never beg anyone, Madam. Especially not to a former servant, or…was it former whore…of my father's?'

At his words, Emma fainted. There was a sudden rush as Anna, Maggie, Miss Foster and even the two men accompanying Atkins went to Emma's aid.

'How dare you? You despicable fiend,' Anna cried, holding Emma in her arms.

Atkins nodded to the other two men and, with a last look at Emma, turned on his heel and walked away.

The journey home was a silent affair, subdued by the incident. Anna informed Thomas of what had taken place as soon as he joined them. Fury at the man's disrespect darkened his face.

Emma didn't speak. She sat beside Anna, gazing out over the countryside as the carriage trundled over the dusty roads.

Once they arrived home, Emma raced upstairs to Sophie. For the next hour, she sat cradling her daughter and crying silent tears.

'I think you should take a tray up to her, Maisie,' Agnes said, slicing a loaf of bread. 'She's frail enough without missin' meals.'

'I will take it, Agnes,' Anna volunteered, coming into the kitchen. 'Papa is playing with Clare.'

Picking up the tray, Anna turned to see Brenton and Ned washing their hands in the scullery. *He came back.*

Brenton lifted his head, and together they drank in the sight of each other. Anna's stomach tingled and her heart beat faster than usual. As Brenton smiled an apology at her, she thought her knees would buckle from under her. Gone was the animosity between them as though it never existed. She nodded in a silent understanding. She was tired of battling against her feelings concerning him. It was time to let fate take its course and perhaps take that leap of faith.

Conscious of the heavy tray in her hands, Anna reluctantly moved on, but one thing was clear in her mind at last. She could no longer deny her feelings for better or worse.

Anna entered Emma's room and saw her sitting quietly on the bed, watching Sophie play on the floor.

She placed the tray on a small table and sat beside her. 'Do you want to talk about it?'

Emma's gaze, full of suffering, rested on Anna. 'That man, he is Marcus's son.'

'I see.'

'He had been living in America for many years, and I met him for the first time when he came home for Christmas two years ago. Marcus didn't like his son, he told me so, but nevertheless he was welcomed when he arrived that Christmas Eve.' Emma gave a small shudder. 'I tried to like Clive, but he isn't a nice person, and nothing at all like his father. Throughout Christmas, he caused problems and was demanding. He drank too much and argued with Marcus. He went out until late at night and slept all day, which was difficult for all of us. The cook never knew how much food would be needed, and Sue, the daily, was terrified of going anywhere near his room.'

Emma rose from the bed and stood by Sophie. 'Marcus was very ill. He had been for some time, and after Christmas, the doctor confined him to his bed. When alone, I started to feel uncomfortable in Clive's presence, and he seemed to enjoy it.' Emma's voice lowered to a murmur. 'For the New Year celebrations, Clive held a large party that lasted two days. It caused a terrible argument. Marcus told him to leave by the end of the week, explaining that I had enough to see to with the running of the house and him being ill without having to attend to Clive and his friends.'

As Emma stroked Sophie's wispy hair, Anna could see her hands shaking. 'Anyway, from then on Clive sought me out at every opportunity. I think he enjoyed my fear of him.'

'You don't have to tell me, Emma, if it upsets you so,' Anna assured her.

'I think I've got to tell someone, Anna. Maybe then, I will be able to put it all behind me. You see, it was such a shock seeing him again today. I honestly thought I never would again. I imagined he'd gone back to America.'

Emma picked up a soft bristled brush and ran it over Sophie's blonde curls. 'Marcus died a few days after their argument, on the tenth of January. A week later, after the funeral, Clive ordered for the house to be packed up. He was to sell it and everything in it. He told me he'd no money, and Marcus had only left him the house and furniture in the will. Clive was disappointed his father didn't have the fortune he believed he owned. He got drunk every night.' Emma came and sat on the bed again. Her voice shook and her pale face highlighted the shadows under her eyes.

Anna took her cold hands between her own, trying to rub some warmth into them.

'Clive came into my room one night and stood at the end of my bed,' Emma continued. 'He just stared at me with such a terrible look on his face. I told him to leave, but he just laughed. Then, he slowly took off his clothes. I couldn't scream. I tried to, but nothing came out.' Emma looked at Anna, her face full of shame and pain. 'He...You can imagine what happened.'

'I'm deeply sorry.' Anna held Emma to her. Sophie crawled up to them and pulled on their skirts.

Bending down, Emma picked her up and cradled her tightly.

'I thank the heavens above that she bears no resemblance to him. I don't think I could have stood it if she had.'

'How did you get away from him?' asked Anna.

'The next day, I packed all my belongings and simply walked away. I walked away from the house that had been my home for years, and I walked away without any references.'

'Oh, Emma.'

'I worked all sorts of jobs. Eventually, I realized I was pregnant. Not long after, I was robbed of everything, and I simply lost the will to live. I didn't care about myself or whether I lived or died.'

'Then we found you.' Anna smiled tenderly.

'Yes, you found me. You and Maisie saved me and my daughter.'

* * *

Birds flew overhead in their journey south to warmer climates and Thomas, Maggie, and Miss Foster packed and returned home. It saddened Anna to see them go. However, a letter from Tom and his pregnant wife, announcing they would visit her this coming Christmas, filled her with happiness. They had been on a honeymoon tour of Europe. She missed Tom dreadfully and wanted to make friends with her new sister-in-law.

September brought the end of the harvesting. The last of the summer vegetables and fruits were stored, pickled, or made into jam to be eaten in the winter

months. The excess was sold in Halifax. Animals
born throughout the spring and summer were weaned
and sold at market, leaving the farm bereft of their
particular noises. A quiet stillness settled over the
land. Animals, both wild and tame, prepared
themselves for the long frosty winter ahead.

Brenton divided his time between Henry's farm
and Anna's. He knew Ned couldn't do all the work by
himself. Together, he and Ned did the work of ten
men. Sometimes, even after dark, they would still be
at their tasks by the light of a lantern. They came into
the house only for their meals and then left again,
spending whole days logging trees and chopping
wood in readiness for the large fires needed in the
house during winter. Anna watched as they checked
and repaired the roofs of all the outbuildings and the
houses on the two farms before the winter gales,
snow, and blizzards descended. The list of jobs to do
before the onset of harsh weather was upon them was
never ending.

Inside the house, the women worked to put it back
in order after the departure of their visitors and the
lazy days of summer. Winter clothes and boots were
brought out and cleaned and polished, chimney
sweeps employed and the last summer blooms picked.

Anna only managed to speak to Brenton briefly
once a day about the necessities of the farm, and that
always took place in the kitchen, in front of the
others. Her heart struggled against her logical mind,
which argued for caution, but the less she saw of him,
the more she thought of him. It amazed her how much
she ached to be with him. Soon, she started to make
excuses to seek him out. Even so, when they were in

each other's company, his eyes told her things that his lips never uttered, and it made her doubt not only herself but him as well.

In the study one morning, Anna bit into a crisp red apple and tutted as the juice ran down her chin. Crunching loudly, she moved aside the curtains and through the open window she sniffed at the cool autumn breeze like a dog chasing a scent. The days were changing—the cycle of life was entering another phase.

Brenton strolled by whistling and she instinctively waved to him. Her heart constricted at his smile. She watched him until he rounded the house. He had made no advance to her in weeks, and she faltered at the thought he might not want her any longer.

Anna abandoned the apple as an ache spread in her chest. Gathering up her skirts, she rushed from the study into the kitchen. The time had come to finish with uncertainties. She would make him discuss the future with her.

She loved him and she had to make him see that she did. He had to believe her.

Maisie came in through the back door with a basket filled with berries tucked under her arm. 'These are the last of the berries.'

'Another summer finished.' Emma smiled, coming into the kitchen with Henry's tray.

Glancing out the opened back door, she viewed the empty yard. Brenton had gone. Anna frowned and turned to Emma. 'Is Henry's cough better? He had a dreadful night.'

Emma sighed. 'The honey and lemon in his tea helped, but he's still not good.'

The four women were quiet at this. Henry was old and frail. Who knew how long he would be with them?

'I think I will go and pick some of the last roses. Henry loves the roses.' Anna picked up Maisie's now empty basket, she went into the scullery to find her garden scissors, gloves, and straw hat. Letting herself out the front door, she strolled down to the flowerbeds. The garden was a source of delight to her. In spring and summer, the large beds were a riot of colour, and for many weeks the house smelt of their fragrances. Putting down the basket, she set to work.

Happily cutting away at dead flowers and selecting fragrant buds for inside, Anna, at first, did not hear the carriage wheels as they slowly rumbled up the drive. Straightening, she took off her gloves and tilted her hat back a little to gaze at the vehicle.

The carriage came to a stop, its door opened, and a tall man climbed out. The gentleman, which he obviously was by his appearance, adjusted his long black coat and turned towards her. From her position at the bottom of the garden, she could not see his face, but for some reason she felt a strange sensation race throughout her body, rooting her to the spot.

As if hypnotized, she watched him walk toward her. As he closed the distance between them, memories flashed through her mind. That walk, the way he held himself, was so familiar. Her daydreams, her nightmares, they were all here. The past had become the present.

'My God, you are more beautiful than before.'

His words sent the fine hairs on the back of her neck standing on end and a quiver to her stomach. Matt Cowan, the man she had loved and lost, was here, at her home, in her little piece of paradise.

Chapter 20

'How are you, Anna?' he asked in his velvety voice.

He looked the same, only a little older, thinner. There were lines at the corners of his nose that ran down to his mouth and a few smaller lines at the corners of his eyes, probably from squinting in the tropical sun. Grey sprinkled his hair, but he still looked distinguished and extremely handsome, although there was a change in him. Besides the weight loss, his eyes were sunken and seemed haunted. Anna's heart raced even though she felt all colour leave her face.

'Why are you here?' It all she could think of to say.

He gave her a slow smile. 'Would you believe me if I said that I could not keep away? I made a most dreadful mistake, my dove.'

'Do not call me that. I am not your anything, not now.' His sudden arrival confused her. She was not sure if she could deal with this situation. Fifteen months. He'd been out of her life for that length of time. She thought she'd never see him again.

'I am not here to hurt you, Anna. I do not want to cause you any problems. I just wanted to see you. Talk to you. Can I put things right between us?'

Anna bit her lip as she tried to decide what to do. He must not go into the house and meet everyone, yet she did not think he was going to go away quickly either.

'Good God, I don't believe it.' Maisie stood a few feet away from them, but they had been so engrossed in each other that they had not heard her approach.

'Maisie.' Matt smiled. 'It is good to see you again.'

'Shame I can't say the same.' She crossed her arms over her chest. 'How did you find us?'

'I called on Aunt Harriet, and she told me,' Matt answered her before turning back to Anna, who still stood as if she had seen a ghost.

Maisie took a step closer to Anna. 'Are you back in England for long?'

Matt kept his gaze on Anna. 'Yes, I am, at least until I have achieved all I need to do.'

'You should not have come here,' Anna whispered, half afraid. She could not drag her gaze from him.

He reached out to her. 'I desperately wanted to see you.'

'You have no place in my life.' She stepped back.

'And what about my daughter?' His voice held a note of accusation. 'Your daughter is mine, is she not? Thomas confided in Aunt Harriet, and she told me in a letter. I returned immediately on the next ship.'

Anna felt herself sway, and Maisie's arms went around her protectively.

'Leave us be,' Maisie cried.

'Anna, please, I do not want to cause trouble.' Matt looked aggrieved. 'Nevertheless, I do so wish to meet my daughter.'

'She's a baby and knows nothing about you.'
Anna's hands shook and she clasped them together. 'I
do not want you here.'

'I just want to meet her. Then I will go, I promise.'

'I'm gettin' Brenton.' Maisie hurried away; her
whole manner showed her disapproval.

'She does not change, does she?' Matt grinned
ruefully. 'She is still devoted.'

'Some people know what the word means and can
do it easily.'

'I supposed I deserved that, but do not forget, it
was you who sent me away.'

'I was doing what you really wanted.' Anna bent
and picked up the cut roses that were now wilting.
'You wanted me, and you wanted your freedom. I
gave you your freedom because you could not have
both.'

'I know now I made a terrible mistake.' He
stepped closer. 'Will you forgive me?'

'You are too late. I do not need you in my life.'

Anna and Matt stared at each other, all the hurt and
emotions coming back to haunt her. It was all too
cruel. She needed no reminder of their shared past.

'Anna?' Brenton's voice came from far away, but
when she turned, he was standing quite close. 'Are
you all right?' A frown creased his stern features. He
stood solid as an oak tree. His blue eyes had narrowed
to chips of ice.

Gathering her wits, Anna smiled sadly at him.
'Yes, I am fine. The past has come back to visit me,
that is all.' She took a deep breath. 'Brenton, this is
Mr. Matt Cowan. Matt, Brenton O'Mara.'

The two men shook hands stiffly, sizing each other up. After the introductions, Matt asked for a drink. Anna noticed a fine sweat beading on his brow. Obviously, this meeting was affecting him more than he wanted to let on.

Once they were seated in the drawing room, Maisie went off to make a tray of tea, leaving the three of them in silence, each with their own thoughts.

'What's goin' on, lass?' Agnes urged, putting spoonful's of fresh tealeaves in the teapot.

'Matt Cowan's come back, the man Anna wanted to marry,' Maisie whispered, taking the tea service off the dresser.

'Clare's father?' Emma asked, cutting up slices of cake. 'I thought he lived in the wilds of the Amazon?'

'Aye, well, I wish he was back in't Amazon,' Maisie fumed. 'He's caused Anna enough trouble before, and now he's back to do it all again. An' he wants to meet Clare.'

'Brenton will have something to say about that.' Agnes's head nodded vigorously. 'Don't forget, he wasn't in the picture before, but he definitely is now, and he won't stand for any carrying on. I can tell you that now.'

When Maisie carried the tea tray into the drawing room, the tension in the atmosphere was tangible. Matt sat back in his chair and wiped his brow with a handkerchief, his hands shook.

'Could you pour please, Maisie? I shall go and see if Clare is awake,' Anna said, rising from her seat.

'Do you think that is wise?' Brenton said, standing also.

'It has to be done, Brenton, so it might as well be done now.' She swept from the room without a glance at Matt, who had slowly stood when Anna did.

For the next hour, Anna ran the gauntlet of emotions. It was so hard to be in the same room with her ex-lover, holding their child, while the new man in her life watched. The sight of Matt holding Clare twisted Anna's heart until she felt it would stop altogether. For the last couple of months, she'd cocooned herself in an ideal existence where the pain of the past no long lingered. Now, it seemed to be unravelling right before her eyes, sending her spiralling into a pit of despair. She couldn't have Matt in her world again.

'Well, it is getting late, and I have things to do.' Brenton rose and looked at her. It was a sure sign that he wanted Cowan to be gone, and his look conveyed that if Cowan had any manners then he should be on his way.

Matt passed Clare to Anna and pushed himself up off the sofa only to stumble and fall to his knees. Anna and Brenton rushed to him and helped him back onto the sofa. Sweat broke out on his forehead and glistened on his upper lip.

'Matt, are you ill?' Anna used her own handkerchief to wipe his brow.

'I—apologize, Anna, for troubling you.' Matt swayed and slumped forward.

Brenton caught him before he toppled.

Anna hurried to the door and shouted for Maisie, who rushed to take Clare from her. 'And bring some water, Maisie.'

337

Brenton ran his hand over his face. 'He needs to leave.'

'Not in this state.' She quickly undid Matt's collar. 'Let me make you comfortable.'

He reached for her hand. 'I...feel bad, Anna, I...should not have come. Silly of me. I knew...'

'Never mind that now.'

Matt's eyes closed. 'I should not have come.'

Maisie brought a glass of water, but Matt was incapable of holding it. Anna tried to help but more spilt down his shirtfront than went in his mouth.

'He needs a doctor,' Brenton said, rocking back on his heels.

'There...is no point...' Matt managed to say before doubling up and groaning in agony.

Alarmed, Anna dithered for a moment, and then sprang into action. 'Help me get him upstairs, Brenton, then go fetch the doctor.'

Brenton was hesitant to touch him. 'What if he is contagious?'

'He has been in the house for an hour. It is too late now.'

Together they shifted him into an upright position and half dragged, half carried his dead weight upstairs. They took him into the spare room.

Maisie helped make him comfortable. 'He's a burnin' up. Get them clothes off him.'

'I'll go for the doctor.' Brenton left them.

Matt tossed and turned in the bed.

'Hush now. Hush now,' soothed Anna, slipping off his boots.

For a moment, he lay still, and Anna breathed a sigh of relief. Then the next minute, he thrashed about again, nearly knocking her sideways.

'Good grief.' Maisie said, grabbing his arms. 'Summat's turning him inside out.'

Anna straightened, rubbing her forehead in anxiety. 'Whatever it is has struck fast and violently.'

They readied the room to nurse him, knowing whatever ailed him would not be cured overnight. Water and towels, fresh sheets and extra lamps were brought in. Maisie lit a small fire in the grate.

'Shall we make a mustard posset for him?'

'Let us a wait until the doctor comes.'

As the setting sun threw gold and orange over the house, the doctor arrived. He made them wait while he examined Matt.

Anna paced the drawing room alone. Brenton settled the animals down for the night and Maisie and Emma put the babies to bed. The doctor entered with a nod to her as he shrugged on his coat. 'I'll be back in the morning. I have a birth to attend now.'

'What is wrong with him?'

'I believe it to be some form of Malaria. Your friend managed to tell me that he'd suffered it before and that his last attack was just before he sailed. I think he wasn't strong enough for the journey.'

Her hand flew to her mouth. 'Malaria?'

The doctor tapped his hat onto his head. 'I'll return in the morning.'

'You cannot leave.' Anna panicked. 'What shall we do? You are needed here.'

'Madam, I have other patients.' He made his way to the front door. 'Bathe him and try to keep him cool

339

and comfortable. That's all anyone can do. I have given him a dose of quinine, but I feel it is too late. Beneath his clothes that man is all skin and bones.' He opened the door and then turned back. His tone grew grim. 'As this is not the first attack he's had, it'll depend on how his body will cope. Whether he lives or dies is in the hands of a better man than me, but I will do all I can and may be successful.'

Slowly, Anna climbed the stairs, her mind in a whirl.

'Anna—Anna?' Matt's voice came to her, weak and disoriented, breaking into her thoughts.

She entered the bedroom and bent over him. 'I am here, Matt.' She wiped his brow, but he drifted off and said no more.

Day flowed into night as Anna tried to keep Matt alive. She lost track of the time, insulated in his room. She spent her time endlessly pouring liquid into his mouth, washing him, and trying to ease his pain. It became an obsession to see him through this ordeal.

Matt drifted in and out of consciousness, not aware of his surroundings. Bit by bit, he faded, as if his former good health never even existed. Anna talked, pleaded, and begged for him to wake up and take some nourishing beef broth, which she knew would make him better—if he would just wake up.

'Don't you dare come back here to die, Matthew Cowan. That's not fair and you've put me through enough.' Powerless, she became angry and then contrite and then angry again. 'Why did you come back? Why? What we had was finished. I coped without you.'

She dashed tears away and gazed out of the window at the darkness. 'You broke my heart. I love Brenton now.'

The second day of Matt's illness dawned while Anna struggled to turn him over so that she could take away his fouled sheets. Looking down on him, Anna could see the change in his appearance. The disease melted the flesh from his body, leaving the skin pulled tightly across his bones. He looked old with many more lines around his mouth and eyes. His skin was the colour of old parchment. Indeed, he looked like a corpse waiting for burial. It shook her to see this normally strong and handsome man reduced as he was now.

Maisie entered the room after breakfast. 'I'll watch him for a minnit, while you get summat to eat.'

'I am not hungry.'

'You'll get to the table now or I'll not be answerable for me actions.' Maisie stood with arms folded and foot tapping. 'I'm just as capable to nurse him, you know.'

Anna was too tired to argue and after a glance at Matt, she left the room and went to wash her face. Downstairs, as she passed the study, she saw Emma seated at the desk. 'What are you looking at?'

'A map.' Emma looked up. 'It is Mr. Cowan's map. It fell out of his coat when I was brushing it.'

Anna edged closer to the desk and gazed down on the well-used map. It had tiny lines and marks all over it. It was obviously a map of Columbia, but what caught her attention were the words, 'Camp Site' and 'Mine Site.' Underneath those two she read a third: 'Dove Mine.' Emotion swamped her.

'He named the mine after me. He always called me his dove, and he called his mine, Dove Mine.'

'There was this too.' Emma held out a framed picture. 'It's you.'

Anna held the small frame gently for it was scratched in places. Staring back at her was her own portrait, the one done by the street artist in York. 'Yes, and somewhere I have one of him.'

Maisie interrupted them. 'He's wakin'.'

Anna scurried back to Matt's side. Tenderly, she lifted his hand and held it to her cheek as his mouth worked to speak. 'I am here, Matt. Right here.'

Matt's bleary eyelids flickered, and then inched open. His tongue darted over dry, cracked lips. 'Anna?'

'Yes. Yes, I am holding your hand.' She patted it, where it lay hot in hers.

'Don't leave...'

'No, no, never. I will stay right here beside you.'

His eyelids fluttered and then closed, only to flicker open again a moment later. 'Lo...love...loved y...you,' he managed to say. Slowly and gracefully, he closed his eyes for the last time. The hand that Anna held went limp.

She stared at him in disbelief, not believing he had slipped away from her, after she had fought so hard to keep him alive. He was Matt, the strong and handsome adventurer. He was the first man to steal her heart away and make her feel what it was like to be in love and to love life. She had borne his child. They had a daughter.

Maisie bent over and gently released Anna's hand from Matt's. At that final break from him, Anna began to shake as shock and exhaustion overcame her.

Pulling the sheet over Matt's head, Maisie then turned to Anna and carefully helped her up from the chair.

Dazed, Anna let Maisie guide her out of the room and across the landing to her bedroom. She was gently pushed onto the dressing stool and left there as Maisie dashed back out again

Weariness overcame her shock. It was finished. A Chapter of her life was closed.

Goodbye, Matt.

Brenton came into the room to find Anna asleep with her head resting on her folded arms on the dressing table. He stopped and studied her for a moment, hoping that Cowan's death hadn't closed Anna's heart for good. Sighing deeply, he bent low, gathered her up into his arms and then delicately laid her down on the bed and covered her with a blanket.

'Brenton?' she whispered.

'Yes, my love?'

'Clare?'

'She's asleep. We'll take care of her. You need rest, and rest you'll get, so don't argue.'

She smiled sleepily. 'I adore you.'

Brenton gazed down at her before bestowing a tiny kiss on her cheek. 'And I you, my precious girl.'

* * *

After sleeping all day, Anna woke when Maisie entered with a tea tray. While she ate the toast and drank a cup of tea, Maisie filled a bath for her.

Soaking in the hot water soothed her muscles and her mind. Matt had appeared and gone so briefly it seemed but a dream. But although she was sorry he'd died, she also knew that a lot of her demons had gone with him. The past was completely behind her now. Her mother, the news of her parentage, Matt, the scandal of her being pregnant was left behind.

While Maisie washed her hair, she spoke of the undertaker arriving and taking Matt's body away. He would organize contacting the Conway's. Anna let all this wash over her as easily as the warm water. She could do no more for Matt. Let his family bury him, for she had already said her goodbyes.

'Look, lass,' Agnes said, as Anna came into the kitchen, feeling better after her bath. 'These packages just arrived. They're from Halifax, the fellow said.' Her eyes danced with excitement as she viewed the assorted boxes.

Anna paused to look at the sides of the boxes. They were from the dressmaker's shop where her father had taken them. She called Emma and Maisie down from upstairs. Together, with growing excitement, they opened the boxes.

Anna pulled a charming dress of fine wool, the shade of dark rust, out of one box and promptly gave it to Agnes. 'There you are, Agnes, compliments of my father,' she told her with a grin.

'What? Oh, no Miss.' Agnes looked horrified. 'I can't take this.'

'Well, you've got to, for this dress is your size. I told father I'd have a dress made for you and—' Picking at random, Anna opened another box, and luckily it was the right one. She held up a long-sleeved dress in deep green, she turned and gave it to Maisie. 'And one for Maisie.'

Maisie's eyes grew wide as she stared at the dress, the finest she'd ever owned. 'Oh, 'tis perfect.'

'Of course, it is,' Anna said with false smugness. 'If I didn't know what kind of dress would suit you, after all these years of knowing you, then something would be wrong with me.' She laughed, light-hearted at the fact that soon she would be talking to Brenton, telling him she loved him.

Next, they watched Emma take out her dress of sky-blue linen. Tears gathered in her eyes as she held it to her. 'It's simply splendid,' she cried, then opened the hatbox, and they all commented on the pretty little bonnet to match.

'Now you, love.' Agnes nodded to Anna.

It had been a long time since Anna had bought new clothes. Opening the last box, a sense of longing for her old life back at the estate overwhelmed her. She supposed it was natural to sometimes miss the life you once lived. The longing only lasted a few fleeting seconds, but it took the shine off receiving her new dress.

'Oh, it's so beautiful,' Emma's voice echoed the others as they gazed at the creation Anna held.

The gown was of the simple lines that anyone knowing Anna would have recognized. The silk material shimmered in the sunlight that fell through the kitchen window. None of the women standing around the table could actually name the colour of the gown. It seemed to be made up in an array colours that all mingled together and created something close to shining mother-of-pearl. Tiny seed pearl buttons formed a neat row down the back of the dress. They were the only ornaments, for the dress would have been spoilt with anything more.

'Go put it on, Miss Anna,' Maisie said in hushed tones. She'd always taken pleasure in the clothes Anna used to wear, but since leaving the estate, Anna wore only dark clothes in pregnancy and for working around the farm. No one here had seen her properly dressed as Maisie had.

Anna paused and then nodded. For the purpose in mind she would wear the dress.

Quietly, so as not to wake Clare, who slept in the cot in the corner, Anna stood in her bedroom and slowly took off the black mourning she'd worn since her mother died. Standing in front of her mirror, she watched the dress fall to the floor. It was like shedding a disguise, another layer of herself, as she prepared to physically transform back to how she used to look. The cold silk of the gown sent shivers along her skin as it settled over her. The silvery-pearl colour deepened the slight tan she acquired over the summer. From helping with farm chores, she'd regained her slimness after Clare's birth, and the gown fit tightly over her corset.

Satin shoes accompanied the gown and she slipped her feet into them. Her hair these days was always tied in a tight bun at the nape of her neck and on impulse Anna took out the pins and shook it free. It fell about her shoulders and hung down her back. It had not been cut for some time and was longer than she ever remembered it being.

Opening a drawer of the dressing table, she took out two pearl combs, swooped up the sides of her hair

and pinned them on top of her head. She stood and
stared at her reflection for a little longer. The
transformation was like stepping back in time. Anna
remembered another occasion when she'd dressed
herself in a gown of blue and had gone to a ball and
fallen in love. That one specific time of her life had
led to her being here today in her own home, living
another kind of life so different from the one before.
Only one thing remained the same, she'd fallen in
love again.

Leaving her room, she walked across the hall and
tapped gently on Henry's door. On hearing his call,
she went in and stood before him. The surprise on his
face brought a smile to her lips.

'Do you think he will say yes, Henry?' Anna asked
calmly. In her mind, she knew what she must do.
What she *wanted* to do.

With a smile as wide as England itself, Henry
nodded. He knew exactly what she meant. 'You could
wear rags, and live in a cave, and he'd still say yes,
me lass.' He gave her a large wink.

'Can you do up the last of the buttons?' She turned
for him to assist her and when he finished, she kissed
his cheek.

Anna gathered the skirts of the dress and went
downstairs. The next few moments would alter her
life. She was going to ask Brenton to marry her.
Nearing the kitchen, she could hear voices and
instantly picked out Brenton's.

Taking a deep breath to still the nerves that
consumed her, Anna walked into the kitchen to stand
before them.

To Gain What's Lost

After the first gasps of admiration, no one said a word. They waited for something, they didn't know what, to happen between Brenton and Anna.

Anna watched the emotions fly across his face. When, at last he looked into her eyes, his own were moist. She thought she would simply die soon if he didn't do or say something. In the end, he closed the few paces between them. Just when she decided she could take no more, Brenton knelt down on bended knee. He took her hand.

'I—I've never in all my life, seen anything so beautiful as you today.' He paused, as if he were having trouble finding the right words. 'I think you might know this, Anna, but still I need to tell you.' He paused again. 'I admire you for all that you are and from the very first moment I met you, my soul was yours.' He smiled tenderly at her, and his voice broke a little as he continued. 'I love you more than I can find words to describe, which is quite an achievement for an Irishman.'

The women smiled tenderly at this, as each one stayed motionless around the kitchen table and watched the beautiful scene unfold before them.

Anna gently lifted Brenton's hands so he rose to stand. She smiled. 'I ignored my feelings for too long, but I was so afraid. I was fearful something might go wrong, and you'd leave my life forever. I denied my feelings, because I'd rather have you as my friend than nothing at all.'

'I will never ever leave you, *acushla*. You mean the moon and the stars, the sun, and the rain to me. I hope you'll do me the grandest honour by becoming my wife?'

Brenton's words fell over Anna with such love and devotion she couldn't respond as emotion clogged her throat. She nodded and smiled through her tears. In seconds they were in each other's arms to the rapturous cheers that echoed around the kitchen and out over the farm.

About the Author

If you enjoyed my story please leave a review online, it helps an author very much, and we appreciate them more than you know.
Thank you
AnneMarie Brear

Australian born AnneMarie Brear writes historical novels and modern romances and sometimes the odd short story, too. Her passions, apart from writing, are travelling, reading, eating her husband's delicious food, reading, researching, and dragging her husband around historical sites looking for inspiration for her next book.

www.annemariebrear.com
Facebook
https://www.facebook.com/annemariebrearauthor
Twitter:
https://twitter.com/annemariebrear
Amazon author page:
http://www.amazon.com/annemariebrear

Printed in Great Britain
by Amazon